THE NEW WESSEX EDITION

General Editor P. N. Furbank

Desperate Remedies

Introduction by C. J. P. Beatty

Far from the Madding Crowd

Introduction by John Bayley

The Hand of Ethelberta

Introduction by Robert Gittings

Jude the Obscure

Introduction by Terry Eagleton

A Laodicean

Introduction by Barbara Hardy

The Mayor of Casterbridge

Introduction by Ian Gregor

A Pair of Blue Eyes

Introduction by Ronald Blythe

The Return of the Native

Introduction by Derwent May

Tess of the d'Urbervilles

Introduction by P. N. Furbank

The Trumpet-Major

Introduction by Barbara Hardy

Two on a Tower

Introduction by F. B. Pinion

Under the Greenwood Tree

Introduction by Geoffrey Grigson

The Well-Beloved

Introduction by J. Hillis Miller

The Woodlanders

Introduction by David Lodge

THE NEW WESSEX EDITION

Two on a Tower

THOMAS HARDY

INTRODUCTION BY

F. B. Pinion

'Ah, my heart! her eyes and she
Have taught thee new astrology.
Howe'er Love's native hours were set,
Whatever starry synod met,
'Tis in the mercy of her eye,
If poor Love shall live or die.'
CRASHAW, *Love's Horoscope*

M

ISBN: 333 33497 3

First edition published elsewhere 1882
New Wessex Edition first published 1975 by
MACMILLAN LONDON LTD
4 Little Essex Street London WC2R 3LF
and Basingstoke
Associated companies in Auckland, Dallas, Delhi, Dublin, Hong Kong, Johannesburg, Lagos, Manzini, Melbourne, Nairobi, New York, Singapore, Tokyo, Washington and Zaria
Second impression 1977
Third impression 1979
Reprinted 1982

CO-ORDINATING EDITORS
Caroline Hobhouse
Edward Leeson

First published in the United States 1977 by
ST MARTIN'S PRESS INC.
175 Fifth Avenue, New York, N.Y. 10010
Library of Congress catalog card no.: 77 70263
ISBN: 0-312-82742-3

Filmset in Photon Times 10 on 11 pt and
printed in Great Britain by
RICHARD CLAY (THE CHAUCER PRESS) LTD
Bungay, Suffolk

Contents

Biography

1840	Hardy born at Higher Bockhampton, near Dorchester. His father and grandfather were master-stonemasons, also keen performers in the band or 'quire' of the local parish church.
1848	Attended school established by his local patroness Julia Augusta Martin. About this time his mother gave him Dryden's *Virgil*, *Rasselas* and *Paul and Virginia*.
1849	Transferred to school in Dorchester. Played fiddle at local weddings and dances.
1856–61	Articled to Dorchester architect John Hicks. Studied Latin and Greek from five to eight in the morning. Began writing verse. Was introduced to modern thought by his friend Horace Moule, son of the Vicar of Fordington.
1862–7	In London, working for the architect Arthur Blomfield. Read widely; studied paintings in National Gallery; became an agnostic.
1867–70	Returned to Dorset for health reasons and was employed by Hicks, and his successor Crickmay, on church restoration.
1868	Completed draft of first novel, 'The Poor Man and the Lady' (later destroyed).
1870	Sent by Crickmay to St Juliot in Cornwall and met future wife Emma Lavinia Gifford. Writing *Desperate Remedies*, his first published novel.
1873	Invited by Leslie Stephen to contribute serial (*Far from the Madding Crowd*) to *Cornhill*.
1874	Married and took rooms in Surbiton.
1876–8	Living at Sturminster Newton; writing *The Return of the Native*.
1878–81	Living in London. Was becoming well known in literary circles. Had serious illness while writing *A Laodicean*.
1881	Took house at Wimborne Minster.
1883	Went to live in Dorchester.
1885	Moved into the house, Max Gate, in Dorchester, which he had built for himself. He and his wife continued to make long annual visits to London.
1888–91	Writing many short stories. Publication of *Tess of the d'Urbervilles* in 1891 created furore.
1892	His father died.
1892–4	Worsening relations with his wife, the trouble being exacerbated by the writing of *Jude the Obscure*. In 1893 they visited Dublin and met Mrs Henniker, with whom he collaborated on a short story and perhaps fell in love.

1895–6	Publication of *Jude* causes scandal. He resolved to give up novel-writing.
1897–8	Writing and revising poems for his first collection, *Wessex Poems*.
1902	Began *The Dynasts*.
1904	His mother died.
1910	Received the Order of Merit.
1912	Making final revision of the Wessex novels. His wife died in November.
1913	In March made penitential pilgrimage to St Juliot and later to his wife's birthplace, Plymouth. Wrote flood of poems 'in expiation'.
1914	Married Florence Dugdale. At outbreak of war joined group of writers pledged to write for the Allied Cause.
1914–28	Wrote and revised the material for several more collections of verse.
1928	Died. His ashes were buried in Westminster Abbey and his heart in his first wife's grave in Stinsford churchyard.

Hardy's Major Works with year of book publication

1871 Desperate Remedies
1872 Under the Greenwood Tree
1873 A Pair of Blue Eyes
1874 Far from the Madding Crowd
1876 The Hand of Ethelberta
1878 The Return of the Native
1880 The Trumpet-Major
1881 A Laodicean
1882 Two on a Tower
1886 The Mayor of Casterbridge
1887 The Woodlanders
1888 Wessex Tales
1891 A Group of Noble Dames
1891 Tess of the d'Urbervilles
1894 Life's Little Ironies
1896 [1895] Jude the Obscure
1897 The Well-Beloved
1898 Wessex Poems
1902 Poems of the Past and the Present
1903 The Dynasts, pt 1
1905 The Dynasts, pt 2
1908 The Dynasts, pt 3
1909 Time's Laughingstocks
1913 A Changed Man and Other Tales
1914 Satires of Circumstance
1917 Moments of Vision
1922 Late Lyrics and Earlier
1923 The Famous Tragedy of the Queen of Cornwall
1925 Human Shows
1928 Winter Words
1952 Our Exploits at West Poley

Acknowledgements

THE General Editor thanks the following for their kind assistance in answering queries: the Librarian of the English Folk Dance and Song Society; Mr John S. Creasey of the Museum of English Rural Life; and the Editor of *Notes and Queries.* He would also like to express a general indebtedness to R. L. Purdy's *Thomas Hardy: a bibliographical study* (Oxford University Press, 1954; reissued 1968); F. B. Pinion's *A Hardy Companion* (Macmillan, 1968); and Denys Kay-Robinson's *Hardy's Wessex Re-appraised* (David & Charles, 1972).

P. N. FURBANK

Introduction

IN January 1882, when Hardy undertook to write *Two on a Tower*, he had reached a point almost exactly midway in his career as a writer of prose fiction. He had shown his creative gifts in a number of works – most of all in *Far from the Madding Crowd* and *The Return of the Native* – but his greatest tragedies were still to come. The kind of 'charity' which inspires them is more clearly and confidently voiced in *Two on a Tower*, their immediate forerunner, than ever before. More than any other of his novels it combines all those elements (including tragedy and humour) which Hardy had in mind when he divided his fiction into three categories: 'Novels of Character and Environment', 'Romances and Fantasies' and 'Novels of Ingenuity'.[1]

Though not ranked among Hardy's major achievements, *Two on a Tower* is certainly one of his most readable and remarkable. It is a moving romance which makes admirable and ingenious use of rather limited resources to provide a story which is economical in presentation and continually enlivened with suspense or surprising turns of event. On reading it in 1920, Mrs Henniker, a novelist herself, found it strange that it was not '*more* talked of', and thought the interest of the story 'wonderfully well maintained'. By Victorian standards it was daring enough; but to embark on a romance conceived with reference to cosmic space was even more venturesome, arguing a knowledge of astronomy which was far from superficial.

Hardy's interest in stellar space went much deeper than the visual as it is seen in the northern sky of *Far from the Madding Crowd* and the southern sky of 'Drummer Hodge'. Both express the 'poetry of motion' felt by their author in 'the panoramic glide of the stars', but pre-eminently these scenes are presented as they appeared to Wessex rustics. One is familiar, the other foreign; Gabriel Oak has learned to tell the time from the direction of the stars, while the drummer is lost in wondering ignorance. Hardy's knowledge of

[1] See below, p. 312.

astronomy began no doubt in boyhood observations and inquiries; when he was fifteen or sixteen, it was extended by *The Popular Educator* and telescopic viewing with Handley Moule at Fordington. Ten years later the new scientific philosophy which had overthrown his belief in Providence turned his researches to recent studies of the universe in its inconceivable dimensions of space and time.

Two poems of the period illustrate his philosophical interest in the world of space. 'At a Lunar Eclipse' (186–) gives a foretaste of *The Dynasts*, emphasising the relative insignificance of the earth, its tragic wars and heroism, its geniuses and 'women fairer than the skies'. The central idea of 'In Vision I Roamed' (1866) is more akin to that of *Two on a Tower*; after sweeping imaginatively through

> ghast heights of sky,
> To the last chambers of the monstrous Dome,

the poet takes comfort in the thought that someone dear to him, though far away, is relatively near.

In *The Return of the Native* Hardy presented a tragic story against a background suggesting the insignificance of mortality with reference to time, whereas in *Two on a Tower* he 'set the emotional history' of two cosmologically 'infinitesimal lives against the stupendous background of the stellar universe', hoping 'to impart to readers the sentiment that of these contrasting magnitudes the smaller might be the greater to them as men'. With the harsh indifference of nature's laws, and the impact of what appears from limited knowledge to be chance in human affairs, these dimensions form the general context of Hardy's tragedy. The Spirit of the Pities is heard against the Spirit of the Years.

Features of the story had appealed to him at various times before he began to plot the novel. The tower on Black Down to the memory of Admiral Hardy was a distant landmark which must have excited Hardy's interest when he set off to his school in Dorchester, partly from its Napoleonic associations, and even more from the glow he felt as a collateral descendant of one of the great figures in the battle of Trafalgar. A jotting among his memoranda for fiction shows that he had this monument in mind for a story in November 1878. Eight years earlier he had made a note on a wife who pined for her husband, though he had treated her roughly; when at last he sent for her, she died for joy at the news. Possibilities could have been suggested by a passage in George Eliot's *The Mill on the Floss*, where Maggie Tulliver, after asking questions on the astronomer in *The Eton Latin Grammar* 'who hated women generally', remarks:

'I suppose it's all astronomers [who hate women]: because, you know, they live up in high towers, and if the women came there, they might talk and hinder them from looking at the stars.'

Hardy must have considered the story in earnest soon after he and his wife moved from Upper Tooting to Wimborne, Dorset, in June 1881. During the first night in their new home they watched Tebbutt's Comet. Soon afterwards he became interested in the high tower a few miles away in Charborough Park; it provided a setting which he chose to disguise, and revived 'the poor man and the lady' motif which had been the subject of his first (unpublished) novel. He probably anticipated the eager expectations which the second transit of Venus would arouse at the end of 1882. There could have been little doubt about the subject of his next novel when he was invited in October 1881 to provide a serial for *The Atlantic Monthly*, for the following month he wrote to the Astronomer Royal requesting permission to visit the observatory at Greenwich. How he obtained it is best told in his own words:

He was requested to state before it could be granted if his application was made for astronomical and scientific reasons or not. He therefore drew up a scientific letter, the gist of which was that he wished to ascertain if it would be possible for him to adapt an old tower, built in a plantation in the West of England for other objects, to the requirements of a telescopic study of the stars by a young man very ardent in that pursuit (this being the imagined situation in the proposed novel). An order to view Greenwich Observatory was promptly sent.[1]

Expressions and facts in the novel show that one of the books Hardy studied was R. A. Proctor's *Essays in Astronomy* (1872). His aim, he told his friend Edmund Gosse, was 'to make science, not the mere padding of a romance' but its 'actual vehicle'.[2]

In devising his story Hardy conformed to two principles which he had observed from the outset of his career as a novelist. The first

[1] F. E. Hardy, *The Life of Thomas Hardy, 1840–1928* (Macmillan, 1962) p. 151.

[2] R. L. Purdy, *Thomas Hardy: a bibliographical study* (Oxford University Press, 1954; reissued 1968) p. 44 n.

he emphasised in a letter of July 1868 to Macmillan, which announced his first attempt to publish a novel: 'as a rule no fiction will considerably interest readers poor or rich unless the passion of love forms a prominent feature in the thread of the story'. The second is found in notes he wrote in the summer preceding his Greenwich visit:

> The real, if unavowed, purpose of fiction is to give pleasure by gratifying the love of the uncommon in human experience. . . .
>
> The writer's problem is, how to strike the balance between the uncommon and the ordinary so as on the one hand to give interest, on the other to give reality.
>
> In working out this problem, human nature must never be made abnormal, which is introducing incredibility. The uncommonness must be in the events, not in the characters; and the writer's art lies in shaping that uncommonness while disguising its unlikelihood, if it be unlikely.[1]

The seeds of romance in the story of a beautiful widow who falls in love with a handsome young astronomer and marries him secretly are obvious; the 'uncommonness' lies in the circumstances which compel a lady of the most laudable principles to rise above self-interest, insist that her husband shall travel abroad to further his career and, finding that she is with child, passively accept a deceived bishop's proposal of marriage without infringing the law. The major problem for Hardy was not so much in devising an ingenious plot as in the theme: two people whose lives we follow with interest will naturally seem more important than the immensities of outer space, but it is extraordinarily difficult for the novelist, however great his astronomical knowledge, to create concurrently rather than intermittently an imaginative awareness of the infinitesimality of those lives in the universe at large.

Readers in the post-Lawrentian era can hardly appreciate a writer's restrictions in the Victorian world. Hardy's audacity had not yet reached its climax, and he had yet to learn how to accommodate his stories to magazine readers. The reception of *Desperate Remedies*, his first published novel, made him realise the danger of offending upper-class moral susceptibilities. Eleven years later, in creating circumstances which made a lady reveal her love despite the restraints of propriety, Hardy knew what risks he was running,

[1] *Life*, p. 150.

but it is doubtful whether he realised his offence in making the same lady, even though a passive victim, a party to the deception of a bishop. This turn of events still disturbs a modern reader. The best that can be said for Hardy is that he draws a veil over it; his excuse that Lady Constantine succumbed to 'convention' remains unconvincing. It could only have rubbed salt into the wound of the contemporary society reader. The editor of *The Atlantic* was perturbed, readers were offended and critics were 'acid'; but Hardy was pleased to find that complaints were countered by 'enthusiastic letter-writing' to him and a greater interest in his latest novel than he had enjoyed for some time.

By January 1882 Hardy had agreed to arrange the story for American serialisation in eight monthly parts, the first to appear in May. This programme required a careful scrutiny of the story as a whole, with readjustments no doubt, before the first instalment was completed and sent off to Boston in February. It was a happy period in Hardy's life, according to Sir George Douglas, who first met him at Wimborne; and this happiness is reflected in the rather high-spirited detachment which occasionally characterises the presentation as well as in the humour of the rustic scenes. The first of these is such that one wishes it were longer; but an eight-part serial imposed limits on all aspects of the novel.

It is typical of Hardy that he accepted the pressures of serial demand, agreed to publication in book form as soon as possible, and later regretted his shortcomings. Professionally he did his best in the circumstances; had he known what interest would develop in his work, he might have pursued a more circumspect policy. The novel appeared in October 1882 before the serial was concluded. The following January he informed Edmund Gosse that,

> though the plan of the story was carefully thought out, the actual writing was lamentably hurried – having been produced month by month, and the MS. despatched to America, where it was printed without my seeing the proofs. It would have been rewritten for the book form if I had not played truant and gone off to Paris.[1]

It seems most unlikely that he seriously contemplated rewriting the novel, for agreement to publish the book was reached as early as July 1882. To promote interest in the work after its publication,

[1] Purdy, p. 44.

Hardy wrote a neat abstract of the story for his publisher, Sampson Low, Marston, Searle & Rivington:

> Being the story of the unforeseen relations into which a lady and a youth many years her junior were drawn by studying the stars together; of her desperate situation through generosity to him; and of the reckless *coup d'audace* by which she effected her deliverance.[1]

The criticism roused by this *coup d'audace* seems to have astonished Hardy, who, in answer to the charge that he was hostile to the Church, pointed out that 'one of the most honourable characters', the hero's friend, is a clergyman, and that the heroine's 'most tender qualities' are inseparable from her religious feelings.

It was at the beginning of June 1882, when he had probably not reached the halfway stage in *Two on a Tower*, that Hardy wrote one of his most famous notes on the artist:

> As, in looking at a carpet, by following one colour a certain pattern is suggested, by following another colour, another; so in life the seer should watch that pattern among general things which his idiosyncrasy moves him to observe, and describe that alone. This is, quite accurately, a going to Nature; yet the result is no mere photograph, but purely the product of the writer's own mind.[2]

Inevitably, in writing for the entertainment of magazine-readers, Hardy included narrative items and links that did not express his personality. Readers familiar with the scene in *Tess of the d'Urbervilles* which expresses Hardy's abhorrence of blood sports may be astonished that he could have detailed Swithin's methods of improvising supper, when he and his wife were forced to take refuge in the tower to avoid recognition by Louis Glanville, as if bird-killing were as unexceptionable to the author as to most countrymen of the period. One can applaud his dexterity in resolving the involutions of the coral-bracelet menace successfully, but it is no more than a trivial device for keeping the reader on tenterhooks. *Two on a Tower* is not one of Hardy's most serious novels. It is a romantic tragi-comedy, but it reveals the main facets of his personality and 'idiosyncratic mode of regard'.

It would be a mistake to overlook his humour; it was part of his rural inheritance. He would enjoy the story of the parson's bride

[1] Purdy, p. 44. [2] *Life*, p. 153.

who couldn't avoid blushing deeply when a certain psalm was sung at her wedding, or of the yokel who, when told to rehearse the articles of his belief during preparations for Confirmation, knew no better than to answer the parson as the irreverent Sir Blount Constantine prompted. This was a colour in Hardy's temperament which was to become more and more interwoven with the tragic pattern until it assumed a rather sombre general hue. As one of his earliest novels, *Under the Greenwood Tree*, illustrates abundantly, his rustics often utter perennial sense in incomparable language which raises a smile and goes straight to its mark. Happily Hardy made such expression the pivotal point for the main turn in the romantic events which precede the tragi-comedy of *Two on a Tower*:

> 'But the young man himself?'
>
> 'Planned, cut out, and finished for the delight of 'ooman!'
>
> 'Yet he must be willing.'
>
> 'That would soon come. If they get up this tower ruling plannards together much longer, their plannards will soon rule them together, in my way o' thinking. If she've a disposition towards the knot, she can soon teach him.'
>
> 'True, true, and lawfully. What before mid ha' been a wrong desire is now a holy wish!'
>
> The scales fell from Swithin St Cleeve's eyes as he heard the words of his neighbours....

The most important pattern Hardy saw in life was the complex web of chance. 'Blind Circumstance' was the god that ruled his universe. His 'mode of regard' was essentially scientific. In such a world the fortunes of people are regulated at critical stages by the interaction of character, environmental opportunities past and present, and events. In the passage already quoted from the jottings on fiction which Hardy wrote in the summer of 1881, it is stressed that anything unusual must be in events, not character. He expressed the same thought more explicitly with reference to his next novel, *The Mayor of Casterbridge*: 'it is not improbabilities of incident but improbabilities of character that matter'. Truth is often even stranger than fiction. Unusual events are possible, and one or two determine the plot of *Two on a Tower*. Had the hero and heroine differed radically in one respect from what they are, had

Viviette not been endowed with a more mature sense of responsibility than Swithin's, for example, their story could not have remained the same, however.

The critical importance of chance is illustrated when Swithin receives the letter outlining the terms of his great-uncle's legacy. Had it arrived a month earlier, there is no telling what effect the prospect of a large annuity might have had on one 'whose love for celestial physics was second to none'. It reached him when he was on his way to his marriage in Bath; 'his bosom's lord sat lightly in his throne', and 'it affected him about as much as the view of horizons shown by sheet-lightning. He saw an immense prospect; it went, and the world was as before.' This is but the first in a series of chances which create the gin in which the heroine finds herself desperately caught. As the tragedy tightens its hold, Hardy's nobler nature is expressed. It is seen in Lady Constantine's sacrifice of her happiness for her husband's future. 'To love St Cleeve so far better than herself as this was to surpass the love of women as conventionally understood', and it was this 'altruism in subjecting her self-love to benevolence' which led to disaster. Superficially Hardy's language may seem detached, but its overtones reveal the depth of imaginative feeling. In Swithin's absence, could Viviette 'singly meet her impending trial, despising the shame', and could he wish to remarry her when she was 'fading to middle-age'? 'A fear sharp as a frost settled down upon her, that in any such scheme as this she would be building upon the sand.' In altruism and self-denial she displays that most excellent gift of charity; in the final trial of her fortitude she falters. Marty South and Tess were to demonstrate these virtues unswervingly, and Hardy's heart went out to all of them in their distresses.

Though not the most tragic, Viviette is perhaps the most attractive of Hardy's heroines. The following passage suggests that an explanation is to be found in his life:

> Lady Constantine, in being nearly ten years his senior, was an object even better calculated to nourish a youth's first passion than a girl of his own age, superiority of experience and ripeness of emotion exercising the same peculiar fascination over him as over other young men in their first ventures in this kind.

Part of the final tragedy of Viviette is her immediate awareness from

Swithin's look that, in losing her beauty's bloom during his long absence, she has lost his heart. The pathos of the situation was known to Hardy from experience. Even as a young boy he had fallen in love with the lady of the local manor who had mothered him, but so great was the change in her appearance when he met her years later in London that he made it the subject of some of his early poems, notably 'Amabel' and 'She, to Him'. The opening lines of the latter prove conclusively that one of the minor themes of *Two on a Tower* struck plaintive chords:

> When you shall see me in the toils of Time,
> My lauded beauties carried off from me,
> My eyes no longer stars as in their prime....

How deep were his resurrected feelings on the subject may be seen in his preface of 1895.

The novel, however, was not planned predominantly as a tragedy. Lady Constantine was destined to be a pawn in a game of dupery which may, from one angle, have appeared to Hardy as one of life's little ironies. She was spared the shame of public gossip and slander, but the off-stage episode of her married life in a bishop's palace leaves one wondering what misery and guilt she suffered, and whether a slightly malicious humour got the better of Hardy's judgement when he planned this phase of the novel. Perhaps he could take the consequential, self-seeking Bishop Helmsdale little more seriously than we can Mr Collins in *Pride and Prejudice*, whom he somewhat resembles. Louis Glanville's intrigue is regarded as 'Puck-like', as if the author's attitude is summed up in the words 'Lord, what fools these mortals be!' Planes and perspectives have changed. The door is closed on tragic feelings, and conspiracy triumphs. Hardy's interest at this period in the fictional possibilities of the Mephistophelian role must be taken into account. He had employed it in his previous novel, *A Laodicean*: it was to be central to his next major story, 'The Romantic Adventures of a Milkmaid', and assume a more Satanic form in Alec d'Urberville. It is seen in Louis Glanville; the plotter or tempter is associated with smoke and sometimes fire, usually with a cigar which glows like a red coal in the dark.

With chance an important element in a writer's philosophy, a predisposition to irony of situation is almost inevitable. In the plot of *Two on a Tower* much depends on the time factor in Swithin's receipt of his great-uncle's letter and in the unexpected arrival of new information on Sir Blount Constantine's death. The tragic consequences of actions to which Lady Constantine would never have consented had she known the truth may indeed be regarded as cruel 'satires of circumstance'. More ordinary and incidental irony occurs when Viviette entertains the Bishop, and the serenity of her manner (arising from her secret marriage) makes her all the more attractive to him. It continues when this self-important dignitary finds a clue for his repulse in the synchronisation of his first proposal and the receipt of the more circumstantial account of her husband's death. The last little irony in Louis Glanville's plans to save his sister (and still, like the brother in 'A Tragedy of Two Ambitions', to exploit her marriage to his advantage) is the Bishop's complacent comment on Lady Constantine's acceptance of him: 'A good and wise woman, she perceived what a true shelter from sadness was offered in this, and was not the one to despise Heaven's gift.'

Hardy could rarely expand within the limits imposed by his serial agreement; and this is particularly noticeable in the economy of scenic effects. His keen observation is seen more often in detail than in landscape. Yet one of the more dominant features of his later novels, the harmonisation of setting and situation, may be glimpsed at intervals. The opening scene seems to augur both happiness and sorrow; in the sunshine of an early winter afternoon the tower is 'bright and cheerful' above a gloomy wood where skeletal trees sob and moan. 'Darker grew the evenings, tearfuller the moonlights, and heavier the dews' when the lovesick hero found he was unable to concentrate on his life work as a result of his lady's absence. When they agreed to marry secretly (not knowing that such a course would wreck his opportunities for a distinguished career), the wind roared and shook the tower until suddenly it reached hurricane force and whirled away the dome.

The insignificance of the individual in space and time was axiomatic, part of 'the pattern of general things', for Hardy. In *Two on a Tower* his main aim was to create an 'emotional history', and by limiting himself to two principal characters he gave himself greater scope for making their romance and tragedy loom large in the reader's imagination. To provide the contrasting viewpoints in a single vision proved (not surprisingly, under the pressure of serialisation) beyond his grasp. With this theme in mind, he chose an ancient camp for the site of his tower, with 'palæolithic dead men' feeding the roots of the trees around its base; Swithin's wedding preparations

accorded well with the prehistoric spot on which they were made. Embedded under his feet were possibly even now rude trinkets that had been worn at bridal ceremonies of the early inhabitants. Little signified those ceremonies to-day.... That his own rite, nevertheless, signified much, was the inconsequent reasoning of Swithin, as it is of many another bridegroom besides....

In its context, this passage shows the irreconcilability of two valid points of view.

The main background, however, is the stellar universe. In his attempt to reveal the relative insignificance of sublunary lives, Hardy chose for his astronomer a youthful enthusiast, so absorbed in his studies that he is detached from the world and consciously insusceptible to a woman's charms. Their first sweeps of space and subsequent discussion emphasise that nothing was made for man, that the universe continues until grandeur is lost eventually in ghastliness, and all human affairs lose their importance; yet, however much Lady Constantine feels 'annihilated' by it, the effect on the reader is little more than conceptual. During their next observations,

Having got closer to immensity than their fellow-creatures, they saw at once its beauty and its frightfulness. They more and more felt the contrast between their own tiny magnitudes and those among which they had recklessly plunged, till they were oppressed with the presence of a vastness they could not cope with even as an idea, and which hung about them as a nightmare.

These reductive impressions are occasional and little more than a backcloth. With one slight exception (ch. 34), celestial immensities are not linked with human plight in moving scenes, as time (geologically or historically) and landscape are in *A Pair of Blue Eyes*, *The Return of the Native* and *Tess of the d'Urbervilles.* A brief and unscientific reference to 'the cruelty of the natural laws' which had been Swithin's study does nothing imaginatively to reinforce an intermittent theme.

To some extent it is reinforced by astronomical allusion. When Swithin realises that, in thinking of the heaven above, he had not perceived 'the better heaven beneath', and proclaims that Viviette's eyes are henceforth to be his stars, we are reminded of expressions (already quoted) from Hardy's early poems. The astronomer's terms and imagery recall his studies. He tells Lady Constantine that the shattering of the lens he had brought from London fills but a degree in the circle of her thoughts but covers the whole circumference of his; to him the streak on her cheek from Louis' whiplash is as 'straight as a meridian'. A long bed of snowdrops 'looked up at him like a nether Milky Way'; the following autumn, when Welland House suffered neglect, tufts of grass in the gravel walks appeared like black stars in the gloaming. Elsewhere in his narration Hardy frequently alludes to the heavens and astronomy. The 'modern Eudoxus' rises above 'the embarrassing horizon of Lady Constantine's great house' and becomes himself when he enlarges on the scintillation of the stars. Distracted by 'the better heaven beneath', he diminishes scientifically to 'a dim vapour of himself'. With marriage, his astronomical ardour is renewed; Viviette finds him absorbed in the adjustment of his telescope, 'the *primum mobile* of his gravitation'. When she insists on their separation for the sake of his career,

> He turn'd and saw the terror in her eyes,
> That yearn'd upon him shining in such wise
> As a star midway in the midnight fix'd.

As this young man travels abroad for the first time and becomes increasingly interested in the southern skies, Viviette, who has stood high in his heaven, sinks like the North Star with his retreat southward. When he returns years later, time has brought changes he never anticipated:

> Her cheeks had lost for ever that firm contour which had been drawn by the vigorous hand of youth, and the masses of hair that were once darkness visible had become touched here and there by a faint grey haze, like the Via Lactea in a midnight sky.

The discipline which characterises the general style of the novel (despite some minor lapses) may be seen in Hardy's other associative imagery. It is never lush or excessive. Concise, apt and often idiosyncratic, it shows a wide range of interests and sensibility. Recollections from his boyhood occur in the reference to muffs 'large as smugglers' tubs' and in the parallel between Swithin's ready response to the question on equatorial manufacturers and the drawing of a weir-hatch which speedily inundated Lady Constantine with the information she sought. Hardy's commonest imagery proclaims the countryman and the poet. How impressively he evokes the evanescent effect of the opportunities conjured up by his great-uncle's letter on Swithin will already have been noticed. The link between the faint grey haze in Viviette's hair and the Via Lactea recalls their first joint observation of the Milky Way, 'stretched over their heads with the luminousness of a frosted web' as they discussed the immense voids of space. A few of the illustrative images show a familiarity with paintings and architectural drawing. Many derive from Shakespeare, more from the Bible; their register extends from 'the mishap of Tobit' to tragic tones and evocations. The aptness of humorous similitudes ranges from the more obvious (in, for example, the clearing of throats like the noise of atmospheric hoes and scrapers) to the wittier, when, with a swift change of aspect as he leaves Lady Constantine to reprimand Swithin, the Bishop appears 'like an evangelized King of Spades come to have it out with the Knave of Hearts'. Smoke from newly lit fires rises out of cottage chimneys 'like the stems of blue trees' in an impressionist picture, while the swaying 'in seconds' of the 'thin straight stems' of trees 'like inverted pendulums' has a fascinating quaintness. Less remarkable but more admirable is the comparison from a writer's experience:

> As the words in which a thought is expressed develop a further thought, so did the fact of her having got so far influence her to go further.

and the fine precision of:

> her intention wheeled this way and that like the balance of a watch. His unexpected proposition had brought about the smartest encounter of inclination with prudence, of impulse with reserve, that she had ever known.

As a reflection of character and mood, the letters form an interesting variety, those from Lady Constantine, the Bishop, and Swithin's misogynist great-uncle being the most memorable. Not surprisingly, Viviette's are moving or tragic. Her 'Romance' nature contrasts favourably with the Laodicean temperament of Hardy's previous heroine. The 'Eve' in her shows itself (never very seriously) in her occasional pique at Swithin's unflattering ingenuousness, in the thought (rapidly following a twinge of conscience) that by marriage she had raised him socially, and in her jealousy of Tabitha Lark. Despite his youth and differences in their social background, the lovers make an excellent match. Their astronomical pursuits dissolve mundane distinctions and promote a sense of equality. Each has a nobility of nature and a readiness to put the interests of the other first. Yet they are far from similar. Their physical contrast has its temperamental parallel. Swithin is an intellectual, remarkably detached from sublunary affairs before he realises what love is; Viviette is warm and affectionate, swayed by generous feelings, 'either lover or *dévote*'. Any realisation she has of the 'ephemeral trivialities' of her problems in the infinite sum of things must be slight and transitory. Ironically, Swithin's scientific outlook, the 'inexorably simple logic' which made him accept Viviette's self-denying wishes literally when he returned after years of absence, contributes to the final catastrophe.

In its concluding stages, the pace of the novel quickens admirably. The account of Swithin's travels and work is kept to an effective minimum, in the interests of both author and reader. Swithin learns enough from England to satisfy the curiosity of the reader before his return. Except for a rather confusing oversight in the chronological annotation at this point, the ending is worked out with commendable artistry. No one is overlooked and, though Hezzy Biles, speaking for the rustic 'chorus', asserts that little has happened at Welland during Swithin's absence – 'when you've said that a few stripling boys and maidens have busted into blooth, and a few married women have plimmed and chimped (my lady among 'em), why, you've said anighst all, Mr San Cleeve' – we learn all that is relevant, not least with reference to Tabitha Lark. Its context may be slightly unrealistic, though Viviette is a religious woman, but the simple question asked by her son in the hearing of Swithin as he ascends the tower, 'You made a mistake, didn't you, mother?'

remains haunting in its dramatic irony. Shocks follow, leading to one of Hardy's most tragic climaxes. The final pages combine story and theme. The 'loneliness' of the southern sky seemed more lonely to Swithin than the 'north stellar region' with which he was familiar; and we are reminded of the 'ephemeral trivialities' of life. On his return, the theme is the effect of time and change. It is largely through Time's revenges, and the immediate effect of physical change in Viviette on Swithin, that the Bishop is avenged. On this note the novel ends, suggesting that, if we can detach ourselves and look at life from a more macrocosmic viewpoint, the tragedy wears a comic aspect.

The topicality of *Two on a Tower* must have increased its interest in 1882–3. The only two transits of Venus in the nineteenth century occurred in December 1874 and December 1882. If Swithin did not have the first of these in mind when he referred to 'the next', the concluding events of the story must be imagined to have taken place after the complete novel was published. It would be unwise to assume that Hardy kept close to contemporary astronomical chronology (no eclipse of the moon fits in with a time scheme relating to either transit of Venus), yet he seems to have utilised two events of 1881, the appearance of Tebbutt's Comet and the publication of important work by an American on variable stars.

The reception of the novel did much to make Hardy realise what a 'fearful price' the contemporary novelist had to pay for 'the privilege of writing in the English language'.[1] Yet he did not mind outraging readers who judged by the letter of the law, for in subsequent editions he took steps to show conclusively that Lady Constantine's child was conceived when she and Swithin knew that their marriage was illegal. On this issue, even after completing *Jude the Obscure*, he preferred an evasive half-truth in his preface of 1895.

F. B. PINION

A star in the text indicates that an explanatory note is to be found at the end of the book, while superior numbers refer to footnotes.

[1] 'Candour in English Fiction' (1890), reprinted in *Thomas Hardy's Personal Writings*, ed. Harold Orel (Macmillan, 1967) p. 130.

TWO ON A TOWER

Thomas Hardy's WESSEX
Fictitious names as Exonbury
Real names as Portsmouth
Miles
Cliff without name
Targan Bay
Dundagel
Nalleney Vale
St. Launce's
Plymouth
OFF WESSEX
Trufal
Penzephyr
Lands End
Bristol Channel
Stancy Castle
Exon Moor
Dunkery Beacon
Quantock Hills
Downstaple
Bristol
Bath
Mendip Hills
Tountall
Glaston
Sedgemoor
OUTER WESSEX
Toneborough
LOWER WESSEX
Tivworthy
Exonbury
River Axe
Idmouth
Tor-upon-Sea
Deadmans Bay
Isle of Slingers
The Beal
The Race
Lightship
The Channel
Christminster
Lumsdon
NORTH WESSEX
Alfredston
Marygreen
MID WESSEX
Marlbury Downs
Batton Castle
Kennetbridge
Castle Royal
Aldbrickham
Inkpen Beacon
Stoke Barehills
Quartershot
Weydon Priors
Icenway House
UPPER WESSEX
Wintoncester
Deansleigh
Southampton
The Great Stonehenge
Plain
Stour Head
Melchester
Shaston
Wingreen
The Chase
Trantridge Cross
Sherton Abbas
Stourcastle
Chaseborough
Vale of Blackmore
Shottsford Forum
Lornton Inn
Ivell
King's Hintock
High Stoy
Bulbarrow
Emminster
Flintcomb-Ash
Warborne
Pilsdon
Chalk Newton
SOUTH WESSEX
Casterbridge
Egdon Heath
Chene Manor
Havenpool
Port Bredy
Blackon
Talbothays
Overcombe
Wellbridge
Anglebury
Budmouth
Knollsea
Sandbourne
The Great Forest
Solentsea
Portsmouth
The Island
Occidens
Meridies
Oriens

Preface

THIS slightly-built romance was the outcome of a wish to set the emotional history of two infinitesimal lives against the stupendous background of the stellar universe, and to impart to readers the sentiment that of these contrasting magnitudes the smaller might be the greater to them as men.

But on the publication of the book people seemed to be less struck with these high aims of the author than with their own opinion, first, that the novel was an 'improper' one in its morals, and, secondly, that it was intended to be a satire on the Established Church of this country. I was made to suffer in consequence from several eminent pens.*

That, however, was thirteen years ago, and, in respect of the first opinion, I venture to think that those who care to read the story now will be quite astonished at the scrupulous propriety observed therein on the relations of the sexes; for though there may be frivolous, and even grotesque touches on occasion, there is hardly a single caress in the book outside legal matrimony, or what was intended so to be.

As for the second opinion, it is sufficient to draw attention, as I did at the time, to the fact that the Bishop is every inch a gentleman, and that the parish priest who figures in the narrative is one of its most estimable characters.

However, the pages must speak for themselves. Some few readers, I trust – to take a serious view – will be reminded by this imperfect story, in a manner not unprofitable to the growth of the social sympathies, of the pathos, misery, long-suffering, and divine tenderness which in real life frequently accompany the passion of such a woman as Viviette for a lover several years her junior.

The scene of the action was suggested by two real spots in the part of the country specified, each of which has a column standing upon it. Certain surrounding peculiarities have been imported into the narrative from both sites, and from elsewhere.

The first edition of the novel was published in 1882, in three volumes.

July 1895 T.H.

CHAPTER ONE

On an early winter afternoon, clear but not cold, when the vegetable world was a weird multitude of skeletons through whose ribs the sun shone freely, a gleaming landau* came to a pause on the crest of a hill in Wessex. The spot was where the old Melchester Road, which the carriage had hitherto followed, was joined by a drive that led round into a park at no great distance off.

The footman alighted, and went to the occupant of the carriage, a lady about eight- or nine-and-twenty. She was looking through the opening afforded by a field-gate at the undulating stretch of country beyond. In pursuance of some remark from her the servant looked in the same direction.

The central feature of the middle distance, as they beheld it, was a circular isolated hill, of no great elevation, which placed itself in strong chromatic contrast with a wide acreage of surrounding arable by being covered with fir-trees. The trees were all of one size and age, so that their tips assumed the precise curve of the hill they grew upon. This pine-clad protuberance was yet further marked out from the general landscape by having on its summit a tower in the form of a classical column, which, though partly immersed in the plantation, rose above the tree-tops to a considerable height. Upon this object the eyes of lady and servant were bent.

'Then there is no road leading near it?' she asked.

'Nothing nearer than where we are now, my lady.'

'Then drive home,' she said after a moment. And the carriage rolled on its way.

A few days later, the same lady, in the same carriage, passed that spot again. Her eyes, as before, turned to the distant tower.

'Nobbs,' she said to the coachman, 'could you find your way home through that field, so as to get near the outskirts of the plantation where the column is?'

The coachman regarded the field. 'Well, my lady,' he observed, 'in dry weather we might drive in there by inching and pinching,* and so get across by Five-and-Twenty Acres, all being well. But the ground is so heavy after these rains that perhaps it would hardly be safe to try it now.'

'Perhaps not,' she assented indifferently. 'Remember it, will you, at a drier time?'

And again the carriage sped along the road, the lady's eyes resting on the segmental* hill, the blue trees that muffled it, and the column that formed its apex, till they were out of sight.

A long time elapsed before that lady drove over the hill again. It was February; the soil was now unquestionably dry, the weather and scene being in other respects much as they had been before. The familiar shape of the column seemed to remind her that at last an opportunity for a close inspection had arrived. Giving her directions she saw the gate opened, and after a little manœuvring the carriage swayed slowly into the uneven field.

Although the pillar stood upon the hereditary estate of her husband the lady had never visited it, owing to its insulation by this well-nigh impracticable ground. The drive to the base of the hill was tedious and jerky, and on reaching it she alighted, directing that the carriage should be driven back empty over the clods, to wait for her on the nearest edge of the field. She then ascended beneath the trees on foot.

The column now showed itself as a much more important erection than it had appeared from the road, or the park, or the windows of Welland House, her residence hard by, whence she had surveyed it hundreds of times without ever feeling a sufficient interest in its details to investigate them. The column had been erected in the eighteenth century, as a substantial memorial of her husband's great-grandfather, a respectable officer who had fallen in the American war,* and the reason of her lack of interest was partly owing to her relations with this husband, of which more anon. It was little beyond the sheer desire for something to do – the chronic desire of her curiously lonely life – that had brought her here now. She was in a mood to welcome anything that would in some measure disperse an almost killing *ennui*. She would have welcomed even a misfortune. She had heard that from the summit of the pillar four counties could be seen. Whatever pleasurable effect was to be derived from looking into four counties she resolved to enjoy today.

The fir-shrouded hill-top was (according to some antiquaries) an old Roman camp, – if it were not (as others insisted) an old British castle,* or (as the rest swore) an old Saxon field of Witenagemote,* – with remains of an outer and an inner vallum,* a winding path leading up between their overlapping ends* by an easy ascent. The spikelets from the trees formed a soft carpet over the route, and occasionally a brake of brambles barred the interspaces of the trunks. Soon she stood immediately at the foot of the column.

It had been built in the Tuscan* order of classic architecture, and was really a tower, being hollow with steps inside. The gloom and solitude which prevailed round the base were remarkable. The sob of the environing trees was here expressively manifest; and moved by the light breeze their thin straight stems rocked in seconds, like inverted pendulums; while some boughs and twigs rubbed the pillar's sides, or occasionally clicked in catching each other. Below the level of their summits the masonry was lichen-stained and mildewed, for the sun never pierced that moaning cloud of blue-black vegetation. Pads of moss grew in the joints of the stone-work, and here and there shade-loving insects had engraved on the mortar patterns of no human style or meaning; but curious and suggestive. Above the trees the case was different: the pillar rose into the sky a bright and cheerful thing, unimpeded, clean and flushed with the sunlight.

The spot was seldom visited by a pedestrian, except perhaps in the shooting season. The rarity of human intrusion was evidenced by the mazes of rabbit-runs,* the feathers of shy birds, the exuviæ* of reptiles; as also by the well-worn paths of squirrels down the sides of trunks, and thence horizontally away. The fact of the plantation being an island in the midst of an arable plain sufficiently accounted for this lack of visitors. Few unaccustomed to such places can be aware of the insulating effect of ploughed ground, when no necessity compels people to traverse it. This rotund hill of trees and brambles, standing in the centre of a ploughed field of some forty or fifty acres, was probably visited less frequently than a rock would have been visited in a lake of equal extent.

She walked round the column to the other side, where she found the door through which the interior was reached. The paint, if it had ever owned any, was all washed from the wood, and down the decaying surface of the boards liquid rust from the nails and hinges had run in red stains. Over the door was a stone tablet, bearing, apparently, letters or words; but the inscription, whatever it was, had been smoothed over with a plaster of lichen.

Here stood this aspiring piece of masonry, erected as the most conspicuous and ineffaceable reminder of a man that could be thought of; and yet the whole aspect of the memorial betokened forgetfulness. Probably not a dozen people within the district knew the name of the person commemorated; while perhaps not a soul remembered whether the column were hollow or solid, whether with or without a tablet explaining its date and purpose. She herself had lived within a mile of it for the last five years, and had never come near it till now.

She hesitated to ascend alone, but finding that the door was not fastened she pushed it open with her foot, and entered. A scrap of writing-paper lay within, and arrested her attention by its freshness. Some human being, then, knew the spot, despite her surmises. But as the paper had nothing on it no clue was afforded; yet feeling herself the proprietor of the column and of all around it her self-assertiveness was sufficient to lead her on. The staircase was lighted by slits in the wall, and there was no difficulty in reaching the top, the steps being quite unworn. The trap-door leading on to the roof was open, and on looking through it an interesting spectacle met her eye.

A youth was sitting on a stool in the centre of the lead flat which formed the summit of the column, his eye being applied to the end of a large telescope that stood before him on a tripod. This sort of presence was unexpected, and the lady started back into the shade of the opening. The only effect produced upon him by her footfall was an impatient wave of the hand, which he did without removing his eye from the instrument, as if to forbid her to interrupt him.

Pausing where she stood the lady examined the aspect of the individual who thus made himself so completely at home on a building which she deemed her unquestioned property. He was a youth who might properly have been characterized by a word the judicious chronicler would not readily use in such a connexion, preferring to reserve it for raising images of the opposite sex. Whether because no deep felicity is likely to arise from the condition, or from any other reason, to say in these days that a youth is beautiful is not to award him that amount of credit which the expression would have carried with it if he had lived in the times of the Classical Dictionary.* So much, indeed, is the reverse the case that the assertion creates an awkwardness in saying anything more about him. The beautiful youth usually verges so perilously on the incipient coxcomb, who is about to become the Lothario or Juan* among the neighbouring maidens, that, for the due understanding of our present young man, his sublime innocence of any thought concerning his own material aspect, or that of others, is most fervently asserted, and must be as fervently believed.

Such as he was, there the lad sat. The sun shone full in his face, and on his head he wore a black velvet skull-cap, leaving to view below it a curly margin of very light shining hair, which accorded well with the flush upon his cheek.

He had such a complexion as that with which Raffaelle* enriches the countenance of the youthful son of Zacharias,* – a complexion which, though clear, is far enough removed from virgin delicacy, and suggests plenty of sun and wind as its accompaniment. His features were sufficiently straight in the contours to correct the beholder's first impression that the head was the head of a girl. Beside him stood a little oak table, and in front was the telescope.

His visitor had ample time to make these observations; and she may have done so all the more keenly through being herself of a totally opposite type. Her hair was black as midnight, her eyes had no less deep a shade, and her complexion showed the richness demanded as a support to these decided features. As she continued to look at the pretty fellow before her, apparently so far abstracted into some speculative world as scarcely to know a real one, a warmer wave of her warm temperament glowed visibly through her, and a qualified observer might from this have hazarded a guess that there was Romance* blood in her veins.

But even the interest attaching to the youth could not arrest her attention for ever, and as he made no further signs of moving his eye from the instrument she broke the silence with –

'What do you see? – something happening somewhere?'

'Yes, quite a catastrophe!' he automatically murmured, without moving round.

'What?'

'A cyclone in the sun.'

The lady paused, as if to consider the weight of that event in the scale of terrene* life.

'Will it make any difference to us here?'* she asked.

The young man by this time seemed to be awakened to the consciousness that somebody unusual was talking to him; he turned, and started.

'I beg your pardon,' he said. 'I thought it was my relative come to look after me! She often comes about this time.'

He continued to look at her and forget the sun, just such a reciprocity of influence* as might have been expected between a dark lady and a flaxen-haired youth making itself apparent in the faces of each.

'Don't let me interrupt your observations,' said she.

'Ah, no,' said he, again applying his eye; whereupon his face lost the animation which her presence had lent it, and became immutable as that of a bust, though superadding to the serenity of repose the sensitiveness of life. The expression that settled on him was one of awe. Not unaptly might it have been said that he was worshipping the sun. Among the various intensities of that worship which have prevailed since the first intelligent being saw the luminary decline westward, as the young man now beheld it doing, his was not the weakest. He was engaged in what may be called a very chastened or schooled form of that first and most natural of adorations.

'But would you like to see it?' he recommenced. 'It is an event that is witnessed only about once in two or three years, though it may occur often enough.'

She assented, and looked through the shaded eye-piece, and saw a whirling mass, in the centre of which the blazing globe seemed to be laid bare to its core. It was a peep into a maelstrom of fire, taking place where nobody had ever been or ever would be.

'It is the strangest thing I ever beheld,' she said. Then he looked again; till wondering who her companion could be she asked, 'Are you often here?'

'Every night when it is not cloudy, and often in the day.'

'Ah, night, of course. The heavens must be beautiful from this point.'

'They are rather more than that.'

'Indeed! Have you entirely taken possession of this column?'

'Entirely.'

'But it is my column,' she said, with smiling asperity.

'Then are you Lady Constantine, wife of the absent Sir Blount Constantine?'

'I am Lady Constantine.'

'Ah, then I agree that it is your ladyship's. But will you allow me to rent it of you for a time, Lady Constantine?'

'You have taken it, whether I allow it or not. However, in the interests of science it is advisable that you continue your tenancy. Nobody knows you are here, I suppose?'

'Hardly anybody.'

He then took her down a few steps into the interior, and showed her some ingenious contrivances for stowing articles away.

'Nobody ever comes near the column, – or, as it's called here, Rings-Hill Speer,'* he continued; 'and when I first came up it nobody had been here for thirty or forty years. The staircase was choked with daws' nests and feathers, but I cleared them out.'

'I understood the column was always kept locked?'

'Yes, it has been so. When it was built, in 1782, the key was given to my great-grandfather, to keep by him in case visitors should happen to want it. He lived just down there where I live now.'

He denoted by a nod a little dell lying immediately beyond the ploughed land which environed them.

'He kept it in his bureau, and as the bureau descended to my grandfather, my mother, and myself, the key descended with it. After the first thirty or forty years, nobody ever asked for it. One day I saw it, lying rusty in its niche, and, finding that it belonged to this column, I took it and came up. I stayed here till it was dark, and the stars came out, and that night I resolved to be an astronomer. I came back here from school several months ago, and I mean to be an astronomer still.'

He lowered his voice, and added:

'I aim at nothing less than the dignity and office of Astronomer Royal,* if I live. Perhaps I shall not live.'

'I don't see why you should suppose that,' said she. 'How long are you going to make this your observatory?'

'About a year longer – till I have obtained a practical familiarity with the heavens. Ah, if I only had a good equatorial!'*

'What is that?'

'A proper instrument for my pursuit. But time is short, and science is infinite,* – how infinite only those who study astronomy fully realize, – and perhaps I shall be worn out before I make my mark.'

She seemed to be greatly struck by the odd mixture in him of scientific earnestness and melancholy mistrust of all things human. Perhaps it was owing to the nature of his studies.

'You are often on this tower alone at night?' she said.

'Yes; at this time of the year particularly, and while there is no moon. I observe from seven or eight till about two in the morning, with a view to my great work on variable stars. But with such a telescope as this – well, I must put up with it!'

'Can you see Saturn's ring and Jupiter's moons?'

He said drily that he could manage to do that, not without some contempt for the state of her knowledge.

'I have never seen any planet or star through a telescope.'

'If you will come the first clear night, Lady Constantine, I will show you any number. I mean, at your express wish; not otherwise.'

'I should like to come, and possibly may at some time. These stars that vary so much – sometimes evening stars, sometimes morning stars, sometimes in the east, and sometimes in the west – have always interested me.'

'Ah – now there is a reason for your not coming. Your ignorance of the realities of astronomy is so satisfactory that I will not disturb it except at your serious request.'

'But I wish to be enlightened.'

'Let me caution you against it.'

'Is enlightenment on the subject, then, so terrible?'

'Yes, indeed.'

She laughingly declared that nothing could have so piqued her curiosity as his statement, and turned to descend. He helped her down the stairs and through the briers. He would have gone further and crossed the open corn-land with her, but she preferred to go alone. He then retraced his way to the top of the column, but, instead of looking longer at the sun, watched her diminishing towards the distant fence, behind which waited the carriage. When in the midst of the field, a dark spot on an area of brown, there crossed her path a moving figure, whom it was as difficult to distinguish from the earth he trod as the caterpillar from its leaf, by reason of the excellent match between his clothes and the clods. He was one of a dying-out generation who retained the principle, nearly unlearnt now, that a man's habiliments should be in harmony with his environment. Lady Constantine and this figure halted beside each other for some minutes; then they went on their several ways.

The brown person was a labouring man known to the world of Welland as Haymoss (the encrusted form of the word Amos, to adopt the phrase of philologists). The reason of the halt had been some inquiries addressed to him by Lady Constantine.

'Who is that – Amos Fry, I think?' she had asked.

'Yes, my lady,' said Haymoss; 'a homely barley driller, born under the eaves of your ladyship's outbuildings, in a manner of speaking, – though your ladyship was neither born nor 'tempted* at that time.'

'Who lives in the old house behind the plantation?'

'Old Gammer* Martin, my lady, and her grandson.'

'He has neither father nor mother, then?'

'Not a single one, my lady.'

'Where was he educated?'

'At Warborne, – a place where they draw up young gam'sters'* brains like rhubarb under a ninepenny pan,* my lady, excusing my common way. They hit* so much learning into en that 'a* could talk like the day of Pentecost;* which is a wonderful thing for a simple boy, and his mother only the plainest ciphering* woman in the world. Warborne Grammar School – that's where 'twas 'a went to. His father, the reverent Pa'son St Cleeve, made a terrible bruckle hit* in 's marrying, in the sight of the high.* He were the curate here, my lady, for a length o' time.'

'Oh, curate,' said Lady Constantine. 'It was before I knew the village.'

'Ay, long and merry ago! And he married Farmer Martin's daughter – Giles Martin, a limberish* man, who used to go rather bad upon his legs, if you can mind?* I knowed the man well enough; who should know en better! The maid was a poor windling* thing, and, though a playward* piece o' flesh when he married her, she socked and sighed,* and went out like a snoff!* Yes, my lady. Well, when Pa'son St Cleeve married this homespun woman the toppermost folk wouldn't speak to his wife. Then he dropped a cuss or two, and said he'd no longer get his living by curing their twopenny souls o' such d— nonsense as that (excusing my common way), and he took to farming straightway, and then 'a dropped down dead in a nor'-west thunderstorm; it being said – hee-hee! – that Master God was in tantrums wi'en for leaving his service, – hee-hee! I give the story as I heard it, my lady, but be dazed* if I believe in such trumpery* about folks in the sky, nor anything else that's said on 'em, good or bad. Well, Swithin, the boy, was sent to the grammar school, as I say for;* but what with having two stations of life in his blood he's good for nothing, my lady. He mopes about – sometimes here and sometimes there; nobody troubles about en.'

Lady Constantine thanked her informant and proceeded onward. To her, as a woman, the most curious feature in the afternoon's incident was that this lad of striking beauty, scientific attainments, and cultivated bearing, should be linked on the maternal side with a local agricultural family through his father's matrimonial eccentricity. A more attractive feature in the case was that the same youth, so capable of being ruined by flattery, blandishment, pleasure, even gross prosperity, should be at present living on in a primitive Eden of unconsciousness,* with aims towards whose accomplishment a Caliban* shape would have been as effective as his own.

CHAPTER TWO

SWITHIN ST CLEEVE lingered on at his post until the more sanguine birds of the plantation, already recovering from their midwinter anxieties, piped a short evening hymn to the vanishing sun.

The landscape was gently concave; with the exception of tower and hill there were no points on which late rays might linger; and hence the dish-shaped fifty acres of tilled land assumed a uniform hue of shade quite suddenly. The one or two stars that appeared were quickly clouded over, and it was soon obvious that there would be no sweeping* the heavens that night. After tying a piece of tarpaulin, which had once seen service on his maternal grandfather's farm, over all the apparatus around him, he went down the stairs in the dark, and locked the door.

With the key in his pocket he descended through the underwood on the side of the slope opposite to that trodden by Lady Constantine, and crossed the field in a line mathematically straight, and in a manner that left no traces, by keeping in the same furrow all the way on tiptoe. In a few minutes he reached a little dell, which occurred quite unexpectedly on the other side of the field-fence, and descended to a venerable thatched house, whose enormous roof, broken up by dormers* as big as haycocks, could be seen even in the twilight. Over the white walls, built of chalk in the lump, outlines of creepers formed dark patterns, as if drawn in charcoal.

Inside the house his maternal grandmother was sitting by a wood fire. Before it stood a pipkin, in which something was evidently kept warm. An eight-legged oak table in the middle of the room was laid for a meal. This woman of eighty, in a large mob cap,* under which she wore a little cap to keep the other clean, retained faculties but little blunted. She was gazing into the flames, with her hands upon her knees, quietly re-enacting in her brain certain of the long chain of episodes, pathetic, tragical, and humorous, which had constituted the parish history for the last sixty years. On Swithin's entry she looked up at him in a sideway direction.

'You should not have waited for me, granny,' he said.

''Tis of no account, my child. I've had a nap while sitting here. Yes, I've had a nap, and went straight back into my old county* again, as usual. The place was as natural as when I left it, – e'en just three-score years ago! All the folks and my old aunt were there, as when I was a child, – yet I suppose if I were really to set out and go there, hardly a soul would be left alive to say to me, dog how art!* But tell Hannah to stir her stumps and serve supper – though I'd fain do it myself, the poor old soul is getting so unhandy!'

Hannah revealed herself to be much nimbler and several years younger than granny, though of this the latter seemed to be oblivious. When the meal was nearly over Mrs Martin produced the contents of the mysterious vessel by the fire, saying that she had caused it to be brought in from the back kitchen, because Hannah was hardly to be trusted with such things, she was becoming so childish.

'What is it, then?' said Swithin. 'Oh, one of your special puddings.' At sight of it, however, he added reproachfully, 'Now, granny!'

Instead of being round, it was in shape an irregular boulder that had been exposed to the weather for centuries – a little scrap pared off here, and a little piece cut away there; the general aim being, nevertheless, to avoid destroying the symmetry of the pudding while taking as much as possible of its substance.

'The fact is,' added Swithin, 'the pudding is half gone!'

'I've only sliced off the merest paring once or twice, to taste if it was well done!' pleaded Granny Martin, with wounded feelings. 'I said to Hannah when she took it up, "Put it here to keep it hot, as there's a better fire than in the back kitchen."'

'Well, I am not going to eat any of it, chopped round like that!' said Swithin decisively, as he rose from the table, pushed away his chair, and went upstairs; the 'other station of life that was in his blood',* and which had been brought out by the grammar school, probably stimulating him.

'Ah, the world is an ungrateful place! 'Twas a pity I didn't take my poor name off this earthly calendar and creep under ground sixty long years ago, instead of leaving my own county to come here!' mourned old Mrs Martin. 'But I told his mother how 'twould be – marrying so many notches above her.* The child was sure to chaw high,* like his father!'

When Swithin had been upstairs a minute or two, however, he altered his mind, and coming down again ate all the pudding, with the aspect of a person undertaking a deed of great magnanimity. The relish with which he did so restored the unison that knew no more serious interruptions than such as this.

'Mr Torkingham has been here this afternoon,' said his grandmother: 'and he wants me to let him meet some of the choir here to-night for practice. They who live at this end of the parish won't go to his house to try over the tunes, because 'tis so far, they say; and so 'tis, poor men. So he's going to see what coming to them will do. He asks if you would like to join.'

'I would if I had not so much to do.'

'But it is cloudy to-night.'

'Yes; but I have calculations without end, granny. Now, don't you tell him I'm in the house, will you? and then he'll not ask for me.'

'But if he should, must I then tell a lie, Lord forgive me?'

'No, you can say I'm upstairs; he must think what he likes. Not a word about the astronomy to any of them, whatever you do. I should be called a visionary, and all sorts.'

'So thou beest, child. Why can't ye do something that's of use?'

At the sound of footsteps Swithin beat a hasty retreat upstairs, where he struck a light, and revealed a table covered with books and papers, while round the walls hung star-maps and other diagrams illustrative of celestial phenomena. In a corner stood a huge paste-board tube, which a close inspection would have shown to be intended for a telescope. Swithin hung a thick cloth over the window in addition to the curtains, and sat down to his papers. On the ceiling was a black stain of smoke, and under this he placed his lamp, evidencing that the midnight oil was consumed on that precise spot very often.

Meanwhile there had entered to the room below a personage who, to judge from her voice and the quick pit-pat of her feet, was a maiden young and blithe. Mrs Martin welcomed her by the title of Miss Tabitha Lark, and inquired what wind had brought her that way; to which the visitor replied that she had come for the singing.

'Sit ye down, then,' said granny. 'And do you still go to the House to read to my lady?'

'Yes, I go and read, Mrs Martin; but as to getting my lady to hearken, that's more than a team of six horses could force her to do.'

The girl had a remarkably smart and fluent utterance, which was probably a cause, or a consequence, of her vocation.

''Tis the same story, then?' said grandmother Martin.

'Yes. Eaten out with listlessness. She's neither sick nor sorry, but how dull and dreary she is, only herself can tell. When I get there in the morning she is sitting in bed, for my lady doesn't care to get up; and then she makes me bring this book and that book, till the bed is heaped up with immense volumes that half bury her, making her look, as she leans upon her elbow, like the stoning of Stephen.* She yawns; then she looks towards the tall glass; then she looks out at the weather, mooning her great black eyes, and fixing them on the sky as if they stuck there, while my tongue goes flick-flack* along, a hundred and fifty words a minute; then she looks at the clock; then she asks me what I've been reading.'

'Ah, poor soul!' said granny. 'No doubt she says in the morning, "Would God it were evening", and in the evening, "Would God it were morning", like the disobedient woman in Deuteronomy.'*

Swithin in the room overhead had suspended his calculations, for the duologue interested him. There now crunched heavier steps outside the door, and his grandmother could be heard greeting sundry local representatives of the bass and tenor voice, who lent a cheerful and well-known personality to the names Sammy Blore, Nat Chapman, Hezekiah Biles, and Haymoss Fry (the latter being one with whom the reader has already a distant acquaintance); besides these came small producers of treble, who had not yet developed into such distinctive units of society as to require particularizing.

'Is the good man come?' asked Nat Chapman. 'No, – I see we be here afore him. And how is it with aged women to-night, Mrs Martin?'

'Tedious traipsing* enough with this one, Nat. Sit ye down. Well, little Freddy, you don't wish in the morning that 'twere evening, and at evening that 'twere morning again, do you, Freddy, trust 'ee for it?'

'Now, who might wish such a thing as that, Mrs Martin? – nobody in this parish?' asked Sammy Blore curiously.

'My lady is always wishing it,' spoke up Miss Tabitha Lark.

'Oh, she! Nobody can be answerable for the wishes of that onnatural tribe of mankind. Not but that the woman's heart-strings is tried in many aggravating ways.'

'Ah, poor woman!' said granny. 'The state she finds herself in – neither maid, wife, nor widow – is not the primest* form of life for keeping in good spirits. How long is it since she has heard from Sir Blount, Tabitha?'

'Two years and more,' said the young woman. 'He went into one side of Africa as it might be three St Martin's days* back. I can mind it, because 'twas my birthday. And he meant to come out the other side. But he didn't. He has never come out at all.'

'For all the world like losing a rat in a barley-mow,'* said Hezekiah. 'He's lost, though you know where he is.'

His comrades nodded.

'Ay, my lady is a walking weariness. I seed her yawn just at the very moment when the fox was halloaed away by Lornton Copse, and the hounds runned en all but past her carriage wheels. If I were she I'd see a little life; though there's no fair, club-walking,* nor feast to speak of, till Easter week, – that's true.'

'She dares not. She's under solemn oath to do no such thing.'

'Be cust if I would keep any such oath! But here's the pa'son, if my ears don't deceive me.'

There was a noise of horse's hoofs without, a stumbling against the door-scraper, a tethering to the window-shutter, a creaking of the door on its hinges, and a voice which Swithin recognized as Mr Torkingham's. He greeted each of the previous arrivals by name, and stated that he was glad to see them all so punctually assembled.

'Ay, sir,' said Haymoss Fry. ''Tis only my jints* that have kept me from assembling myself* long ago. I'd assemble upon the top of Welland Steeple,* if 'tweren't for my jints. I assure 'ee, Pa'son Tarkenham, that in the clitch* o' my knees, where the rain used to come through when I was cutting clots* for the new lawn in old my lady's time, 'tis as if rats wez gnawing every now and then. When a feller's young he's too small in the brain to see how soon a constitution can be squandered, worse luck!'

'True,' said Biles, to fill the time while the parson was engaged in finding the Psalms. 'A man's a fool till he's forty. Often have I thought, when hay-pitching, and the small of my back seeming no stouter than a harnet's,* "The devil send* that I had but the making of labouring men for a twelvemonth!" I'd gie every man-jack two good backbones, even if the alteration was as wrong as forgery.'

'Four, – four backbones,' said Haymoss decisively.

'Yes, four,' threw in Sammy Blore, with additional weight of experience. 'For you want one in front for breast-ploughing* and such like, one at the right side for ground-dressing,* and one at the left side for turning mixens.'*

'Well; then next I'd move every man's wyndpipe* a good span away from his glutchpipe,* so that at harvest time he could fetch breath in 's drinking, without being choked and strangled as he is now. Thinks I, when I feel the victuals going—'

'Now, we'll begin,' interrupted Mr Torkingham, his mind returning to this world again on concluding his search for a psalm.

Thereupon the racket of chair-legs on the floor signified that they were settling into their seats, – a disturbance which Swithin took advantage of by going on tiptoe across the floor above, and putting sheets of paper over knot-holes in the boarding at points where carpet was lacking, that his lamp-light might not shine down. The absence of a ceiling beneath rendered his position virtually that of one suspended in the same apartment.

The parson announced Psalm fifty-third to the tune of 'Devizes', and his voice burst forth with

> 'The Lord look'd down from Heav'n's high tower
> The sons of men to view',*

in notes of rigid cheerfulness.

In this start, however, he was joined only by the girls and boys, the men furnishing but an accompaniment of ahas and hems. Mr Torkingham stopped, and Sammy Blore spoke, –

'Beg your pardon, sir, – if you'll deal mild with us a moment. What with the wind and walking, my throat's as rough as a grater;* and not knowing you were going to hit up* that minute, I hadn't hawked,* and I don't think Hezzy and Nat had, either, – had ye, souls?'

'I hadn't got thorough ready, that's true,' said Hezekiah.

'Quite right of you, then, to speak,' said Mr Torkingham. 'Don't mind explaining; we are here for practice. Now clear your throats, then, and at it again.'

There was a noise as of atmospheric hoes and scrapers, and the bass contingent at last got under way with a time of its own:

'The Lard looked down vrom Heav'n's high tower!'

'Ah, that's where we are so defective – the pronunciation,' interrupted the parson. 'Now repeat after me: "The Lord look'd down from Heav'n's high tower."'

The choir repeated like an exaggerative echo: 'The Lawd look'd daown from Heav'n's high towah!'

'Better!' said the parson, in the strenuously sanguine tones of a man who got his living by discovering a bright side in things where it was not very perceptible to other people. 'But it should not be given with quite so extreme an accent; or we may be called affected by other parishes. And, Nathaniel Chapman, there's a jauntiness in your manner of singing which is not quite becoming. Why don't you sing more earnestly?'

'My conscience won't let me, sir. They say every man for himself: but, thank God, I'm not so mean as to lessen old fokes' chances by being earnest at my time o' life, and they so much nearer the need o't.'

'It's bad reasoning, Nat, I fear. Now, perhaps we had better sol-fa* the tune. Eyes on your books, please. *Doe! doe-ray-mee—*'

'I can't sing like that, not I!' said Sammy Blore, with condemnatory astonishment. 'I can sing genuine music, like F and G; but not anything so much out of the order of nater* as that.'

'Perhaps you've brought the wrong book, sir?' chimed in Haymoss, kindly. 'I've knowed music early in life and late, – in short, ever since Luke Sneap broke his new fiddle-bow in the wedding psalm, when Pa'son Wilton brought home his bride (you can mind the time, Sammy? – when we sung "His wife, like a fair fertile vine, her lovely fruit shall bring",* when the young woman turned as red as a rose, not knowing 'twas coming). I've knowed music ever since then, I say, sir, and never heard the like o' that. Every martel* note had his name of A, B, C, at that time.'

'Yes, yes, men; but this is a more recent system!'

'Still, you can't alter a old-established note that's A or B by nater,' rejoined Haymoss, with yet deeper conviction that Mr Torkingham was getting off his head. 'Now sound A, neighbour Sammy, and let's have a slap at* Heav'n's high tower again, and show the Pa'son the true way!'

Sammy produced a private tuning-fork, black and grimy, which, being about seventy years of age, and wrought before pianoforte builders had sent up the pitch to make their instruments brilliant,* was nearly a note flatter than the parson's. While an argument as to the true pitch was in progress there came a knocking without.

'Somebody's at the door!' said a little treble girl.

'Thought I heard a knock before!' said the relieved choir.

The latch was lifted, and a man asked from the darkness, 'Is Mr Torkingham here?'

'Yes, Mills. What do you want?'

It was the parson's man.

'O, if you please,' said Mills, showing an advanced margin of himself round the door, 'Lady Constantine wants to see you very particular, sir, and could you call on her after dinner, if you ben't engaged with poor folks? She's just had a letter, – so they say, – and it's about that, I believe.'

Finding, on looking at his watch, that it was necessary to start at once if he meant to see her that night, the parson cut short the practising, and, naming another night for meeting, he withdrew. All the singers assisted him on to his cob, and watched him till he disappeared over the edge of the Bottom.

CHAPTER THREE

MR TORKINGHAM trotted briskly onward to his house, a distance of about a mile, each cottage, as it revealed its half-buried position by its single light, appearing like a one-eyed night creature watching him from an ambush. Leaving his horse at the parsonage he performed the remainder of the journey on foot, crossing the park towards Welland House by a stile and path till he struck into the drive near the north door of the mansion.

This drive, it may be remarked, was also the common highway to the lower village, and hence Lady Constantine's residence and park, as is occasionally the case with old-fashioned manors, possessed none of the exclusiveness found in some aristocratic settlements. The parishioners looked upon the park avenue as their natural thoroughfare, particularly for christenings, weddings, and funerals, which passed the squire's mansion with due considerations as to the scenic effect of the same from the manor windows. Hence the house of Constantine, when going out from its breakfast, had been continually crossed on the doorstep for the last two hundred years by the houses of Hodge and Giles* in full cry to dinner. At present these collisions were but too infrequent, for though the villagers passed the north front door as regularly as ever, they seldom met a Constantine. Only one was there to be met, and she had no zest for outings before noon.

The long, low front of the Great House, as it was called by the parish, stretching from end to end of the terrace, was in darkness as the vicar slackened his pace before it, and only the distant fall of water disturbed the stillness of the manorial precincts.

On gaining admittance he found Lady Constantine waiting to receive him. She wore a heavy dress of velvet and lace, and being the only person in the spacious apartment she looked small and isolated. In her left hand she held a letter and a couple of at-home cards.* The soft dark eyes which she raised to him as he entered – large, and melancholy by circumstance far more than by quality –

were the natural indices of a warm and affectionate, perhaps slightly voluptuous temperament, languishing for want of something to do, cherish, or suffer for.

Mr Torkingham seated himself. His boots, which had seemed elegant in the farm-house, appeared rather clumsy here, and his coat, that was a model of tailoring when he stood amid the choir, now exhibited decidedly strained relations with his limbs. Three years had passed since his induction to the living of Welland, but he had never as yet found means to establish that reciprocity with Lady Constantine which usually grows up, in the course of time, between parsonage and manor-house, – unless, indeed, either side should surprise the other by showing respectively a weakness for awkward modern ideas on landownership, or on church formulas, which had not been the case here. The present meeting, however, seemed likely to initiate such a reciprocity.

There was an appearance of confidence on Lady Constantine's face; she said she was so very glad that he had come, and looking down at the letter in her hand was on the point of pulling it from its envelope; but she did not. After a moment she went on more quickly: 'I wanted your advice, or rather your opinion, on a serious matter, – on a point of conscience.' Saying which she laid down the letter and looked at the cards.

It might have been apparent to a more penetrating eye than the vicar's that Lady Constantine, either from timidity, misgiving, or reconviction, had swerved from her intended communication, or perhaps decided to begin at the other end.

The parson, who had been expecting a question on some local business or intelligence, at the tenor of her words altered his face to the higher branch of his profession.

'I hope I may find myself of service, on that or any other question,' he said gently.

'I hope so. You may possibly be aware, Mr Torkingham, that my husband, Sir Blount Constantine, was, not to mince matters, a mistaken – somewhat jealous man. Yet you may hardly have discerned it in the short time you knew him.'

'I had some little knowledge of Sir Blount's character in that respect.'

'Well, on this account my married life with him was not of the most comfortable kind.' (Lady Constantine's voice dropped to a more pathetic note.) 'I am sure I gave him no cause for suspicion; though had I known his disposition sooner I should hardly have dared to marry him. But his jealousy and doubt of me were not so strong as to divert him from a purpose of his, – a mania for African lion-hunting, which he dignified by calling it a scheme of geographical discovery; for he was inordinately anxious to make a name for himself in that field. It was the one passion that was stronger than his mistrust of me. Before going away he sat down with me in this room, and read me a lecture, which resulted in a very rash offer on my part. When I tell it to you, you will find that it provides a key to all that is unusual in my life here. He bade me consider what my position would be when he was gone; hoped that I should remember what was due to him, – that I would not so behave towards other men as to bring the name of Constantine into suspicion; and charged me to avoid levity of conduct in attending any ball, rout,* or dinner to which I might be invited. I, in some contempt for his low opinion of me, volunteered, there and then, to live like a cloistered nun during his absence; to go into no society whatever, – scarce even to a neighbour's dinner-party; and demanded bitterly if that would satisfy him. He said yes, held me to my word, and gave me no loophole for retracting it. The inevitable fruits of precipitancy have resulted to me: my life has become a burden. I get such invitations as these' (holding up the cards), 'but I so invariably refuse them that they are getting very rare.... I ask you, can I honestly break that promise to my husband?'

Mr Torkingham seemed embarrassed. 'If you promised Sir Blount Constantine to live in solitude till he comes back, you are, it seems to me, bound by that promise. I fear that the wish to be released from your engagement is to some extent a reason why it should be kept. But your own conscience would surely be the best guide, Lady Constantine?'

'My conscience is quite bewildered with its responsibilities,' she continued, with a sigh. 'Yet it certainly does sometimes say to me that – that I ought to keep my word. Very well; I must go on as I am going, I suppose.'

'If you respect a vow, I think you must respect your own,' said the parson, acquiring some further firmness. 'Had it been wrung from you by compulsion, moral or physical, it would have been open to you to break it. But as you proposed a vow when your husband only required a good intention, I think you ought to adhere to it; or what is the pride worth that led you to offer it?'

'Very well,' she said, with resignation. 'But it was quite a work of supererogation on my part.'

'That you proposed it in a supererogatory spirit does not lessen your obligation, having once put yourself under that obligation. St Paul, in his Epistle to the Hebrews, says, "An oath for confirmation is an end of all strife."* And you will readily recall the words in Ecclesiastes, "Pay that which thou hast vowed. Better is it that thou shouldest not vow than that thou shouldest vow and not pay."* Why not write to Sir Blount, tell him the inconvenience of such a bond, and ask him to release you?'

'No; never will I. The expression of such a desire would, in his mind, be a sufficient reason for disallowing it. I'll keep my word.'

Mr Torkingham rose to leave. After she had held out her hand to him, when he had crossed the room, and was within two steps of the door, she said, 'Mr Torkingham.' He stopped. 'What I have told you is only the least part of what I sent for you to tell you.'

Mr Torkingham walked back to her side. 'What is the rest of it, then?' he asked, with grave surprise.

'It is a true revelation, as far as it goes; but there is something more. I have received this letter, and I wanted to say – something.'

'Then say it now, my dear lady.'

'No,' she answered, with a look of utter inability. 'I cannot speak of it now! Some other time. Don't stay. Please consider this conversation as private. Good-night.'

CHAPTER FOUR

IT was a bright starlight night, a week or ten days later. There had been several such nights since the occasion of Lady Constantine's promise to Swithin St Cleeve to come and study astronomical phenomena on the Rings-Hill column; but she had not gone there. This evening she sat at a window, the blind of which had not been drawn down. Her elbow rested on a little table, and her cheek on her hand. Her eyes were attracted by the brightness of the planet Jupiter, as he rode in the ecliptic* opposite, beaming down upon her as if desirous of notice.

Beneath the planet could be still discerned the dark edges of the park landscape against the sky. As one of its features, though nearly screened by the trees which had been planted to shut out the fallow tracts of the estate, rose the upper part of the column. It was hardly visible now, even if visible at all; yet Lady Constantine knew from daytime experience its exact bearing from the window at which she leaned. The knowledge that there it still was, despite its rapid envelopment by the shades, led her lonely mind to her late meeting on its summit with the young astronomer, and to her promise to honour him with a visit for learning some secrets about the scintillating bodies overhead. The curious juxtaposition of youthful ardour and old despair that she had found in the lad would have made him interesting to a woman of perception, apart from his fair hair and early-Christian* face. But such is the heightening touch of memory that his beauty was probably richer in her imagination than in the real. It was a moot point to consider whether the temptations that would be brought to bear upon him in his course would exceed the staying power of his nature. Had he been a wealthy youth he would have seemed one to tremble for. In spite of his attractive ambitions and gentlemanly bearing she thought it would possibly be better for him if he never became known outside his lonely tower, – forgetting that he had received such intellectual enlargement as would probably make his continuance in Welland seem, in his own eye, a slight upon his father's branch of his family, whose social standing had been, only a few years earlier, but little removed from her own.

Suddenly she flung a cloak about her and went out on the terrace. She passed down the steps to the lower lawn, through the door to the open park, and there stood still. The tower was now discernible. As the words in which a thought is expressed develop a further thought, so did the fact of her having got so far influence her to go further. A person who had casually observed her gait would have thought it irregular; and the lessenings and increasings of speed with which she proceeded in the direction of the pillar could be accounted for only by a motive much more disturbing than an intention to look through a telescope. Thus she went on till, leaving the park, she crossed the turnpike-road, and entered the large field in the middle of which a fir-clad hill stood like Mont St Michel* in its bay.

The stars were so bright as distinctly to show her the place, and now she could see a faint light at the top of the column, which rose like a shadowy finger pointing to the upper constellations. There was no wind, in a human sense; but a steady stertorous breathing from the fir-trees showed that, now as always, there was movement in apparent stagnation. Nothing but an absolute vacuum could paralyze their utterance.

The door of the tower was shut. It was something more than the freakishness which is engendered by a sickening monotony that had led Lady Constantine thus far, and hence she made no ado about admitting herself. Three years ago, when her every action was a thing of propriety, she had known of no possible purpose which could have led her abroad in a manner such as this.

She ascended the tower noiselessly. On raising her head above the hatchway she beheld Swithin bending over a scroll of paper which lay on the little table beside him. The small lantern that illuminated it showed also that he was warmly wrapped up in a coat and thick cap, behind him standing the telescope on its frame.

What was he doing? She looked over his shoulder upon the paper, and saw figures and signs. When he had jotted down something he went to the telescope again.

'What are you doing to-night?' she said in a low voice.

Swithin started, and turned. The faint lamp-light was sufficient to reveal her face to him.

'Tedious work, Lady Constantine,' he answered, without betraying much surprise. 'Doing my best to watch phenomenal stars, as I may call them.'

'You said you would show me the heavens if I could come on a starlight night. I have come.'

Swithin, as a preliminary, swept round the telescope to Jupiter, and exhibited to her the glory of that orb. Then he directed the instrument to the less bright shape of Saturn.

'Here,' he said, warming up to the subject, 'we see a world which is to my mind by far the most wonderful in the solar system. Think of streams of satellites or meteors* racing round and round the planet like a fly-wheel,* so close together as to seem solid matter!' He entered further and further into the subject, his ideas gathering momentum as he went on, like his pet heavenly bodies.

When he paused for breath she said, in tones very different from his own, 'I ought now to tell you that, though I am interested in the stars, they were not what I came to see you about. . . . I first thought of disclosing the matter to Mr Torkingham; but I altered my mind, and decided on you.'

She spoke in so low a voice that he might not have heard her. At all events, abstracted by his grand theme, he did not heed her. He continued, –

'Well, we will get outside the solar system altogether, – leave the whole group of sun, primary and secondary planets quite behind us in our flight, as a bird might leave its bush and sweep into the whole forest. Now what do you see, Lady Constantine?' He levelled the achromatic* at Sirius.

She said that she saw a bright star, though it only seemed a point of light now as before.

'That's because it is so distant that no magnifying will bring its size up to zero.* Though called a fixed star, it is, like all fixed stars, moving with inconceivable velocity; but no magnifying will show that velocity as anything but rest.'

And thus they talked on about Sirius, and then about other stars

> . . . in the scrowl
> Of all those beasts, and fish, and fowl,
> With which, like Indian plantations,
> The learned stock the constellations,*

till he asked her how many stars she thought were visible to them at that moment.

She looked around over the magnificent stretch of sky that their high position unfolded. 'O, thousands, – hundreds of thousands,' she said absently.

'No. There are only about three thousand. Now, how many do you think are brought within sight by the help of a powerful telescope?'

'I won't guess.'

'Twenty millions. So that, whatever the stars were made for, they were not made to please our eyes. It is just the same in everything; nothing is made for man.'

'Is it that notion which makes you so sad for your age?' she asked, with almost maternal solicitude. 'I think astronomy is a bad study for you. It makes you feel human insignificance too plainly.'

'Perhaps it does. However,' he added more cheerfully, 'though I feel the study to be one almost tragic in its quality, I hope to be the new Copernicus.* What he was to the solar system I aim to be to the systems beyond.'

Then, by means of the instrument at hand, they travelled together from the earth to Uranus, and the mysterious outskirts of the solar system; from the solar system to a star in the Swan,* the nearest fixed star in the northern sky; from the star in the Swan to remoter stars; thence to the remotest visible; till the ghastly chasm which they had bridged by a fragile line of sight was realized by Lady Constantine.

'We are now traversing distances beside which the immense line stretching from the earth to the sun is but an invisible point,' said the youth. 'When, just now, we had reached a planet whose remoteness is a hundred times the remoteness of the sun from the earth, we were only a two thousandth part of the journey to the spot at which we have optically arrived now.'

'O, pray don't; it overpowers me!' she replied, not without seriousness. 'It makes me feel that it is not worth while to live; it quite annihilates me.'

'If it annihilates your ladyship to roam over these yawning spaces just once, think how it must annihilate me to be, as it were, in constant suspension amid them night after night.'

'Yes. . . . It was not really this subject that I came to see you upon, Mr St Cleeve,' she began a second time. 'It was a personal matter.'

'I am listening, Lady Constantine.'

'I will tell it you. Yet no, – not this moment. Let us finish this grand subject first; it dwarfs mine.'

It would have been difficult to judge from her accents whether she was afraid to broach her own matter, or really interested in his. Or a certain youthful pride that he evidenced at being the elucidator of such a large theme, and at having drawn her there to hear and observe it, may have inclined her to indulge him for kindness' sake.

Thereupon he took exception to her use of the word 'grand' as descriptive of the actual universe:

'The imaginary picture of the sky as the concavity of a dome whose base extends from horizon to horizon of our earth is grand, simply grand, and I wish I had never got beyond looking at it in that way. But the actual sky is a horror.'

'A new view of our old friends, the stars,' she said, smiling up at them.

'But such an obviously true one!' said the young man. 'You would hardly think, at first, that horrid monsters lie up there waiting to be discovered by any moderately penetrating mind – monsters to which those of the oceans bear no sort of comparison.'

'What monsters may they be?'

'Impersonal monsters, namely, Immensities. Until a person has thought out the stars and their interspaces, he has hardly learnt that there are things much more terrible than monsters of shape, namely, monsters of magnitude without known shape. Such monsters are the voids and waste places of the sky. Look, for instance, at those pieces of darkness in the Milky Way,' he went on, pointing with his finger to where the galaxy stretched across over their heads with the luminousness of a frosted web. 'You see that dark opening in it near the Swan? There is a still more remarkable one south of the equator, called the Coal Sack,* as a sort of nickname that has a farcical force from its very inadequacy. In these our sight plunges quite beyond any twinkler we have yet visited. Those are deep wells for the human mind to let itself down into, leave alone* the human body! and think of the side caverns and secondary abysses to right and left as you pass on!'

Lady Constantine was heedful and silent.

He tried to give her yet another idea of the size of the universe; never was there a more ardent endeavour to bring down the immeasurable to human comprehension! By figures of speech and apt comparisons he took her mind into leading-strings,* compelling her to follow him into wildernesses of which she had never in her life even realized the existence.

'There is a size at which dignity begins,' he exclaimed; 'further on there is a size at which grandeur begins; further on there is a size at which solemnity begins; further on, a size at which awfulness begins; further on, a size at which ghastliness begins. That size faintly approaches the size of the stellar universe. So am I not right in saying that those minds who exert their imaginative powers to bury themselves in the depths of that universe merely strain their faculties to gain a new horror?'

Standing, as she stood, in the presence of the stellar universe, under the very eyes of the constellations, Lady Constantine apprehended something of the earnest youth's argument.

'And to add a new weirdness to what the sky possesses in its size and formlessness, there is involved the quality of decay. For all the wonder of these everlasting stars, eternal spheres, and what not, they are not everlasting, they are not eternal; they burn out like candles. You see that dying one in the body of the Greater Bear?* Two centuries ago it was as bright as the others. The senses may become terrified by plunging among them as they are, but there is a pitifulness even in their glory. Imagine them all extinguished, and your mind feeling its way through a heaven of total darkness, occasionally striking against the black, invisible cinders of those stars. . . . If you are cheerful, and wish to remain so, leave the study of astronomy alone. Of all the sciences, it alone deserves the character of the terrible.'

'I am not altogether cheerful.'

'Then if, on the other hand, you are restless and anxious about the future, study astronomy at once. Your troubles will be reduced amazingly. But your study will reduce them in a singular way, by reducing the importance of everything. So that the science is still terrible, even as a panacea. It is quite impossible to think at all adequately of the sky – of what the sky substantially is, without feeling it as a juxtaposed nightmare. It is better – far better – for men to forget the universe than to bear it clearly in mind! ... But you say the universe was not really what you came to see me about. What was it, may I ask, Lady Constantine?'

She mused, and sighed, and turned to him with something pathetic in her.

'The immensity of the subject you have engaged me on has completely crushed my subject out of me! Yours is celestial; mine lamentably human! And the less must give way to the greater.'

'But is it, in a human sense, and apart from macrocosmic* magnitudes, important?' he inquired, at last attracted by her manner; for he began to perceive, in spite of his prepossession, that she had really something on her mind.

'It is as important as personal troubles usually are.'

Notwithstanding her preconceived notion of coming to Swithin as employer to dependant, as *châtelaine** to page, she was falling into confidential intercourse with him. His vast and romantic endeavours lent him a personal force and charm which she could not but apprehend. In the presence of the immensities that his young mind had, as it were, brought down from above to hers, they became unconsciously equal. There was, moreover, an inborn liking in Lady Constantine to dwell less on her permanent position as a county lady than on her passing emotions as a woman.

'I will postpone the matter I came to charge you with,' she resumed, smiling. 'I must reconsider it. Now I will return.'

'Allow me to show you out through the trees and across the fields?'

She said neither a distinct yes nor no; and, descending the tower, they threaded the firs and crossed the ploughed field. By an odd coincidence he remarked, when they drew near the Great House –

'You may possibly be interested in knowing, Lady Constantine, that that medium-sized star you see over there, low down in the south, is precisely over Sir Blount Constantine's head in the middle of Africa.'

'How very strange that you should have said so!' she answered. 'You have broached for me the very subject I had come to speak of.'

'On a domestic matter?' he said, with surprise.

'Yes. What a small matter it seems now, after our astronomical stupendousness! and yet on my way to you it so far transcended the ordinary matters of my life as the subject you have led me up to transcends this. But', with a little laugh, 'I will endeavour to sink down to such ephemeral trivialities as human tragedy, and explain, since I have come. The point is, I want a helper: no woman ever wanted one more. For days I have wanted a trusty friend who could go on a secret errand for me. It is necessary that my messenger should be educated, should be intelligent, should be silent as the grave. Do you give me your solemn promise as to the last point, if I confide in you?'

'Most emphatically, Lady Constantine.'

'Your right hand upon the compact.'

He gave his hand, and raised hers to his lips. In addition to his respect for her as the lady of the manor, there was the admiration of twenty years for twenty-eight or nine in such relations.

'I trust you,' she said. 'Now, beyond the above conditions, it was specially necessary that my agent should have known Sir Blount Constantine well by sight when he was at home. For the errand is concerning my husband; I am much disturbed at what I have heard about him.'

'I am indeed sorry to know it.'

'There are only two people in the parish who fulfil all the conditions, – Mr Torkingham, and yourself. I sent for Mr Torkingham, and he came. I could not tell him. I felt at the last moment that he wouldn't do. I have come to you because I think you will do. This is it: my husband has led me and all the world to believe that he is in Africa, hunting lions. I have had a mysterious letter informing me that he has been seen in London, in very peculiar circumstances. The truth of this I want ascertained. Will you go on the journey?'

'Personally, I would go to the end of the world for you, Lady Constantine; but—'

'No buts!'

'How can I leave?'

'Why not?'

'I am preparing a work on variable stars. There is one of these which I have exceptionally observed for several months, and on this my great theory is mainly based. It has been hitherto called irregular; but I have detected a periodicity* in its so-called irregularities which, if proved, would add some very valuable facts to those known on this subject, one of the most interesting, perplexing, and suggestive in the whole field of astronomy. Now, to clinch my theory, there should be a sudden variation this week, – or at latest next week, – and I have to watch every night not to let it pass. You see my reason for declining, Lady Constantine.'

'Young men are always so selfish!' she said.

'It might ruin the whole of my year's labour if I leave now!' returned the youth, greatly hurt. 'Could you not wait a fortnight longer?'

'No, – no. Don't think that I have asked you, pray. I have no wish to inconvenience you.'

'Lady Constantine, don't be angry with me! Will you do this, – watch the star for me while I am gone? If you are prepared to do it effectually, I will go.'

'Will it be much trouble?'

'It will be some trouble. You would have to come here every clear evening about nine. If the sky were not clear, then you would have to come at four in the morning, should the clouds have dispersed.'

'Could not the telescope be brought to my house?'

Swithin shook his head.

'Perhaps you did not observe its real size, – that it was fixed to a frame-work? I could not afford to buy an equatorial, and I have been obliged to rig up an apparatus of my own devising, so as to make it in some measure answer the purpose of an equatorial. It *could* be moved, but I would rather not touch it.'

'Well, I'll go to the telescope,' she went on, with an emphasis that was not wholly playful. 'You are the most ungallant youth I ever met with; but I suppose I must set that down to science. Yes, I'll go to the tower at nine every night.'

'And alone? I should prefer to keep my pursuits there unknown.'

'And alone,' she answered, quite overborne by his inflexibility.

'You will not miss the morning observation, if it should be necessary?'

'I have given my word.'

'And I give mine. I suppose I ought not to have been so exacting!' He spoke with that sudden emotional sense of his own insignificance which made these alternations of mood possible. 'I will go anywhere – do anything for you – this moment – to-morrow or at any time. But you must return with me to the tower, and let me show you the observing process.'

They retraced their steps, the tender hoar-frost taking the imprint of their feet, while two stars in the Twins* looked down upon their two persons through the trees, as if those two persons could bear some sort of comparison with them. On the tower the instructions were given. When all was over, and he was again conducting her to the Great House she said –

'When can you start?'

'Now,' said Swithin.

'So much the better. You shall go up by the night mail.'

CHAPTER FIVE

ON the third morning after the young man's departure Lady Constantine opened the post-bag anxiously. Though she had risen before four o'clock, and crossed to the tower through the gray half-light when every blade and twig were furred with rime, she felt no languor. Expectation could banish at cock-crow the eye-heaviness which apathy had been unable to disperse all the day long.

There was, as she had hoped, a letter from Swithin St Cleeve.

DEAR LADY CONSTANTINE, – I have quite succeeded in my mission, and shall return to-morrow at 10 P.M. I hope you have not failed in the observations. Watching the star through an opera-glass Sunday night I fancied some change had taken place, but I could not make myself sure. Your memoranda for that night I await with impatience. Please don't neglect to write down, *at the moment*, all remarkable appearances both as to colour and intensity; and be very exact as to time, which correct in the way I showed you. – I am, dear Lady Constantine, yours most faithfully,

SWITHIN ST CLEEVE

Not another word in the letter about his errand; his mind ran on nothing but this astronomical subject. He had succeeded in his mission, and yet he did not even say yes or no to the great question, – whether or not her husband was masquerading in London at the address she had given.

'Was ever anything so provoking!' she cried.

However, the time was not long to wait. His way homeward would lie within a stone's-throw of the manor-house, and though for certain reasons she had forbidden him to call at the late hour of his arrival, she could easily intercept him in the avenue. At twenty minutes past ten she went out into the drive, and stood in the dark. Seven minutes later she heard his footstep, and saw his outline in the slit of light between the avenue-trees. He had a valise in one hand, a great-coat on his arm, and under his arm a parcel which seemed to be very precious, from the manner in which he held it.

'Lady Constantine?' he asked softly.

'Yes,' she said, in her excitement holding out both her hands, though he had plainly not expected her to offer one.

'Did you watch the star?'

'I'll tell you everything in detail; but, pray, your errand first!'

'Yes, it's all right. Did you watch every night, – not missing one?'

'I forgot to go – twice,' she murmured contritely.

'O, Lady Constantine!' he cried in dismay. 'How could you serve me so! what shall I do?'

'Please forgive me! Indeed, I could not help it. I had watched and watched, and nothing happened; and somehow my vigilance relaxed when I found nothing was likely to take place in the star.'

'But the very circumstance of it not having happened made it all the more likely every day.'

'Have you – seen—' she began imploringly.

Swithin sighed, lowered his thoughts to sublunary things, and told briefly the story of his journey. Sir Blount Constantine was not in London at the address which had been anonymously sent her. It was a mistake of identity. The person who had been seen there Swithin had sought out. He resembled Sir Blount strongly; but he was a stranger.

'How can I reward you!' she exclaimed, when he had done.

'In no way but by giving me your good wishes in what I am going to tell you on my own account.' He spoke in tones of mysterious exultation. 'This parcel is going to make my fame!'

'What is it?'

'A huge object-glass* for the great telescope I am so busy about! Such a magnificent aid to science has never entered this county before, you may depend.'

He produced from under his arm the carefully cuddled-up package, which was in shape a round flat disk, like a dinner-plate, tied in paper.

Proceeding to explain his plans to her more fully he walked with her towards the door by which she had emerged. It was a little side wicket* through a wall dividing the open park from the garden terraces. Here for a moment he placed his valise and parcel on the coping of the stone balustrade, till he had bidden her farewell. Then he turned, and in laying hold of his bag by the dim light pushed the parcel over the parapet. It fell smash upon the paved walk ten or a dozen feet beneath.

'O, good heavens!' he cried in anguish.

'What?'

'My object-glass broken!'

'Is it of much value?'

'It cost all I possess!'

He ran round by the steps to the lower lawn, Lady Constantine following, as he continued, 'It is a magnificent eight-inch first quality object lens! I took advantage of my journey to London to get it! I have been six weeks making the tube of milled board; and as I had not enough money by twelve pounds for the lens, I borrowed it of my grandmother out of her last annuity payment. What can be, can be done!'

'Perhaps it is not broken.'

He felt on the ground, found the parcel, and shook it. A clicking noise issued from inside. Swithin smote his forehead with his hand, and walked up and down like a mad fellow.

'My telescope! I have waited nine months for this lens. Now the possibility of setting up a really powerful instrument is over! It is too cruel – how could it happen! ... Lady Constantine, I am ashamed of myself, – before you. O but, Lady Constantine, if you only knew what it is to a person engaged in science to have the means of clinching a theory snatched away at the last moment! It is I against the world; and when the world has accidents on its side in addition to its natural strength, what chance for me!'

The young astronomer leant against the wall, and was silent. His misery was of an intensity and kind with that of Palissy,* in these struggles with an adverse fate.

'Don't mind it, – pray don't!' said Lady Constantine. 'It is dreadfully unfortunate! You have my whole sympathy. Can it be mended?'

'Mended, – no, no!'

'Cannot you do with your present one a little longer?'

'It is altogether inferior, cheap, and bad!'

'I'll get you another, – yes, indeed, I will! Allow me to get you another as soon as possible. I'll do anything to assist you out of your trouble; for I am most anxious to see you famous. I know you will be a great astronomer, in spite of this mishap! Come, say I may get a new one.'

Swithin took her hand. He could not trust himself to speak.

Some days later a little box of peculiar kind came to the Great House. It was addressed to Lady Constantine, 'with great care'. She had it partly opened and taken to her own writing-room; and after lunch, when she had dressed for walking, she took from the box a paper parcel like the one which had met with the accident. This she hid under her mantle as if she had stolen it; and going out slowly across the lawn passed through the little door before spoken of, and was soon hastening in the direction of the Rings-Hill column.

There was a bright sun overhead on that afternoon of early spring, and its rays shed an unusual warmth on south-west aspects, though shady places still retained the look and feel of winter. Rooks were already beginning to build new nests or to mend up old ones, and clamorously called in neighbours to give opinions on difficulties in their architecture. Lady Constantine swerved once from her path, as if she had decided to go to the homestead where Swithin lived; but on second thoughts she bent her steps to the column.

Drawing near it she looked up; but by reason of the height of the parapet nobody could be seen thereon who did not stand on tiptoe. She thought, however, that her young friend might possibly see her if he were there, and come down; and that he was there she soon ascertained by finding the door unlocked, and the key inside. No movement, however, reached her ears from above, and she began to ascend.

Meanwhile affairs at the top of the column had progressed as follows. The afternoon being exceptionally fine Swithin had ascended about two o'clock, and, seating himself at the little table which he had constructed on the spot, he began reading over his notes and examining some astronomical journals that had reached him in the morning. The sun blazed into the hollow roof-space as into a tub, and the sides kept out every breeze. Though the month was February below it was May in the abacus* of the column. This state of the atmosphere, and the fact that on the previous night he had pursued his observations till past two o'clock, produced in him at the end of half an hour an overpowering inclination to sleep. Spreading on the lead-work a thick rug which he kept up there, he flung himself down against the parapet, and was soon in a state of unconsciousness.

It was about ten minutes afterwards that a soft rustle of silken clothes came up the spiral staircase, and, hesitating onwards, reached the orifice, where appeared the form of Lady Constantine. She did not at first perceive that he was present, and stood still to reconnoitre. Her eye glanced over his telescope, now wrapped up, his table and papers, his observing-chair, and his contrivances for making the best of a deficiency of instruments. All was warm, sunny, and silent, except that a solitary bee, which had somehow got within the hollow of the abacus, was singing round inquiringly, unable to discern that ascent was the only mode of escape. In another moment she beheld the astronomer, lying in the sun like a sailor in the main-top.

Lady Constantine coughed slightly; he did not awake. She then entered, and, drawing the parcel from beneath her cloak, placed it on the table. After this she waited, looking for a long time at his sleeping face, which had a very interesting appearance. She seemed reluctant to leave, yet wanted resolution to wake him; and, pencilling his name on the parcel, she withdrew to the staircase, where the brushing of her dress decreased to silence as she receded round and round on her way to the base.

Swithin still slept on, and presently the rustle began again in the far-down interior of the column. The door could be heard closing, and the rustle came nearer, showing that she had shut herself in, – no doubt to lessen the risk of an accidental surprise by any roaming villager. When Lady Constantine reappeared at the top, and saw the parcel still untouched and Swithin asleep as before, she exhibited some disappointment; but she did not retreat.

Looking again at him her eyes became so sentimentally fixed on his face that it seemed as if she could not withdraw them. There lay, in the shape of an Antinous,* no *amoroso*,* no gallant, but a guileless philosopher. His parted lips were lips which spoke, not of love, but of millions of miles; those were eyes which habitually gazed, not into the depths of other eyes, but into other worlds. Within his temples dwelt thoughts, not of woman's looks, but of stellar aspects and the configuration of constellations.

Thus, to his physical attractiveness was added the attractiveness of mental inaccessibility. The ennobling influence of scientific pursuits was demonstrated by the speculative purity which expressed itself in his eyes whenever he looked at her in speaking, and in the childlike faults of manner which arose from his obtuseness to their difference of sex. He had never, since becoming a man, looked even so low as to the level of a Lady Constantine. His heaven at present was truly in the skies, and not in that only other place where they say it can be found, in the eyes of some daughter of Eve. Would any Circe or Calypso* – and if so, what one? – ever check this pale-haired scientist's nocturnal sailings into the interminable spaces overhead, and hurl all his mighty calculations on cosmic force and stellar fire into Limbo?* O the pity of it, if such should be the case!

She became much absorbed in these very womanly reflections; and at last Lady Constantine sighed, perhaps she herself did not exactly know why. Then a very soft expression lighted on her lips and eyes, and she looked at one jump ten years more youthful than before – quite a girl in aspect, younger than he. On the table lay his implements, among them a pair of scissors which, to judge from the shreds around, had been used in cutting curves in thick paper for some calculating process.

What whim, agitation, or attraction prompted the impulse, nobody knows; but she took the scissors and, bending over the sleeping youth, cut off one of the curls, or rather crooks, – for they hardly reached a curl, – into which each lock of his hair chose to twist itself in the last inch of its length. The hair fell upon the rug. She picked it up quickly, returned the scissors to the table, and, as if her dignity had suddenly become ashamed of her fantasies, hastened through the door and descended the staircase.

CHAPTER SIX

WHEN his nap had naturally exhausted itself Swithin awoke. He awoke without any surprise, for he not unfrequently gave to sleep in the day-time what he had stolen from it in the night watches. The first object that met his eyes was the parcel on the table, and, seeing his name inscribed thereon, he made no scruple to open it.

The sun flashed upon a lens of surprising magnitude, polished to such a smoothness that the eye could scarcely meet its reflections. Here was a crystal in whose depths were to be seen more wonders than had been revealed by the crystals of all the Cagliostros.*

Swithin, hot with joyousness, took this treasure to his telescope manufactory at the homestead; then he started off for the Great House.

On gaining its precincts he felt shy of calling, never having received any hint or permission to do so; while Lady Constantine's mysterious manner of leaving the parcel seemed to demand a like mysteriousness in his approaches to her. All the afternoon he lingered about uncertainly, in the hope of intercepting her on her return from a drive, occasionally walking with an indifferent lounge across glades commanded by the windows, that if she were indoors she might know he was near. But she did not show herself during the daylight. Still impressed by her playful secrecy he carried on the same idea after dark, by returning to the house and passing through the garden door on to the lawn front, where he sat on the parapet that breasted the terrace.

Now she frequently came out here for a melancholy saunter after dinner, and to-night was such an occasion. Swithin went forward, and met her at nearly the spot where he had dropped the lens some nights earlier.

'I have come to see you, Lady Constantine. How did the glass get on my table?'

She laughed as lightly as a girl; that he had come to her in this way was plainly no offence thus far.

'Perhaps it was dropped from the clouds by a bird,' she said.

'Why should you be so good to me?' he cried.

'One good turn deserves another,' answered she.

'Dear Lady Constantine! Whatever discoveries result from this shall be ascribed to you as much as to me. Where should I have been without your gift?'

'You would possibly have accomplished your purpose just the same, and have been so much the nobler for your struggle against ill-luck. I hope that now you will be able to proceed with your large telescope as if nothing had happened.'

'O yes, I will, certainly. I am afraid I showed too much feeling, the reverse of stoical, when the accident occurred. That was not very noble of me.'

'There is nothing unnatural in such feeling at your age. When you are older you will smile at such moods, and at the mishaps that give rise to them.'

'Ah, I perceive you think me weak in the extreme,' he said, with just a shade of pique. 'But you will never realize that an incident which filled but a degree in the circle of your thoughts covered the whole circumference of mine. No person can see exactly what and where another's horizon is.'

They soon parted, and she re-entered the house, where she sat reflecting for some time, till she seemed to fear that she had wounded his feelings. She awoke in the night, and thought and thought on the same thing, till she had worked herself into a feverish fret* about it. When it was morning she looked across at the tower, and sitting down, impulsively wrote the following note: –

DEAR MR ST CLEEVE, – I cannot allow you to remain under the impression that I despised your scientific endeavours in speaking as I did last night. I think you were too sensitive to my remark. But perhaps you were agitated with the labours of the day, and I fear that watching so late at night must make you very weary. If I can help you again, please let me know. I never realized the grandeur of astronomy till you showed me how to do so. Also let me know about the new telescope. Come and see me! After your great kindness in being my messenger I can never do enough for you. I wish you had a mother or sister, and pity your loneliness! I am lonely too. – Yours truly,

VIVIETTE CONSTANTINE

She was so anxious that he should get this letter the same day that she ran across to the column with it during the morning, preferring to be her own emissary in so curious a case. The door, as she had expected, was locked; and, slipping the letter under it, she went home again. During lunch her ardour in the cause of Swithin's hurt feelings cooled down, till she exclaimed to herself, as she sat at her lonely table, 'What could have possessed me to write in that way!'

After lunch she went faster to the tower than she had gone in the early morning, and peeped eagerly into the chink under the door. She could discern no letter, and, on trying the latch, found that the door would open. The letter was gone, Swithin having obviously arrived in the interval.

She blushed a blush which seemed to say, 'I am getting foolishly interested in this young man.' She had, in short, in her own opinion, somewhat overstepped the bounds of dignity. Her instincts did not square well with the formalities of her existence, and she walked home despondently.

Had a concert, bazaar, lecture, or Dorcas meeting* required the patronage and support of Lady Constantine at this juncture, the circumstance would probably have been sufficient to divert her mind from Swithin St Cleeve and astronomy for some little time. But as none of these incidents were within the range of expectation – Welland House and parish lying far from large towns and watering-places* – the void in her outer life continued, and with it the void in her life within.

The youth had not answered her letter; neither had he called upon her in response to the invitation she had regretted, with the rest of the epistle, as being somewhat too warmly informal for black and white. To speak tenderly to him was one thing, to write another – that was her feeling immediately after the event; but his counter-move of silence and avoidance, though probably the result of pure unconsciousness on his part, completely dispersed such self-considerations now. Her eyes never fell upon the Rings-Hill column without a solicitous wonder arising as to what he was doing. A true woman, she would assume the remotest possibility to be the most likely contingency, if the possibility had the recommendation of being tragical; and she now feared that something was wrong with Swithin St Cleeve. Yet there was not the least doubt that he had become so immersed in the business of the new telescope as to forget everything else.

On Sunday, between the services, she walked to Little Welland, chiefly for the sake of giving a run to a house-dog, a large St Bernard, of whom she was fond. The distance was but short, and she returned along a narrow lane, divided from the river by a hedge, through whose leafless twigs the ripples flashed silver lights into her eyes. Here she discovered Swithin, leaning over a gate, his eyes bent upon the stream.

The dog first attracted his attention; then he heard her, and turned round. She had never seen him looking so despondent.

'You have never called, though I invited you,' said Lady Constantine.

'My great telescope won't work!' he replied lugubriously.

'I am sorry for that. So it has made you quite forget me?'

'Ah, yes; you wrote me a very kind letter, which I ought to have answered. Well, I *did* forget, Lady Constantine. My new telescope won't work, and I don't know what to do about it at all!'

'Can I assist you any further?'

'No, I fear not. Besides, you have assisted me already.'

'What would really help you out of all your difficulties? Something would, surely?'

He shook his head.

'There must be some solution to them?'

'O yes,' he replied, with a hypothetical gaze into the stream; '*some* solution of course – an equatorial, for instance.'

'What's that?'

'Briefly, an impossibility. It is a splendid instrument, with an object-lens of, say, eight or nine inches aperture, mounted with its axis parallel to the earth's axis, and fitted up with graduated circles for denoting right ascensions and declinations;* besides having special eye-pieces, a finder, and all sorts of appliances, clock-work to make the telescope follow the motion in right ascension – I cannot tell you half the conveniences. Ah, an equatorial is a thing indeed!'

'An equatorial is the one instrument required to make you quite happy?'

'Well, yes.'

'I'll see what I can do.'

'But, Lady Constantine,' cried the amazed astronomer, 'an equatorial such as I describe costs as much as two grand pianos!'

She was rather staggered at this news; but she rallied gallantly, and said, 'Never mind. I'll make inquiries.'

'But it could not be put on the tower without people seeing it! It would have to be fixed to the masonry. And there must be a dome of some kind to keep off the rain. A tarpaulin might do.'

Lady Constantine reflected. 'It would be a great business, I see,' she said. 'Though as far as the fixing and roofing go, I would of course consent to your doing what you like with the old column. My workmen could fix it, could they not?'

'O yes. But what would Sir Blount say, if he came home and saw the goings on?'

Lady Constantine turned aside to hide a sudden displacement of blood from her cheek. 'Ah – my husband!' she whispered. . . . 'I am just now going to church,' she added in a repressed and hurried tone. 'I will think of this matter.'

In church it was with Lady Constantine as with the Lord Angelo of Vienna* in a similar situation – Heaven had her empty words only, and her invention* heard not her tongue. She soon recovered from the momentary consternation into which she had fallen at Swithin's abrupt query. The possibility of that young astronomer becoming a renowned scientist by her aid was a thought which gave her secret pleasure. The course of rendering him instant material help began to have a great fascination for her; it was a new and unexpected channel for her cribbed and confined* emotions. With experiences so much wider than his, Lady Constantine saw that the chances were perhaps a million to one against Swithin St Cleeve ever being Astronomer Royal, or Astronomer Extraordinary* of any sort; yet the remaining chance in his favour was one of those possibilities which, to a woman of bounding intellect and venturesome fancy, are pleasanter to dwell on than likely issues that have no savour of high speculation in them. The equatorial question was a great one; and she had caught such a large spark from his enthusiasm that she could think of nothing so piquant as how to obtain the important instrument.

When Tabitha Lark arrived at the Great House next day, instead of finding Lady Constantine in bed, as formerly, she discovered her in the library, poring over what astronomical works she had been able to unearth from the worm-eaten shelves. As these publications were, for a science of such rapid development, somewhat venerable, there was not much help of a practical kind to be gained from them. Nevertheless, the equatorial retained a hold upon her fancy, till she became as eager to see one on the Rings-Hill column as Swithin himself.

The upshot of it was that Lady Constantine sent a messenger that evening to Welland Bottom, where the homestead of Swithin's grandmother was situated, requesting the young man's presence at the house at twelve o'clock next day.

He hurriedly returned an obedient reply, and the promise was enough to lend great freshness to her manner next morning, instead of the leaden air which was too frequent with her before the sun reached the meridian, and sometimes after. Swithin had, in fact, arisen as an attractive little intervention between herself and despair.

CHAPTER SEVEN

A FOG defaced all the trees of the park that morning; the white atmosphere adhered to the ground like a fungoid growth from it, and made the turfed undulations look slimy and raw. But Lady Constantine settled down in her chair to await the coming of the late curate's son with a serenity which the vast blanks outside could neither baffle nor destroy.

At two minutes to twelve the door-bell rang, and a look overspread the lady's face that was neither maternal, sisterly, nor amorous; but partook in an indescribable manner of all three kinds. The door was flung open and the young man was ushered in, the fog still clinging to his hair, in which she could discern a little notch where she had nipped off the curl.

A speechlessness that socially was a defect in him was to her view a piquant attribute just now. He looked somewhat alarmed.

'Lady Constantine, have I done anything, that you have sent—?' he began breathlessly, as he gazed in her face, with parted lips.

'O no, of course not! I have decided to do something, – nothing more,' she smilingly said, holding out her hand, which he rather gingerly touched. 'Don't look so concerned. Who makes equatorials?'

This remark was like the drawing of a weir-hatch, and she was speedily inundated* with all she wished to know concerning astronomical opticians. When he had imparted the particulars he waited, manifestly burning to know whither these inquiries tended.

'I am not going to buy you one,' she said gently.

He looked as if he would faint.

'Certainly not. I do not wish it. I – could not have accepted it,' faltered the young man.

'But I am going to buy one for *myself*. I lack a hobby, and I shall choose astronomy. I shall fix my equatorial on the column.'

Swithin brightened up.

'And I shall let you have the use of it whenever you choose. In brief, Swithin St Cleeve shall be Lady Constantine's Astronomer Royal; and she – and she—'

'Shall be his Queen.'* The words came not much the worse for being uttered only in the tone of one anxious to complete a tardy sentence.

'Well, that's what I have decided to do,' resumed Lady Constantine. 'I will write to these opticians at once.'

There seemed to be no more for him to do than to thank her for the privilege, whenever it should be available, which he promptly did, and then made as if to go. But Lady Constantine detained him with, 'Have you ever seen my library?'

'No; never.'

'You don't say you would like to see it.'

'But I should.'

'It is the third door on the right. You can find your way in, and you can stay there as long as you like.'

Swithin then left the morning-room for the apartment designated, and amused himself in that 'soul of the house', as Cicero* defined it, till he heard the lunch-bell sounding from the turret, when he came down from the library steps, and thought it time to go home. But at that moment a servant entered to inquire whether he would or would not prefer to have his lunch brought in to him there; at his affirmative a large tray arrived on the stomach of a footman, and Swithin was greatly surprised to see a whole pheasant placed at his disposal.

Having breakfasted at eight that morning, and having been much in the open air afterwards, the Adonis*-astronomer's appetite assumed grand proportions. How much of that pheasant he might consistently eat without hurting his dear patroness Lady Constantine's feelings, when he could readily eat it all, was a problem in which the reasonableness of a larger and larger quantity argued itself inversely as a smaller and smaller quantity remained. When, at length, he had finally decided on a terminal point in the body of the bird, the door was gently opened.

'O, you have not finished?' came to him over his shoulder, in a considerate voice.

'O yes, thank you, Lady Constantine,' he said, jumping up.

'Why did you prefer to lunch in this awkward, dusty place?'

'I thought – it would be better,' said Swithin simply.

'There is fruit in the other room, if you like to come. But perhaps you would rather not?'

'O yes, I should much like to,' said Swithin, walking over his napkin, and following her as she led the way to the adjoining apartment.

Here, while she asked him what he had been reading, he modestly ventured on an apple,* in whose flavour he recognized the familiar taste of old friends robbed from her husband's orchards in his childhood, long before Lady Constantine's advent on the scene. She supposed he had confined his search to his own sublime subject, astronomy?

Swithin suddenly became older to the eye, as his thoughts reverted to the topic thus reintroduced. 'Yes,' he informed her. 'I seldom read any other subject. In these days the secret of productive study is to avoid well.'

'Did you find any good treatises?'

'None. The theories in your books are almost as obsolete as the Ptolemaic System.* Only fancy, that magnificent Cyclopædia, leather-bound, and stamped, and gilt, and wide margined, and bearing the blazon of your house in magnificent colours, says that the twinkling of the stars is probably caused by heavenly bodies passing in front of them in their revolutions.'

'And is it not so? That was what I learned when I was a girl.'

The modern Eudoxus* now rose above the embarrassing horizon of Lady Constantine's great house, magnificent furniture, and awe-inspiring footman and butler. He became quite natural, all his self-consciousness fled, and his eye spoke into hers no less than his lips to her ears, as he said, 'How such a theory can have lingered on to this day beats conjecture! François Arago,* as long as forty or fifty years ago, conclusively established the fact that scintillation is the simplest thing in the world, – merely a matter of atmosphere. But I won't speak of this to you now. The comparative absence of scintillation in warm countries was noticed by Humboldt.* Then, again, the scintillations vary. No star flaps his wings like Sirius when he lies low! He flashes out emeralds and rubies, amethystine flames and sapphirine colours, in a manner quite marvellous to behold, and this is only *one* star! So, too, do Arcturus, and Capella,* and lesser luminaries.... But I tire you with this subject?'

'On the contrary, you speak so beautifully that I could listen all day.'

The astronomer threw a searching glance upon her for a moment; but there was no satire in the warm soft eyes which met his own with a luxurious contemplative interest. 'Say some more of it to me,' she continued, with a mien not far removed from coaxing.

After some hesitation the subject returned again to his lips, and he said some more – indeed, much more; Lady Constantine often throwing in an appreciative remark or question, often meditatively regarding him, in pursuance of ideas not exactly based on his words, and letting him go on as he would.

Before he left the house the new astronomical project was set in train. The top of the column was to be roofed in, to form a proper observatory; and on the ground that he knew better than any one else how this was to be carried out, she requested him to give precise directions on the point, and to superintend the whole. A wooden cabin was to be erected at the foot of the tower, to provide better accommodation for casual visitors to the observatory than the spiral staircase and lead-flat* afforded. As this cabin would be completely buried in the dense fir foliage which enveloped the lower part of the column and its pedestal, it would be no disfigurement to the general appearance. Finally, a path was to be made across the surrounding fallow, by which she might easily approach the scene of her new study.

When he was gone she wrote to the firm of opticians concerning the equatorial for whose reception all this was designed.

The undertaking was soon in full progress; and by degrees it became the talk of the hamlets round that Lady Constantine had given up melancholy for astronomy, to the great advantage of all who came in contact with her. One morning, when Tabitha Lark had come as usual to read, Lady Constantine chanced to be in a quarter of the house to which she seldom wandered; and while here she heard her maid talking confidentially to Tabitha in the adjoining room on the curious and sudden interest which Lady Constantine had acquired in the moon and stars.

'They do say all sorts of trumpery,' observed the handmaid. 'They say – though 'tis little better than mischief, to be sure – that it isn't the moon, and it isn't the stars, and it isn't the plannards,* that my lady cares for, but for the pretty lad who draws 'em down from the sky to please her; and being a married example,* and what with sin and shame knocking at every poor maid's door afore you can say, "Hands off, my dear," to the civilest young man, she ought to set a better pattern.'

Lady Constantine's face flamed up vividly.

'If Sir Blount were to come back all of a sudden – O, my!'

Lady Constantine grew cold as ice.

'There's nothing in it,' said Tabitha scornfully. 'I could prove it any day.'

'Well, I wish I had half her chance!' sighed the lady's maid. And no more was said on the subject then.

Tabitha's remark showed that the suspicion was quite in embryo as yet. Nevertheless, saying nothing to reveal what she had overheard, immediately after the reading Lady Constantine flew like a bird to where she knew that Swithin might be found.

He was in the plantation, setting up little sticks to mark where the wooden cabin was to stand. She called him to a remote place under the funereal trees.

'I have altered my mind,' she said. 'I can have nothing to do with this matter.'

'Indeed?' said Swithin, surprised.

'Astronomy is not my hobby any longer. And you are not my Astronomer Royal.'

'O Lady Constantine!' cried the youth, aghast. 'Why, the work is begun! I thought the equatorial was ordered.'

She dropped her voice, though a Jericho shout* would not have been overheard: 'Of course astronomy is my hobby privately, and you are to be my Astronomer Royal, and I still furnish the observatory; but not to the outer world. There is a reason against my indulgence in such scientific fancies openly; and the project must be arranged in this wise. The whole enterprise is yours: you rent the tower of me: you build the cabin: you get the equatorial. I simply give permission, since you desire it. The path that was to be made from the hill to the park is not to be thought of. There is to be no communication between the house and the column. The equatorial will arrive addressed to you, and its cost I will pay through you. My name must not appear, and I vanish entirely from the undertaking. . . . This blind is necessary,' she added, sighing. 'Good-bye!'

'But you *do* take as much interest as before, and it *will* be yours just the same?' he said, walking after her. He scarcely comprehended the subterfuge, and was absolutely blind as to its reason.

'Can you doubt it? But I dare not do it openly.'

With this she went away; and in due time there circulated through the parish an assertion that it was a mistake to suppose Lady Constantine had anything to do with Swithin St Cleeve or his star-gazing schemes. She had merely allowed him to rent the tower of her for use as his observatory, and to put some temporary fixtures on it for that purpose.

After this Lady Constantine lapsed into her former life of loneliness; and by these prompt measures the ghost of a rumour which had barely started into existence was speedily laid to rest. It had probably originated in her own dwelling, and had gone but little further. Yet, despite her self-control, a certain north window of the Great House, that commanded an uninterrupted view of the upper ten feet of the column, revealed her to be somewhat frequently gazing from it at a rotundity which had begun to appear on the summit. To those with whom she came in contact she sometimes addressed such remarks as, 'Is young Mr St Cleeve getting on with his observatory? I hope he will fix his instruments without damaging the column, which is so interesting to us as being in memory of my dear husband's great-grandfather – a truly brave man.'

On one occasion her building-steward ventured to suggest to her that, Sir Blount having deputed to her the power to grant short leases in his absence, she should have a distinctive agreement with Swithin, as between landlord and tenant, with a stringent clause against his driving nails into the stonework of such an historical memorial. She replied that she did not wish to be severe on the last representative of such old and respected parishioners as St Cleeve's mother's family had been, and of such a well-descended family as his father's; so that it would only be necessary for the steward to keep an eye on Mr St Cleeve's doings.

Further, when a letter arrived at the Great House from Hilton & Pimm's, the opticians, with information that the equatorial was ready and packed, and that a man would be sent with it to fix it, she replied to that firm to the effect that their letter should have been addressed to Mr St Cleeve, the local astronomer, on whose behalf she had made the inquiries; that she had nothing more to do with the matter; that he would receive the instrument and pay the bill, – her guarantee being given for the latter performance.

CHAPTER EIGHT

LADY CONSTANTINE then had the pleasure of beholding a waggon, laden with packing-cases, moving across the field towards the pillar; and not many days later Swithin, who had never come to the Great House since the luncheon, met her in a path which he knew to be one of her promenades.

'The equatorial is fixed, and the man gone,' he said, half in doubt as to his speech, for her commands to him not to recognize her agency or patronage still puzzled him. 'I respectfully wish – you could come and see it, Lady Constantine.'

'I would rather not; I cannot.'

'Saturn is lovely; Jupiter is simply sublime; I can see double stars in the Lion and in the Virgin,* where I had seen only a single one before. It is all I required to set me going!'

'I'll come. But – you need say nothing about my visit. I cannot come to-night, but I will some time this week. Yet only this once, to try the instrument. Afterwards you must be content to pursue your studies alone.'

Swithin seemed but little affected at this announcement. 'Hilton & Pimm's man handed me the bill,' he continued.

'How much is it?'

He told her. 'And the man who has built the hut and dome, and done the other fixing, has sent in his.' He named this amount also.

'Very well. They shall be settled with. My debts must be paid with my money, which you shall have at once, – in cash, since a cheque would hardly do. Come to the house for it this evening. But no, no – you must not come openly; such is the world. Come to the window – the window that is exactly in a line with the long snowdrop bed, in the south front – at eight to-night, and I will give you what is necessary.'

'Certainly, Lady Constantine,' said the young man.

At eight that evening accordingly, Swithin entered like a spectre upon the terrace to seek out the spot she had designated. The equatorial had so entirely absorbed his thoughts that he did not trouble himself seriously to conjecture the why and wherefore of her secrecy. If he casually thought of it he set it down in a general way to an intensely generous wish on her part not to lessen his influence among the poorer inhabitants by making him appear the object of patronage.

While he stood by the long snowdrop bed, which looked up at him like a nether Milky Way,* the French casement* of the adjoining window softly opened, and a hand bordered by a glimmer of lace was stretched forth, from which he received a crisp little parcel, – bank-notes, apparently. He knew the hand, and held it long enough to press it to his lips, the only form which had ever occurred to him of expressing his gratitude to her without the incumbrance of clumsy words, a vehicle at the best of times but rudely suited to such delicate merchandise. The hand was hastily withdrawn, as if the treatment had been unexpected. Then seemingly moved by second thoughts she bent forward and said, 'Is the night good for observations?'

'Perfect.'

She paused. 'Then I'll come to-night,' she at last whispered. 'It makes no difference to me, after all. Wait just one moment.'

He waited, and she presently emerged, muffled up like a nun; whereupon they left the terrace and struck across the park together.

Very little was said by either till they were crossing the fallow, when he asked if his arm would help her. She did not take the offered support just then; but when they were ascending the prehistoric earthwork, under the heavy gloom of the fir-trees, she seized it, as if rather influenced by the oppressive solitude than by fatigue.

Thus they reached the foot of the column, ten thousand spirits in prison seeming to gasp their griefs from the funereal boughs overhead, and a few twigs scratching the pillar with the drag of impish claws as tenacious as those figuring in St Anthony's temptation.*

'How intensely dark it is just here!' she whispered. 'I wonder you can keep in the path. Many ancient Britons lie buried there doubtless.'

He led her round to the other side, where, feeling his way with his hands, he suddenly left her, appearing a moment after with a light.

'What place is this?' she exclaimed.

'This is the new wood cabin,' said he.

She could just discern the outline of a little house, not unlike a bathing-machine* without wheels.

'I have kept lights ready here,' he went on, 'as I thought you might come any evening, and possibly bring company.'

'Don't criticize me for coming alone,' she exclaimed with sensitive promptness. 'There are social reasons for what I do of which you know nothing.'

'Perhaps it is much to my discredit that I don't know.'

'Not at all. You are all the better for it. Heaven forbid that I should enlighten you. Well, I see this is the hut. But I am more curious to go to the top of the tower, and make discoveries.'

He brought a little lantern from the cabin, and lighted her up the winding staircase to the temple of that sublime mystery on whose threshold he stood as priest.

The top of the column was quite changed. The tub-shaped space within the parapet, formerly open to the air and sun, was now arched over by a light dome of lath-work* covered with felt. But this dome was not fixed. At the line where its base descended to the parapet there were half a dozen iron balls, precisely like cannon-shot, standing loosely in a groove, and on these the dome rested its whole weight. In the side of the dome was a slit, through which the wind blew and the North Star* beamed, and towards it the end of the great telescope was directed. This latter magnificent object, with its circles, axes, and handles complete, was securely fixed in the middle of the floor.

'But you can only see one part of the sky through that slit,' said she.

The astronomer stretched out his arm, and the whole dome turned horizontally round, running on the balls with a rumble like thunder. Instead of the star Polaris,* which had first been peeping in through the slit, there now appeared the countenances of Castor and Pollux.* Swithin then manipulated the equatorial, and put it through its capabilities in like manner.

She was enchanted; being rather excitable she even clapped her hands just once. She turned to him: 'Now are you happy?'

'But it is all *yours*, Lady Constantine.'

'At this moment. But that's a defect which can soon be remedied.

When is your birthday?'

'Next month, – the seventh.'

'Then it shall all be yours, – a birthday present.'

The young man protested; it was too much.

'No, you must accept it all, – equatorial, dome, stand, hut, and everything that has been put here for this astronomical purpose. The possession of these apparatus would only compromise me. Already they are reputed to be yours, and they must be made yours. There is no help for it. If ever' (here her voice lost some firmness), – 'if ever you go away from me, – from this place, I mean, – and marry, and settle in a new home elsewhere for good, and forget me, you must take these things, equatorial and all, and never tell your wife or anybody how they came to be yours.'

'I wish I could do something more for you!' exclaimed the much-moved astronomer. 'If you could but share my fame, – supposing I get any, which I may die before doing, – it would be a little compensation. As to my going away and marrying, I certainly shall not. I may go away, but I shall never marry.'

'Why not?'

'A beloved science is enough wife for me, – combined, perhaps, with a little warm friendship with one of kindred pursuits.'

'Who is the friend of kindred pursuits?'

'Yourself I should like it to be.'

'You would have to become a woman before I could be that, publicly; or I a man,' she replied, with dry melancholy.

'Why I a woman, or you a man, dear Lady Constantine?'

'I cannot explain. No; you must keep your fame and your science all to yourself, and I must keep my – troubles.'

Swithin, to divert her from melancholy – not knowing that in the expression of her melancholy thus and now she found much pleasure, – changed the subject by asking if they should take some observations.

'Yes; the scenery is well hung to-night,' she said, looking out upon the heavens.

Then they proceeded to scan the sky, roving from planet to star, from single stars to double stars, from double to coloured stars, in the cursory manner of the merely curious. They plunged down to that at other times invisible multitude in the back rows of the celestial theatre: remote layers of constellations whose shapes were new and singular; pretty twinklers which for infinite ages had spent their beams without calling forth from a single earthly poet a single line, or being able to bestow a ray of comfort on a single benighted traveller.

'And to think,' said Lady Constantine, 'that the whole race of shepherds, since the beginning of the world, – even those immortal shepherds who watched near Bethlehem,* – should have gone into their graves without knowing that for one star that lighted them in their labours, there were a hundred as good behind trying to do so! . . . I have a feeling for this instrument not unlike the awe I should feel in the presence of a great magician in whom I really believed. Its powers are so enormous, and weird, and fantastical, that I should have a personal fear in being with it alone. Music drew an angel down,* said the poet: but what is that to drawing down worlds!'

'I often experience a kind of fear of the sky after sitting in the observing-chair a long time,' he answered. 'And when I walk home afterwards I also fear it for what I know is there, but cannot see, as one naturally fears the presence of a vast formless something that only reveals a very little of itself. That's partly what I meant by saying that magnitude, which up to a certain point has grandeur, has beyond it ghastliness.'

Thus the interest of their sidereal* observations led them on, till the knowledge that scarce any other human vision was travelling within a hundred million miles of their own gave them such a sense of the isolation of that faculty as almost to be a sense of isolation in respect of their whole personality, causing a shudder at its absoluteness. At night, when human discords and harmonies are hushed, in a general sense, for the greater part of twelve hours, there is nothing to moderate the blow with which the infinitely great, the stellar universe, strikes down upon the infinitely little, the mind of the beholder; and this was the case now. Having got closer to immensity than their fellow-creatures, they saw at once its beauty and its frightfulness. They more and more felt the contrast between their own tiny magnitudes and those among which they had recklessly plunged, till they were oppressed with the presence of a vastness they could not cope with even as an idea, and which hung about them like a nightmare.

He stood by her while she observed; she by him when they changed places. Once that Swithin's emancipation from a trammelling body had been effected by the telescope, and he was well away in space, she felt her influence over him diminishing to nothing. He was quite unconscious of his terrestrial neighbourings, and of herself as one of them. It still further reduced her towards unvarnished* simplicity in her manner to him.

The silence was broken only by the ticking of the clock-work which gave diurnal* motion to the instrument. The stars moved on, the end of the telescope followed, but their tongues stood still. To expect that he was ever voluntarily going to end the pause by speech was apparently futile. She laid her hand upon his arm.

He started, withdrew his eye from the telescope, and brought himself back to the earth by a visible – almost painful – effort.

'Do come out of it,' she coaxed, with a softness in her voice which any man but unpractised Swithin would have felt to be exquisite. 'I feel that I have been so foolish as to put in your hands an instrument to effect my own annihilation. Not a word have you spoken for the last ten minutes.'

'I have been mentally getting on with my great theory. I hope soon to be able to publish it to the world. What, are you going? I will walk with you, Lady Constantine. When will you come again?'

'When your great theory is published to the world.'

CHAPTER NINE

LADY CONSTANTINE, if narrowly observed at this time, would have seemed to be deeply troubled in conscience, and particularly after the interview above described. Ash-Wednesday* occurred in the calendar a few days later, and she went to morning service with a look of genuine contrition on her emotional and yearning countenance.

Besides herself the congregation consisted only of the parson, clerk,* school-children, and three old people living on alms, who sat under the reading-desk; and thus, when Mr Torkingham blazed forth the denunciatory sentences of the Commination,* nearly the whole force of them seemed to descend upon her own shrinking shoulders. Looking across the empty pews she saw through the one or two clear panes of the window opposite a youthful figure in the churchyard, and the very feeling against which she had tried to pray returned again irresistibly.

When she came out and had crossed into the private walk, Swithin came forward to speak to her. This was a most unusual circumstance, and argued a matter of importance.

'I have made an amazing discovery in connexion with the variable stars,' he exclaimed. 'It will excite the whole astronomical world, and the world outside but little less. I had long suspected the true secret of their variability; but it was by the merest chance on earth that I hit upon a proof of my guess. Your equatorial has done it, my good, kind Lady Constantine, and our fame is established for ever!'

He sprang into the air, and waved his hat in his triumph.

'O, I am so glad – so rejoiced!' she cried. 'What is it? But don't stop to tell me. Publish it at once in some paper; nail your name to it, or somebody will seize the idea and appropriate it, – forestall you in some way. It will be Adams and Leverrier* over again.'

'If I may walk with you I will explain the nature of the discovery. It accounts for the occasional green tint of Castor, and every difficulty. I said I would be the Copernicus of the stellar system, and I have begun to be. Yet who knows?'

'Now don't be so up and down! I shall not understand your explanation, and I would rather not know it. I shall reveal it if it is very grand. Women, you know, are not safe depositaries of such valuable secrets. You may walk with me a little way, with great pleasure. Then go and write your account, so as to insure your ownership of the discovery.... But how you have watched!' she cried, in a sudden accession of anxiety, as she turned to look more closely at him. 'The orbits of your eyes are leaden, and your eyelids are red and heavy. Don't do it – pray don't. You will be ill, and break down.'

'I have, it is true, been up a little late this last week,' he said cheerfully. 'In fact, I couldn't tear myself away from the equatorial; it is such a wonderful possession that it keeps me there till daylight. But what does that matter, now I have made the discovery?'

'Ah, it *does* matter! Now, promise me – I insist – that you will not commit such imprudences again; for what should I do if my Astronomer Royal were to die?'

She laughed, but far too apprehensively to be effective as a display of levity.

They parted, and he went home to write out his paper. He promised to call as soon as his discovery was in print. Then they waited for the result.

It is impossible to describe the tremulous state of Lady Constantine during the interval. The warm interest she took in Swithin St Cleeve – many would have said dangerously warm interest – made his hopes her hopes; and though she sometimes admitted to herself that great allowance was requisite for the overweening confidence of youth in the future, she permitted herself to be blinded to probabilities for the pleasure of sharing his dreams. It seemed not unreasonable to suppose the present hour to be the beginning of realization to her darling wish that this young man should become famous. He had worked hard, and why should he not be famous early? His very simplicity in mundane affairs afforded a strong presumption that in things celestial he might be wise. To obtain support for this hypothesis she had only to think over the lives of many eminent astronomers.

She waited feverishly for the flourish of trumpets from afar, by which she expected the announcement of his discovery to be greeted. Knowing that immediate intelligence of the outburst would be brought to her by himself, she watched from the windows of the Great House each morning for a sight of his figure hastening down the glade.

But he did not come.

A long array of wet days passed their dreary shapes before her, and made the waiting still more tedious. On one of these occasions she ran across to the tower, at the risk of a severe cold. The door was locked.

Two days after she went again. The door was locked still. But this was only to be expected in such weather. Yet she would have gone on to his house, had there not been one reason too many against such precipitancy. As astronomer and astronomer there was no harm in their meetings; but as woman and man she feared them.

Ten days passed without a sight of him; ten blurred and dreary days, during which the whole landscape dripped like a mop: the park trees swabbed the gravel from the drive, while the sky was a zinc-coloured archivault* of immovable cloud. It seemed as if the whole science of astronomy had never been real, and that the heavenly bodies, with their motions, were as theoretical as the lines and circles of a bygone mathematical problem.

She could content herself no longer with fruitless visits to the column, and when the rain had a little abated she walked to the nearest hamlet, and in a conversation with the first old woman she met contrived to lead up to the subject of Swithin St Cleeve by talking about his grandmother.

'Ah, poor old heart; 'tis a bad time for her, my lady!' exclaimed the dame.

'What?'

'Her grandson is dying; and such a gentleman through and through!'

'What! . . . O, it has something to do with that dreadful discovery!'

'Discovery, my lady?'

She left the old woman with an evasive answer, and with a breaking heart crept along the road. Tears brimmed as she walked, and by the time that she was out of sight sobs burst forth tumultuously.

'I am too fond of him!' she moaned; 'but I can't help it; and I don't care if it's wrong, – I don't care!'

Without further considerations as to who beheld her doings she instinctively went straight towards Mrs Martin's. Seeing a man coming she calmed herself sufficiently to ask him through her dropped veil how poor Mr St Cleeve was that day. But she only got the same reply: 'They say he is dying, my lady.'

When Swithin had parted from Lady Constantine, on the previous Ash-Wednesday, he had gone straight to the homestead and prepared his account of 'A New Astronomical Discovery'. It was written perhaps in too glowing a rhetoric for the true scientific tone of mind; but there was no doubt that his assertion met with a most startling aptness all the difficulties which had accompanied the received theories on the phenomena attending those changeable suns of marvellous systems so far away. It accounted for the nebulous mist that surrounds some of them at their weakest time; in short, took up a position of probability which has never yet been successfully assailed.

The papers were written in triplicate, and carefully sealed up with blue wax. One copy was directed to Greenwich,* another to the Royal Society,* another to a prominent astronomer. A brief statement of the essence of the discovery was also prepared for the leading daily paper.

He considered these documents, embodying as they did two years of his constant thought, reading, and observation, too important to be entrusted for posting to the hands of a messenger; too important to be sent to the sub-post-office at hand. Though the day was wet, dripping wet, he went on foot with them to a chief office, five miles off,* and registered them. Quite exhausted by the walk after his long night-work, wet through, yet sustained by the sense of a great achievement, he called at a bookseller's for the astronomical periodicals to which he subscribed; then, resting for a short time at an inn, he plodded his way homewards, reading his papers as he went, and planning how to enjoy a repose on his laurels of a week or more.

On he strolled through the rain, holding the umbrella vertically over the exposed page to keep it dry while he read. Suddenly his eye was struck by an article. It was the review of a pamphlet by an American astronomer, in which the author announced a conclusive discovery with regard to variable stars.*

The discovery was precisely the discovery of Swithin St Cleeve. Another man had forestalled his fame by a period of about six weeks.

Then the youth found that the goddess Philosophy,* to whom he had vowed to dedicate his whole life, would not in return support him through a single hour of despair. In truth, the impishness of circumstance* was newer to him than it would have been to a philosopher of threescore-and-ten. In a wild wish for annihilation he flung himself down on a patch of heather that lay a little removed from the road, and in this humid bed remained motionless, while time passed by unheeded.

The March rain pelted him mercilessly, the beaded moisture from the heavily charged locks of heath penetrated him through back and sides, and clotted his hair to unsightly tags and tufts. When he awoke it was dark. He thought of his grandmother, and of her possible alarm at missing him. On attempting to rise, he found that he could hardly bend his joints, and that his clothes were as heavy as lead from saturation. His teeth chattering and his knees trembling he pursued his way home, where his appearance excited great concern. He was obliged at once to retire to bed, and the next day he was delirious from the chill.

It was about ten days after this unhappy occurrence that Lady Constantine learnt the news, as above described, and hastened along to the homestead in that state of anguish in which the heart is no longer under the control of the judgment, and self-abandonment, even to error, verges on heroism.

On reaching the house in Welland Bottom the door was opened to her by old Hannah, who wore an assiduously sorrowful look; and Lady Constantine was shown into the large room, – so wide that the beams bent in the middle, – where she took her seat in one of a methodic range of chairs, beneath a portrait of the Reverend Mr St Cleeve, her astronomer's erratic father.

The eight unwatered dying plants, in the row of eight flower-pots, denoted that there was something wrong in the house. Mrs Martin came downstairs fretting, her wonder at beholding Lady Constantine not altogether displacing the previous mood of grief.

'Here's a pretty kettle of fish, my lady!' she exclaimed.

Lady Constantine said, 'Hush!' and pointed inquiringly upward.

'He is not overhead, my lady,' replied Swithin's grandmother. 'His bedroom is at the back of the house.'

'How is he now?'

'He is better, just at this moment; and we are more hopeful. But he changes so.'

'May I go up? I know he would like to see me.'

Her presence having been made known to the sufferer she was conducted upstairs to Swithin's room. The way thither was through the large chamber he had used as a study and for the manufacture of optical instruments. There lay the large pasteboard telescope that had been just such a failure as Crusoe's large boat;* there were his diagrams, maps, globes, and celestial apparatus of various sorts. The absence of the worker through illness or death is sufficient to touch the prosiest workshop and tools with the hues of pathos, and it was with a swelling bosom that Lady Constantine passed through this arena of his youthful activities to the little chamber where he lay.

Old Mrs Martin sat down by the window, and Lady Constantine bent over Swithin.

'Don't speak to me!' she whispered. 'It will weaken you; it will excite you. If you do speak, it must be very softly.'

She took his hand, and one irrepressible tear fell upon it.

'Nothing will excite me now, Lady Constantine,' he said; 'not even your goodness in coming. My last excitement was when I lost the battle. . . . Do you know that my discovery has been forestalled? It is that that's killing me.'

'But you are going to recover; you are better, they say. Is it so?'

'I think I am, to-day. But who can be sure?'

'The poor boy was so upset at finding that his labour had been thrown away,' said his grandmother, 'that he lay down in the rain, and chilled his life out.'

'How could you do it?' Lady Constantine whispered. 'O, how could you think so much of renown, and so little of me? Why, for every discovery made there are ten behind that await making. To commit suicide like this, as if there were nobody in the world to care for you!'

'It was done in my haste, and I am very, very sorry for it! I beg both you and all my few friends never, never to forgive me! It would kill me with self-reproach if you were to pardon my rashness!'

At this moment the doctor was announced, and Mrs Martin went downstairs to receive him. Lady Constantine thought she would remain to hear his report, and for this purpose withdrew, and sat down in a nook of the adjoining work-room of Swithin, the doctor meeting her as he passed through it into the sick chamber.

He was there a torturingly long time; but at length he came out to the room she waited in, and crossed it on his way downstairs. She rose and followed him to the stairhead.

'How is he?' she anxiously asked. 'Will he get over it?'

The doctor, not knowing the depth of her interest in the patient, spoke with the blunt candour natural towards a comparatively indifferent inquirer.

'No, Lady Constantine,' he replied; 'there's a change for the worse.'

And he retired down the stairs.

Scarcely knowing what she did Lady Constantine ran back to Swithin's side, flung herself upon the bed, and in a paroxysm of sorrow kissed him.

CHAPTER TEN

THE placid inhabitants of the parish of Welland, including warbling waggoners, lone shepherds, ploughmen, the blacksmith, the carpenter, the gardener at the Great House, the steward and agent, the parson, clerk, and so on, were hourly expecting the announcement of St Cleeve's death. The sexton had been going to see his brother-in-law, nine miles distant, but promptly postponed the visit for a few days, that there might be the regular professional hand present to toll the bell in a note of due fulness and solemnity; an attempt by a deputy, on a previous occasion of his absence, having degenerated into a miserable stammering clang that was a disgrace to the parish.

But Swithin St Cleeve did not decease, a fact of which, indeed, the habituated reader will have been well aware ever since the rain came down upon the young man in the ninth chapter, and led to his alarming illness. Though, for that matter, so many maimed histories are hourly enacting themselves in this dun-coloured world as to lend almost a priority of interest to narratives concerning those

> 'Who lay great bases for eternity
> Which prove more short than waste or ruining'.*

How it arose that he did not die was in this wise; and his example affords another instance of that reflex rule of the vassal soul over the sovereign body, which, operating so wonderfully in elastic natures, and more or less in all, originally gave rise to the legend that supremacy lay on the other side.

The evening of the day after the tender, despairing, farewell kiss of Lady Constantine, when he was a little less weak than during her visit, he lay with his face to the window. He lay alone, quiet and resigned. He had been thinking, sometimes of her and other friends, but chiefly of his lost discovery. Although nearly unconscious at the time, he had yet been aware of that kiss, as the delicate flush which followed it upon his cheek would have told; but he had attached little importance to it as between woman and man. Had he been dying of love instead of wet weather, perhaps the impulsive act of that handsome lady would have been seized on as a proof that his love was returned. As it was her kiss seemed but the evidence of a naturally demonstrative kindliness, felt towards him chiefly because he was believed to be leaving her for ever.

The reds of sunset passed, and dusk drew on. Old Hannah came upstairs to pull down the blinds, and as she advanced to the window he said to her, in a faint voice, 'Well, Hannah, what news to-day?'

'O, nothing, sir,' Hannah replied, looking out of the window with sad apathy, 'only that there's a comet, they say.'

'A WHAT?' said the dying astronomer, starting up on his elbow.

'A comet – that's all, Master Swithin,' repeated Hannah, in a lower voice, fearing she had done harm in some way.

'Well, tell me, tell me!' cried Swithin. 'Is it Gambart's?* Is it Charles the Fifth's,* or Halley's,* or Faye's,* or whose?'

'Hush!' said she, thinking St Cleeve slightly delirious again. ''Tis God A'mighty's, of course. I haven't seed en* myself; but they say he's getting bigger every night, and that he'll be the biggest one known for fifty years when he's full growed. There, you must not talk any more now, or I'll go away.'

Here was an amazing event, little noise as it had made in the happening. Of all phenomena that he had longed to witness during his short astronomical career, those appertaining to comets had excited him most. That the magnificent comet of 1811* would not return again for thirty centuries had been quite a permanent regret with him. And now, when the bottomless abyss of death seemed yawning beneath his feet, one of these much-desired apparitions, as large, apparently, as any of its tribe, had chosen to show itself.

'O, if I could but live to see that comet through my equatorial!' he cried.

Compared with comets, variable stars, which he had hitherto made his study, were, from their remoteness, uninteresting. They were to the former as the celebrities of Ujiji or Unyamwesi* to the celebrities of his own country. Members of the solar system, these dazzling and perplexing rangers, the fascination of all astronomers, rendered themselves still more fascinating by the sinister suspicion attaching to them of being possibly the ultimate destroyers of the human race. In his physical prostration St Cleeve wept bitterly at not being hale and strong enough to welcome with proper honour the present specimen of these desirable visitors.

The strenuous wish to live and behold the new phenomenon, supplanting the utter weariness of existence that he had heretofore experienced, gave him a new vitality. The crisis passed; there was a turn for the better; and after that he rapidly mended. The comet had in all probability saved his life. The limitless and complex wonders of the sky resumed their old power over his imagination; the possibilities of that unfathomable blue ocean* were endless. Finer feats than ever he would perform were to be achieved in its investigation. What Lady Constantine had said, that for one discovery made ten awaited making, was strikingly verified by the sudden appearance of this splendid marvel.

The windows of St Cleeve's bedroom faced the west, and nothing would satisfy him but that his bed should be so pulled round as to give him a view of the low sky, in which the as yet minute tadpole of fire was recognizable. The mere sight of it seemed to lend him sufficient resolution to complete his own cure forthwith. His only fear now was lest, from some unexpected cause or other, the comet would vanish before he could get to the observatory on Rings-Hill Speer.

In his fervour to begin observing he directed that an old telescope, which he had used in his first celestial attempts, should be tied at one end to the bed-post, and at the other fixed near his eye as he reclined. Equipped only with this rough improvisation he began to take notes. Lady Constantine was forgotten, till one day, suddenly, wondering if she knew of the important phenomenon, he revolved in his mind whether as a fellow-student and sincere friend of his she ought not to be sent for, and instructed in the use of the equatorial.

But though the image of Lady Constantine, in spite of her kindness and unmistakably warm heart, had been obscured in his mind by the heavenly body, she had not so readily forgotten him. Too shy to repeat her visit after so nearly betraying her secret, she yet, every day, by the most ingenious and subtle means that could be devised by a woman who feared for herself, but could not refrain from tampering with danger, ascertained the state of her young friend's health. On hearing of the turn in his condition she rejoiced on his account, and became yet more despondent on her own. If he had died she might have mused on him as her dear departed saint without much sin: but his return to life was a delight that bewildered and dismayed.

One evening a little later on he was sitting at his bedroom window as usual, waiting for a sufficient decline of light to reveal the comet's form, when he beheld, crossing the field contiguous to the house, a figure which he knew to be hers. He thought she must be coming to see him on the great comet question, to discuss which with so delightful and kind a comrade was an expectation full of pleasure. Hence he keenly observed her approach, till something happened that surprised him.

When, at the descent of the hill, she had reached the stile that admitted to Mrs Martin's garden, Lady Constantine stood quite still for a minute or more, her gaze bent on the ground. Instead of coming on to the house she went heavily and slowly back, almost as if in pain; and then at length, quickening her pace, she was soon out of sight. She appeared in the path no more that day.

CHAPTER ELEVEN

WHY had Lady Constantine stopped and turned?

A misgiving had taken sudden possession of her. Her true sentiment towards St Cleeve was too recognizable by herself to be tolerated.

That she had a legitimate interest in him as a young astronomer was true; that her sympathy on account of his severe illness had been natural and commendable was also true. But the superfluous feeling was what filled her with trepidation.

Superfluities have been defined as things you cannot do without, and this particular emotion, that came not within her rightful measure, was in danger of becoming just such a superfluity with her. In short, she felt there and then that to see St Cleeve again would be an impropriety; and by a violent effort she retreated from his precincts, as he had observed.

She resolved to ennoble her conduct from that moment of her life onwards. She would exercise kind patronage towards Swithin without once indulging herself with his company. Inexpressibly dear to her deserted heart he was becoming, but for the future he should at least be hidden from her eyes. To speak plainly, it was growing a serious question whether, if he were not hidden from her eyes, she would not soon be plunging across the ragged boundary which divides the permissible from the forbidden.

By the time that she had drawn near home the sun was going down. The heavy, many-chevroned* church, now subdued by violet shadow except where its upper courses caught the western stroke of flame-colour, stood close to her grounds, as in many other parishes, though the village of which it formerly was the nucleus had become quite depopulated: its cottages had been demolished to enlarge the park, leaving the old building to stand there alone, like a standard without an army.

It was Friday night, and she heard the organist practising voluntaries within. The hour, the notes, the even-song of the birds, and her own previous emotions, combined to influence her devotionally. She entered, turning to the right and passing under the chancel arch, where she sat down and viewed the whole empty length, east and west. The semi-Norman* arches with their multitudinous notchings, were still visible by the light from the tower window, but the lower portion of the building was in obscurity, except where the feeble glimmer from the candle of the organist spread a glow-worm radiance around. The player, who was Miss Tabitha Lark, continued without intermission to produce her wandering sounds, unconscious of any one's presence except that of the youthful blower* at her side.

The rays from the organist's candle illuminated but one small fragment of the chancel outside the precincts of the instrument, and that was the portion of the eastern wall whereon the ten commandments were inscribed. The gilt letters shone sternly into Lady Constantine's eyes; and she, being as impressionable as a turtle-dove, watched a certain one of those commandments on the second table,* till its thunder* broke her spirit with blank contrition.

She knelt down, and did her utmost to eradicate those impulses towards St Cleeve which were inconsistent with her position as the wife of an absent man, though not unnatural in her as his victim.

She knelt till she seemed scarcely to belong to the time she lived in, which lost the magnitude that the nearness of its perspective lent it on ordinary occasions and took its actual rank in the long line of other centuries. Having once got out of herself, seen herself from afar off, she was calmer, and went on to register a magnanimous vow. She would look about for some maiden fit and likely to make St Cleeve happy; and this girl she would endow with what money she could afford, that the natural result of their apposition should do him no worldly harm. The interest of her, Lady Constantine's, life should be in watching the development of love between Swithin and the ideal maiden.

The very painfulness of the scheme to her susceptible heart made it pleasing to her conscience; and she wondered that she had not before this time thought of a stratagem which united the possibility of benefiting the astronomer with the advantage of guarding against peril to both Swithin and herself. By providing for him a suitable helpmate she would preclude the dangerous awakening in him of sentiments reciprocrating her own.

Arrived at a point of exquisite misery through this heroic intention, Lady Constantine's tears moistened the books upon which her forehead was bowed. And as she heard her feverish heart throb against the desk, she firmly believed the wearing impulses of that heart would put an end to her sad life, and momentarily recalled the banished image of St Cleeve to apostrophise him in the thoughts that paraphrased the quaint lines of Heine's *Lieb' Liebchen*: –

'Dear my love, press thy hand to my breast, and tell
If thou tracest the knocks in that narrow cell;
A carpenter dwells there; cunning is he,
And slyly he's shaping a coffin for me!'*

Lady Constantine was disturbed by a break in the organist's meandering practice, and raising her head she saw a person standing by the player. It was Mr Torkingham, and what he said was distinctly audible. He was inquiring for herself.

'I thought I saw Lady Constantinc walk this way,' he rejoined to Tabitha's negative. 'I am very anxious indeed to meet with her.'

She went forward. 'I am here,' she said. 'Don't stop playing, Miss Lark. What is it, Mr Torkingham?'

Tabitha thereupon resumed her playing, and Mr Torkingham joined Lady Constantine.

'I have some very serious intelligence to break to your ladyship,' he said. 'But – I will not interrupt you here.' (He had seen her rise from her knees to come to him.) 'I will call at the House the first moment you can receive me after reaching home.'

'No, tell me here,' she said, seating herself.

He came close, and placed his hand on the poppy-head* of the seat.

'I have received a communication,' he resumed haltingly, 'in which I am requested to prepare you for the contents of a letter that you will receive to-morrow morning.'

'I am quite ready.'

'The subject is briefly this, Lady Constantine: that you have been a widow for more than eighteen months.'

'Dead!'

'Yes. Sir Blount was attacked by dysentery and malarious fever, on the banks of the Zouga* in South Africa, so long ago as last October twelvemonths, and it carried him off. Of the three men who were with him, two succumbed to the same illness, a hundred miles further on; while the third, retracing his steps into a healthier district, remained there with a native tribe, and took no pains to make the circumstances known. It seems to be only by the mere accident of his having told some third party that we know of the matter now. This is all I can tell you at present.'

She was greatly agitated for a few moments; and the Table of the Law opposite, which now seemed to appertain to another dispensation, glistened indistinctly upon a vision still obscured by the old tears.

'Shall I conduct you home?' asked the parson.

'No thank you,' said Lady Constantine. 'I would rather go alone.'

CHAPTER TWELVE

ON the afternoon of the next day Mr Torkingham, who occasionally dropped in to see St Cleeve, called again as usual; after duly remarking on the state of the weather, congratulating him on his sure though slow improvement, and answering his inquiries about the comet, he said, 'You have heard, I suppose, of what has happened to Lady Constantine?'

'No! Nothing serious?'

'Yes, it is serious.' The parson informed him of the death of Sir Blount, and of the accidents which had hindered all knowledge of the same, – accidents favoured by the estrangement of the pair and the cessation of correspondence between them for some time.

His listener received the news with the concern of a friend, Lady Constantine's aspect in his eyes depending but little on her condition matrimonially.

'There was no attempt to bring him home when he died?'

'O no. The climate necessitates instant burial. We shall have more particulars in a day or two, doubtless.'

'Poor Lady Constantine, – so good and so sensitive as she is! I suppose she is quite prostrated by the bad news.'

'Well, she is rather serious, – not prostrated. The household is going into mourning.'

'Ah, no, she would not be quite prostrated,' murmured Swithin, recollecting himself. 'He was unkind to her in many ways. Do you think she will go away from Welland?'

That the vicar could not tell. But he feared that Sir Blount's affairs had been in a seriously involved condition, which might necessitate many and unexpected changes.

Time showed that Mr Torkingham's surmises were correct.

During the long weeks of early summer, through which the young man still lay imprisoned, if not within his own chamber, within the limits of the house and garden, news reached him that Sir Blount's mismanagement and eccentric behaviour were resulting in serious consequences to Lady Constantine; nothing less, indeed, than her almost complete impoverishment. His personalty* was swallowed up in paying his debts, and the Welland estate was so heavily charged with annuities to his distant relatives that only a mere pittance was left for her. She was reducing the establishment to the narrowest compass compatible with decent gentility. The horses were sold one by one; the carriages also; the greater part of the house was shut up, and she resided in the smallest rooms. All that was allowed to remain of her former contingent of male servants were an odd man* and a boy. Instead of using a carriage she now drove about in a donkey-chair,* the said boy walking in front to clear the way and keep the animal in motion; while she wore, so his informants reported, not an ordinary widow's cap or bonnet, but something even plainer, the black material being drawn tightly round her face, giving her features a small, demure, devout cast, very pleasing to the eye.

'Now, what's the most curious thing in this, Mr San Cleeve,' said Sammy Blore, who, in calling to inquire after Swithin's health, had imparted some of the above particulars, 'is that my lady seems not to mind being a poor woman half so much as we do at seeing her so. 'Tis a wonderful gift, Mr San Cleeve, wonderful, to be able to guide yerself, and not let loose yer soul in blasting at such a misfortune. I should go and drink neat* regular, as soon as I had swallered my breakfast, till my innerds was burnt out like a' old copper, if it had happened to me; but my lady's plan is best. Though I only guess how one feels in such losses, to be sure, for I never had nothing to lose.'

Meanwhile the observatory was not forgotten; nor that visitant of singular shape and habits which had appeared in the sky from no one knew whence, trailing its luminous streamer,* and proceeding on its way in the face of a wondering world, till it should choose to vanish as suddenly as it had come.

When, about a month after the above dialogue took place, Swithin was allowed to go about as usual, his first pilgrimage was to the Rings-Hill Speer. Here he studied at leisure what he had come to see.

On his return to the homestead, just after sunset, he found his grandmother and Hannah in a state of great concern. The former was looking out for him against the evening light, her face showing itself worn and rutted, like an old highway, by the passing of many days. Her information was that in his absence Lady Constantine had called in her driving-chair, to inquire for him. Her ladyship had wished to observe the comet through the great telescope, but had found the door locked when she applied at the tower. Would he kindly leave the door unfastened to-morrow, she had asked, that she might be able to go to the column on the following evening for the same purpose? She did not require him to attend.

During the next day he sent Hannah with the key to Welland House, not caring to leave the tower open. As evening advanced and the comet grew distinct, he doubted if Lady Constantine could handle the telescope alone with any pleasure or profit to herself. Unable, as a devotee to science, to rest under this misgiving, he crossed the field in the furrow that he had used ever since the corn was sown, and entered the plantation. His unpractised mind never once guessed that her stipulations against his coming might have existed along with a perverse hope that he would come.

On ascending he found her already there. She sat in the observing-chair: the warm light from the west, which flowed in through the opening of the dome, brightened her face, and her face only, her robes of sable lawn rendering the remainder of her figure almost invisible.

'You have come!' she said with shy pleasure. 'I did not require you. But never mind.' She extended her hand cordially to him.

Before speaking he looked at her with a great new interest in his eye. It was the first time that he had seen her thus, and she was altered in more than dress. A soberly-sweet expression sat on her face. It was of a rare and peculiar shade – something that he had never seen before in woman.

'Have you nothing to say?' she continued. 'Your footsteps were audible to me from the very bottom, and I knew they were yours. You look almost restored.'

'I am almost restored,' he replied, respectfully pressing her hand. 'A reason for living arose, and I lived.'

'What reason?' she inquired, with a rapid blush.

He pointed to the rocket-like object in the western sky.

'O, you mean the comet. Well, you will never make a courtier!

You know, of course, what has happened to me; that I have no longer a husband – have had none for a year and a half. Have you also heard that I am now quite a poor woman? Tell me what you think of it.'

'I have thought very little of it since I heard that you seemed to mind poverty but little. There is even this good in it, that I may now be able to show you some little kindness for all those you have done me, my dear lady.'

'Unless for economy's sake, I go and live abroad, – at Dinan, Versailles, or Boulogne.'

Swithin, who had never thought of such a contingency, was earnest in his regrets; without, however, showing more than a sincere friend's disappointment.

'I did not say it was absolutely necessary,' she continued. 'I have, in fact, grown so homely and home-loving, I am so interested in the place and the people here, that, in spite of advice, I have almost determined not to let the house; but to continue the less business-like but pleasanter alternative of living humbly in a part of it, and shutting up the rest.'

'Your love of astronomy is getting as strong as mine!' he said ardently. 'You could not tear yourself away from the observatory!'

'You might have supposed me capable of a little human feeling as well as scientific, in connection with the observatory.'

'Dear Lady Constantine, by admitting that your astronomer has also a part of your interest—'

'Ah, you did not find it out without my telling!' she said, with a playfulness which was scarcely playful, a warmer accession of colour being visible in her face. 'I diminish myself in your esteem by reminding you.'

'You might do anything in this world without diminishing yourself in my esteem, after the goodness you have shown. And more than that, no misrepresentation, no rumour, no damning appearance whatever, would ever shake my loyalty to you.'

'But you put a very matter-of-fact construction on my motives sometimes. You see me in such a hard light that I have to drop hints in quite a manœuvring manner to let you know I am as sympathetic as other people. I sometimes think you would rather have me die than have your equatorial stolen. Confess that your admiration for me was based on my house and position in the county! Now I am shorn of all that glory, such as it was, and am a widow, and am poorer than my tenants, and can no longer buy telescopes, and am unable, from the narrowness of my circumstances, to mix in circles that people formerly said I adorned, I fear I have lost the little hold I once had over you.'

'You are as unjust now as you have been generous hitherto,' said St Cleeve, with tears in his eyes at the gentle banter of the lady, which he, poor innocent, read as her real opinions. Seizing her hand he continued, in tones between reproach and anger, 'I swear to you that I have but two devotions, two thoughts, two hopes, and two blessings in this world, and that one of them is yourself!'

'And the other?'

'The pursuit of astronomy.'

'And astronomy stands first.'

'I have never ordinated* two such dissimilar ideas! And why should you deplore your altered circumstances, my dearest lady? Your widowhood, if I may take the liberty to speak on such a subject, is, though I suppose a sadness, not perhaps an unmixed evil. For though your pecuniary troubles have been discovered to the world and yourself by it, your happiness in marriage was, as you have confided to me, not great; and you are now left free as a bird to follow your own hobbies.'

'I wonder you recognize that.'

'But perhaps,' he added, with a sigh of regret, 'you will again fall a prey to some man, some uninteresting country squire or other, and be lost to the scientific world after all.'

'If I fall a prey to any man, it will not be to a country squire. But don't go on with this, for heaven's sake! You may think what you like in silence.'

'We are forgetting the comet,' said St Cleeve. He turned, and set the instrument in order for observation, and wheeled round the dome.

While she was looking at the nucleus of the fiery plume, that now filled so large a space of the sky as completely to dominate it, Swithin dropped his gaze upon the field, and beheld in the dying light a number of labourers crossing directly towards the column.

'What do you see?' Lady Constantine asked, without ceasing to observe the comet.

'Some of the work-folk are coming this way. I know what they are coming for, – I promised to let them look at the comet through the glass.'

'They must not come up here,' she said decisively.

'They shall await your time.'

'I have a special reason for wishing them not to see me here. If you ask why, I can tell you. They mistakenly suspect my interest to be less in astronomy than in the astronomer, and they must have no showing for such a wild notion. What can you do to keep them out?'

'I'll lock the door,' said Swithin. 'They will then think I am away.' He ran down the staircase, and she could hear him hastily turning the key. Lady Constantine sighed.

'What weakness, what weakness!' she said to herself. 'That envied power of self-control, where is it? That power of concealment which a woman should have – where? To run such risks, to come here alone, – O, if it were known! But I was always so, always!'

She jumped up, and followed him downstairs.

CHAPTER THIRTEEN

HE was standing immediately inside the door at the bottom, though it was so dark she could hardly see him. The villagers were audibly talking just without.

'He's sure to come, rathe* or late,' resounded up the spiral in the vocal note of Hezzy Biles. 'He wouldn't let such a fine show as the comet makes to-night go by without peeping at it, – not Master Cleeve! Did ye bring along the flagon, Haymoss? Then we'll sit down inside his little board-house here, and wait. He'll come afore bed-time. Why, his spy-glass will stretch out that there comet as long as Welland Lane!'

'I'd as soon miss the great peep-show that comes every year to Greenhill Fair* as a sight of such a immortal spectacle as this!' said Amos Fry.

'"Immortal spectacle", – where did ye get that choice mossel, Haymoss?' inquired Sammy Blore. 'Well, well, the Lord save good scholars – and take just a bit o' care of them that bain't!* As 'tis so dark in the hut, suppose we draw out the bench into the front here, souls?'

The bench was accordingly brought forth, and in order to have a back to lean against they placed it exactly across the door into the spiral staircase.

'Now, have ye got any backy?* If ye haven't, I have,' continued Sammy Blore. A striking of matches followed, and the speaker concluded comfortably, 'Now, we shall do very well.'

'And what do this comet mean?' asked Haymoss. 'That some great tumult is going to happen, or that we shall die of a famine?'*

'Famine – no!' said Nat Chapman. 'That only touches such as we, and the Lord only concerns himself with born gentlemen. It isn't to be supposed that a strange fiery lantern like that would be lighted up for folks with ten or a dozen shillings a week* and their gristing,* and a load o' thorn faggots* when we can get 'em. If 'tis a token that he's getting hot about the ways of anybody in this parish, 'tis about my Lady Constantine's, since she is the only one of a figure worth such a hint.'

'As for her income, – that she's now lost.'

'Ah, well; I don't take in all I hear.'

Lady Constantine drew close to St Cleeve's side, and whispered, trembling, 'Do you think they will wait long? Or can we get out?'

Swithin felt the awkwardness of the situation. The men had placed the bench close to the door, which, owing to the stairs within, opened outwards; so that at the first push by the pair inside to release themselves the bench must have gone over, and sent the smokers sprawling on their faces. He whispered to her to ascend the column and wait till he came.

'And have the dead man left her nothing? Hey? And have he carried his inheritance into's grave? And will his skeleton lie warm on account o't? Hee-hee!' said Haymoss.

''Tis all swallered up,' observed Hezzy Biles. 'His goings-on made her miserable till 'a died, and if I were the woman I'd have my randys* now. He ought to have bequeathed to her our young gent, Mr St Cleeve, as some sort of amends. I'd up and marry en, if I were she; since her downfall has brought 'em quite near together, and made him as good as she in rank, as he was afore in bone and breeding.'

'D'ye think she will?' asked Sammy Blore. 'Or is she meaning to enter upon a virgin life for the rest of her days?'

'I don't want to be unreverent to her ladyship; but I really don't think she is meaning any such waste of a comely carcase. I say she's rather meaning to commit flat matrimony wi' somebody or other, and one young gentleman in particular.'

'But the young man himself?'

'Planned, cut out, and finished for the delight of 'ooman!'*

'Yet he must be willing.'

'That would soon come. If they get up this tower ruling plannards together much longer, their plannards will soon rule them* together, in my way o' thinking. If she've a disposition towards the knot, she can soon teach him.'

'True, true, and lawfully. What before mid ha'* been a wrong desire is now a holy wish!'

The scales fell from Swithin St Cleeve's eyes as he heard the words of his neighbours. How suddenly the truth dawned upon him; how it bewildered him, till he scarcely knew where he was; how he recalled the full force of what he had only half apprehended at earlier times, particularly of that sweet kiss she had impressed on his lips when she supposed him dying, – these vivid realizations are difficult to tell in slow verbiage. He could remain there no longer, and with an electrified heart he retreated up the spiral.

He found Lady Constantine half way to the top, standing by a loop-hole;* and when she spoke he discovered that she was almost in tears. 'Are they gone?' she asked.

'I fear they will not go yet,' he replied, with a nervous fluctuation of manner that had never before appeared in his bearing towards her.

'What shall I do?' she asked. 'I ought not to be here; nobody knows that I am out of the house. O, this is a mistake! I must go home somehow.'

'Did you hear what they were saying?'

'No,' said she. 'What is the matter? Surely you are disturbed? What did they say?'

'It would be the exaggeration of frankness in me to tell you.'

'Is it what a woman ought not to be made acquainted with?'

'It is, in this case. It is so new and so indescribable an idea to me – that' – he leant against the concave wall, quite tremulous with strange incipient sentiments.

'What sort of an idea?' she asked gently.

'It is – an awakening. In thinking of the heaven above, I did not perceive – the—'

'Earth beneath?'*

'The better heaven beneath. Pray, dear Lady Constantine, give me your hand for a moment.'

She seemed startled, and the hand was not given.

'I am so anxious to get home,' she repeated. 'I did not mean to stay here more than five minutes!'

'I fear I am much to blame for this accident,' he said. 'I ought not to have intruded here. But don't grieve! I will arrange for your escape, somehow. Be good enough to follow me down.'

They redescended, and, whispering to Lady Constantine to remain a few stairs behind, he began to rattle and unlock the door.

The men precipitately removed their bench, and Swithin stepped out, the light of the summer night being still enough to enable them to distinguish him.

'Well, Hezekiah, and Samuel, and Nat, how are you?' he said boldly.

'Well, sir, 'tis much as before wi' me,' replied Nat. 'One hour a week wi' God A'mighty and the rest with the devil, as a chap may say. And really, now yer poor father's gone, I'd as lief that* that Sunday hour should pass like the rest; for Pa'son Tarkenham do tease a feller's conscience that much, that church is no hollerday at all to the limbs, as it was in yer reverent father's time! But we've been waiting here, Mr San Cleeve, supposing ye had not come.'

'I have been staying at the top, and fastened the door not to be disturbed. Now I am sorry to disappoint you, but I have another engagement this evening, so that it would be inconvenient to admit you. To-morrow evening, or any evening but this, I will show you the comet and any stars you like.'

They readily agreed to come the next night, and prepared to depart. But what with the flagon, and the pipes, and the final observations, getting away was a matter of time. Meanwhile a cloud, which nobody had noticed, arose from the north overhead, and large drops of rain began to fall so rapidly that the conclave entered the hut till it should be over. St Cleeve strolled off under the firs.

The next moment there was a rustling through the trees at another point, and a man and woman appeared. The woman took shelter under a tree, and the man, bearing wraps and umbrellas, came forward.

'My lady's man and maid,' said Sammy.

'Is her ladyship here?' asked the man.

'No. I reckon her ladyship keeps more kissable company,' replied Nat Chapman.

'Pack o' stuff!' said Blore.

'Not here? Well, to be sure! We can't find her anywhere in the wide house! I've been sent to look for her with these overclothes and umbrella. I've suffered horse-flesh traipsing up and down, and can't find her nowhere. Lord, Lord, where can she be, and two months' wages owing to me!'

'Why so anxious, Anthony Green, as I think yer name is shaped? You be not a married man?' said Hezzy.

‘’Tis what they call me, neighbours, whether or no.’

‘But surely you was a bachelor chap by late, afore her ladyship got rid of the regular servants and took ye?’

‘I were; but that’s past!’

‘And how came ye to bow yer head to ’t, Anthony? ’Tis what you never was inclined to. You was by no means a doting man in early time.’

‘Well, had I been left to my own free choice, ’tis as like as not I should ha’ shunned forming such kindred, being at that time a poor day man, or weekly, at my highest luck in hiring. But ’tis wearing work to hold out against the custom of the country, and the woman wanting ’ee to stand by her and save her from unborn shame;* so, since common usage would have it, I let myself be carried away by opinion, and took her. Though she’s never once thanked me for covering her confusion, that’s true! But, ’tis the way of the lost when safe, and I don’t complain. Here she is, just behind, under the tree, if you’d like to see her? – a very nice homespun woman to look at, too, for all her few weather stains. . . . Well, well, where can my lady be? And I the trusty jineral man* – ’tis more than my place is worth to lose her! Come forward, Gloriana, and talk nicely to the work-folk.’

While the woman was talking the rain increased so much that they all retreated further into the hut. St Cleeve, who had impatiently stood a little way off, now saw his opportunity, and, putting in his head, said, ‘The rain beats in; you had better shut the door. I must ascend and close up the dome.’

Slamming the door upon them without ceremony he quickly went to Lady Constantine in the column, and telling her they could now pass the villagers unseen he gave her his arm. Thus he conducted her across the front of the hut into the shadows of the firs.

‘I will run to the house and harness your little carriage myself,’ he said tenderly. ‘I will then take you home in it.’

‘No; please don’t leave me alone under these dismal trees!’ Neither would she hear of his getting her any wraps; and, opening her little sunshade to keep the rain out of her face, she walked with him across the insulating field, after which the trees of the park afforded her a sufficient shelter to reach home without much damage.

Swithin was too greatly affected by what he had overheard to speak much to her on the way, and protected her as if she had been a shorn lamb. After a farewell which had more meaning than sound in it, he hastened back to Rings-Hill Speer. The work-folk were still in the hut, and, by dint of friendly converse and a sip at the flagon, had so cheered Mr and Mrs Anthony Green that they neither thought nor cared what had become of Lady Constantine.

St Cleeve's sudden sense of new relations with that sweet patroness had taken away in one half-hour his natural ingenuousness. Henceforth he could act a part.

'I have made all secure at the top,' he said, putting his head into the hut. 'I am now going home. When the rain stops, lock this door and bring the key to my house.'

CHAPTER FOURTEEN

THE laboured resistance which Lady Constantine's judgment had offered to her rebellious affection ere she learnt that she was a widow, now passed into a bashfulness that rendered her almost as unstable of mood as before. But she was one of that mettle – fervid, cordial, and spontaneous – who had not the heart to spoil a passion; and her affairs having gone to rack and ruin by no fault of her own she was left to a painfully narrowed existence which lent even something of rationality to her attachment. Thus it was that her tender and unambitious soul found comfort in her reverses.

As for St Cleeve, the tardiness of his awakening was the natural result of inexperience combined with devotion to a hobby. But, like a spring bud hard in bursting, the delay was compensated by after speed. At once breathlessly recognizing in this fellow-watcher of the skies* a woman who loved him, in addition to the patroness and friend, he truly translated the nearly forgotten kiss she had given him in her moment of despair.

Lady Constantine, in being nearly ten years his senior, was an object even better calculated to nourish a youth's first passion than a girl of his own age, superiority of experience and ripeness of emotion exercising the same peculiar fascination over him as over other young men in their first ventures in this kind.

The alchemy which thus transmuted an abstracted astronomer into an eager lover – and, must it be said? spoilt a promising young physicist to produce a common-place inamorato* – may be almost described as working its change in one short night. Next morning he was so fascinated with the novel sensation that he wanted to rush off at once to Lady Constantine, and say, 'I love you true!'* in the intensest tones of his mental condition, to register his assertion in her heart before any of those accidents which 'creep in 'twixt vows, and change decrees of kings,'* should occur to hinder him. But his embarrassment at standing in a new position towards her would not allow him to present himself at her door in any such hurry. He waited on as helplessly as a girl for a chance of encountering her.

But though she had tacitly agreed to see him on any reasonable occasion, Lady Constantine did not put herself in his way. She even kept herself out of his way. Now that for the first time he had learnt to feel a strong impatience for their meeting, her shyness for the first time led her to delay it. But given two people living in one parish, who long from the depths of their hearts to be in each other's company, what resolves of modesty, policy, pride, or apprehension will keep them for any length of time apart?

One afternoon he was watching the sun from his tower, half echoing the Greek astronomer's* wish that he might be set close to that luminary for the wonder of beholding it in all its glory, under the slight penalty of being consumed the next instant. He glanced over the high-road between the field and the park (which sublunary features now too often distracted his attention from his telescope), and saw her passing along that way.

She was seated in the donkey-carriage that had now taken the place of her landau, the white animal looking no larger than a cat at that distance. The buttoned boy, who represented both coachman and footman, walked alongside the animal's head at a solemn pace; the dog stalked at the distance of a yard behind the vehicle, without indulging in a single gambol; and the whole turn-out resembled in dignity a dwarfed state procession.

Here was an opportunity but for two obstructions: the boy, who might be curious; and the dog, who might bark and attract the attention of any labourers or servants near. Yet the risk was to be run, and, knowing that she would soon turn up a certain shady lane at right angles to the road she had followed, he ran hastily down the staircase, crossed the barley (which now covered the field) by the path not more than a foot wide that he had trodden for himself, and got into the lane at the other end. By slowly walking along in the direction of the turnpike-road he soon had the satisfaction of seeing her coming. To his surprise he also had the satisfaction of perceiving that neither boy nor dog was in her company.

They both blushed as they approached, she from sex, he from inexperience. One thing she seemed to see in a moment, that in the interval of her absence St Cleeve had become a man; and as he greeted her with this new and maturer light in his eyes she could not hide her embarrassment, or meet their fire.

'I have just sent my page across to the column with your book on Cometary Nuclei,' she said softly; 'that you might not have to come to the house for it. I did not know I should meet you here.'

'Didn't you wish me to come to the house for it?'

'I did not, frankly. You know why, do you not?'

'Yes, I know. Well, my longing is at rest. I have met you again. But are you unwell, that you drive out in this chair?'

'No; I walked out this morning, and am a little tired.'

'I have been looking for you night and day. Why do you turn your face aside? You used not to be so.' Her hand rested on the side of the chair, and he took it. 'Do you know that since we last met, I have been thinking of you – daring to think of you – as I never thought of you before?'

'Yes, I know it.'

'How did you know?'

'I saw it in your face when you came up.'

'Well, I suppose I ought not to think of you so. And yet, had I not learned to, I should never fully have felt how gentle and sweet you are. Only think of my loss if I had lived and died without seeing more in you than in astronomy! But I shall never leave off doing so now. When you talk I shall love your understanding; when you are silent I shall love your face. But how shall I know that you care to be so much to me?'

Her manner was disturbed as she recognized the impending self-surrender, which she knew not how to resist, and was not altogether at ease in welcoming.

'O, Lady Constantine,' he continued, bending over her, 'give me some proof more than mere seeming and inference, which are all I have at present, that you don't think this I tell you of presumption in me! I have been unable to do anything since I last saw you for pondering uncertainly on this. Some proof, or little sign, that we are one in heart!'

A blush settled again on her face; and half in effort, half in spontaneity, she put her finger on her cheek. He almost devotionally kissed the spot.

'Does that suffice?' she asked, scarcely giving her words voice.

'Yes; I am convinced.'

'Then that must be the end. Let me drive on; the boy will be back again soon.' She spoke hastily and looked askance to hide the heat of her cheek.

'No; the tower door is open, and he will go to the top, and waste his time in looking through the telescope.'

'Then you should rush back, for he will do some damage.'

'No; he may do what he likes, tinker and spoil the instrument, destroy my papers, – anything, so that he will stay there and leave us alone.'

She glanced up with pained pleasure.

'You never used to feel like that!' There was keen self-reproach in her voice. 'You were once so devoted to your science that the thought of an intruder into your temple would have driven you wild. Now you don't care; and who is to blame? Ah, not you, not you!'

The animal ambled on with her, and he, leaning on the side of the little vehicle, kept her company.

'Well, don't let us think of that,' he said. 'I offer myself and all my energies, frankly and entirely, to you, my dear, dear lady, whose I shall be always! But my words in telling you this will only injure my meaning instead of emphasizing it. In expressing, even to myself, my thoughts of you, I find that I fall into phrases which, as a critic, I should hitherto have heartily despised for their commonness. What's the use of saying, for instance, as I have just said, that I give myself entirely to you, and shall be yours always, – that you have my devotion, my highest homage? Those words have been used so frequently in a flippant manner that honest use of them is not distinguishable from the unreal.' He turned to her, and added, smiling, 'Your eyes are to be my stars for the future.'

'Yes, I know it, – I know it, and all you would say! I dreaded even while I hoped for this, my dear young friend,' she replied, her eyes being full of tears. 'I am injuring you; who knows that I am not ruining your future, – I who ought to know better? Nothing can come of this, – nothing must, – and I am only wasting your time. Why have I drawn you off from a grand celestial study to study poor lonely me? Say you will never despise me, when you get older, for this episode in our lives. But you will, – I know you will! All men do, when they have been attracted in their unsuspecting youth, as I have attracted you. I ought to have kept my resolve.'

'What was that?'

'To bear anything rather than draw you from your high purpose; to be like the noble citizen of old Greece,* who, attending a sacrifice, let himself be burnt to the bone by a coal that jumped into his sleeve rather than disturb the sacred ceremony.'

'But can I not study and love both?'

'I hope so, – I earnestly hope so. But you'll be the first if you do, and I am the responsible one if you do not.'

'You speak as if I were quite a child, and you immensely older. Why, how old do you think I am? I am twenty.'

'You seem younger. Well, that's so much the better. Twenty sounds strong and firm. How old do you think I am?'

'I have never thought of considering.' He innocently turned to scrutinize her face. She winced a little. But the instinct was premature. Time had taken no liberties with her features as yet; nor had trouble very roughly handled her.

'I will tell you,' she replied, speaking almost with physical pain, yet as if determination should carry her through. 'I am nine-and-twenty – nearly – I mean a little more, a few months – a year – more. Am I not a fearful deal older than you?'

'At first it seems a great deal,' he answered, musing. 'But it doesn't seem much when one gets used to it.'

'Nonsense!' she exclaimed. 'It *is* a good deal.'

'Very well, then, sweetest Lady Constantine, let it be,' he said gently.

'You should not let it be! A polite man would have flatly contradicted me.... O I am ashamed of this!' she added a moment after, with a subdued, sad look upon the ground. 'I am speaking by the card* of the outer world, which I have left behind utterly; no such lip service is known in your sphere. I care nothing for those things, really; but that which is called the Eve in us* will out sometimes. Well, we will forget that now, as we must, at no very distant date, forget all the rest of this.'

He walked beside her thoughtfully awhile, with his eyes also bent on the road. 'Why must we forget it all?' he inquired.

'It is only an interlude.'

'An interlude! It is no interlude to me. O how can you talk so lightly of this, Lady Constantine? And yet, if I were to go away from here, I might, perhaps, soon reduce it to an interlude! Yes,' he resumed impulsively, 'I will go away. Love dies, and it is just as well to strangle it in its birth; it can only die once! I'll go.'

'No, no!' she said, looking up apprehensively. 'I misled you. It is no interlude to me, – it is tragical. I only meant that from a worldly point of view it is an interlude, which we should try to forget. But the world is not all. You will not go away?'

But he continued drearily, 'Yes, yes, I see it all; you have enlightened me. It will be hurting your prospects even more than mine, if I stay. Now, Sir Blount is dead, you are free again, – may marry where you will, but for this fancy of ours. I'll leave Welland before harm comes of my staying.'

'Don't decide to do a thing so rash!' she begged, seizing his hand and looking miserable at the effect of her words. 'I shall have nobody left in the world to care for! And now I have given you the great telescope, and lent you the column, it would be ungrateful to go away! I was wrong; believe me that I did not mean that it was a mere interlude to *me*. O if you only knew how very, very far it is from that! It is my doubt of the result to you that makes me speak so slightingly.'

They were now approaching cross-roads, and casually looking up they beheld, thirty or forty yards beyond the crossing, Mr Torkingham, who was leaning over a gate, his back being towards them. As yet he had not recognized their approach.

The master-passion had already supplanted St Cleeve's natural ingenuousness by subtlety.

'Would it be well for us to meet Mr Torkingham just now?' he began.

'Certainly not,' she said hastily, and pulling the rein she instantly drove down the right-hand road. 'I cannot meet anybody!' she murmured. 'Would it not be better that you leave me now? – not for my pleasure, but that there may arise no distressing tales about us before we know – how to act in this – this –' (she smiled faintly at him) 'heartaching extremity!'

They were passing under a huge oak-tree whose limbs, irregular with shoulders, knuckles, and elbows, stretched horizontally over the lane in a manner recalling Absalom's death.* A slight rustling was perceptible amid the leafage as they drew out from beneath it, and turning up his eyes Swithin saw that very buttoned page whose advent they had dreaded looking down with interest at them from a perch not much higher than a yard above their heads. He had a bunch of oak-apples in one hand, plainly the object of his climb, and was furtively watching Lady Constantine with the hope that she might not see him. But that she had already done, though she did not reveal it, and, fearing that the latter words of their conversation had been overheard, they spoke not till they had passed the next turning.

She stretched out her hand to his. 'This must not go on,' she said imploringly. 'My anxiety as to what may be said of such methods of meeting makes me too unhappy. See what has happened!' She could not help smiling. 'Out of the frying-pan into the fire! After meanly turning to avoid the parson we have rushed into a worse publicity. It is too humiliating to have to avoid people, and lowers both you and me. The only remedy is not to meet.'

'Very well,' said Swithin, with a sigh. 'So it shall be.'

And with smiles that might more truly have been tears they parted there and then.

CHAPTER FIFTEEN

THE summer passed away, and autumn with its infinite suite of tints came creeping on. Darker grew the evenings, tearfuller the moonlights, and heavier the dews. Meanwhile the comet had waxed to its largest dimensions, – so large that not only the nucleus but a portion of the tail had been visible in broad day. It was now on the wane, though every night the equatorial still afforded an opportunity of observing the singular object which would soon disappear altogether from the heavens for perhaps thousands of years.*

But the astronomer of the Rings-Hill Speer was no longer a match for his celestial materials. Scientifically he had become but a dim vapour of himself; the lover had come into him like an armed man,* and cast out the student, and his intellectual situation was growing a life-and-death matter.

The resolve of the pair had been so far kept: they had not seen each other in private for three months. But on one day in October he ventured to write a note to her: –

'I can do nothing! I have ceased to study, ceased to observe. The equatorial is useless to me. This longing I have for you absorbs my life, and outweighs my intentions. The power to labour in the grandest of fields has left me. I struggle against the weakness till I think of the cause, and then I bless her. But the very desperation of my mind has suggested a remedy; and this I would inform you of at once.

'Can you come to me, since I must not come to you? I will wait to-morrow night at the edge of the plantation by which you would enter to the column. I will not detain you; my plan can be told in ten words.'

The night after posting this missive to her he waited at the spot mentioned.

It was a melancholy evening for going abroad. A blusterous wind had risen during the day, and still continued to increase. Yet he stood watchful in the darkness, and was ultimately rewarded by discerning a shady muffled shape that embodied itself from the field, accompanied by the scratching of silk over stubble. There was no longer any disguise as to the nature of their meeting. It was a lovers' assignation, pure and simple; and boldly realizing it as such he clasped her in his arms.

'I cannot bear this any longer!' he exclaimed. 'Three months since I saw you alone! Only a glimpse of you in church, or a bow from the distance, in all that time! O dearest, what a fearful struggle this keeping apart has been!'

'Yet I should have had strength to persist, since it seemed best,' she murmured when she could speak, 'had not your words on your condition so alarmed and saddened me. This inability of yours to work, or study, or observe, – it is terrible! So terrible a sting is it to my conscience that your hint about a remedy has brought me instantly.'

'Yet I don't altogether mind it, since it is you, my dear, who have displaced the work; and yet the loss of time nearly distracts me, when I have neither the power to work nor the delight of your company.'

'But your remedy! O, I cannot help guessing it! Yes; you are going away!'

'Let us ascend the column; we can speak more at ease there. Then I will explain all. I would not ask you to climb so high but the hut is not yet furnished.'

He entered the cabin at the foot, and having lighted a small lantern, conducted her up the hollow staircase to the top, where he closed the slides of the dome to keep out the wind, and placed the observing-chair for her.

'I can stay only five minutes,' she said, without sitting down. 'You said it was important that you should see me, and I have come. I assure you it is at a great risk. If I am seen here at this time I am ruined for ever. But what would I not do for you? O Swithin, your remedy – is it to go away? There is no other; and yet I dread that like death!'

'I can tell you in a moment, but I must begin at the beginning. All this ruinous idleness and distraction is caused by the misery of our not being able to meet with freedom. The fear that something may snatch you from me keeps me in a state of perpetual apprehension.'

'It is too true also of me! I dread that some accident may happen, and waste my days in meeting the trouble half-way.'

'So our lives go on, and our labours stand still. Now for the remedy. Dear Lady Constantine, allow me to marry you.'

She started, and the wind without shook the building, sending up a yet intenser moan from the firs.

'I mean, marry you quite privately. Let it make no difference whatever to our outward lives for years, for I know that in my present position you could not possibly acknowledge me as husband publicly. But by marrying at once we secure the certainty that we cannot be divided by accident, coaxing, or artifice; and, at ease on that point, I shall embrace my studies with the old vigour, and you yours.'

Lady Constantine was so agitated at the unexpected boldness of such a proposal from one hitherto so boyish and deferential that she sank into the observing-chair, her intention to remain for only a few minutes being quite forgotten.

She covered her face with her hands. 'No, no, – I dare not!' she whispered.

'But is there a single thing else left to do?' he pleaded, kneeling down beside her, less in supplication than in abandonment. 'What else can we do?'

'Wait till you are famous.'

'But I cannot be famous unless I strive, and this distracting condition prevents all striving!'

'Could you not strive on if I – gave you a promise, a solemn promise, to be yours when your name is fairly well known?'

St Cleeve breathed heavily. 'It will be a long, weary time,' he said. 'And even with your promise I shall work but half-heartedly. Every hour of study will be interrupted with "Suppose this or this happens"; "Suppose somebody persuades her to break her promise"; worse still, "Suppose some rival maligns me, and so seduces her away." No, Lady Constantine, dearest, best as you are, that element of distraction would still remain, and where that is, no sustained energy is possible. Many erroneous things have been written and said by the sages, but never did they float a greater fallacy than that love serves as a spur to win the loved one by patient toil.'

'I cannot argue with you,' she said weakly.

'My only possible other chance would lie in going away,' he resumed after a moment's reflection, with his eyes on the lantern flame, which waved and smoked in the currents of air that leaked into the dome from the fierce wind-stream without. 'If I might take away the equatorial, supposing it possible that I could find some suitable place for observing in the southern hemisphere, – say, at the Cape, – I *might* be able to apply myself to serious work again, after the lapse of a little time. The southern constellations offer a less exhausted field for investigation. I wonder if I might!'

'You mean,' she answered uneasily, 'that you might apply yourself to work when your recollection of me began to fade, and my life to become a matter of indifference to you? ... Yes, go! No, – I cannot bear it! The remedy is worse than the disease. I cannot let you go away!'

'Then how can you refuse the only condition on which I can stay, without ruin to my purpose and scandal to your name? Dearest, agree to my proposal, as you love both me and yourself!'

He waited, while the fir-trees rubbed and prodded the base of the tower, and the wind roared around and shook it; but she could not find words to reply.

'Would to God,' he burst out, 'that I might perish here, like Winstanley* in his lighthouse! Then the difficulty would be solved for you.'

'You are so wrong, so very wrong, in saying so!' she exclaimed passionately. 'You may doubt my wisdom, pity my short-sightedness; but there is one thing you do know, – that I love you dearly!'

'You do, – I know it!' he said, softened in a moment. 'But it seems such a simple remedy for the difficulty that I cannot see how you can mind adopting it, if you care so much for me as I do for you.'

'Should we live ... just as we are, exactly, ... supposing I agreed?' she faintly inquired.

'Yes, that is my idea.'

'Quite privately, you say. How could – the marriage be quite private?'

'I would go away to London and get a licence. Then you could come to me, and return again immediately after the ceremony. I could return at leisure, and not a soul in the world would know what had taken place. Think, dearest, with what a free conscience you could then assist me in my efforts to plumb these deeps above us!

Any feeling that you may now have against clandestine meetings as such would then be removed, and our hearts would be at rest.'

There was a certain scientific practicability even in his love-making, and it here came out excellently. But she sat on with suspended breath, her heart wildly beating, while he waited in open-mouthed expectation. Each was swayed by the emotion within them, much as the candle-flame was swayed by the tempest without. It was the most critical evening of their lives.

The pale rays of the little lantern fell upon her beautiful face, snugly and neatly bound in by her black bonnet; but not a beam of the lantern leaked out into the night to suggest to any watchful eye that human life at its highest excitement was beating within the dark and isolated tower; for the dome had no windows, and every shutter that afforded an opening for the telescope was closed. Predilections and misgivings so equally strove within her still youthful breast that she could not utter a word; her intention wheeled this way and that like the balance of a watch. His unexpected proposition had brought about the smartest encounter of inclination with prudence, of impulse with reserve, that she had ever known.

Of all the reasons that she had expected him to give for his urgent request to see her this evening, an offer of marriage was probably the last. Whether or not she had ever amused herself with hypothetical fancies on such a subject, and it was only natural that she should vaguely have done so, – the courage in her *protégé* coolly to advance it, without a hint from herself that such a proposal would be tolerated, showed her that there was more in his character than she had reckoned on: and the discovery almost frightened her. The humour, attitude, and tenor of her attachment had been of quite an unpremeditated quality, unsuggestive of any such audacious solution to their distresses as this.

'I repeat my question, dearest,' he said, after her long pause. 'Shall it be done? Or shall I exile myself, and study as best I can, in some distant country, out of sight and sound?'

'Are those the only alternatives? Yes, yes; I suppose they are!' She waited yet another moment, bent over his kneeling figure, and kissed his forehead. 'Yes; it shall be done,' she whispered. 'I will marry you.'

'My angel, I am content!'

He drew her yielding form to his heart, and her head sank upon his shoulder, as he pressed his two lips continuously upon hers. To such had the study of celestial physics brought them in the space of eight months, one week, and a few odd days.

'I am weaker than you, – far the weaker,' she went on, her tears falling. 'Rather than lose you out of my sight I will marry without stipulation or condition. But – I put it to your kindness – grant me one little request.'

He instantly assented.

'It is that, in consideration of my peculiar position in this county, – O, you can't understand it! – you will not put an end to the absolute secrecy of our relationship without my full assent. Also, that you will never come to Welland House without first discussing with me the advisability of the visit, accepting my opinion on the point. There, see how a timid woman tries to fence herself in!'

'My dear lady-love, neither of those two high-handed courses should I have taken, even had you not stipulated against them. The very essence of our marriage plan is that those two conditions are kept. I see as well as you do, even more than you do, how important it is that for the present – ay, for a long time hence – I should still be but the curate's lonely son, unattached to anybody or anything, with no object of interest but his science; and you the recluse lady of the manor, to whom he is only an acquaintance.'

'See what deceits love sows in honest minds!'

'It would be a humiliation to you at present that I could not bear if a marriage between us were made public; an inconvenience without any compensating advantage.'

'I am so glad you assume it without my setting it before you! Now I know you are not only good and true, but politic and trustworthy.'

'Well, then, here is our covenant. My lady swears to marry me; I, in return for such great courtesy, swear never to compromise her by intruding at Welland House, and to keep the marriage concealed till I have won a position worthy of her.'

'Or till I request it to be made known,' she added, possibly foreseeing a contingency which had not occurred to him.

'Or till you request it,' he repeated.

'It is agreed,' murmured Lady Constantine.

CHAPTER SIXTEEN

AFTER this there only remained to be settled between them the practical details of the project.

These were that he should leave home in a couple of days, and take lodgings either in the distant city of Bath or in a convenient suburb of London, till a sufficient time should have elapsed to satisfy legal requirements;* that on a fine morning at the end of this time she should hie away to the same place, and be met at the station by St Cleeve, armed with the marriage licence; whence they should at once proceed to the church fixed upon for the ceremony; returning home independently in the course of the next two or three days.

While these tactics were under discussion the two-and-thirty winds of heaven* continued, as before, to beat about the tower, though their onsets appeared to be somewhat lessening in force. Himself now calmed and satisfied, Swithin, as is the wont of humanity, took serener views of Nature's crushing mechanics without, and said, 'The wind doesn't seem disposed to put the tragic period to our hopes and fears that I spoke of in my momentary despair.'

'The disposition of the wind is as vicious as ever,' she answered, looking into his face with pausing thoughts on, perhaps, other subjects than that discussed. 'It is your mood of viewing it that has changed. "There is nothing either good or bad, but thinking makes it so."'*

And, as if flatly to stultify Swithin's assumption, a circular hurricane, exceeding in violence any that had preceded it, seized hold upon Rings-Hill Speer at that moment with the determination of a conscious agent. The first sensation of a resulting catastrophe was conveyed to their intelligence by the flapping of the candle-flame against the lantern-glass; then the wind, which hitherto they had heard rather than felt, rubbed past them like a fugitive. Swithin beheld around and above him, in place of the concavity of the dome, the open heaven, with its racing clouds, remote horizon, and intermittent gleam of stars. The dome that had covered the tower had been whirled off bodily; and they heard it descend crashing upon the trees.

Finding himself untouched Swithin stretched out his arms towards Lady Constantine, whose apparel had been seized by the spinning air, nearly lifting her off her legs. She, too, was as yet unharmed. Each held the other for a moment, when, fearing that something further would happen, they took shelter in the staircase.

'Dearest, what an escape!' he said, still holding her.

'What is the accident?' she asked. 'Has the whole top really gone?'

'The dome has been blown off the roof.'

As soon as it was practicable he relit the extinguished lantern, and they emerged again upon the leads, where the extent of the disaster became at once apparent. Saving the absence of the enclosing hemisphere all remained the same. The dome, being constructed of wood, was light by comparison with the rest of the structure, and the wheels which allowed it horizontal, or, as Swithin expressed it, azimuth motion, denied it a firm hold upon the walls; so that it had been lifted off them like a cover from a pot. The equatorial stood in the midst as it had stood before.

Having executed its grotesque purpose the wind sank to comparative mildness. Swithin took advantage of this lull by covering up the instruments with cloths, after which the betrothed couple prepared to go downstairs.

But the events of the night had not yet fully disclosed themselves. At this moment there was a sound of footsteps and a knocking at the door below.

'It can't be for me!' said Lady Constantine. 'I retired to my room before leaving the house, and told them on no account to disturb me.'

She remained at the top while Swithin went down the spiral. In the gloom he beheld Hannah.

'O Master Swithin, can ye come home! The wind have blowed down the only chimley that don't smoke, and the pinion-end* with it; and the old ancient house, that have been in your family so long as the memory of man, is naked to the world! It is a mercy that your grammer were not killed, sitting by the hearth, poor old soul, and soon to walk wi' God, – for 'a 's* getting wambling on her pins,*

Mr Swithin, as aged folks do. As I say, 'a was all but murdered by the elements, and doing no' more harm than the babes in the wood, nor speaking one harmful word. And the fire and smoke were blowed all across house like Sodom and Gomorrah;* and your poor reverent father's features scorched to flakes, looking like the vilest ruffian, and the gilt frame spoiled! Every flitch,* every eye-piece, and every chine* is buried under the walling; and I fed them pigs with my own hands, Master Swithin, little thinking they would come to this end. Do ye collect yourself, Mr Swithin, and come at once!'

'I will, – I will. I'll follow you in a moment. Do you hasten back again and assist.'

When Hannah had departed the young man ran up to Lady Constantine, to whom he explained the accident. After sympathizing with old Mrs Martin Lady Constantine added, 'I thought something would occur to mar our scheme!'

'I am not quite sure of that yet.'

On a short consideration with him she agreed to wait at the top of the tower till he could come back and inform her if the accident were really so serious as to interfere with his plan for departure. He then left her, and there she sat in the dark, alone, looking over the parapet, and straining her eyes in the direction of the homestead.

At first all was obscurity; but when he had been gone about ten minutes lights began to move to and fro in the hollow where the house stood, and shouts occasionally mingled with the wind, which retained some violence yet, playing over the trees beneath her as on the strings of a lyre. But not a bough of them was visible, a cloak of blackness covering everything netherward; while overhead the windy sky looked down with a strange and disguised face, the three or four stars that alone were visible being so dissociated by clouds that she knew not which they were. Under any other circumstances Lady Constantine might have felt a nameless fear in thus sitting aloft on a lonely column, with a forest groaning under her feet, and palæolithic dead men* feeding its roots; but the recent passionate decision stirred her pulses to an intensity beside which the ordinary tremors of feminine existence asserted themselves in vain. The apocalyptic* effect of the scene surrounding her was, indeed, not inharmonious, and afforded an appropriate background to her intentions.

After what seemed to her an interminable space of time, quick steps in the staircase became audible above the roar of the firs, and in a few instants St Cleeve again stood beside her.

The case of the homestead was serious. Hannah's account had not been exaggerated in substance: the gable end of the house was open to the garden; the joists, left without support, had dropped, and with them the upper floor. By the help of some labourers, who lived near, and Lady Constantine's man Anthony, who was passing at the time, the homestead had been propped up, and protected for the night by some rick-cloths; but Swithin felt that it would be selfish in the highest degree to leave two lonely old women to themselves at this juncture. 'In short,' he concluded despondently, 'I cannot go to stay in Bath or London just now; perhaps not for another fortnight!'

'Never mind,' she said. 'A fortnight hence will do as well.'

'And I have these for you,' he continued. 'Your man Green was passing my grandmother's on his way back from Warborne, where he had been, he says, for any letters that had come for you by the evening post. As he stayed to assist the other men I told him I would go on to your house with the letters he had brought. Of course I did not tell him I should see you here.'

'Thank you. Of course not. Now I'll return at once.'

In descending the column her eye fell upon the superscription of one of the letters, and she opened and glanced over it by the lantern light. She seemed startled, and, musing, said, 'The postponement of our – intention must be, I fear, for a long time. I find that after the end of this month I cannot leave home safely, even for a day.' Perceiving that he was about to ask why, she added, 'I will not trouble you with the reason now; it would only harass you. It is only a family business, and cannot be helped.'

'Then we cannot be married till – God knows when!' said Swithin blankly. 'I cannot leave home till after the next week or two; you cannot leave home unless within that time. So what are we to do?'

'I do not know.'

'My dear, dear one, don't let us be beaten like this! Don't let a well-considered plan be overthrown by a mere accident! Here's a remedy. Do *you* go and stay the requisite time in the parish we are to be married in, instead of me. When my grandmother is again well housed I can come to you, instead of you to me, as we first said.

Then it can be done within the time.'

Reluctantly, shyly, and yet with a certain gladness of heart, she gave way to his proposal that they should change places in the programme. There was much that she did not like in it, she said. It seemed to her as if she were taking the initiative by going and attending to the preliminaries. It was the man's part to do that, in her opinion, and was usually undertaken by him.

'But,' argued Swithin, 'there are cases in which the woman does give the notices, and so on; that is to say, when the man is absolutely hindered from doing so; and ours is such a case. The seeming is nothing; I know the truth, and what does it matter? You do not refuse – retract your word to be my wife, because, to avoid a sickening delay, the formalities require you to attend to them in place of me?'

She did not refuse, she said. In short she agreed to his entreaty. They had, in truth, gone so far in their dream of union that there was no drawing back now. Whichever of them was forced by circumstances to be the protagonist in the enterprise, the thing must be done. Their intention to become husband and wife, at first halting and timorous, had accumulated momentum with the lapse of hours, till it now bore down every obstacle in its course.

'Since you beg me to, – since there is no alternative between my going and a long postponement,' she said, as they stood in the dark porch of Welland House before parting, – 'since I am to go first, and seem to be the pioneer in this adventure, promise me, Swithin, promise your Viviette, that in years to come, when perhaps you may not love me so warmly as you do now—'

'That will never be.'

'Well, hoping it will not, dear, but supposing it should, promise me that you will never reproach me as the one who took the initiative when it should have been yourself, forgetting that it was at your request; promise that you will never say I showed immodest readiness to do so, or anything which may imply your obliviousness of the fact that I act in obedience to necessity and your earnest prayer.'

Need it be said that he promised never to reproach her with that or any other thing as long as they should live? The few details of the reversed arrangement were soon settled, Bath being the place finally decided on. Then, with a warm audacity which events had encouraged, he pressed her to his breast, and she silently entered the house. He returned to the homestead, there to attend to the unexpected duties of repairing the havoc wrought by the gale.

That night, in the solitude of her chamber, Lady Constantine reopened and read the subjoined letter – one of those handed to her by St Cleeve: –

—— Street, Piccadilly,
October 15, 18–

Dear Viviette, – You will be surprised to learn that I am in England, and that I am again out of harness – unless you should have seen the latter in the papers. Rio Janeiro may do for monkeys, but it won't do for me. Having resigned the appointment I have returned here, as a preliminary step to finding another vent for my energies; in other words, another milch cow for my sustenance. I knew nothing whatever of your husband's death till two days ago; so that any letter from you on the subject, at the time it became known, must have miscarried. Hypocrisy at such a moment is worse than useless, and I therefore do not condole with you, particularly as the event, though new to a banished man like me, occurred so long since. You are better without him, Viviette, and are now just the limb for doing something for yourself, notwithstanding the threadbare state in which you seem to have been cast upon the world. You are still young, and, as I imagine (unless you have vastly altered since I beheld you), good-looking: therefore make up your mind to retrieve your position by a match with one of the local celebrities; and you would do well to begin drawing neighbouring covers* at once. A genial squire, with more weight than wit, more realty* than weight, and more personalty than realty (considering the circumstances), would be best for you. You might make a position for us both by some such alliance; for, to tell the truth, I have had but in-and-out luck so far. I shall be with you in little more than a fortnight, when we will talk over the matter seriously, if you don't object. – Your affectionate brother,

Louis

It was this allusion to her brother's coming visit which had caught her eye in the tower staircase, and led to a modification in the wedding arrangement.

Having read the letter through once Lady Constantine flung it aside with an impatient little stamp that shook the decaying old floor and casement. Its contents produced perturbation, misgiving, but not retreat. The deep glow of enchantment shed by the idea of a private union with her beautiful young lover killed the pale light of cold reasoning from an indifferently good relative.

'O, no,' she murmured, as she sat, covering her face with her hand. 'Not for wealth untold could I give him up now!'

No argument, short of Apollo in person* from the clouds, would have influenced her. She made her preparations for departure as if nothing had intervened.

CHAPTER SEVENTEEN

In her days of prosperity Lady Constantine had often gone to the city of Bath, either frivolously, for shopping purposes, or musico-religiously, to attend choir festivals in the Abbey; so there was nothing surprising in her reverting to an old practice. That the journey might appear to be of a somewhat similar nature she took with her the servant who had been accustomed to accompany her on former occasions, though the woman, having now left her service, and settled in the village as the wife of Anthony Green, with a young child on her hands, could with some difficulty leave home. Lady Constantine overcame the anxious mother's scruples by providing that young Green should be well cared for; and knowing that she could count upon this woman's fidelity, if upon anybody's, in case of an accident (for it was chiefly Lady Constantine's exertions that had made an honest wife of Mrs Green), she departed for a fortnight's absence.

The next day found mistress and maid settled in lodgings in an old plum-coloured brick street,* which a hundred years ago could boast of rank and fashion among its residents, though now the broad fan-light over each broad door admitted the sun to the hall of a lodging-house keeper only. The lamp-posts were still those that had done duty with oil lights; and rheumatic old coachmen and postilions,* that once had driven and ridden gloriously from London to Land's End, ornamented with their bent persons and bow legs the pavement in front of the chief inns, in the sorry hope of earning sixpence to keep body and soul together.

'We are kept well informed on the time o' day, my lady,' said Mrs Green, as she pulled down the blinds in Lady Constantine's room on the evening of their arrival. 'There's a church exactly at the back of us, and I hear every hour strike.'

Lady Constantine said she had noticed that there was a church quite near.

'Well, it is better to have that at the back than other folks' winders.* And if your ladyship wants to go there it won't be far to walk.'

'That's what occurred to me,' said Lady Constantine, '*if* I should want to go.'

During the ensuing days she felt to the utmost the tediousness of waiting merely that time might pass. Not a soul knew her there, and she knew not a soul, a circumstance which, while it added to her sense of secrecy, intensified her solitude. Occasionally she went to a shop, with Green as her companion. Though there were purchases to be made, they were by no means of a pressing nature, and but poorly filled up the vacancies of those strange, speculative days, – days surrounded by a shade of fear, yet poetized by sweet expectation.

On the thirteenth day she told Green that she was going to take a walk, and leaving the house she passed by the obscurest streets to the Abbey. After wandering about beneath the aisles till her courage was screwed* to its highest, she went out at the other side, and, looking timidly round to see if anybody followed, walked on till she came to a certain door, which she reached just at the moment when her heart began to sink to its very lowest, rendering all the screwing up in vain.

Whether it was because the month was October, or from any other reason, the deserted aspect of the quarter in general sat especially on this building. Moreover the pavement was up, and heaps of stone and gravel obstructed the footway. Nobody was coming, nobody was going, in that thoroughfare; she appeared to be the single one of the human race bent upon marriage business, which seemed to have been unanimously abandoned by all the rest of the world as proven folly. But she thought of Swithin, his blonde hair, ardent eyes, and eloquent lips, and was carried onward by the very reflection.

Entering the surrogate's* room Lady Constantine managed, at the last juncture, to state her errand in tones so collected as to startle even herself; to which her listener replied also as if the whole thing were the most natural in the world. When it came to the affirmation that she had lived fifteen days in the parish, she said with dismay –

'O no! I thought the fifteen days meant the interval of residence before the marriage takes place. I have lived here only thirteen days and a half. Now I must come again!'

'Ah – well – I think you need not be so particular,' said the surrogate. 'As a matter of fact, though the letter of the law requires fifteen days' residence, many people make five sufficient. The provision is inserted, as you doubtless are aware, to hinder runaway marriages as much as possible, and secret unions, and other such objectionable practices. You need not come again.'

That evening Lady Constantine wrote to Swithin St Cleeve the last letter of the fortnight: –

MY DEAREST, – Do come to me as soon as you can. By a sort of favouring blunder I have been able to shorten the time of waiting by a day. Come at once, for I am almost broken down with apprehension. It seems rather rash at moments, all this, and I wish you were here to reassure me. I did not know I should feel so alarmed. I am frightened at every footstep, and dread lest anybody who knows me should accost me, and find out why I am here. I sometimes wonder how I could have agreed to come and enact your part, but I did not realize how trying it would be. You ought not to have asked me, Swithin; upon my word, it was too cruel of you, and I will punish you for it when you come! But I won't upbraid; for O I want you so! I hope the homestead is repaired that has cost me all this sacrifice of modesty. If it were anybody in the world but *you* in question I would rush home, without waiting here for the end of it, – I really think I would! But, dearest, no. I must show my strength now, or let it be for ever hid. The barriers of ceremony are broken down between us, and it is for the best that I am here.

And yet, at no point of this trying prelude need Lady Constantine have feared for her strength. Deeds in this connexion demand the particular kind of courage that such perfervid women are endowed with, the courage of their emotions, in which young men are often lamentably deficient. Her fear was, in truth, the fear of being discovered in an unwonted position; not of the act itself. And though her letter was in its way a true exposition of her feeling, had it been necessary to go through the whole legal process over again she would have been found equal to the emergency.

It had been for some days a point of anxiety with her what to do with Green during the morning of the wedding. Chance unexpectedly helped her in this difficulty. The day before the purchase of the licence Green came to Lady Constantine with a letter in her hand from her husband Anthony, her face as long as a fiddle.

'I hope there's nothing the matter?' said Lady Constantine.

'The child's took bad, my lady!' said Mrs Green, with suspended floods of water in her eyes. 'I love the child better than I shall love all them that's coming put together; for he's been a good boy to his mother ever since twelve weeks afore he was born! 'Twas he, a tender deary, that made Anthony marry me, and thereby turned hisself from a little calamity to a little blessing! For, as you well know, the man were a backward man in the church part o' matrimony, my lady; though he'll do anything when he's forced a bit by his manly feelings. And now to lose the child – hoo-hoo-hoo! What shall I doo!'

'Well, you want to go home at once, I suppose?'

Mrs Green explained, between her sobs, that such was her desire; and though this was a day or two sooner than her mistress had wished to be left alone she consented to Green's departure. So during the afternoon her woman went off, with directions to prepare for Lady Constantine's return in two or three days. But as the exact day of her return was uncertain no carriage was to be sent to the station to meet her, her intention being to hire one from the hotel.

Lady Constantine was now left in utter solitude to await her lover's arrival.

CHAPTER EIGHTEEN

A MORE beautiful October morning than that of the next day never beamed upon the Welland groves. The yearly dissolution of leafage was setting in apace. The foliage of the park trees rapidly resolved itself into the multitude of complexions which mark the subtle grades of decay, reflecting wet lights of such innumerable hues that it was a wonder to think their beauties only a repetition of scenes that had been exhibited there on scores of previous Octobers, and had been allowed to pass away without a single dirge from the imperturbable beings who walked among them. Far in the shadows semi-opaque screens of blue haze made mysteries of the commonest gravel-pit, dingle, or recess.

The wooden cabin at the foot of Rings-Hill Speer had been furnished by Swithin as a sitting and sleeping apartment, some little while before this time; for he had found it highly convenient, during night observations at the top of the column, to remain on the spot all night, not to disturb his grandmother by passing in and out of the house, and to save himself the labour of incessantly crossing the field.

He would much have liked to tell her the secret, and, had it been his own to tell, would probably have done so; but sharing it with an objector who knew not his grandmother's affection so well as he did himself, there was no alternative to holding his tongue. The more effectually to guard it he decided to sleep at the cabin during the two or three nights previous to his departure, leaving word at the homestead that in a day or two he was going on an excursion.

It was very necessary to start early. Long before the great eye of the sun was lifted high enough to glance into the Welland glades, St Cleeve arose from his bed in the cabin and prepared to depart, cooking his breakfast upon a little stove in the corner. The young rabbits littered during the foregoing summer watched his preparations through the open door from the grey dawn without, as he bustled, half dressed, in and out under the boughs, and among the blackberries and brambles that grew around.

It was a strange place for a bridegroom to perform his toilet in, but, considering the unconventional nature of the marriage, a not inappropriate one. What events had been enacted in that earthen camp since it was first thrown up, nobody could say; but the primitive simplicity of the young man's preparations accorded well with the prehistoric spot on which they were made. Embedded under his feet were possibly even now rude trinkets that had been worn at bridal ceremonies of the early inhabitants. Little signified* those ceremonies to-day, or the happiness or otherwise of the contracting parties. That his own rite, nevertheless, signified much, was the inconsequent reasoning of Swithin, as it is of many another bridegroom besides; and he, like the rest, went on with his preparations in that mood which sees in his stale repetition the wondrous possibilities of an untried move.

Then through the wet cobwebs, that hung like movable diaphragms on each blade and bough, he pushed his way down to the furrow which led from the secluded fir-tree island to the wide world beyond the field.

He was not a stranger to enterprise, and still less to the contemplation of enterprise; but an enterprise such as this he had never even outlined. That his dear lady was troubled at the situation he had placed her in by not going himself on that errand, he could see from her letter; but, believing an immediate marriage with her to be the true way of restoring to both that equanimity necessary to serene philosophy, he held it of little account how the marriage was brought about, and happily began his journey towards her place of sojourn.

He passed through a little copse before leaving the parish, the smoke from newly lit fires rising like the stems of blue trees out of the few cottage chimneys. Here he heard a quick, familiar footstep in the path ahead of him, and, turning the corner of the bushes, confronted the foot-post on his way to Welland. In answer to St Cleeve's inquiry if there was anything for himself the postman handed out one letter, and proceeded on his route.

Swithin opened and read the letter as he walked, till it brought him to a standstill by the importance of its contents.

They were enough to agitate a more phlegmatic youth than he.

He leant over the wicket which came in his path, and endeavoured to comprehend the sense of the whole.

The large long envelope contained, first, a letter from a solicitor in a northern town, informing him that his paternal great-uncle, who had recently returned from the Cape (whither he had gone in an attempt to repair a broken constitution), was now dead and buried. This great-uncle's name was like a new creation to Swithin. He had held no communication with the young man's branch of the family for innumerable years, – never, in fact, since the marriage of Swithin's father with the simple daughter of Welland Farm. He had been a bachelor to the end of his life, and had amassed a fairly good professional fortune by a long and extensive medical practice in the smoky, dreary, manufacturing town in which he had lived and died. Swithin had always been taught to think of him as the embodiment of all that was unpleasant in man. He was narrow, sarcastic, and shrewd to unseemliness. That very shrewdness had enabled him, without much professional profundity, to establish his large and lucrative connexion, which lay almost entirely among a class who neither looked nor cared for drawing-room courtesies.

However, what Dr St Cleeve had been as a practitioner matters little. He was now dead, and the bulk of his property had been left to persons with whom this story has nothing to do. But Swithin was informed that out of it there was a bequest of £600 a year to himself, – payment of which was to begin with his twenty-first year, and continue for his life, unless he should marry before reaching the age of twenty-five. In the latter precocious and objectionable event his annuity would be forfeited. The accompanying letter, said the solicitor, would explain all.

This, the second letter, was from his uncle to himself, written about a month before the former's death, and deposited with his will, to be forwarded to his nephew when that event should have taken place. Swithin read, with the solemnity that such posthumous epistles inspire, the following words from one who, during life, had never once addressed him: –

DEAR NEPHEW, – You will doubtless experience some astonishment at receiving a communication from one whom you have never personally known, and who, when this comes into your hands, will be beyond the reach of your knowledge. Perhaps I am the loser by this life-long mutual ignorance. Perhaps I am much to blame for it; perhaps not. But such reflections are profitless at this date: I have written with quite other views than to work up a sentimental regret on such an amazingly remote hypothesis as that the fact of a particular pair of people not meeting, among the millions of other pairs of people who have never met, is a great calamity either to the world in general or to themselves.

The occasion of my addressing you is briefly this: Nine months ago a report casually reached me that your scientific studies were pursued by you with great ability, and that you were a young man of some promise as an astronomer. My own scientific proclivities rendered the report more interesting than it might otherwise have been to me; and it came upon me quite as a surprise that any issue of your father's marriage should have so much in him, or you might have seen more of me in former years than you are ever likely to do now. My health had then begun to fail, and I was starting for the Cape, or I should have come myself to inquire into your condition and prospects. I did not return till six months later, and as my health had not improved I sent a trusty friend to examine into your life, pursuits, and circumstances, without your own knowledge, and to report his observations to me. This he did. Through him I learnt, of favourable news: –

(1) That you worked assiduously at the science of astronomy.

(2) That everything was auspicious in the career you had chosen.

Of unfavourable news: –

(1) That the small income at your command, even when eked out by the sum to which you would be entitled on your grandmother's death and the freehold of the homestead, would be inadequate to support you becomingly as a scientific man, whose lines of work were of a nature not calculated to produce emoluments for many years, if ever.

(2) That there was something in your path worse than narrow means, and that that something was *a woman.*

To save you, if possible, from ruin on these heads, I take the preventive measures detailed below.

The chief step is, as my solicitor will have informed you, that, at the age of twenty-five, the sum of £600 a year be settled on you for life, provided you have not married before reaching that age; – a yearly gift of an equal sum to be also provisionally made to you in the interim – and, *vice versâ*, that if you have married before reaching the age of twenty-five you will receive nothing from the date of the marriage.

One object of my bequest is that you may have resources sufficient to enable you to travel and study the Southern constellations. When at the Cape, after hearing of your pursuits, I was much struck with the importance of those constellations to an astronomer just pushing into notice.

There is more to be made of the Southern hemisphere than ever has been made of it yet; the mine is not so thoroughly worked as the Northern, and thither your studies should tend.

The only other preventive step in my power is that of exhortation, at which I am not an adept. Nevertheless, I say to you, Swithin St Cleeve, don't make a fool of yourself, as your father did. If your studies are to be worth anything, believe me, they must be carried on without the help of a woman. Avoid her, and every one of the sex, if you mean to achieve any worthy thing. Eschew all of that sort for many a year yet. Moreover, I say, the lady of your acquaintance avoid in particular. I have heard nothing against her moral character hitherto; I have no doubt it has been excellent. She may have many good qualities, both of heart and of mind. But she has, in addition to her original disqualification as a companion for you (that is, that of sex), these two special drawbacks: she is much older than yourself –

'*Much* older!' said Swithin resentfully.

– and she is so impoverished that the title she derives from her late husband is a positive objection. Beyond this, frankly, I don't think well of her. I don't think well of any woman who dotes upon a man so much younger than herself. To care to be the first fancy of a young fellow like you shows no great common sense in her. If she were worth her salt she would have too much pride to be intimate with a youth in your unassured position, to say no worse. She is old enough to know that a *liaison* with her may, and almost certainly would, be your ruin; and, on the other hand, that a marriage would be preposterous, – unless she is a complete goose, and in that case there is even more reason for avoiding her than if she were in her few senses.

A woman of honourable feeling, nephew, would be careful to do nothing to hinder you in your career, as this putting of herself in your way most certainly will. Yet I hear that she professes a great anxiety on this same future of yours as a physicist. The best way in which she can show the reality of her anxiety is by leaving you to yourself. Perhaps she persuades herself that she is doing you no harm. Well, let her have the benefit of the possible belief; but depend upon it that in truth she gives the lie to her conscience by maintaining such a transparent fallacy. Women's brains are not formed for assisting at any profound science: they lack the power to see things except in the concrete. She'll blab your most secret plans and theories to every one of her acquaintance –

'She's got none!' said Swithin, beginning to get warm.

– and make them appear ridiculous by announcing them before they are matured. If you attempt to study with a woman, you'll be ruled by her to entertain fancies instead of theories, air-castles* instead of intentions, qualms instead of opinions, sickly prepossessions instead of reasoned conclusions. Your wide heaven of study, young man, will soon reduce itself to the miserable narrow expanse of her face, and your myriad of stars to her two trumpery eyes.

An experienced woman waking a young man's passions just at a moment when he is endeavouring to shine intellectually, is doing little else than committing a crime.

Like a certain philosopher I would, upon my soul, have all young men from eighteen to twenty-five kept under barrels; seeing how often, in the lack of some such sequestering process, the woman sits down before each as his destiny, and too frequently enervates his purpose, till he abandons the most promising course ever conceived!

But no more. I now leave your fate in your own hands. Your well-wishing relative,

JOCELYN ST CLEEVE,
Doctor in Medicine

As coming from a bachelor and hardened misogynist of seventy-two, the opinions herein contained were nothing remarkable: but their practical result in restricting the sudden endowment of Swithin's researches by conditions which turned the favour into a harassment was, at this unique moment, discomfiting and distracting in the highest degree.

Sensational, however, as the letter was, the passionate intention of the day was not hazarded for more than a few minutes thereby. The truth was, the caution and bribe came too late, too unexpectedly, to be of influence. They were the sort of thing which required fermentation to render them effective. Had St Cleeve received the exhortation a month earlier; had he been able to run over in his mind, at every wakeful hour of thirty consecutive nights, a private catechism on the possibilities opened up by this annuity, there is no telling what might have been the stress of such a web of perplexity upon him, a young man whose love for celestial physics was second to none. But to have held before him, at the last moment, the picture of a future advantage that he had never once thought of, or discounted for present staying power, it affected him about as much as the view of horizons shown by sheet-lightning. He saw an immense prospect; it went, and the world was as before.

He caught the train at Warborne, and moved rapidly towards

Bath; not precisely in the same key as when he had dressed in the hut at dawn, but, as regarded the mechanical part of the journey, as unhesitatingly as before.

And with the change of scene even his gloom left him; his bosom's lord sat lightly in his throne.* St Cleeve was not sufficiently in mind of poetical literature to remember that wise poets are accustomed to read that lightness of bosom inversely. Swithin thought it an omen of good fortune; and as thinking is causing in not a few such cases, he was perhaps, in spite of poets, right.

CHAPTER NINETEEN

AT the station Lady Constantine appeared, standing expectant, and dressed as if she had never been married at all; he saw her face from the window of the carriage long before she saw him. He no sooner saw her than he was satisfied to his heart's content with his prize. If his great-uncle had offered him from the grave a kingdom instead of her, he would not have accepted it.

Swithin jumped out, and nature never painted in a woman's face more devotion than appeared in my lady's at that moment. To both the situation seemed like a beautiful allegory, not to be examined too closely, lest its defects of correspondence with real life should be apparent.

They almost feared to shake hands in public, so much depended upon their passing that morning without molestation. A fly* was called and they drove away.

'Take this,' she said, handing him a folded paper. 'It belongs to you rather than to me.'

At crossings, and other occasional pauses, pedestrians turned their faces and looked at the pair (for no reason but that, among so many, there were naturally a few of the sort who have eyes to note what incidents come in their way as they plod on); but the two in the vehicle could not but fear that these innocent beholders had special detective designs on them.

'You look so dreadfully young!' she said with humorous fretfulness, as they drove along (Swithin's cheeks being amazingly fresh from the morning air). 'Do try to appear a little haggard, that the parson mayn't ask us awkward questions!'

Nothing further happened, and they were set down opposite a shop about fifty yards from the church door, at five minutes to eleven.

'We will dismiss the fly,' she said. 'It will only attract idlers.'

On turning the corner and reaching the church they found the door ajar; but the building contained only two persons, a man and a woman, – the clerk and his wife, as they learnt. Swithin asked when the clergyman would arrive.

The clerk looked at his watch, and said, 'At just on eleven o'clock.'

'He ought to be here,' said Swithin.

'Yes,' replied the clerk, as the hour struck. 'The fact is, sir, he is a deppity,* and apt to be rather wandering in his wits as regards time and such like, which have stood in the way of the man's getting a benefit.* But no doubt he'll come.'

'The regular incumbent is away, then?'

'He's gone for his bare pa'son's fortnight, – that's all; and we was forced to put up with a weak-talented man or none. The best men goes into the brewing, or into the shipping now-a-days, you see, sir; doctrines being rather shaddery* at present, and your money's worth not sure in our line. So we church officers be left poorly provided with men for odd jobs. I'll tell ye what, sir; I think I'd better run round to the gentleman's lodgings, and try to find him?'

'Pray do,' said Lady Constantine.

The clerk left the church; his wife busied herself with dusting at the further end, and Swithin and Viviette were left to themselves. The imagination travels so rapidly, and a woman's forethought is so assumptive, that the clerk's departure had no sooner doomed them to inaction than it was borne in upon Lady Constantine's mind that she would not become the wife of Swithin St Cleeve, either to-day or on any other day. Her divinations were continually misleading her, she knew: but a hitch at the moment of marriage surely had a meaning in it.

'Ah, – the marriage is not to be!' she said to herself. 'This is a fatality.'

It was twenty minutes past, and no parson had arrived. Swithin took her hand.

'If it cannot be to-day, it can be to-morrow,' he whispered.

'I cannot say,' she answered. 'Something tells me *no.*'

It was almost impossible that she could know anything of the deterrent force exercised on Swithin by his dead uncle that morning. Yet her manner tallied so curiously well with such knowledge that he was struck by it, and remained silent.

'You have a black tie,' she continued, looking at him.

'Yes,' replied Swithin. 'I bought it on my way here.'

'Why could it not have been less sombre in colour?'

'My great-uncle is dead.'

'You had a great-uncle? You never told me.'

'I never saw him in my life. I have only heard about him since his death.'

He spoke in as quiet and measured a way as he could, but his heart was sinking. She would go on questioning; he could not tell her an untruth. She would discover particulars of that great-uncle's provision for him, which he, Swithin, was throwing away for her sake, and she would refuse to be his for his own sake. His conclusion at this moment was precisely what hers had been five minutes sooner: they were never to be husband and wife.

But she did not continue her questions, for the simplest of all reasons: hasty footsteps were audible in the entrance, and the parson was seen coming up the aisle, the clerk behind him wiping the beads of perspiration from his face. The somewhat sorry clerical specimen shook hands with them, and entered the vestry; and the clerk came up and opened the book.

'The poor gentleman's memory is a bit topsy-turvy,' whispered the latter. 'He had got it in his mind that 'twere a funeral, and I found him wandering about the cemetery a-looking for us. However, all's well as ends well.' And the clerk wiped his forehead again.

'How ill-omened!' murmured Viviette.

But the parson came out robed at this moment, and the clerk put on his ecclesiastical countenance and looked in his book. Lady Constantine's momentary languor passed; her blood resumed its courses with a new spring. The grave utterances of the church then rolled out upon the palpitating pair, and no couple ever joined their whispers thereto with more fervency than they.

Lady Constantine (as she continued to be called by the outside world, though she liked to think herself the Mrs St Cleeve that she legally was) had told Green that she might be expected at Welland in a day, or two, or three, as circumstances should dictate. Though the time of return was thus left open it was deemed advisable, by both Swithin and herself, that her journey back should not be deferred after the next day, in case any suspicions might be aroused. As for St Cleeve, his comings and goings were of no consequence. It was seldom known whether he was at home or abroad, by reason of his frequent seclusion at the column.

Late in the afternoon of the next day he accompanied her to the Bath station, intending himself to remain in that city till the following morning. But when a man or youth has such a tender article on his hands as a thirty-hour bride it is hardly in the power of his strongest reason to set her down at a railway, and send her off like a superfluous portmanteau. Hence the experiment of parting so soon after their union proved excruciatingly severe to these. The evening was dull; the breeze of autumn crept fitfully through every slit and aperture in the town; not a soul in the world seemed to notice or care about anything they did. Lady Constantine sighed; and there was no resisting it, – he could not leave her thus. He decided to get into the train with her, and keep her company for at least a few stations on her way.

It drew on to be a dark night, and seeing that there was no serious risk after all, he prolonged his journey with her so far as the junction at which the branch line to Warborne forked off. Here it was necessary to wait a few minutes, before either he could go back or she could go on. They wandered outside the station doorway into the gloom of the road, and there agreed to part.

While she yet stood holding his arm a phaeton* sped towards the station-entrance, where, in ascending the slope to the door, the horse suddenly jibbed. The gentleman who was driving, being either impatient, or possessed with a theory that all jibbers may be started by severe whipping, applied the lash; as a result of it, the horse thrust round the carriage to where they stood, and the end of the driver's sweeping whip cut across Lady Constantine's face with such severity as to cause her an involuntary cry. Swithin turned her round to the lamplight, and discerned a streak of blood on her cheek.

By this time the gentleman who had done the mischief, with many words of regret, had given the reins to his man and dismounted.

'I will go to the waiting-room for a moment,' whispered Viviette hurriedly; and, loosing her hand from his arm, she pulled down her veil and vanished inside the building.

The stranger came forward and raised his hat. He was a slightly built and apparently town-bred man of twenty-eight or thirty; his manner of address was at once careless and conciliatory.

'I am greatly concerned at what I have done,' he said. 'I sincerely trust that your wife' – but observing the youthfulness of Swithin, he withdrew the word suggested by the manner of Swithin towards Lady Constantine – 'I trust the lady was not seriously cut?'

'I trust not,' said Swithin, with some vexation.

'Where did the lash touch her?'

'Straight down her cheek.'

'Do let me go to her, and learn how she is, and humbly apologize.'

'I'll inquire.'

He went to the ladies' room, in which Viviette had taken refuge. She met him at the door, her handkerchief to her cheek, and Swithin explained that the driver of the phaeton had sent to make inquiries.

'I cannot see him!' she whispered. 'He is my brother Louis! He is, no doubt, going on by the train to my house. Don't let him recognize me! We must wait till he is gone.'

Swithin thereupon went out again, and told the young man that the cut on her face was not serious, but that she could not see him; after which they parted. St Cleeve then heard him ask for a ticket for Warborne, which confirmed Lady Constantine's view that he was going on to her house. When the branch train had moved off Swithin returned to his bride, who waited in a trembling state within.

On being informed that he had departed she showed herself much relieved.

'Where does your brother come from?' said Swithin.

'From London, immediately. Rio before that. He has a friend or two in this neighbourhood, and visits here occasionally. I have seldom or never spoken to you of him, because of his long absence.'

'Is he going to settle near you?'

'No, nor anywhere, I fear. He is, or rather was, in the diplomatic service. He was first a clerk in the Foreign Office, and was afterwards appointed attaché at Rio Janeiro. But he has resigned the appointment. I wish he had not.'

Swithin asked why he resigned.

'He complained of the banishment, and the climate, and everything that people complain of who are determined to be dissatisfied, – though, poor fellow, there is some ground for his complaints.

Perhaps some people would say that he is idle. But he is scarcely that; he is rather restless than idle, so that he never persists in anything. Yet if a subject takes his fancy he will follow it up with exemplary patience till something diverts him.'

'He is not kind to you, is he, dearest?'

'Why do you think that?'

'Your manner seems to say so.'

'Well, he may not always be kind. But look at my face; does the mark show?'

A streak, straight as a meridian, was visible down her cheek. The blood had been brought almost to the surface, but was not quite through, that which had originally appeared thereon having possibly come from the horse. It signified that to-morrow the red line would be a livid one.

Swithin informed her that her brother had taken a ticket for Warborne, and she at once perceived that he was going on to visit her at Welland, though from his letter she had not expected him so soon by a few days. 'Meanwhile,' continued Swithin, 'you can now get home only by the late train, having missed that one.'

'But, Swithin, don't you see my new trouble? If I go to Welland House to-night, and find my brother just arrived there, and he sees this cut on my face, – which I suppose you described to him—'

'I did.'

'He will know I was the lady with you!'

'Whom he called my wife. I wonder why we look husband and wife already!'

'Then what am I to do? For the ensuing three or four days I bear in my face a clue to his discovery of our secret.'

'Then you must not be seen. We must stay at an inn here.'

'O no!' she said timidly. 'It is too near home to be quite safe. We might not be known; but *if* we were!'

'We can't go back to Bath now. I'll tell you, dear Viviette, what we must do. We'll go on to Warborne in separate carriages; we'll rejoin each other outside Warborne station; thence we'll walk to the column in the dark, and I'll keep you a captive in the cabin till the scar has disappeared.'

As there was nothing which better recommended itself this course was decided on; and after taking from her trunk the articles that might be required for an incarceration of two or three days they left the said trunk at the cloak-room, and went on by the last train, which reached Warborne about ten o'clock.

It was only necessary for Lady Constantine to cover her face with the thick veil that she had provided for this escapade, to walk out of the station without fear of recognition. St Cleeve came forth from another compartment, and they did not rejoin each other till they had reached a shadowy bend in the old turnpike road, beyond the irradiation of the Warborne lamplight.

The walk to Welland was long. It was the walk which Swithin had taken in the rain when he had learnt the fatal forestalment of his stellar discovery; but now he was moved by a less desperate mood, and blamed neither God nor man. They were not pressed for time, and passed along the silent, lonely way with that sense rather of predestination than of choice in their proceedings which the presence of night sometimes imparts. Reaching the park gate they found it open, and from this they inferred that her brother Louis had arrived.

Leaving the house and park on their right they traced the highway yet a little further, and plunging through the stubble of the opposite field, drew near the isolated earthwork bearing the plantation and tower, which together rose like a flattened dome and lantern from the lighter-hued plain of stubble. It was far too dark to distinguish firs from other trees by the eye alone, but the peculiar dialect of sylvan language* which the piny multitude used would have been enough to proclaim their class at any time. In the lovers' stealthy progress up the slopes a dry stick here and there snapped beneath their feet, seeming like a shot of alarm.

On being unlocked the hut was found precisely as Swithin had left it two days before. Lady Constantine was thoroughly wearied, and sat down, while he gathered a handful of twigs and spikelets from the masses strewn without and lit a small fire, first taking the precaution to blind the little window and relock the door.

Lady Constantine looked curiously around by the light of the blaze. The hut was about the size of some Delia's or Amanda's powder-closet in Georgian times:* in one corner stood the stove, with a little table and chair, a small cupboard hard by, a pitcher of water, a rack overhead, with various articles, including a kettle and a gridiron; while the remaining three or four feet at the other end of the room was curtained off as a dormitory, for Swithin's use during late observations in the tower overhead.

'It is not much of a palace to offer you,' he remarked, smiling. 'But at any rate, it is a refuge.'

The cheerful firelight dispersed in some measure Lady Constantine's anxieties. 'If we only had something to eat!' she said.

'Dear me,' cried St Cleeve, blankly. 'That's a thing I never thought of.'

'Nor I, till now,' she replied.

He reflected with misgiving.

'Beyond a small loaf of bread in the cupboard I have nothing. However, just outside the door there are lots of those little rabbits, about the size of rats, that the keepers call runners. And they are as tame as possible. But I fear I could not catch one now. Yet, dear Viviette, wait a minute; I'll try. You must not be starved.'

He softly let himself out, and was gone some time. When he reappeared, he produced, not a rabbit, but four sparrows and a thrush.

'I could do nothing in the way of a rabbit without setting a wire,' he said. 'But I have managed to get these by knowing where they roost.'

He showed her how to prepare the birds, and, having set her to roast them by the fire, departed with the pitcher, to replenish it at the brook which flowed near the homestead in the neighbouring Bottom.

'They are all asleep at my grandmother's,' he informed her when he re-entered, panting, with the dripping pitcher. 'They imagine me to be a hundred miles off.'

The birds were now ready, and the table was spread. With this fare, eked out by dry toast from the loaf, and moistened with cups of water from the pitcher, to which Swithin added a little wine from the flask he had carried on his journey, they were forced to be content for their supper.

CHAPTER TWENTY

WHEN Lady Constantine awoke the next morning Swithin was nowhere to be seen. Before she was quite ready for breakfast she heard the key turn in the door, and felt startled, till she remembered that the comer could hardly be anybody but he. He brought a basket with provisions, an extra cup-and-saucer, and so on. In a short space of time the kettle began singing on the stove, and the morning meal was ready.

The sweet resinous air from the firs blew in upon them as they sat at breakfast; the birds hopped round the door (which, somewhat riskily, they ventured to keep open); and at their elbow rose the lank column into an upper realm of sunlight, which only reached the cabin in fitful darts and flashes through the trees.

'I could be happy here for ever,' said she, clasping his hand. 'I wish I could never see my great gloomy house again, since I am not rich enough to throw it open, and live there as I ought to do. Poverty of this sort is not unpleasant at any rate. What are you thinking of?'

'I am thinking about my outing this morning. On reaching my grandmother's she was only a little surprised to see me. I was obliged to breakfast there, or appear to do so, to divert suspicion; and this food is supposed to be wanted for my dinner and supper. There will of course be no difficulty in my obtaining an ample supply for any length of time, as I can take what I like from the buttery* without observation. But as I looked in my grandmother's face this morning, and saw her looking affectionately in mine, and thought how she had never concealed anything from me, and had always had my welfare at heart, I felt – that I should like to tell her what we have done.'

'O no, – please not, Swithin!' she exclaimed piteously.

'Very well,' he answered. 'On no consideration will I do so without your consent.' And no more was said on the matter.

The morning was passed in applying wet rag and other remedies to the purple line on Viviette's cheek; and in the afternoon they set up the equatorial under the replaced dome, to have it in order for night observations.

The evening was clear, dry, and remarkably cold by comparison with the daytime weather. After a frugal supper they replenished the stove with charcoal from the homestead, which they also burnt during the day, – an idea of Viviette's, that the smoke from a wood fire might not be seen more frequently than was consistent with the occasional occupation of the cabin by Swithin, as heretofore.

At eight o'clock she insisted upon his ascending the tower for observations, in strict pursuance of the idea on which their marriage had been based, namely, that of restoring regularity to his studies.

The sky had a new and startling beauty that night. A broad, fluctuating, semicircular arch of vivid white light spanned the northern quarter of the heavens, reaching from the horizon to the star Eta in the Greater Bear. It was the Aurora Borealis,* just risen up for the winter season out of the freezing seas of the north, where every autumn vapour was now undergoing rapid congelation.

'O, let us sit and look at it!' she said; and they turned their backs upon the equatorial and the southern glories of the heavens to this new beauty in a quarter which they seldom contemplated.

The lustre of the fixed stars was diminished to a sort of blueness. Little by little the arch grew higher against the dark void, like the form of the Spirit-maiden in the shades of Glenfinlas,* till its crown drew near the zenith, and threw a tissue over the whole waggon and horses of the great northern constellation.* Brilliant shafts radiated from the convexity of the arch, coming and going silently. The temperature fell, and Lady Constantine drew her wrap more closely around her.

'We'll go down,' said Swithin. 'The cabin is beautifully warm. Why should we try to observe to-night? Indeed, we cannot; the Aurora light overpowers everything.'

'Very well. To-morrow night there will be no interruption. I shall be gone.'

'You leave me to-morrow, Viviette?'

'Yes; to-morrow morning.'

The truth was that, with the progress of the hours and days, the conviction had been borne in upon Viviette more and more forcibly that not for kingdoms and principalities could she afford to risk the discovery of her presence here by any living soul.

'But let me see your face, dearest,' he said. 'I don't think it will be safe for you to meet your brother yet.'

As it was too dark to see her face on the summit where they sat they descended the winding staircase; and in the cabin Swithin examined the damaged cheek. The line, though so far attenuated as not to be observable by any one but a close observer, had not quite disappeared. But in consequence of her reiterated and almost tearful anxiety to go, and as there was a strong probability that her brother had left the house, Swithin decided to call at Welland next morning, and reconnoitre with a view to her return.

Getting up and locking her in he crossed the dewy stubble into the park. The house was silent and deserted; and only one stalk of smoke ascended from the chimneys. Notwithstanding that the hour was nearly nine he knocked at the door.

'Is Lady Constantine at home?' asked Swithin, with a disingenuousness now habitual, yet unknown to him six months before.

'No, Mr St Cleeve; my lady has not returned from Bath. We expect her every day.'

'Nobody staying in the house?'

'My lady's brother has been here; but he is gone on to Budmouth. He will come again in two or three weeks, I understand.'

This was enough. Swithin said he would call again, and returned to the cabin, where, waking Viviette, who was not by nature an early riser, he waited on the column till she was ready to breakfast. When this had been shared they prepared to start.

A long walk was before them. Warborne station lay five miles distant, and the next station above that nine miles. They were bound for the latter; their plan being that she should there take the train to the junction where the whip accident had occurred, claim her luggage, and return with it to Warborne, as if from Bath.

The morning was cool and the walk not wearisome. When once they had left behind the stubble-field of their environment and the parish of Welland, they sauntered on comfortably, Lady Constantine's spirits rising as she withdrew further from danger.

They parted by a little brook, about half a mile from the station; Swithin to return to Welland by the way he had come.

Lady Constantine telegraphed from the junction to Warborne for a carriage to be in readiness to meet her on her arrival; and then, waiting for the down train, she travelled smoothly home, reaching Welland House about five minutes sooner than Swithin reached the column hard by, after footing it all the way from where they had parted.

CHAPTER TWENTY-ONE

FROM that day forward their life resumed its old channel in general outward aspect.

Perhaps the most remarkable feature in their exploit was its comparative effectiveness as an expedient for the end design, – that of restoring calm assiduity to the study of astronomy. Swithin took up his old position as the lonely philosopher* at the column, and Lady Constantine lapsed back to immured existence at the house, with apparently not a friend in the parish. The enforced narrowness of life which her limited resources necessitated was now an additional safeguard against the discovery of her relations with St Cleeve. Her neighbours seldom troubled her; as much, it must be owned, from a tacit understanding that she was not in a position to return invitations as from any selfish coldness engendered by her want of wealth.

At the first meeting of the secretly united pair after their short honeymoon they were compelled to behave as strangers to each other. It occurred in the only part of Welland which deserved the name of a village street, and all the labourers were returning to their midday meal, with those of their wives who assisted at outdoor work. Before the eyes of this innocent though quite untrustworthy group, Swithin and his Viviette could only shake hands in passing, though she contrived to say to him in an undertone, 'My brother does not return yet for some time. He has gone to Paris. I will be on the lawn this evening, if you can come.' It was a fluttered smile that she bestowed on him, and there was no doubt that every fibre of her heart vibrated afresh at meeting, with such reserve, one who stood in his close relation to her.

The shades of night fell early now, and Swithin was at the spot of appointment about the time that he knew her dinner would be over. It was just where they had met at the beginning of the year, but many changes had resulted since then. The flower-beds that had used to be so neatly edged were now jagged and leafy; black stars appeared on the pale surface of the gravel walks, denoting tufts of grass that grew unmolested there. Lady Constantine's external affairs wore just that aspect which suggests that new blood may be advantageously introduced into the line; and new blood had been introduced, in good sooth,* – with what social result remained to be seen.

She silently entered on the scene from the same window which had given her passage in months gone by. They met with a concerted embrace, and St Cleeve spoke his greeting in whispers.

'We are quite safe, dearest,' said she.

'But the servants?'

'My meagre staff consists of only two women and the boy; and they are away in the other wing. I thought you would like to see the inside of my house, after showing me the inside of yours. So we will walk through it instead of staying out here.'

She let him in through the casement, and they strolled forward softly, Swithin with some curiosity, never before having gone beyond the library and adjoining room. The whole western side of the house was at this time shut up, her life being confined to two or three small rooms in the south-east corner. The great apartments through which they now whisperingly walked wore already that funereal aspect that comes from disuse and inattention. Triangular cobwebs already formed little hammocks for the dust in corners of the wainscot, and a close smell of wood and leather, seasoned with mouse-droppings, pervaded the atmosphere. So seldom was the solitude of these chambers intruded on by human feet that more than once a mouse stood and looked the twain in the face from the arm of a sofa, or the top of a cabinet, without any great fear.

Swithin had no residential ambition whatever, but he was interested in the place. 'Will the house ever be thrown open to gaiety, as it was in old times?' said he.

'Not unless you make a fortune,' she replied laughingly. 'It is mine for my life, as you know; but the estate is so terribly saddled with annuities to Sir Blount's distant relatives, one of whom will succeed me here, that I have practically no more than my own little private income to exist on.'

'And are you bound to occupy the house?'

'Not bound to. But I must not let it on lease.'

'And was there any stipulation in the event of your re-marriage?'

'It was not mentioned.'

'It is satisfactory to find that you lose nothing by marrying me, at all events, dear Viviette.'

'I hope you lose nothing either – at least, of consequence.'

'What have I to lose?'

'I meant your liberty. Suppose you become a popular physicist (popularity seems cooling towards art and coquetting with science now-a-days), and a better chance offers, and one who would make you a newer and brighter wife than I am comes in your way. Will you never regret this? Will you never despise me?'

Swithin answered by a kiss, and they again went on; proceeding like a couple of burglars, lest they should draw the attention of the cook or Green.

In one of the upper rooms his eyes were attracted by an old chamber organ,* which had once been lent for use in the church. He mentioned his recollection of the same, which led her to say, 'That reminds me of something. There is to be a confirmation in our parish in the spring, and you once told me that you had never been confirmed. What shocking neglect! Why was it?'

'I hardly know. The confusion resulting from my father's death caused it to be forgotten, I suppose.'

'Now, dear Swithin, you will do this to please me, – be confirmed on the present occasion?'

'Since I have done without the virtue of it so long, might I not do without it altogether?'

'No, no!' she said earnestly. 'I do wish it, indeed. I am made unhappy when I think you don't care about such serious matters. Without the Church to cling to, what have we?'

'Each other. But seriously, I should be inverting the established order of spiritual things; people ought to be confirmed before they are married.'

'That's really of minor consequence. Now, don't think slightingly of what so many good men have laid down as necessary to be done. And, dear Swithin, I somehow feel that a certain levity which has perhaps shown itself in our treatment of the sacrament of marriage – by making a clandestine adventure of what is, after all, a solemn rite – would be well atoned for by a due seriousness in other points of religious observance. This opportunity should therefore not be passed over. I thought of it all last night; and you are a parson's son, remember, and he would have insisted on it if he had been alive. In short, Swithin, do be a good boy, and observe the Church's ordinances.'

Lady Constantine, by virtue of her temperament, was necessarily either lover or *dévote*,* and she vibrated so gracefully between these two conditions that nobody who had known the circumstances could have condemned her inconsistencies. To be led into difficulties by those mastering emotions of hers, to aim at escape by turning round and seizing the apparatus of religion – which could only rightly be worked by the very emotions already bestowed elsewhere – it was, after all, but Convention's palpitating attempt to preserve the comfort of her creature's conscience in the trying quandary to which the conditions of sex had given rise. As Viviette could not be confirmed herself, and as Communion Sunday* was a long way off, she urged Swithin thus.

'And the new bishop is such a good man,' she continued. 'I used to have a slight acquaintance with him when he was a parish priest.'

'Very well, dearest. To please you I'll be confirmed. My grandmother, too, will be delighted, no doubt.'

They continued their ramble: Lady Constantine first advancing into rooms with the candle, to assure herself that all was empty, and then calling him forward in a whisper. The stillness was broken only by these whispers, or by the occasional crack of a floorboard beneath their tread. At last they sat down, and, shading the candle with a screen, she showed him the faded contents of this and that drawer or cabinet, or the wardrobe of some member of the family who had died young early in the century, when muslin reigned supreme, when waists were close to arm-pits, and muffs as large as smugglers' tubs.

These researches among habilimental* hulls* and husks, whose human kernels had long ago perished, went on for about half an hour; when the companions were startled by a loud ringing at the front-door bell.

CHAPTER TWENTY-TWO

LADY CONSTANTINE flung down the old-fashioned lacework, whose beauties she had been pointing out to Swithin, and exclaimed, 'Who can it be? Not Louis, surely?'

They listened. An arrival was such a phenomenon at this unfrequented mansion, and particularly a late arrival, that no servant was on the alert to respond to the call; and the visitor rang again, more loudly than before. Sounds of the tardy opening and shutting of a passage-door from the kitchen quarter then reached their ears, and Viviette went into the corridor to hearken more attentively. In a few minutes she returned to the wardrobe-room in which she had left Swithin.

'Yes; it is my brother!' she said with difficult composure. 'I just caught his voice. He has no doubt come back from Paris to stay. This is a rather vexatious, indolent way he has, never to write to prepare me!'

'I can easily go away,' said Swithin.

By this time, however, her brother had been shown into the house, and the footsteps of the page were audible, coming in search of Lady Constantine.

'If you will wait there a moment,' she said, directing St Cleeve into her bedchamber which adjoined; 'you will be quite safe from interruption, and I will quickly come back.' Taking the light she left him.

Swithin waited in darkness. Not more than ten minutes had passed when a whisper in her voice came through the keyhole. He opened the door.

'Yes; he is come to stay!' she said. 'He is at supper now.'

'Very well; don't be flurried, dearest. Shall I stay too, as we planned?'

'O, Swithin, I fear not!' she replied anxiously. 'You see how it is. To-night we have broken the arrangement that you should never come here; and this is the result. Will it offend you if – I ask you to leave?'

'Not in the least. Upon the whole, I prefer the comfort of my little cabin and homestead to the gauntness and alarms of this place.'

'There, now, I fear you are offended!' she said, a tear collecting in her eye. 'I wish I was going back with you to the cabin! How happy we were, those three days of our stay there! But it is better, perhaps, just now, that you should leave me. Yes, these rooms are oppressive. They require a large household to make them cheerful. . . . Yet, Swithin,' she added, after reflection, 'I will not request you to go. Do as you think best. I will light a night-light, and leave you here to consider. For myself, I must go downstairs to my brother at once, or he'll wonder what I am doing.'

She kindled the little light, and again retreated, closing the door upon him.

Swithin sat and waited some time; till he considered that upon the whole it would be preferable to leave. With this intention he emerged and went softly along the dark passage towards the extreme end, where there was a little crooked staircase that would conduct him down to a disused side door. Descending this stair he duly arrived at the other side of the house, facing the quarter whence the wind blew, and here he was surprised to catch the noise of rain beating against the windows. It was a state of weather which fully accounted for the visitor's impatient ringing.

St Cleeve was in a minor kind of dilemma. The rain reminded him that his hat and great-coat had been left downstairs, in the front part of the house; and though he might have gone home without either in ordinary weather it was not a pleasant feat in the pelting winter rain. Retracing his steps to Viviette's room he took the light, and opened a closet-door that he had seen ajar on his way down. Within the closet hung various articles of apparel, upholstery lumber of all kinds filling the back part. Swithin thought he might find here a cloak of hers to throw round him, but finally took down from a peg a more suitable garment, the only one of the sort that was there. It was an old moth-eaten great-coat, heavily trimmed with fur; and in removing it a companion cap of sealskin was disclosed.

'Whose can they be?' he thought, and a gloomy answer suggested itself. 'Pooh,' he then said (summoning the scientific side of his nature), 'matter is matter, and mental association only a delusion.'

Putting on the garments he returned the light to Lady Constantine's bedroom, and again prepared to depart as before.

Scarcely, however, had he regained the corridor a second time, when he heard a light footstep – seemingly Viviette's – again on the front landing. Wondering what she wanted with him further he waited, taking the precaution to step into the closet till sure it was she.

The figure came onward, bent to the keyhole of the bedroom door, and whispered (supposing him still inside), 'Swithin, on second thoughts I think you may stay with safety.'

Having no further doubt of her personality he came out with thoughtless abruptness from the closet behind her, and looking round suddenly she beheld his shadowy fur-clad outline. At once she raised her hands in horror, as if to protect herself from him; she uttered a shriek, and turned shudderingly to the wall, covering her face.

Swithin would have picked her up in a moment, but by this time he could hear footsteps rushing upstairs, in response to her cry. In consternation, and with a view of not compromising her, he effected his retreat as fast as possible, reaching the bend of the corridor just as her brother Louis appeared with a light at the other extremity.

'What's the matter, for heaven's sake, Viviette?' said Louis.

'My husband!' she involuntarily exclaimed.

'What nonsense!'

'O yes, it is nonsense,' she added, with an effort. 'It was nothing.'

'But what was the cause of your cry?'

She had by this time recovered her reason and judgment. 'O, it was a trick of the imagination,' she said, with a faint laugh. 'I live so much alone that I get superstitious – and – I thought for the moment I saw an apparition.'

'Of your late husband?'

'Yes. But it was nothing; it was the outline of the – tall clock and the chair behind. Would you mind going down, and leaving me to go into my room for a moment?'

She entered the bedroom, and her brother went downstairs. Swithin thought it best to leave well alone, and going noiselessly out of the house plodded through the rain homeward. It was plain that agitations of one sort and another had so weakened Viviette's nerves as to lay her open to every impression. That the clothes he had borrowed were some cast-off garments of the late Sir Blount had occurred to St Cleeve in taking them; but in the moment of returning to her side he had forgotten this, and the shape they gave to his figure had obviously been a reminder of too sudden a sort for her. Musing thus he walked along as if he were still, as before, the lonely student, dissociated from all mankind, and with no shadow of right or interest in Welland House or its mistress.

The great-coat and cap were unpleasant companions; but Swithin having been reared, or having reared himself, in the scientific school of thought, would not give way to his sense of their weirdness. To do so would have been treason to his own beliefs and aims.

When nearly home, at a point where his track converged on another path, there approached him from the latter a group of indistinct forms. The tones of their speech revealed them to be Hezzy Biles, Nat Chapman, Fry, and other labourers. Swithin was about to say a word to them, till recollecting his disguise he deemed it advisable to hold his tongue, lest his attire should tell a too dangerous tale as to where he had come from. By degrees they drew closer, their walk being in the same direction.

'Good-night, strainger,' said Nat.

The stranger did not reply.

All of them paced on abreast of him, and he could perceive in the gloom that their faces were turned inquiringly upon his form. Then a whisper passed from one to another of them; then Chapman, who was the boldest, dropped immediately behind his heels, and followed there for some distance, taking close observations of his outline, after which the men grouped again and whispered. Thinking it best to let them pass on Swithin slackened his pace, and they went ahead of him, apparently without much reluctance.

There was no doubt that they had been impressed by the clothes he wore; and having no wish to provoke similar comments from his grandmother and Hannah, Swithin took the precaution, on arriving at Welland Bottom, to enter the homestead by the out-house. Here he deposited the cap and coat in secure hiding, afterwards going round to the front and opening the door in the usual way.

In the entry he met Hannah, who said –

'Only to hear what have been seed to-night, Mr Swithin! The

work-folk have dropped in to tell us!'

In the kitchen were the men who had outstripped him on the road. Their countenances, instead of wearing the usual knotty irregularities, had a smoothed-out expression of blank concern. Swithin's entrance was unobtrusive and quiet, as if he had merely come down from his study upstairs, and they only noticed him by enlarging their gaze, so as to include him in the audience.

'We was in a deep talk at the moment,' continued Blore, 'and Natty had just brought up that story about old Jeremiah Paddock's crossing the park one night at one o'clock in the morning, and seeing Sir Blount a-shutting my lady out-o'-doors; and we was saying that it seemed a true return that he should perish in a foreign land; when we happened to look up, and there was Sir Blount a-walking along.'

'Did it overtake you, or did you overtake it?' whispered Hannah sepulchrally.

'I don't say 'twas *it*,' returned Sammy. 'God forbid that I should drag in a resurrection word about what perhaps was still solid manhood, and has to die! But he, or it, closed in upon us, as 'twere.'

'Yes, closed in upon us!' said Haymoss.

'And I said "Good-night, straigner",' added Chapman.

'Yes, "Good-night, strainger", – that wez yer words, Natty. I support 'ee in it.'

'And then he closed in upon us still more.'

'We closed in upon he, rather,' said Chapman.

'Well, well; 'tis the same thing in such matters! And the form was Sir Blount's. My nostrils told me, for – there, 'a smelled. Yes, I could smell 'n, being to leeward.'

'Lord, lord, what unwholesome scandal's this about the ghost of a respectable gentleman?' said Mrs Martin, who had entered from the sitting-room.

'Now, wait, ma'am. I don't say 'twere a low smell, mind ye. 'Twere a high smell, a sort of gamey flaviour, calling to mind venison and hare, just as you'd expect of a great squire, – not like a poor man's 'natomy, at all; and that was what strengthened my faith that 'twas Sir Blount.'

('The skins that old coat was made of,' ruminated Swithin.)

'Well, well; I've not held out against the spectre o' starvation these five-and-twenty year on nine shillings a week, to be afeard of a walking vapour, sweet or savoury,' said Hezzy. 'So here's homealong.'

'Bide a bit longer, and I'm going too,' contined Fry. 'Well, when I found 'twas Sir Blount my spet dried up within my mouth; for neither hedge nor bush were there for refuge against any foul spring 'a might have made at us.'

''Twas very curious; but we had likewise mentioned his name just afore, in talking of the confirmation that's shortly coming on,' said Hezzy.

'Is there soon to be a confirmation?'

'Yes. In this parish – the first time in Welland church for twenty years. As I say, I had told 'em that he was confirmed the same year that I went up to have it done, as I have very good cause to mind. When we went to be examined, the pa'son said to me, "Rehearse the articles of thy belief." Mr Blount (as he was then) was nighest me, and he whispered, "Women and wine." "Women and wine," says I to the pa'son: and for that I was sent back till next confirmation, Sir Blount never owning that he was the rascal.'

'Confirmation was a sight different at that time,' mused Biles. 'The Bishops didn't lay it on so strong then as they do now. Now-a-days, yer Bishop gives both hands to every Jack-rag and Tom-straw* that drops the knee afore him; but 'twas six chaps to one blessing when we was boys. The Bishop o' that time would stretch out his palms and run his fingers over our row of crowns as off-hand as a bank gentleman telling* money or a thimble-rigger* at a fair. The great lords of the Church in them days wasn't particular to a soul or two more or less; and, for my part, I think living was easier for 't.'

'The new Bishop, I hear, is a bachelor-man; or a widow gentleman is it?' asked Mrs Martin.

'Bachelor, I believe, ma'am. Mr San Cleeve, making so bold, you've never faced him yet, I think?'

Mrs Martin shook her head.

'No; it was a piece of neglect. I hardly know how it happened,' she said.

'I am going to, this time,' said Swithin and turned the chat to other matters.

CHAPTER TWENTY-THREE

SWITHIN could not sleep that night for thinking of his Viviette. Nothing told so significantly of the conduct of her first husband towards the poor lady as the abiding dread of him which was revealed in her by any sudden revival of his image or memory. But for that consideration her almost childlike terror at Swithin's inadvertent disguise would have been ludicrous.

He waited anxiously through several following days for an opportunity of seeing her, but none was afforded. Her brother's presence in the house sufficiently accounted for this. At length he ventured to write a note, requesting her to signal to him in a way she had done once or twice before, – by pulling down a blind in a particular window of the house, one of the few visible from the top of the Rings-Hill column; this to be done on any evening when she could see him after dinner on the terrace.

When he had levelled the glass at that window for five successive nights he beheld the blind in the position suggested. Three hours later, quite in the dusk, he repaired to the place of appointment.

'My brother is away this evening,' she explained, 'and that's why I can come out. He is only gone for a few hours, nor is he likely to go for longer just yet, for he's no money. He keeps himself a good deal in my company, which has made it unsafe for me to venture near you.'

'Has he any suspicion?'

'None, apparently. But he rather depresses me.'

'How, Viviette?' Swithin feared, from her manner, that this was something serious.

'I would rather not tell.'

'But— Well, never mind.'

'Yes, Swithin, I will tell you. There should be no secrets between us. He urges upon me the necessity of marrying, day after day.'

'For money and position, of course.'

'Yes. But I take no notice. I let him go on.'

'Really, this is sad!' said the young man. 'I must work harder than ever, or you will never be able to own me.'

'O yes, in good time!' she cheeringly replied.

'I shall be very glad to have you always near me. I felt the gloom of our position keenly when I was obliged to disappear that night, without assuring you it was only I who stood there. Why were you so frightened at those old clothes I borrowed?'

'Don't ask, – don't ask!' she said, burying her face on his shoulder. 'I don't want to speak of that. There was something so ghastly and so uncanny in your putting on such garments that I wish you had been more thoughtful, and had left them alone.'

He assured her that he did not stop to consider whose they were. 'By the way, they must be sent back,' he said.

'No; I never wish to see them again! I cannot help feeling that your putting them on was ominous.'

'Nothing is ominous in serene philosophy,' he said, kissing her. 'Things are either causes, or they are not causes.* When can you see me again?'

In such wise the hour passed away. The evening was typical of others which followed it at irregular intervals through the winter. And during the intenser months of the season frequent falls of snow lengthened, even more than other difficulties had done, the periods of isolation between the pair. Swithin adhered with all the more strictness to the letter of his promise not to intrude into the house, from his sense of her powerlessness to compel him to keep out should he choose to rebel. A student of the greatest forces in nature, he had, like many others of his sort, no personal force to speak of in a social point of view, mainly because he took no interest in human ranks and formulas; and hence he was as docile as a child in her hands wherever matters of that kind were concerned.

Her brother wintered at Welland; but whether because his experience of tropic climes had unfitted him for the brumal* rigours of Britain, or for some other reason, he seldom showed himself out of doors, and Swithin caught but passing glimpses of him. Now and then Viviette managed to pay a hasty visit to the hut; and at other times her impulsive affection would overcome her sense of risk, and she would press Swithin to call on her at all costs. This he would by no means do. It was obvious to his more logical mind that the secrecy to which they had bound themselves must be kept in its fulness, or might as well be abandoned altogether.

He was now sadly exercised on the subject of his uncle's will. There had as yet been no pressing reasons for a full and candid reply to the solicitor who had communicated with him, owing to the fact that the payments were not to begin till Swithin was one-and-twenty; but time was going on, and something definite would have to be done soon. To own to his marriage and consequent disqualification for the bequest was easy in itself; but it involved telling at least one man what both Viviette and himself had great reluctance in telling anybody. Moreover he wished Viviette to know nothing of his loss in making her his wife. All he could think of doing for the present was to write a postponing letter to his uncle's lawyer, and wait events.

The one practical comfort of this dreary winter-time was his perception of a returning ability to work with the regularity and much of the spirit of earlier days.

One bright night in April there was an eclipse of the moon, and Mr Torkingham, by arrangement, brought to the observatory several labouring men and boys, to whom he had promised a sight of the phenomenon through the telescope. The coming confirmation, fixed for May, was again talked of; and St Cleeve learnt from the parson that the Bishop had arranged to stay the night at the vicarage, and was to be invited to a grand luncheon at Welland House immediately after the ordinance.

This seemed like a going back into life again as regarded the mistress of that house; and St Cleeve was a little surprised that, in his communications with Viviette, she had mentioned no such probability. The next day he walked round the mansion, wondering how in its present state any entertainment could be given therein.

He found that the shutters had been opened, which had restored an unexpected liveliness to the aspect of the windows. Two men were putting a chimney-pot on one of the chimney-stacks, and two more were scraping green mould from the front wall. He made no inquiries on that occasion. Three days later he strolled thitherward again. Now a great cleaning of window-panes was going on, Hezzy Biles and Sammy Blore being the operators, for which purpose their services must have been borrowed from the neighbouring farmer. Hezzy dashed water at the glass with a force that threatened to break it in, the broad face of Sammy being discernible inside, smiling at the onset. In addition to these, Anthony Green and another were weeding the gravel walks, and putting fresh plants into the flower-beds. Neither of these reasonable operations was a great undertaking, singly looked at; but the life Viviette had latterly led and the mood in which she had hitherto regarded the premises, rendered it somewhat significant. Swithin, however, was rather curious than concerned at the proceedings, and returned to his tower with feelings of interest not entirely confined to the worlds overhead.

Lady Constantine may or may not have seen him from the house; but the same evening, which was fine and dry, while he was occupying himself in the observatory with cleaning the eye-pieces of the equatorial, skull-cap on head, observing-jacket on, and in other ways primed for sweeping, the customary stealthy step on the winding staircase brought her form in due course into the rays of the bull's-eye lantern.* The meeting was all the more pleasant to him from being unexpected, and he at once lit up a larger lamp in honour of the occasion.

'It is but a hasty visit,' she said when, after putting up her mouth to be kissed, she had seated herself in the low chair used for observations, panting a little with the labour of ascent. 'But I hope to be able to come more freely soon. My brother is still living on with me. Yes, he is going to stay until the confirmation is over. After the confirmation he will certainly leave. So good it is of you, dear, to please me by agreeing to the ceremony. The Bishop, you know, is going to lunch with us. It is a wonder he has promised to come, for he is a man averse to society, and mostly keeps entirely with the clergy on these confirmation tours, or circuits, or whatever they call them. But Mr Torkingham's house is so very small, and mine is so close at hand, that this arrangement to relieve him of the fuss of one meal, at least, naturally suggested itself; and the Bishop has fallen in with it very readily. How are you getting on with your observations? Have you not wanted me dreadfully, to write down notes?'

'Well, I have been obliged to do without you, whether or no. See here, – how much I have done.' And he showed her a book ruled in columns, headed 'Object', 'Right Ascension', 'Declination', 'Features', 'Remarks', and so on.

She looked over this and other things, but her mind speedily winged its way back to the confirmation. 'It is so new to me,' she said, 'to have persons coming to the house, that I feel rather anxious. I hope the luncheon will be a success.'

'You know the Bishop?' said Swithin.

'I have not seen him for many years. I knew him when I was quite a girl, and he held the little living of Puddle-sub-Mixen, near us; but after that time, and ever since I have lived here, I have seen nothing of him. There has been no confirmation in this village, they say, for twenty years. The other bishop used to make the young men and women go to Warborne; he wouldn't take the trouble to come to such an out-of-the-way parish as ours.'

'This cleaning and preparation that I observe going on must be rather a tax upon you?'

'My brother Louis sees to it, and, what is more, bears the expense.'

'Your brother?' said Swithin, with surprise.

'Well, he insisted on doing so,' she replied, in a hesitating, despondent tone. 'Though he had to borrow the money for it. He has been active in the whole matter, and was the first to suggest the invitation. I should not have thought of it.'

'Well, I will hold aloof till it is all over.'

'Thanks, dearest, for your considerateness. I wish it was not still advisable! But I shall see you on the day, and watch my own philosopher all through the service from the corner of my pew! . . . I hope you are well prepared for the rite, Swithin?' she added, turning tenderly to him. 'It would perhaps be advisable for you to give up this astronomy till the confirmation is over, in order to devote your attention exclusively to that more serious matter.'

'More serious! Well, I will do the best I can. I am sorry to see that you are less interested in astronomy than you used to be, Viviette.'

'No; it is only that these preparations for the Bishop unsettle my mind from study. Now put on your other coat and hat, and come with me a little way.'

CHAPTER TWENTY-FOUR

THE morning of the confirmation was come. It was mid-May time, bringing with it weather not, perhaps, quite so blooming as that assumed to be natural to the month by the joyous poets* of three hundred years ago; but a very tolerable, well-wearing May, that the average rustic would willingly have compounded for* in lieu of Mays occasionally fairer, but usually more foul.

Among the larger shrubs and flowers which composed the outworks of the Welland gardens, the lilac, the laburnum, and the guelder-rose hung out their respective colours of purple, yellow, and white; whilst within these, belted round from every disturbing gale, rose the columbine, the peony, the larkspur, and the Solomon's seal.* The animate things that moved amid this scene of colour were plodding bees, gadding butterflies, and numerous sauntering young feminine candidates for the impending confirmation, who, having gaily bedecked themselves for the ceremony, were enjoying their own appearance by walking about in twos and threes till it was time to start.

Swithin St Cleeve, whose preparations were somewhat simpler than those of the village belles, waited till his grandmother and Hannah had set out, and then, locking the door, followed towards the distant church. On reaching the churchyard gate he met Mr Torkingham, who shook hands with him in the manner of a man with several irons in the fire, and telling Swithin where to sit, disappeared to hunt up some candidates who had not yet made themselves visible.

Casting his eyes round for Viviette, and seeing nothing of her, Swithin went on to the church porch and looked in. From the north side of the nave smiled a host of girls, gaily uniform in dress, age, and a temporary repression of their natural tendency to 'skip like a hare over the meshes of good counsel'.* Their white muslin dresses, their round white caps, from beneath whose borders hair-knots and curls of various shades of brown escaped upon their low shoulders, as if against their will, lighted up the dark pews and grey stone-work to an unwonted warmth and life. On the south side were the young men and boys, – heavy, angular, and massive, as indeed was rather necessary, considering what they would have to bear at the hands of wind and weather before they returned to that mouldy nave for the last time.

Over the heads of all these he could see into the chancel to the square pew on the north side, which was attached to Welland House. There he discerned Lady Constantine already arrived, her brother Louis sitting by her side.

Swithin entered and seated himself at the end of a bench, and she, who had been on the watch, at once showed by subtle signs her consciousness of the presence of the young man who had reversed the ordained sequence of the Church services* on her account. She appeared in black attire, though not strictly in mourning, a touch of red in her bonnet setting off the richness of her complexion without making her gay. Handsomest woman in the church she decidedly was; and yet a disinterested spectator who had known all the circumstances would probably have felt that, the future considered, Swithin's more natural mate would have been one of the muslin-clad maidens who were to be presented to the Bishop with him that day.

When the Bishop had arrived and gone into the chancel, and blown his nose, the congregation were sufficiently impressed by his presence to leave off looking at one another.

The Right Reverend Cuthbert Helmsdale, D.D., ninety-fourth occupant of the episcopal throne of the diocese, revealed himself to be a personage of dark complexion, whose darkness was thrown still further into prominence by the lawn* protuberances that now rose upon his two shoulders like the Eastern and Western hemispheres.* In stature he seemed to be tall and imposing, but something of this aspect may have been derived from his robes.

The service was, as usual, of a length which severely tried the tarrying powers of the young people assembled; and it was not till the youth of all the other parishes had gone up that the turn came for the Welland bevy. Swithin and some older ones were nearly the last. When, at the heels of Mr Torkingham, he passed Lady Constantine's pew, he lifted his eyes from the red lining of that gentleman's hood sufficiently high to catch hers. She was abstracted, tearful, – regarding him with all the rapt mingling of religion, love, fervour, and hope which such women can feel at such times, and which men know nothing of. How fervidly she watched the Bishop place his hand on her beloved youth's head; how she saw the great episcopal ring glistening in the sun among Swithin's brown curls; how she waited to hear if Dr Helmsdale uttered the form 'this thy child' which he used for the younger ones, or 'this thy servant' which he used for those older; and how, when he said 'this thy *child*', she felt a prick of conscience, like a person who had entrapped an innocent youth into marriage for her own gratification, till she remembered that she had raised his social position thereby, – all this could only have been told in its entirety by herself.

As for Swithin, he felt ashamed of his own utter lack of the high enthusiasm which beamed so eloquently from her eyes. When he passed her again, on the return journey from the Bishop to his seat, her face was warm with a blush which her brother might have observed had he regarded her.

Whether he had observed it or not, as soon as St Cleeve had sat himself down again Louis Glanville turned and looked hard at the young astronomer. This was the first time that St Cleeve and Viviette's brother had been face to face in a distinct light, their first meeting having occurred in the dusk of a railway-station. Swithin was not in the habit of noticing people's features; he scarcely ever observed any detail of physiognomy in his friends, a generalization from their whole aspect forming his idea of them; and he now only noted a man of perhaps thirty, who lolled a good deal, and in whose small dark eyes seemed to be concentrated the activity that the rest of his frame decidedly lacked. This gentleman's eyes were henceforward, to the end of the service, continually fixed upon Swithin; but as this was their natural direction, from the position of his seat, there was no great strangeness in the circumstance.

Swithin wanted to say to Viviette, 'Now I hope you are pleased; I have conformed to your ideas of my duty, leaving my fitness out of consideration'; but as he could only see her bonnet and forehead it was not possible even to look the intelligence.* He turned more to the left, where the organ stood, with Miss Tabitha Lark seated behind it.

It being now sermon-time the youthful blower had fallen asleep over the handle of his bellows, and Tabitha pulled out her handkerchief intending to flap him awake with it. With the handkerchief tumbled out a whole family of unexpected articles: a silver thimble; a photograph; a little purse; a scent-bottle; some loose halfpence; nine green gooseberries; a key. They rolled to Swithin's feet, and, passively obeying his first instinct, he picked up as many of the articles as he could find, and handed them to her amid the smiles of the neighbours.

Tabitha was half-dead with humiliation at such an event happening under the very eyes of the Bishop on this glorious occasion; she turned pale as a sheet, and could hardly keep her seat. Fearing she might faint Swithin, who had genuinely sympathized, bent over and whispered encouragingly, 'Don't mind it, Tabitha. Shall I take you out into the air?' She declined his offer, and presently the sermon came to an end.

Swithin lingered behind the rest of the congregation sufficiently long to see Lady Constantine, accompanied by her brother, the Bishop, the Bishop's chaplain, Mr Torkingham, and several other clergy and ladies, cross the churchyard and enter to the luncheon in Welland House; the whole group talking with a vivacity all the more intense, as it seemed, from the recent two hours' enforced repression of their social qualities within the adjacent building.

The young man stood till he was left quite alone in the churchyard, and then went slowly homeward over the hill, perhaps a trifle depressed at the impossibility of being near Viviette in this her one day of gaiety, and joining in the conversation of those who surrounded her.

Not that he felt much jealousy of her situation, as his wife, in comparison with his own. He had so clearly understood from the beginning that, in the event of marriage, their outward lives were to run on as before, that to rebel now would have been unmanly in himself and cruel to her, by adding to embarrassments that were great enough already. His momentary doubt was of his own strength to achieve sufficiently high things to render him, in relation to her, other than a patronized young favourite, whom she had married at an immense sacrifice of position. Now, at twenty, he was doomed to isolation even from a wife; could it be that at, say thirty, he would be welcomed everywhere?

But with motion through the sun and air his mood assumed a lighter complexion, and on reaching home he remembered with interest that Venus was in a favourable aspect* for observation that afternoon.

CHAPTER TWENTY-FIVE

MEANWHILE the interior of Welland House was rattling with the progress of the ecclesiastical luncheon.

The Bishop, who sat at Lady Constantine's side, seemed enchanted with her company, and from the beginning she engrossed his attention almost entirely. The truth was that the circumstance of her not having her whole soul centred on the success of the repast and the pleasure of Bishop Helmsdale, imparted to her, in a great measure, the mood to ensure both. Her brother Louis it was who had laid out the plan of entertaining the Bishop, to which she had assented but indifferently. She was secretly bound to another, on whose career she had staked all her happiness. Having thus other interests she evinced to-day the ease of one who hazards nothing, and there was no sign of that preoccupation with housewifely contingencies which so often makes the hostess hardly recognizable as the charming woman who graced a friend's home the day before. In marrying Swithin Lady Constantine had played her card, – recklessly, impulsively, ruinously, perhaps; but she had played it; it could not be withdrawn; and she took this morning's luncheon as an episode that could result in nothing to her beyond the day's entertainment.

Hence, by that power of indirectness to accomplish in an hour what strenuous aiming will not effect in a lifetime, she fascinated the Bishop to an unprecedented degree. A bachelor, he rejoiced in the commanding period of life that stretches between the time of waning impulse and the time of incipient dotage, when a woman can reach the male heart neither by awakening a young man's passion nor an old man's infatuation. He must be made to admire, or he can be made to do nothing. Unintentionally that is how Viviette operated on her guest.

Lady Constantine, to external view, was in a position to desire many things, and of a sort to desire them. She was obviously, by nature, impulsive to indiscretion. But instead of exhibiting activities to correspond, recently gratified affection lent to her manner just now a sweet serenity, a truly Christian contentment, which it puzzled the learned Bishop exceedingly to find in a warm young widow, and increased his interest in her every moment. Thus matters stood when the conversation veered round to the morning's confirmation.

'That was a singularly engaging young man who came up among Mr Torkingham's candidates,' said the Bishop to her somewhat abruptly.

But abruptness does not catch a woman without her wit. 'Which one?' she said innocently.

'That youth with the "corn-coloured" hair, as a poet of the new school* would call it, who sat just at the side of the organ. Do you know who he is?'

In answering Viviette showed a little nervousness, for the first time that day.

'O yes. He is the son of an unfortunate gentleman who was formerly curate here, – a Mr St Cleeve.'

'I never saw a handsomer young man in my life,' said the Bishop. Lady Constantine blushed. 'There was a lack of self-consciousness, too, in his manner of presenting himself, which very much won me. A Mr St Cleeve, do you say? A curate's son? His father must have been St Cleeve of All Angels,* whom I knew. How comes he to be staying on here? What is he doing?'

Mr Torkingham, who kept one ear on the Bishop all the lunch-time, finding that Lady Constantine was not ready with an answer, hastened to reply: 'Your lordship is right. His father was an All Angels' man. The youth is rather to be pitied.'

'He was a man of talent,' affirmed the Bishop. 'But I quite lost sight of him.'

'He was curate to the late vicar,' resumed the parson, 'and was much liked by the parish: but, being erratic in his tastes and tendencies, he rashly contracted a marriage with the daughter of a farmer, and then quarrelled with the local gentry for not taking up* his wife. This lad was an only child. There was enough money to educate him, and he is sufficiently well provided for to be independent of the world so long as he is content to live here with great economy. But of course this gives him few opportunities of bettering himself.'

'Yes, naturally,' replied the Bishop of Melchester. 'Better have been left entirely dependent on himself. These half-incomes do men little good, unless they happen to be either weaklings or geniuses.'

Lady Constantine would have given the world to say, 'He *is* a genius, and the hope of my life'; but it would have been decidedly risky, and in another moment was unnecessary, for Mr Torkingham said, 'There is a certain genius in this young man, I sometimes think.'

'Well, he really looks quite out of the common,' said the Bishop.

'Youthful genius is sometimes disappointing,' observed Viviette, not believing it in the least.

'Yes,' said the Bishop. 'Though it depends, Lady Constantine, on what you understand by disappointing. It may produce nothing visible to the world's eye, and yet may complete its development within to a very perfect degree. Objective achievements, though the only ones which are counted, are not the only ones that exist and have value; and I for one should be sorry to assert that, because a man of genius dies as unknown to the world as when he was born, he therefore was an instance of wasted material'.

Objective achievements were, however, those that Lady Constantine had a weakness for in the present case, and she asked her more experienced guest if he thought early development of a special talent a good sign in youth.

The Bishop thought it well that a particular bent should not show itself too early, lest disgust* should result.

'Still,' argued Lady Constantine rather firmly (for she felt this opinion of the Bishop's to be one throwing doubt on Swithin), 'sustained fruition is compatible with early bias.* Tycho Brahe* showed quite a passion for the solar system when he was but a youth, and so did Kepler;* and James Ferguson* had a surprising knowledge of the stars by the time he was eleven or twelve.'

'Yes; sustained fruition,' conceded the Bishop (rather liking the words), 'is certainly compatible with early bias. Fénelon* preached at fourteen.'

'He – Mr St Cleeve – is not in the church,' said Lady Constantine.

'He is a scientific young man, my lord,' explained Mr Torkingham.

'An astronomer,' she added, with suppressed pride.

'An astronomer! Really, that makes him still more interesting than being handsome and the son of a man I knew. How and where does he study astronomy?'

'He has a beautiful observatory. He has made use of an old column that was erected on this manor to the memory of one of the Constantines. It has been very ingeniously adapted for his purpose, and he does very good work there. I believe he occasionally sends up a paper to the Royal Society, or Greenwich, or somewhere, and to astronomical periodicals.'

'I should have had no idea, from his boyish look, that he had advanced so far,' the Bishop answered. 'And yet I saw on his face that within there was a book* worth studying. His is a career I should very much like to watch.'

A thrill of pleasure chased through Lady Constantine's heart at this praise of her chosen one. It was an unwitting compliment to her taste and discernment in singling him out for her own, despite its temporary inexpediency.

Her brother Louis now spoke. 'I fancy he is as interested in one of his fellow-creatures as in the science of astronomy,' observed the cynic drily.

'In whom?' said Lady Constantine quickly.

'In the fair maiden who sat at the organ, – a pretty girl, rather. I noticed a sort of by-play going on between them occasionally, during the sermon, which meant mating, if I am not mistaken.'

'She!' cried Lady Constantine. 'She is only a village girl, a dairyman's daughter, – Tabitha Lark, who used to come to read to me.'

'She may be a savage, for all that I know: but there is something between those two young people, nevertheless.'

The Bishop looked as if he had allowed his interest in a stranger to carry him too far, and Mr Torkingham was horrified at the irreverent and easy familiarity of Louis Glanville's talk in the presence of a consecrated bishop. As for Viviette, her tongue lost all its volubility. She felt quite faint at heart, and hardly knew how to control herself.

'I have never noticed anything of the sort,' said Mr Torkingham.

'It would be a matter for regret,' said the Bishop, 'if he should follow his father in forming an attachment that would be a hindrance to him in any honourable career; though perhaps an early marriage, intrinsically considered, would not be bad for him. A youth who looks as if he had come straight from old Greece may be exposed to many temptations, should he go out into the world without a friend or counsellor to guide him.'

Despite her sudden jealousy Viviette's eyes grew moist at the picture of her innocent Swithin going into the world without a friend or counsellor. But she was sick in soul and disquieted still by Louis's dreadful remarks, who, unbeliever as he was in human virtue, could have no reason whatever for representing Swithin as engaged in a private love affair if such were not his honest impression.

She was so absorbed during the remainder of the luncheon that she did not even observe the kindly light that her presence was shedding on the right reverend ecclesiastic by her side. He reflected it back in tones duly mellowed by his position; the minor clergy caught up the rays thereof, and so the gentle influence played down the table.

The company soon departed when luncheon was over; and the remainder of the day passed in quietness, the Bishop being occupied in his room at the vicarage with writing letters or a sermon. Having a long journey before him the next day he had expressed a wish to be housed for the night without ceremony, and would have dined alone with Mr Torkingham but that, by a happy thought, Lady Constantine and her brother were asked to join them.

However, when Louis crossed the churchyard and entered the vicarage drawing-room at seven o'clock, his sister was not in his company. She was, he said, suffering from a headache, and much regretted that she was on that account unable to come. At this intelligence the social sparkle disappeared from the Bishop's eye, and he sat down to table, endeavouring to mould into the form of episcopal serenity an expression which was really one of common human disappointment.

In his simple statement Louis Glanville had by no means expressed all the circumstances which accompanied his sister's refusal, at the last moment, to dine at her neighbour's house. Louis had strongly urged her to bear up against her slight indisposition – if it were that, and not disinclination – and come along with him on just this one occasion, pernaps a more important episode in her life than she was aware of. Viviette thereupon knew quite well that he alluded to the favourable impression she was producing on the Bishop, notwithstanding that neither of them mentioned the Bishop's name. But she did not give way, though the argument waxed strong between them; and Louis left her in no very amiable mood, saying, 'I don't believe you have any more headache than I have, Viviette. It is some provoking whim of yours – nothing more.'

In this there was a substratum of truth. When her brother had left her, and she had seen him from the window entering the vicarage gate, Viviette seemed to be much relieved, and sat down in her bedroom till the evening grew dark, and only the lights shining through the trees from the parsonage dining-room revealed to the eye where that dwelling stood. Then she arose, and putting on the cloak she had used so many times before for the same purpose, she locked her bedroom door (to be supposed within, in case of the accidental approach of a servant), and let herself privately out of the house.

Lady Constantine paused for a moment under the vicarage windows, till she could sufficiently well hear the voices of the diners to be sure that they were actually within, and then went on her way, which was towards the Rings-Hill column. She appeared a mere spot, hardly distinguishable from the sod, as she crossed the open ground, and soon became absorbed in the black mass of the fir plantation.

Meanwhile the conversation at Mr Torkingham's dinner-table was not of a highly exhilarating quality. The parson, in long self-communing during the afternoon, had decided that the Diocesan Synod,* whose annual session at Melchester had occurred in the month previous, would afford a solid and unimpeachable subject to launch during the meal, whenever conversation flagged; and that it would be one likely to win the respect of his spiritual chieftain for himself as the introducer. Accordingly, in the further belief that you could not have too much of a good thing, Mr Torkingham not only acted upon his idea, but at every pause rallied to the synod point with unbroken firmness. Everything which had been discussed at that last session – such as the introduction of the lay element into the councils of the church, the reconstitution of the ecclesiastical courts, church patronage, the tithe question* – was revived by Mr Torkingham, the excellent remarks which the Bishop had made in his addresses on those subjects were quoted back to him.

As for Bishop Helmsdale himself, his instincts seemed to be to allude in a debonair spirit to the incidents of the past day – to the flowers in Lady Constantine's beds, the date of her house – perhaps with a view of hearing a little more about their owner from Louis, who would very readily have followed the Bishop's lead had the parson allowed him room. But this Mr Torkingham seldom did, and about half-past nine they prepared to separate.

Louis Glanville had risen from the table, and was standing by the window, looking out upon the sky, and privately yawning, the topics discussed having been hardly in his line.

'A fine night,' he said at last.

'I suppose our young astronomer is hard at work now,' said the Bishop, following the direction of Louis's glance towards the clear sky.

'Yes,' said the parson; 'he is very assiduous whenever the nights are good for observation. I have occasionally joined him in his tower, and looked through his telescope with great benefit to my ideas of celestial phenomena. I have not seen what he has been doing lately.'

'Suppose we stroll that way?' said Louis. 'Would you be interested in seeing the observatory, Bishop?'

'I am quite willing to go,' said the Bishop, 'if the distance is not too great. I should not be at all averse to making the acquaintance of so exceptional a young man as this Mr St Cleeve seems to be; and I have never seen the inside of an observatory in my life.'

The intention was no sooner formed than it was carried out, Mr Torkingham leading the way.

CHAPTER TWENTY-SIX

HALF an hour before this time Swithin St Cleeve had been sitting in his cabin at the base of the column. working out some figures from observations taken on preceding nights, with a view to a theory that he had in his head on the motions of certain so-called fixed stars.

The evening being a little chilly a small fire was burning in the stove, and this and the shaded lamp before him lent a remarkably cosy air to the chamber. He was awakened from his reveries by a scratching at the window-pane like that of the point of an ivy leaf, which he knew to be really caused by the tip of his sweetheart-wife's forefinger. He rose and opened the door to admit her, not without astonishment as to how she had been able to get away from her friends.

'Dearest Viv, why, what's the matter?' he said, perceiving that her face, as the lamplight fell on it, was sad, and even stormy.

'I thought I would run across to see you. I have heard something so – so – to your discredit, and I know it can't be true! I know you are constancy itself; but your constancy produces strange effects in people's eyes!'

'Good heavens! Nobody has found us out—'

'No, no – it is not that. You know, Swithin, that I am always sincere, and willing to own if I am to blame in anything. Now will you prove to me that you are the same by owning some fault to me?'

'Yes, dear, indeed; directly I can think of one worth owning.'

'I wonder one does not rush upon your tongue in a moment!'

'I confess that I am sufficiently a Pharisee* not to experience that spontaneity.'

'Swithin, don't speak so affectedly, when you know so well what I mean! Is it nothing to you that, after all our vows for life, you have thought it right to – flirt with a village girl?'

'O Viviette!' interrupted Swithin, taking her hand, which was hot and trembling. 'You who are full of noble and generous feelings, and regard me with devoted tenderness that has never been surpassed by woman, – how can you be so greatly at fault? *I* flirt, Viviette? By thinking that you injure yourself in my eyes. Why, I am so far from doing so that I continually pull myself up for watching you too jealously, as to-day, when I have been dreading the effect upon you of other company in my absence, and thinking that you rather shut the gates against me when you have big-wigs to entertain.'

'Do you, Swithin?' she cried. It was evident that the honest tone of his words was having a great effect in clearing away the clouds. She added with an uncertain smile, 'But how can I believe that, after what was seen to-day? My brother, not knowing in the least that I had an iota of interest in you, told me that he witnessed the signs of an attachment between you and Tabitha Lark in church, this morning.'

'Ah!' cried Swithin, with a burst of laughter. 'Now I know what you mean, and what has caused this misunderstanding! How dear of you, Viviette, to come at once and have it out with me, instead of brooding over it with dark imaginings, and thinking bitter things of me, as many women would have done!' He succinctly told the whole story of his little adventure with Tabitha that morning; and the sky was clear on both sides. 'When shall I be able to claim you,' he added, 'and put an end to all such painful accidents as these?'

She partially sighed. Her perception of what the outside world was made of, latterly somewhat obscured by solitude and her lover's company, had been revived to-day by her entertainment of the Bishop, clergymen, and, more particularly, clergymen's wives; and it did not diminish her sense of the difficulties in Swithin's path to see anew how little was thought of the greatest gifts, mental and spiritual, if they were not backed up by substantial temporalities. However, the pair made the best of their future that circumstances permitted, and the interview was at length drawing to a close when there came, without the slightest forewarning, a smart rat-tat-tat upon the little door.

'O I am lost!' breathed Viviette, seizing his arm. 'Why was I so incautious?'

'It is nobody of consequence,' whispered Swithin assuringly. 'Somebody from my grandmother, probably, to know when I am coming home.'

They were unperceived so far, for the only window which gave light to the hut was screened by a curtain. At that moment they heard the sound of their visitors' voices, and, with a consternation as great as her own, Swithin discerned the tones of Mr Torkingham and the Bishop of Melchester.

'Where shall I get? What shall I do?' said the poor lady, clasping her hands.

Swithin looked around the cabin, and a very little look was required to take in all its resources. At the doorway end, as previously explained, were a table, stove, chair, cupboard, and so on; while the other was completely occupied by a diminutive Arabian bedstead,* hung with curtains of pink-and-white chintz. On the inside of the bed there was a narrow channel, about a foot wide, between it and the wall of the hut. Into this cramped retreat Viviette slid herself, and stood trembling behind the curtains.

By this time the knock had been repeated more loudly, the light through the window-blind unhappily revealing the presence of some inmate. Swithin smoothed the bed a little, threw open the door, and Mr Torkingham introduced his visitors.

The Bishop shook hands with the young man, told him he had known his father, and at Swithin's invitation, weak as it was, entered the cabin, the vicar and Louis Glanville remaining on the threshold, not to inconveniently crowd the limited space within.

Bishop Helmsdale looked benignantly around the apartment, and said, 'Quite a settlement in the backwoods – quite: far enough from the world to afford the votary of science the seclusion he needs, and not so far as to limit his resources. A hermit might apparently live here in as much solitude as in a primeval forest.'

'His lordship has been good enough to express an interest in your studies,' said Mr Torkingham to St Cleeve. 'And we have come to ask you to let us see the observatory.'

'With great pleasure,' stammered Swithin.

'Where is the observatory?' inquired the Bishop, peering round again.

'The staircase is just outside this door,' Swithin answered. 'I am at your lordship's service, and will show you up at once.'

'And this is your little bed, for use when you work late,' said the Bishop.

'Yes; I am afraid it is rather untidy,' Swithin apologized.

'And here are your books,' the Bishop continued, turning to the table and the shaded lamp. 'You take an observation at the top, I presume, and come down here to record your observations.'

The young man explained his precise processes as well as his state of mind would let him, and while he was doing so Mr Torkingham and Louis waited patiently without, looking sometimes into the night, and sometimes through the door at the interlocutors, and listening to their scientific converse. When all had been exhibited here below Swithin lit his lantern, and, inviting his visitors to follow, led the way up the column, experiencing no small sense of relief as soon as he heard the footsteps of all three tramping on the stairs behind him. He knew very well that, once they were inside the spiral, Viviette was out of danger, her knowledge of the locality enabling her to find her way with perfect safety through the plantation, and into the park home.

At the top he uncovered his equatorial, and, for the first time at ease, explained to them its beauties, and revealed by its help the glories of those stars that were eligible for inspection. The Bishop spoke as intelligently as could be expected on a topic not peculiarly his own; but, somehow, he seemed rather more abstracted in manner now than when he had arrived. Swithin thought that perhaps the long clamber up the stairs, coming after a hard day's work, had taken his spontaneity out of him, and Mr Torkingham was afraid that his lordship was getting bored. But this did not appear to be the case; for though he said little he stayed on some time longer, examining the construction of the dome after relinquishing the telescope; while occasionally Swithin caught the eyes of the Bishop fixed hard on him.

'Perhaps he sees some likeness of my father in me,' the young man thought; and the party making ready to leave at this time he conducted them to the bottom of the tower.

Swithin was not prepared for what followed their descent. All were standing at the foot of the staircase. The astronomer, lantern in hand, offered to show them the way out of the plantation, to which Mr Torkingham replied that he knew the way very well, and would not trouble his young friend. He strode forward with the words, and Louis followed him, after waiting a moment and finding that the Bishop would not take the precedence. The latter and Swithin were thus left together for one moment, whereupon the Bishop turned.

'Mr St Cleeve,' he said in a strange voice, 'I should like to speak to you privately, before I leave to-morrow morning. Can you meet me – let me see – in the churchyard, at half-past ten o'clock?'

'O yes, my lord, certainly,' said Swithin. And before he had recovered from his surprise the Bishop had joined the others in the shades of the plantation.

Swithin immediately opened the door of the hut, and scanned the nook behind the bed. As he had expected his bird had flown.

CHAPTER TWENTY-SEVEN

ALL night the astronomer's mind was on the stretch with curiosity as to what the Bishop could wish to say to him. A dozen conjectures entered his brain, to be abandoned in turn as unlikely. That which finally seemed the most plausible was that the Bishop, having become interested in his pursuits, and entertaining friendly recollections of his father, was going to ask if he could do anything to help him on in the profession he had chosen. Should this be the case, thought the suddenly sanguine youth, it would seem like an encouragement to that spirit of firmness which had led him to reject his late uncle's offer because it involved the renunciation of Lady Constantine.

At last he fell asleep; and when he awoke it was so late that the hour was ready to solve what conjecture could not. After a hurried breakfast he paced across the fields, entering the churchyard by the south gate precisely at the appointed minute.

The inclosure was well adapted for a private interview, being bounded by bushes of laurel and alder nearly on all sides. He looked round; the Bishop was not there, nor any living creature save himself. Swithin sat down upon a tombstone to await Bishop Helmsdale's arrival.

While he sat he fancied he could hear voices in conversation not far off, and further attention convinced him that they came from Lady Constantine's lawn, which was divided from the churchyard by a high wall and shrubbery only. As the Bishop still delayed his coming, though the time was nearly eleven, and as the lady whose sweet voice mingled with those heard from the lawn was his personal property, Swithin became exceedingly curious to learn what was going on within that screened promenade. A way of doing so occurred to him. The key was in the church door; he opened it, entered, and ascended to the belfry in the west tower. At the back of this was a window commanding a full view of Viviette's garden front.

The flowers were all in gayest bloom, and the creepers on the walls of the house were bursting into tufts of young green. A broad gravel-walk ran from end to end of the façade, terminating in a large conservatory. In the walk were three people pacing up and down. Lady Constantine's was the central figure, her brother being on one side of her, and on the other a stately form in a corded shovel-hat* of glossy beaver and black breeches. This was the Bishop. Viviette carried over her shoulder a sunshade lined with red, which she twirled idly. They were laughing and chatting gaily, and when the group approached the churchyard many of their remarks entered the silence of the church tower through the ventilator of the window.

The conversation was general, yet interesting enough to Swithin. At length Louis stepped upon the grass and picked up something that had lain there, which turned out to be a bowl: throwing it forward he took a second, and bowled it towards the first, or jack.* The Bishop, who seemed to be in a sprightly mood, followed suit, and bowled one in a curve towards the jack, turning and speaking to Lady Constantine as he concluded the feat. As she had not left the gravelled terrace he raised his voice, so that the words reached Swithin distinctly.

'Do you follow us?' he asked gaily.

'I am not skilful,' she said. 'I always bowl narrow.'

The Bishop meditatively paused.

'This moment reminds one of the scene in *Richard the Second*,'* he said. 'I mean the Duke of York's garden, where the queen and her two ladies play, and the queen says –

"What sport shall we devise here in this garden,
To drive away the heavy thought of care?"

To which her lady answers, "Madam, we'll play at bowls."'

'That's an unfortunate quotation for you,' said Lady Constantine; 'for if I don't forget, the queen declines, saying, "'Twill make me think the world is full of rubs,* and that my fortune runs against the bias."'*

'Then I cite *mal à propos*.* But it is an interesting old game, and might have been played at that very date on this very green.'

The Bishop lazily bowled another, and while he was doing it Viviette's glance rose by accident to the belfry window, where she recognized Swithin's face. Her surprise was only momentary; and waiting till both her companions' backs were turned she smiled and blew him a kiss. In another minute she had another opportunity, and blew him another; afterwards blowing him one a third time.

Her blowings were put a stop to by the Bishop and Louis throwing down the bowls and rejoining her in the path, the house clock at the moment striking half-past eleven.

'This is a fine way of keeping an engagement,' said Swithin to himself. 'I have waited an hour while you indulge in those trifles!'

He fumed, turned, and behold somebody was at his elbow: Tabitha Lark. Swithin started, and said, 'How did you come here, Tabitha?'

'In the course of my calling, Mr St Cleeve,' said the smiling girl. 'I come to practise on the organ. When I entered I saw you up here through the tower arch, and I crept up to see what you were looking at. The Bishop is a striking man, is he not?'

'Yes, rather,' said Swithin.

'I think he is much devoted to Lady Constantine, and I am glad of it. Aren't you?'

'O yes – very,' said Swithin, wondering if Tabitha had seen the tender little salutes between Lady Constantine and himself.

'I don't think she cares much for him,' added Tabitha judicially. 'Or, even if she does, she could be got away from him in no time by a younger man.'

'Pooh, that's nothing,' said Swithin impatiently.

Tabitha then remarked that her blower had not come to time, and that she must go to look for him; upon which she descended the stairs, and left Swithin again alone.

A few minutes later the Bishop suddenly looked at his watch, Lady Constantine having withdrawn towards the house. Apparently apologizing to Louis the Bishop came down the terrace, and through the door into the churchyard. Swithin hastened downstairs and joined him in the path under the sunny wall of the aisle.

Their glances met, and it was with some consternation that Swithin beheld the change that a few short minutes had wrought in that episcopal countenance. On the lawn with Lady Constantine the rays of an almost perpetual smile had brightened his dark aspect like flowers in a shady place: now the smile was gone as completely as yesterday; the lines of his face were firm; his dark eyes and whiskers were overspread with gravity; and as he gazed upon Swithin from the repose of his stable figure it was like an evangelized King of Spades come to have it out with the Knave of Hearts.

To return for a moment to Louis Glanville. He had been somewhat struck with the abruptness of the Bishop's departure, and more particularly by the circumstance that he had gone away by the private door into the churchyard instead of by the regular exit on the other side. True, great men were known to suffer from absence of mind, and Bishop Helmsdale, having a dim sense that he had entered by that door yesterday, might have unconsciously turned thitherward now. Louis, upon the whole, thought little of the matter, and being now left quite alone on the lawn, he seated himself in an arbour and began smoking.

The arbour was situated against the churchyard wall. The atmosphere was as still as the air of a hot-house; only fourteen inches of brickwork divided Louis from the scene of the Bishop's interview with St Cleeve, and as voices on the lawn had been audible to Swithin in the churchyard, voices in the churchyard could be heard without difficulty from that close corner of the lawn. No sooner had Louis lit a cigar than the dialogue began.

'Ah, you are here, St Cleeve,' said the Bishop gruffly, hardly replying to Swithin's good morning. 'I fear I am a little late. Well, my request to you to meet me may have seemed somewhat unusual, seeing that we were strangers till a few hours ago.'

'I don't mind that, if your lordship wishes to see me.'

'I thought it best to see you regarding your confirmation yesterday; and my reason for taking a more active step with you than I should otherwise have done is that I have some interest in you through having known your father when we were undergraduates. His rooms were on the same staircase with mine at All Angels, and we were friendly till time and affairs separated us even more completely than usually happens. However, about your presenting yourself for confirmation.' (The Bishop's voice grew stern.) 'If I had known yesterday morning what I knew twelve hours later, I wouldn't have confirmed you at all.'

'Indeed, my lord!'

'Yes, I say it, and I mean it. I visited your observatory last night.'

'You did, my lord.'

'In inspecting it I noticed something which I may truly describe as extraordinary. I have had young men present themselves to me who turned out to be notoriously unfit, either from giddiness, from being profane or intemperate, or from some bad quality or other. But I never remember a case which equalled the cool culpability of this. While infringing the first principles of social decorum you might at least have respected the ordinance sufficiently to have stayed away from it altogether. Now I have sent for you here to see if a last entreaty and a direct appeal to your sense of manly uprightness will have any effect in inducing you to change your course of life.'

The voice of Swithin in his next remark showed how tremendously this attack of the Bishop had told upon his feelings. Louis, of course, did not know the reason why the words should have affected him precisely as they did; to any one in the secret the double embarrassment arising from misapprehended ethics and inability to set matters right, because his word of secrecy to another was inviolable, would have accounted for the young man's emotion sufficiently well.

'I am very sorry your lordship should have seen anything objectionable,' said Swithin. 'May I ask what it was?'

'You know what it was. Something in your chamber, which forced me to the above conclusions. I disguised my feelings of sorrow at the time for obvious reasons, but I never in my whole life was so shocked!'

'At what, my lord?'

'At what I saw.'

'Pardon me, Bishop Helmsdale, but you said just now that we are strangers; so what you saw in my cabin concerns me only.'

'There I contradict you. Twenty-four hours ago that remark would have been plausible enough; but by presenting yourself for confirmation at my hands you invited my investigation into your principles.'

Swithin sighed. 'I admit it,' he said.

'And what do I find them?'

'You say reprehensible. But you might at least let me hear the proof!'

'I can do more, sir. I can let you see it!'

There was a pause. Louis Glanville was so highly interested that he stood upon the seat of the arbour, and looked through the leafage over the wall. The Bishop had produced an article from his pocket.

'What is it?' said Swithin, laboriously scrutinizing the thing as if he did not know what it was full well.

'Why, don't you see?' said the Bishop, holding it out between his finger and thumb in Swithin's face. 'A bracelet, – a coral bracelet. I found the wanton object on the bed in your cabin! And of the sex of the owner there can be no doubt. More than that, she was concealed behind the curtains, for I saw them move.' In the decision of his opinion the Bishop threw the coral bracelet down on a tombstone.

'Nobody was in my room, my lord, who had not a perfect right to be there,' said the younger man.

'Well, well, that's a matter of assertion. Now don't get into a passion, and say to me in your haste what you'll repent of saying afterwards.'

'I am not in a passion, I assure your lordship. I am too sad for passion.'

'Very well; that's a hopeful sign. Now I would ask you, as one man of another, do you think that to come to me, the Bishop of this large and important diocese, as you came yesterday, and pretend to be something that you are not, is quite upright conduct, leave alone religious? Think it over. We may never meet again. But bear in mind what your Bishop and spiritual head says to you, and see if you cannot mend before it is too late.'

Swithin was meek as Moses,* but he tried to appear sturdy. 'My lord, I am in a difficult position,' he said mournfully; 'how difficult, nobody but myself can tell. I cannot explain; there are insuperable reasons against it. But will you take my word of assurance that I am not so bad as I seem? Some day I will prove it. Till then I only ask you to suspend your judgment on me.'

The Bishop shook his head incredulously and went towards the vicarage, as if he had lost his hearing. Swithin followed him with his eyes, and Louis followed the direction of Swithin's. Before the Bishop had reached the vicarage entrance Lady Constantine crossed in front of him. She had a basket on her arm, and was, in fact, going to visit some of the poorer cottages. Who could believe the Bishop now to be the same man that he had been a moment before? The darkness left his face as if he had come out of a cave; his look was all sweetness, and shine, and gaiety, as he again greeted Viviette.

CHAPTER TWENTY-EIGHT

THE conversation which arose between the Bishop and Lady Constantine was of that lively and reproductive kind which cannot be ended during any reasonable halt of two people going in opposite directions. He turned, and walked with her along the laurel-screened lane that bordered the churchyard, till their voices died away in the distance. Swithin then aroused himself from his thoughtful regard of them, and went out of the churchyard by another gate.

Seeing himself now to be left alone on the scene, Louis Glanville descended from his post of observation in the arbour. He came through the private doorway, and on to that spot among the graves where the Bishop and St Cleeve had conversed. On the tombstone still lay the coral bracelet which Dr Helmsdale had flung down there in his indignation; for the agitated, introspective mood into which Swithin had been thrown had banished from his mind all thought of securing the trinket and putting it in his pocket.

Louis picked up the little red scandal-breeding thing, and while walking on with it in his hand he observed Tabitha Lark approaching the church, in company with the young blower whom she had gone in search of to inspire her organ-practising within. Louis immediately put together, with that rare diplomatic keenness of which he was proud, the little scene he had witnessed between Tabitha and Swithin during the confirmation, and the Bishop's stern statement as to where he had found the bracelet. He had no longer any doubt that it belonged to her.

'Poor girl!' he said to himself, and sang in an undertone –

> 'Tra deri, dera,
> L'histoire n'est pas nouvelle!'*

When she drew nearer Louis called her by name. She sent the boy into the church, and came forward, blushing at having been called by so fine a gentleman. Louis held out the bracelet.

'Here is something I have found, or somebody else has found,' he said to her. 'I won't state where. Put it away, and say no more about it. I will not mention it either. Now go on into the church where you are going, and may Heaven have mercy on your soul, my dear.'

'Thank you, sir,' said Tabitha, with some perplexity, yet inclined to be pleased, and only recognizing in the situation the fact that Lady Constantine's humorous brother was making her a present.

'You are much obliged to me?'

'O yes!'

'Well, Miss Lark, I've discovered a secret, you see.'

'What may that be, Mr Glanville?'

'That you are in love.'

'I don't admit it, sir. Who told you so?'

'Nobody. Only I put two and two together. Now take my advice. Beware of lovers! They are a bad lot, and bring young women to tears.'

'Some do, I dare say. But some don't.'

'And you think that in your particular case the latter alternative will hold good? We generally think we shall be lucky ourselves, though all the world before us, in the same situation, have been otherwise.'

'O yes, or we should die outright of despair.'

'Well, I don't think you will be lucky in your case.'

'Please how do you know so much, since my case has not yet arrived?' asked Tabitha, tossing her head a little disdainfully, but less than she might have done if he had not obtained a charter for his discourse by giving her the bracelet.

'Fie, Tabitha!'

'I tell you it has not arrived!' she said, with some anger. 'I have not got a lover, and everybody knows I haven't, and it's an insinuating thing for you to say so!'

Louis laughed, thinking how natural it was that a girl should so emphatically deny circumstances that would not bear curious inquiry.

'Why, of course I meant myself,' he said soothingly. 'So, then, you will not accept me?'

'I didn't know you meant yourself,' she replied. 'But I won't accept you. And I think you ought not to jest on such subjects.'

'Well, perhaps not. However, don't let the Bishop see your

bracelet, and all will be well. But mind, lovers are deceivers.'

Tabitha laughed, and they parted, the girl entering the church. She had been feeling almost certain that, having accidentally found the bracelet somewhere, he had presented it in a whim to her as the first girl he met. Yet now she began to have momentary doubts whether he had not been labouring under a mistake, and had imagined her to be the owner. The bracelet was not valuable; it was, in fact, a mere toy, – the pair of which this was one being a little present made to Lady Constantine by Swithin on the day of their marriage; and she had not worn them with sufficient frequency out of doors for Tabitha to recognize either as positively her ladyship's. But when, out of sight of the blower, the girl momentarily tried it on in a corner by the organ, it seemed to her that the ornament was possibly Lady Constantine's. Now that the pink beads shone before her eyes on her own arm she remembered having seen a bracelet with just such an effect gracing the wrist of Lady Constantine upon one occasion. A temporary self-surrender to the sophism that if Mr Louis Glanville chose to give away anything belonging to his sister, she, Tabitha, had a right to take it without question, was soon checked by a resolve to carry the tempting strings of coral to her ladyship that evening, and inquire the truth about them. This decided on she slipped the bracelet into her pocket, and played her voluntaries with a light heart.

Bishop Helmsdale did not tear himself away from Welland till about two o'clock that afternoon, which was three hours later than he had intended to leave. It was with a feeling of relief that Swithin, looking from the top of the tower, saw the carriage drive out from the vicarage into the turnpike road,* and whirl the right reverend gentleman again towards Warborne. The coast being now clear of him Swithin meditated how to see Viviette, and explain what had happened. With this in view he waited where he was till evening came on.

Meanwhile Lady Constantine and her brother dined by themselves at Welland House. They had not met since the morning, and as soon as they were left alone Louis said, 'You have done very well so far; but you might have been a little warmer.'

'Done well?' she asked, with surprise.

'Yes, with the Bishop. The difficult question is how to follow up our advantage. How are you to keep yourself in sight of him?'

'Heavens, Louis! You don't seriously mean that the Bishop of Melchester has any feelings for me other than friendly?'

'Viviette, this is affectation. You know he has as well as I do.'

She sighed. 'Yes,' she said. 'I own I had a suspicion of the same thing. What a misfortune!'

'A misfortune? Surely the world is turned upside down! You will drive me to despair about our future if you see things so awry. Exert yourself to do something, so as to make of this accident a stepping-stone to higher things.* The gentleman will give us the slip if we don't pursue the friendship at once.'

'I cannot have you talk like this,' she cried impatiently. 'I have no more thought of the Bishop than I have of the Pope. I would much rather not have had him here to lunch at all. You said it would be necessary to do it, and an opportunity, and I thought it my duty to show some hospitality when he was coming so near, Mr Torkingham's house being so small. But of course I understood that the opportunity would be one for you in getting to know him, your prospects being so indefinite at present; not one for me.'

'If you don't follow up this chance of being spiritual queen of Melchester, you will never have another of being anything. Mind this, Viviette: you are not so young as you were. You are getting on to be a middle-aged woman, and your black hair is precisely of the sort which time quickly turns grey. You must make up your mind to grizzled* bachelors or widowers. Young marriageable men won't look at you; or if they do just now, in a year or two more they'll despise you as an antiquated party.'

Lady Constantine perceptibly paled. 'Young men what?' she asked. 'Say that again.'

'I said it was no use to think of young men; they won't look at you much longer; or if they do, it will be to look away again very quickly.'

'You imply that if I were to marry a man younger than myself he would speedily acquire a contempt for me? How much younger must a man be than his wife – to get that feeling for her?' She was resting her elbow on the chair as she faintly spoke the words, and covered her eyes with her hand.

'An exceedingly small number of years,' said Louis drily. 'Now the Bishop is at least twenty years older than you, and on that account, no less than on others, is an excellent match. You would be head of the church in this diocese: what more can you require after these years of miserable obscurity? In addition, you would escape that minor thorn in the flesh of bishops' wives, of being only "Mrs" while their husbands are peers.'

She was not listening; his previous observation still detained her thoughts.

'Louis,' she said, 'in the case of a woman marrying a man much younger than herself, does he get to dislike her, even if there has been a social advantage to him in the union?'

'Yes, – not a whit less. Ask any person of experience. But what of that? Let's talk of our own affairs. You say you have no thought of the Bishop. And yet if he had stayed here another day or two he would have proposed to you straight off.'

'Seriously, Louis, I could not accept him.'

'Why not?'

'I don't love him.'

'Oh, oh, I like those words!' cried Louis, throwing himself back in his chair and looking at the ceiling in satirical enjoyment. 'A woman who at two-and-twenty married for convenience, at thirty talks of not marrying without love; the rule of inverse, that is, in which more requires less, and less requires more. As your only brother, older than yourself, and more experienced, I insist that you encourage the Bishop.'

'Don't quarrel with me, Louis!' she said piteously. 'We don't know that he thinks anything of me, – we only guess.'

'I know it, – and you shall hear how I know. I am of a curious and conjectural nature, as you are aware. Last night, when everybody had gone to bed, I stepped out for a five minutes' smoke on the lawn, and walked down to where you get near the vicarage windows. While I was there in the dark one of them opened, and Bishop Helmsdale leant out. The illuminated oblong of your window shone him full in the face between the trees, and presently your shadow crossed it. He waved his hand, and murmured some tender words, though what they were exactly I could not hear.'

'What a vague, imaginary story, – as if he could know my

shadow! Besides, a man of the Bishop's dignity wouldn't have done such a thing. When I knew him as a younger man he was not at all romantic, and he's not likely to have grown so now.'

'That's just what he is likely to have done. No lover is so extreme a specimen of the species as an old lover. Come, Viviette, no more of this fencing.* I have entered into the project heart and soul – so much that I have postponed my departure till the matter is well under way.'

'Louis – my dear Louis – you will bring me into some disagreeable position!' said she, clasping her hands. 'I do entreat you not to interfere or do anything rash about me. The step is impossible. I have something to tell you some day. I must live on, and endure—'

'Everything except this penury,' replied Louis, unmoved. 'Come, I have begun the campaign by inviting Bishop Helmsdale, and I'll take the responsibility of carrying it on. All I ask of you is not to make a ninny of yourself. Come, give me your promise!'

'No, I cannot, – I don't know how to! I only know one thing, – that I am in no hurry—'

'"No hurry" be hanged! Agree, like a good sister, to charm the Bishop.'

'I must consider!' she replied, with perturbed evasiveness.

It being a fine evening Louis went out of the house to enjoy his cigar in the shrubbery. On reaching his favourite seat he found he had left his cigar-case behind him; he immediately returned for it. When he approached the window by which he had emerged he saw Swithin St Cleeve standing there in the dusk, talking to Viviette inside.

St Cleeve's back was towards Louis, but, whether at a signal from her or by accident, he quickly turned and recognized Glanville; whereupon raising his hat to Lady Constantine the young man passed along the terrace-walk and out by the churchyard door.

Louis rejoined his sister. 'I didn't know you allowed your lawn to be a public thoroughfare for the parish,' he said.

'I am not exclusive, especially since I have been so poor,' replied she.

'Then do you let everybody pass this way, or only that illustrious youth because he is so good-looking?'

'I have no strict rule in the case. Mr St Cleeve is an acquaintance of mine, and he can certainly come here if he chooses.' Her colour rose somewhat, and she spoke warmly.

Louis was too cautious a bird to reveal to her what had suddenly dawned upon his mind – that his sister, in common with the (to his thinking) unhappy Tabitha Lark, had been foolish enough to get interested in this phenomenon of the parish, this scientific Adonis. But he resolved to cure at once her tender feeling, if it existed, by letting out a secret which would inflame her dignity against the weakness.

'A good-looking young man,' he said, with his eyes where Swithin had vanished. 'But not so good as he looks. In fact a regular young sinner.'

'What do you mean?'

'Oh, only a little feature I discovered in St Cleeve's history. But I suppose he has a right to sow his wild oats as well as other young men.'

'Tell me what you allude to, – do, Louis.'

'It is hardly fit that I should. However, the case is amusing enough. I was sitting in the arbour to-day, and was an unwilling listener to the oddest interview I ever heard of. Our friend the Bishop discovered, when we visited the observatory last night, that our astronomer was not alone in his seclusion. A lady shared his romantic cabin with him; and finding this, the Bishop naturally enough felt that the ordinance of confirmation had been profaned. So his lordship sent for Master Swithin this morning, and meeting him in the churchyard read him such an excommunicating* lecture as I warrant he won't forget in his lifetime. Ha-ha-ha! 'Twas very good, – very.'

He watched her face narrowly while he spoke with such seeming carelessness. Instead of the agitation of jealousy that he had expected to be aroused by this hint of another woman in the case, there was a curious expression, more like embarrassment than anything else which might have been fairly attributed to the subject. 'Can it be that I am mistaken?' he asked himself.

The possibility that he might be mistaken restored Louis to good-humour, and lights having been brought he sat with his sister for some time, talking with purpose of Swithin's low rank on one side, and the sordid struggles that might be in store for him. St Cleeve being in the uphappy case of deriving his existence through two channels of society, it resulted that he seemed to belong to either this or that according to the altitude of the beholder. Louis threw the light entirely on Swithin's agricultural side, bringing out old Mrs Martin and her connexions and her ways of life with luminous distinctness, till Lady Constantine became greatly depressed. She, in her hopefulness, had almost forgotten, latterly, that the bucolic element, so incisively represented by Messrs Hezzy Biles, Haymoss Fry, Sammy Blore, and the rest entered into his condition at all; to her he had been the son of his academic father alone.

But she would not reveal the depression to which she had been subjected by this resuscitation of the homely half of poor Swithin, presently putting an end to the subject by walking hither and thither about the room.

'What have you lost?' said Louis, observing her movements.

'Nothing of consequence,—a bracelet.'

'Coral?' he inquired calmly.

'Yes. How did you know it was coral? You have never seen it, have you?'

He was about to make answer; but the amazed enlightenment which her announcement had produced in him through knowing where the Bishop had found such an article, led him to reconsider himself. Then, like an astute man, by no means sure of the dimensions of the intrigue he might be uncovering, he said carelessly, 'I found such a one in the churchyard to-day. But I thought it appeared to be of no great rarity, and I gave it to one of the village girls who were passing by.'

'Did she take it? Who was she?' said the unsuspecting Viviette.

'Really, I don't remember. I suppose it is of no consequence?'

'O no; its value is nothing, comparatively. It was only one of a pair such as young girls wear.' Lady Constantine could not add that, in spite of this, she herself valued it as having been Swithin's present, and the best he could afford.

Panic-struck by his ruminations, although revealing nothing by his manner, Louis soon after went up to his room, professedly to write letters. He gave vent to a low whistle when he was out of hearing. He of course remembered perfectly well to whom he had given the corals, and resolved to seek out Tabitha the next morning to ascertain whether she could possibly have owned such a trinket as well as his sister, – which at present he very greatly doubted, though fervently hoping that she might.

CHAPTER TWENTY-NINE

THE effect upon Swithin of the interview with the Bishop had been a very marked one. He felt that he had good ground for resenting that dignitary's tone in haughtily assuming that all must be sinful which at the first blush appeared to be so, and in narrowly refusing a young man the benefit of a single doubt. Swithin's assurance that he would be able to explain all some day had been taken in contemptuous incredulity.

'He may be as virtuous as his prototype Timothy;* but he's an opinionated old fogey all the same,' said St Cleeve petulantly.

Yet, on the other hand, Swithin's nature was so fresh and ingenuous, notwithstanding that recent affairs had somewhat denaturalized him, that for a man in the Bishop's position to think him immoral was almost as overwhelming as if he had actually been so, and at moments he could scarcely bear existence under so gross a suspicion. What was his union with Lady Constantine worth to him when, by reason of it, he was thought a reprobate by almost the only man who had professed to take an interest in him?

Certainly, by contrast with his air-built image of himself as a worthy astronomer, received by all the world, and the envied husband of Viviette, the present imputation was humiliating. The glorious light of this tender and refined passion seemed to have become debased to burlesque hues by pure accident, and his æsthetic no less than his ethic taste was offended by such an anti-climax. He who had soared amid the remotest grandeurs of nature had been taken to task on a rudimentary question of morals, which had never been a question with him at all. This was what the exigencies of an awkward attachment had brought him to; but he blamed the circumstances, and not for one moment Lady Constantine.

Having now set his heart against a longer concealment he was disposed to think that an excellent way of beginning a revelation of their marriage would be by writing a confidential letter to the Bishop, detailing the whole case. But it was impossible to do this on his own responsibility. He still recognized the understanding entered into with Viviette, before the marriage, to be as binding as ever, – that the initiative in disclosing their union should come from her. Yet he hardly doubted that she would take that initiative when he told her of his extraordinary reprimand in the churchyard.

This was what he had come to do when Louis saw him standing at the window. But before he had said half-a-dozen words to Viviette she motioned him to go on, which he mechanically did, ere he could sufficiently collect his thoughts on its advisability or otherwise. He did not, however, go far. While Louis and his sister were discussing him in the drawing-room he lingered musing in the churchyard, hoping that she might be able to escape and join him in the consultation he so earnestly desired.

She at last found opportunity to do this. As soon as Louis had left the room and shut himself in upstairs she ran out by the window in the direction Swithin had taken. When her footsteps began crunching on the gravel he came forward from the churchyard door.

They embraced each other in haste, and then, in a few short panting words, she explained to him that her brother had heard and witnessed the interview on that spot between himself and the Bishop, and had told her the substance of the Bishop's accusation, not knowing she was the woman in the cabin.

'And what I cannot understand is this,' she added; 'how did the Bishop discover that the person behind the bed-curtains was a woman and not a man?'

Swithin explained that the Bishop had found the bracelet on the bed, and had brought it to him in the churchyard.

'O Swithin, what do you say? Found the coral bracelet? What did you do with it?'

Swithin clapped his hand to his pocket.

'Dear me! I recollect – I left it where it lay on Reuben Heath's tombstone.'

'O my dear, dear Swithin!' she cried miserably. 'You have compromised me by your forgetfulness. I have claimed the article as mine. My brother did not tell me that the Bishop brought it from the cabin. What can I, can I do, that neither the Bishop nor my brother may conclude *I* was the woman there?'

'But if we announce our marriage—'

'Even as your wife, the position was too undignified – too I don't know what – for me ever to admit that I was there! Right or wrong, I must declare the bracelet was not mine. Such an escapade – why, it would make me ridiculous in the county; and anything rather than that!'

'I was in hope that you would agree to let our marriage be known,' said Swithin, with some disappointment. 'I thought that these circumstances would make the reason for doing so doubly strong.'

'Yes. But there are, alas, reasons against it still stronger! Let me have my way.'

'Certainly, dearest. I promised that before you agreed to be mine. My reputation – what is it! Perhaps I shall be dead and forgotten before the next Transit of Venus!'*

She soothed him tenderly, but could not tell him why she felt the reasons against any announcement as yet to be stronger than those in favour of it. How could she, when her feeling had been cautiously fed and developed by her brother Louis's unvarnished exhibition of Swithin's material position in the eyes of the world? – that of a young man, the scion of a family of farmers recently her tenants, living at the homestead with his grandmother, Mrs Martin.

To soften her refusal she said in declaring it, 'One concession, Swithin, I certainly will make. I will see you oftener. I will come to the cabin and tower frequently; and will contrive, too, that you come to the house occasionally. During the last winter we passed whole weeks without meeting; don't let us allow that to happen again.'

'Very well, dearest,' said Swithin good-humouredly. 'I don't care so terribly much for the old man's opinion of me, after all. For the present, then, let things be as they are.'

Nevertheless, the youth felt her refusal more than he owned; but the unequal temperament of Swithin's age, so soon depressed on his own account, was also soon to recover on hers, and it was with almost a child's forgetfulness of the past that he took her view of the case.

When he was gone she hastily re-entered the house. Her brother had not reappeared from upstairs; but she was informed that Tabitha Lark was waiting to see her, if her ladyship would pardon the said Tabitha for coming so late. Lady Constantine made no objection, and saw the young girl at once.

When Lady Constantine entered the waiting-room, behold, in Tabitha's outstretched hand lay the coral ornament which had been causing Viviette so much anxiety.

'I guessed, on second thoughts, that it was yours, my lady,' said Tabitha, with rather a frightened face; 'and so I have brought it back.'

'But how did you come by it, Tabitha?'

'Mr Glanville gave it to me; he must have thought it was mine. I took it, fancying at the moment that he handed it to me because I happened to come by first after he had found it.'

Lady Constantine saw how the situation might be improved so as to effect her deliverance from this troublesome little web of evidence.

'O, you can keep it,' she said brightly. 'It was very good of you to bring it back. But keep it for your very own. Take Mr Glanville at his word, and *don't explain.* And, Tabitha, divide the strands into two bracelets; there are enough of them to make a pair.'

The next morning, in pursuance of his resolution, Louis wandered round the grounds till he saw the girl for whom he was waiting enter the church. He accosted her over the wall. But, puzzling to view, a coral bracelet blushed on each of her young arms, for she had promptly carried out the suggestion of Lady Constantine.

'You are wearing it, I see, Tabitha, with the other,' he murmured. 'Then you mean to keep it?'

'Of course, I mean to keep what's mine.'

'You are sure it is not Lady Constantine's? I find she has one like it.'

'Quite sure. But if you doubt me you had better take it to her, sir, and ask her,' said the saucy girl.

'O no; that's not necessary,' replied Louis, considerably shaken in his convictions.

When Louis met his sister, a short time after, he did not catch her, as he had intended to do, by saying suddenly, 'I have found your bracelet. I know who has got it.'

'You cannot have found it,' she replied quietly, 'for I have discovered that it was never lost,' and stretching out both her hands she revealed one on each, Viviette having performed the same operation with her remaining bracelet that she had advised Tabitha to do with the other.

Louis was mystified, but by no means convinced. In spite of this attempt to hoodwink him his mind returned to the subject every hour of the day. There was no doubt that either Tabitha or Viviette had been with Swithin in the cabin. He recapitulated every case that had occurred during his visit to Welland in which his sister's manner had been of a colour to justify the suspicion that it was she. There was that strange incident in the corridor, when she had screamed at what she described to be a shadowy resemblance to her late husband; how very improbable that this fancy should have been the only cause of her agitation! Then he had noticed, during Swithin's confirmation, a blush upon her cheek when he passed her on his way to the Bishop, and the fervour in her glance during the few moments of the imposition of hands. Then he suddenly recalled the night at the railway station, when the accident with the whip took place, and how, when he reached Welland House an hour later, he had found no Viviette there. Running thus from incident to incident he increased his suspicions without being able to cull from the circumstances anything amounting to evidence; but evidence he now determined to acquire without saying a word to any one.

His plan was of a cruel kind: to set a trap into which the pair would blindly walk if any secret understanding existed between them of the nature he suspected.

CHAPTER THIRTY

LOUIS began his stratagem by calling at the tower one afternoon, as if on the impulse of the moment.

After a friendly chat with Swithin, whom he found there (having watched him enter), Louis invited the young man to dine the same evening at the House, that he might have an opportunity of showing him some interesting old scientific works in folio,* which, according to Louis's account, he had stumbled on in the library. Louis set no great bait for St Cleeve in this statement, for old science was not old art which, having perfected itself, has died and left its secret hidden in its remains. But Swithin was a responsive fellow, and readily agreed to come; being, moreover, always glad of a chance of meeting Viviette *en famille*.* He hoped to tell her of a scheme that had lately suggested itself to him as likely to benefit them both: that he should go away for a while, and endeavour to raise sufficient funds to visit the great observatories of Europe, with an eye to a post in one of them. Hitherto the only bar to the plan had been the exceeding narrowness of his income, which, though sufficient for his present life, was absolutely inadequate to the requirements of a travelling astronomer.

Meanwhile Louis Glanville had returned to the House and told his sister in the most innocent manner that he had been in the company of St Cleeve that afternoon, getting a few wrinkles* on astronomy; that they had grown so friendly over the fascinating subject as to leave him no alternative but to invite St Cleeve to dine at Welland the same evening, with a view to certain researches in the library afterwards.

'I could quite make allowances for any youthful errors into which he may have been betrayed,' Louis continued sententiously, 'since, for a scientist, he is really admirable. No doubt the Bishop's caution will not be lost upon him; and as for his birth and connexions – those he can't help.'

Lady Constantine showed such alacrity in adopting the idea of having Swithin to dinner, and she ignored his 'youthful errors' so completely, as almost to betray herself. In fulfilment of her promise to see him oftener she had been intending to run across to Swithin on that identical evening. Now the trouble would be saved in a very delightful way by the exercise of a little hospitality which Viviette herself would not have dared to suggest.

Dinner-time came and with it Swithin, exhibiting rather a blushing and nervous manner that was, unfortunately, more likely to betray their cause than was Viviette's own more practised bearing. Throughout the meal Louis sat like a spider in the corner of his web, observing them narrowly, and at moments flinging out an artful thread here and there, with a view to their entanglement. But they underwent the ordeal marvellously well. Perhaps the actual tie between them, through being so much closer and of so much more practical a nature than even their critic supposed it, was in itself a protection against their exhibiting that ultra-reciprocity of manner which, if they had been merely lovers, might have betrayed them.

After dinner the trio duly adjourned to the library as had been planned, and the volumes were brought forth by Louis with the zest of a bibliophilist.* Swithin had seen most of them before, and thought but little of them; but the pleasure of staying in the house made him welcome any reason for doing so, and he willingly looked at whatever was put before him, from Bertius's Ptolemy* to Rees's Cyclopædia.*

The evening thus passed away, and it began to grow late. Swithin who, among other things, had planned to go to Greenwich next day to view the Royal Observatory, would every now and then start up and prepare to leave for home, when Glanville would unearth some other volume and so detain him yet another half-hour.

'By George!' he said, looking at the clock when Swithin was at last really about to depart. 'I didn't know it was so late. Why not stay here to-night, St Cleeve? It is very dark, and the way to your place is an awkward cross-cut over the fields.'

'It would not inconvenience us at all, Mr St Cleeve, if you would care to stay,' said Lady Constantine.

'I am afraid – the fact is, I wanted to take an observation at twenty minutes past two,' began Swithin.

'O, now, never mind your observation,' said Louis. 'That's only an excuse. Do that to-morrow night. Now you will stay. It is settled. Viviette, say he must stay, and we'll have another hour of these charming intellectual researches.'

Viviette obeyed with delightful ease. 'Do stay, Mr St Cleeve!' she said sweetly.

'Well, in truth I can do without the observation,' replied the young man as he gave way. 'It is not of the greatest consequence.'

Thus it was arranged; but the researches among the tomes were not prolonged to the extent that Louis had suggested. In three-quarters of an hour from that time they had all retired to their respective rooms; Lady Constantine's being on one side of the west corridor, Swithin's opposite, and Louis's at the further end.

Had a person followed Louis when he withdrew, that watcher would have discovered, on peeping through the key-hole of his door, that he was engaged in one of the oddest of occupations for such a man, – sweeping down from the ceiling, by means of a walking-cane, a long cobweb which lingered on high in the corner. Keeping it stretched upon the cane he gently opened the door, and set the candle in such a position on the mat that the light shone down the corridor. Thus guided by its rays he passed out slipperless, till he reached the door of St Cleeve's room, where he applied the dangling spider's thread in such a manner that it stretched across like a tight-rope from jamb* to jamb, barring, in its fragile way, entrance and egress. The operation completed he retired again, and, extinguishing his light, went through his bedroom window out upon the flat roof of the portico to which it gave access.

Here Louis made himself comfortable in his chair and smoking-cap,* enjoying the fragrance of a cigar for something like half-an-hour. His position commanded a view of the two windows of Lady Constantine's room, and from these a dim light shone continuously. Having the window partly open at his back, and the door of his room also scarcely closed, his ear retained a fair command of any noises that might be made.

In due time faint movements became audible; whereupon, returning to his room, he re-entered the corridor and listened intently. All was silent again, and darkness reigned from end to end. Glanville, however, groped his way along the passage till he again reached Swithin's door, where he examined, by the light of a wax-match he had brought, the condition of the spider's thread. It was gone; somebody had carried it off bodily, as Samson carried off the pin and the web.* In other words, a person had passed through the door.

Still holding the faint wax-light in his hand Louis turned to the door of Lady Constantine's chamber, where he observed first that, though it was pushed together so as to appear fastened to cursory view, the door was not really closed by about a quarter of an inch. He dropped his light and extinguished it with his foot. Listening he heard a voice within – Viviette's voice, in a subdued murmur, though speaking earnestly.

Without any hesitation Louis then returned to Swithin's door, opened it, and walked in. The starlight from without was sufficient, now that his eyes had become accustomed to the darkness, to reveal that the room was unoccupied, and that nothing therein had been disturbed.

With a heavy tread Louis came forth, walked loudly across the corridor, knocked at Lady Constantine's door, and called 'Viviette!'

She heard him instantly, replying 'Yes' in startled tones. Immediately afterwards she opened her door, and confronted him in her dressing-gown, with a light in her hand. 'What is the matter, Louis?' she said.

'I am greatly alarmed. Our visitor is missing.'

'Missing? What, Mr St Cleeve?'

'Yes. I was sitting up to finish a cigar, when I thought I heard a noise in this direction. On coming to his room I find he is not there.'

'Good Heaven! I wonder what has happened!' she exclaimed, in apparently intense alarm.

'I wonder,' said Glanville grimly.

'Suppose he is a somnambulist! If so, he may have gone out and broken his neck. I have never heard that he is one, but they say that sleeping in strange places disturbs the minds of people who are given to that sort of thing, and provokes them to it.'

'Unfortunately for your theory his bed has not been touched.'

'O, what then can it be?'

Her brother looked her full in the face. 'Viviette!' he said sternly.

She seemed puzzled. 'Well?' she replied, in simple tones.

'I heard voices in your room,' he continued.

'Voices?'

'A voice, – yours.'

'Yes, you may have done so. It was mine.'

'A listener is required for a speaker.'

'True, Louis.'

'Well, to whom were you speaking?'

'To God.'

'Viviette! I am ashamed of you.'

'I was saying my prayers.'

'Prayers – to God! To St Swithin,* rather!'

'What do you mean, Louis?' she asked, flushing up warm, and drawing back from him. 'It was a form of prayer I use, particularly when I am in trouble. It was recommended to me by the Bishop, and Mr Torkingham commends it very highly.'

'On your honour, if you have any,' he said bitterly, 'whom have you there in your room?'

'No human being.'

'Flatly, I don't believe you.'

She gave a dignified little bow, and, waving her hand into the apartment, said, 'Very well; then search and see.'

Louis entered, and glanced round the room, behind the curtains, under the bed, out of the window – a view from which showed that escape thence would have been impossible, – everywhere, in short, capable or incapable of affording a retreat to humanity; but discovered nobody. All he observed was that a light stood on the low table by her bedside; that on the bed lay an open Prayer-Book, the counterpane being unpressed, except into a little pit beside the Prayer-Book, apparently where her head had rested in kneeling.

'But where is St Cleeve?' he said, turning in bewilderment from these evidences of innocent devotion.

'Where can he be?' she chimed in, with real distress. 'I should so much like to know. Look about for him. I am quite uneasy!'

'I will, on one condition: that you own that you love him.'

'Why should you force me to that?' she murmured. 'It would be no such wonder if I did.'

'Come, you do.'

'Well, I do.'

'Now I'll look for him.'

Louis took a light and turned away, astonished that she had not indignantly resented his intrusion and the nature of his questioning.

At this moment a slight noise was heard on the staircase, and they could see a figure rising step by step, and coming forward against the long lights of the staircase window. It was Swithin, in his ordinary dress, and carrying his boots in his hand. When he beheld them standing there so motionless, he looked rather disconcerted, but came on towards his room.

Lady Constantine was too agitated to speak, but Louis said, 'I am glad to see you again. Hearing a noise a few minutes ago I came out to learn what it could be. I found you absent, and we have been very much alarmed.'

'I am very sorry,' said Swithin, with contrition. 'I owe you a hundred apologies: but the truth is that on entering my bedroom I found the sky remarkably clear, and though I told you that the observation I was to make was of no great consequence, on thinking it over alone I felt it ought not to be allowed to pass; so I was tempted to run across to the observatory, and make it, as I had hoped, without disturbing anybody. If I had known that I should alarm you I would not have done it for the world.'

Swithin spoke very earnestly to Louis, and did not observe the tender reproach in Viviette's eyes when he showed by his tale his decided notion that the prime use of dark nights lay in applying them to the furtherance of practical astronomy.

Everything being now satisfactorily explained the three retired to their several chambers, and Louis heard no more noises that night, or rather morning; his attempts to solve the mystery of Viviette's life here and her relations with St Cleeve having thus far resulted chiefly in perplexity. True, an admission had been wrung from her; and even without such an admission it was clear that she had a tender feeling for Swithin. How to extinguish that romantic folly it now became his object to consider.

CHAPTER THIRTY-ONE

SWITHIN'S midnight excursion to the tower in the cause of science led him to oversleep himself, and when the brother and sister met at breakfast in the morning he did not appear.

'Don't disturb him, – don't disturb him,' said Louis laconically. 'Hullo, Viviette, what are you reading there that makes you flame up so?'

She was glancing over a letter that she had just opened, and at his words looked up with misgiving.

The incident of the previous night left her in great doubt as to what her bearing towards him ought to be. She had made no show of resenting his conduct at the time, from a momentary supposition that he must know all her secret; and afterwards, finding that he did not know it, it seemed too late to affect indignation at his suspicions. So she preserved a quiet neutrality. Even had she resolved on an artificial part she might have forgotten to play it at this instant, the letter being of a kind to banish previous considerations.

'It is a letter from Bishop Helmsdale,' she faltered.

'Well done! I hope for your sake it is an offer.'

'That's just what it is.'

'No, – surely?' said Louis, beginning a laugh of surprise.

'Yes,' she returned indifferently. 'You can read it, if you like.'

'I don't wish to pry into a communication of that sort.'

'Oh, you may read it,' she said, tossing the letter across to him.

Louis thereupon read as under: –

THE PALACE, MELCHESTER,
June 28, 18–

MY DEAR LADY CONSTANTINE – During the two or three weeks that have elapsed since I experienced the great pleasure of renewing my acquaintance with you, the varied agitation of my feelings has clearly proved that my only course is to address you by letter, and at once. Whether the subject of my communication be acceptable to you or not, I can at least assure you that to suppress it would be far less natural, and upon the whole less advisable, than to speak out frankly, even if afterwards I hold my peace for ever.

The great change in my experience during the past year or two – the change, that is, which has resulted from my advancement to a bishopric – has frequently suggested to me, of late, that a discontinuance in my domestic life of the solitude of past years was a question which ought to be seriously contemplated. But whether I should ever have contemplated it without the great good fortune of my meeting with you is doubtful. However, the thing has been considered at last, and without more ado I candidly ask if you would be willing to give up your life at Welland, and relieve my household loneliness here by becoming my wife.

I am far from desiring to force a hurried decision on your part, and will wait your good pleasure patiently, should you feel any uncertainty at the moment as to the step. I am quite disqualified, by habits and experience, for the delightful procedure of urging my suit in the ardent terms which would be so appropriate towards such a lady, and so expressive of my inmost feeling. In truth, a prosy cleric of one-and-fifty wants encouragement to make him eloquent. Of this, however, I can assure you: that if admiration, esteem, and devotion can compensate in any way for the lack of those qualities which might be found to burn with more outward brightness in a younger man, those it is in my power to bestow for the term of my earthly life. Your steady adherence to church principles and your interest in ecclesiastical polity (as was shown by your bright questioning on those subjects during our morning walk round your grounds) have indicated strongly to me the grace and appropriateness with which you would fill the position of a bishop's wife, and how greatly you would add to his reputation, should you be disposed to honour him with your hand. Formerly there have been times when I was of opinion – and you will rightly appreciate my candour in owning it – that a wife was an impediment to a bishop's due activities; but constant observation has convinced me that, far from this being the truth, a meet consort infuses life into episcopal influence and teaching.

Should you reply in the affirmative I will at once come to see you, and with your permission will, among other things, show you a few plain, practical rules which I have interested myself in drawing up for our future guidance. Should you refuse to change your condition on my account, your decision will, as I need hardly say, be a great blow to me. In any event, I could not do less than I have done, after giving the subject my full consideration. Even if there be a slight deficiency of warmth on your part, my earnest hope is that a mind comprehensive as yours will perceive the immense power for good that you might exercise in the position in which a union with me would place you, and allow that perception to weigh in determining your answer.

I remain, my dear Lady Constantine, with the highest respect and affection, – Yours always,

C. MELCHESTER

'Well, you will not have the foolhardiness to decline, now that the question has actually been popped, I should hope,' said Louis, when he had done reading.

'Certainly I shall,' she replied.

'You will really be such a flat,* Viviette?'

'You speak without much compliment. I have not the least idea of accepting him.'

'Surely you will not let your infatuation for that young fellow carry you so far, after my acquainting you with the shady side of his character? You call yourself a religious woman, say your prayers out loud, follow up the revived methods in church practice, and what not; and yet you can think with partiality of a person who, far from having any religion in him, breaks the most elementary commandments in the decalogue.'

'I cannot agree with you,' she said, turning her face askance, for she knew not how much of her brother's language was sincere, and how much assumed, the extent of his discoveries with regard to her secret ties being a mystery. At moments she was disposed to declare the whole truth, and have done with it. But she hesitated, and left the words unsaid; and Louis continued his breakfast in silence.

When he had finished, and she had eaten little or nothing, he asked once more, 'How do you intend to answer that letter? Here you are, the poorest woman in the county, abandoned by people who used to be glad to know you, and leading a life as dismal and dreary as a nun's, when an opportunity is offered you of leaping at once into a leading position in this part of England. Bishops are given to hospitality; you would be welcomed everywhere. In short, your answer must be yes.'

'And yet it will be no,' she said, in a low voice. She had at length learnt, from the tone of her brother's latter remarks, that at any rate he had no knowledge of her actual marriage, whatever indirect ties he might suspect her guilty of.

Louis could restrain himself no longer at her answer. 'Then

conduct your affairs your own way. I know you to be leading a life that won't bear investigation, and I'm hanged if I'll stay here any longer!'

Saying which, Glanville jerked back his chair, and strode out of the room. In less than a quarter of an hour, and before she had moved a step from the table, she heard him leaving the house.

CHAPTER THIRTY-TWO

WHAT to do she could not tell. The step which Swithin had entreated her to take, objectionable and premature as it had seemed in a county aspect, would at all events have saved her from this dilemma. Had she allowed him to tell the Bishop his simple story in its fulness, who could say but that that divine might have generously bridled his own impulses, entered into the case with sympathy, and forwarded with zest their designs for the future, owing to his interest of old in Swithin's father, and in the naturally attractive features of the young man's career.

A puff of wind from the open window, wafting the Bishop's letter to the floor, aroused her from her reverie. With a sigh she stooped and picked it up, glanced at it again; then arose, and with the deliberateness of inevitable action wrote her reply: –

WELLAND HOUSE,
June 29, 18–

MY DEAR BISHOP OF MELCHESTER – I confess to you that your letter, so gracious and flattering as it is, has taken your friend somewhat unawares. The least I can do in return for its contents is to reply as quickly as possible.

There is no one in the world who esteems your high qualities more than myself, or who has greater faith in your ability to adorn the episcopal seat that you have been called on to fill. But to your question I can give only one reply, and that is an unqualified negative. To state this unavoidable decision distresses me, without affectation; and I trust you will believe that, though I decline the distinction of becoming your wife, I shall never cease to interest myself in all that pertains to you and your office; and shall feel the keenest regret if this refusal should operate to prevent a lifelong friendship between us. – I am, my dear Bishop of Melchester, ever sincerely yours,

VIVIETTE CONSTANTINE

A sudden revulsion from the subterfuge of writing as if she were still a widow, wrought in her mind a feeling of dissatisfaction with the whole scheme of concealment; and pushing aside the letter she allowed it to remain unfolded and unaddressed. In a few minutes she heard Swithin approaching, when she put the letter out of the way and turned to receive him.

Swithin entered quietly, and looked round the room. Seeing with unexpected pleasure that she was there alone, he came over and kissed her. Her discomposure at some foregone event was soon obvious.

'Has my staying caused you any trouble?' he asked in a whisper. 'Where is your brother this morning?'

She smiled through her perplexity as she took his hand. 'The oddest things happen to me, dear Swithin,' she said. 'Do you wish particularly to know what has happened now?'

'Yes, if you don't mind telling me.'

'I do mind telling you. But I must. Among other things I am resolving to give way to your representations, – in part, at least. It will be best to tell the Bishop everything, and my brother, if not other people.'

'I am truly glad to hear it, Viviette,' said he cheerfully. 'I have felt for a long time that honesty is the best policy.'

'I at any rate feel it now. But it is a policy that requires a great deal of courage!'

'It certainly requires some courage, – I should not say a great deal; and indeed, as far as I am concerned, it demands less courage to speak out than to hold my tongue.'

'But, you silly boy, you don't know what has happened. The Bishop has made me an offer of marriage.'

'Good gracious, what an impertinent old man! What have you done about it, dearest?'

'Well, I have hardly accepted him,' she replied, laughing. 'It is this event which has suggested to me that I should make my refusal a reason for confiding our situation to him.'

'What would you have done if you had not been already appropriated?'

'That's an inscrutable mystery. He is a worthy man; but he has very pronounced views about his own position, and some other undesirable qualities. Still, who knows? You must bless your stars that you have secured me. Now let us consider how to draw up our confession to him. I wish I had listened to you at first, and allowed you to take him into our confidence before his declaration arrived. He may possibly resent the concealment now. However, this cannot be helped.'

'I tell you what, Viviette,' said Swithin, after a thoughtful pause, 'if the Bishop is such an earthly sort of man as this, a man who goes falling in love, and wanting to marry you, and so on, I am not disposed to confess anything to him at all. I fancied him altogether different from that.'

'But he's none the worse for it, dear.'

'I think he is – to lecture me and love you, all in one breath!'

'Still, that's only a passing phase; and you first proposed making a confidant of him.'

'I did.... Very well. Then we are to tell nobody but the Bishop?'

'And my brother Louis. I must tell him; it is unavoidable. He suspects me in a way I could never have credited of him!'

Swithin, as was before stated, had arranged to start for Greenwich that morning, permission having been accorded him by the Astronomer Royal to view the Observatory; and their final decision was that, as he could not afford time to sit down with her, and write to the Bishop in collaboration, each should, during the day, compose a well-considered letter, disclosing their position from his and her own point of view; Lady Constantine leading up to her confession by her refusal of the Bishop's hand. It was necessary that she should know what Swithin contemplated saying, that her statements might precisely harmonize. He ultimately agreed to send her his letter by the next morning's post, when, having read it, she would in due course despatch it with her own.

As soon as he had breakfasted Swithin went his way, promising to return from Greenwich by the end of the week.

Viviette passed the remainder of that long summer day, during which her young husband was receding towards the capital, in an almost motionless state. At some instants she felt exultant at the idea of announcing her marriage and defying general opinion. At another her heart misgave her, and she was tormented by a fear lest Swithin should some day accuse her of having hampered his deliberately-shaped plan of life by her intrusive romanticism. That was often the trick of men who had sealed by marriage, in their inexperienced youth, a love for those whom their maturer judgment would have rejected as too obviously disproportionate in years.

However, it was now too late for these lugubrious thoughts; and, bracing herself, she began to frame the new reply to Bishop Helmsdale – the plain, unvarnished tale* that was to supplant the undivulging answer first written. She was engaged on this difficult problem till daylight faded in the west, and the broad-faced moon edged upwards, like a plate of old gold,* over the elms towards the village. By that time Swithin had reached Greenwich; her brother had gone she knew not whither; and she and loneliness dwelt solely, as before, within the walls of Welland House.

At this hour of sunset and moonrise the new parlour-maid entered, to inform her that Mr Cecil's head clerk, from Warborne, particularly wished to see her.

Mr Cecil was her solicitor, and she knew of nothing whatever that required his intervention just at present. But he would not have sent at this time of day without excellent reasons, and she directed that the young man might be shown in where she was. On his entry the first thing she noticed was that in his hand he carried a newspaper.

'In case you should not have seen this evening's paper, Lady Constantine, Mr Cecil has directed me to bring it to you at once, on account of what appears there in relation to your ladyship. He has only just seen it himself.'

'What is it? How does it concern me?'

'I will point it out.'

'Read it yourself to me. Though I am afraid there's not enough light.'

'I can see very well here,' said the lawyer's clerk, stepping to the window. Folding back the paper he read: –

'NEWS FROM SOUTH AFRICA

'CAPE TOWN, *May 17* (*viâ* Plymouth). – A correspondent of the *Cape Chronicle* states that he has interviewed an Englishman just arrived from the interior, and learns from him that a considerable misapprehension exists in England concerning the death of the traveller and hunter, Sir Blount Constantine—'

'O, he's living! My husband is alive,' she cried, sinking down in nearly a fainting condition.

'No, my lady. Sir Blount is dead enough, I am sorry to say.

'Dead, did you say?'

'Certainly, Lady Constantine; there is no doubt of it.'

She sat up, and her intense relief almost made itself perceptible like a fresh atmosphere in the room. 'Yes. Then what did you come for?' she asked calmly.

'That Sir Blount has died is unquestionable,' replied the lawyer's clerk gently. 'But there has been some mistake about the date of his death.'

'He died of malarious fever on the banks of the Zouga, October 24, 18–.'

'No; he only lay ill there a long time, it seems. It was a companion who died at that date. But I'll read the account to your ladyship, with your permission: –

'The decease of this somewhat eccentric wanderer did not occur at the time hitherto supposed, but only in last December. The following is the account of the Englishman alluded to, given as nearly as possible in his own words: During the illness of Sir Blount and his friend by the Zouga, three of the servants went away, taking with them a portion of his clothing and effects; and it must be they who spread the report of his death at this time. After his companion's death he mended, and when he was strong enough he and I travelled on to a healthier district. I urged him not to delay his return to England; but he was much against going back there again, and became so rough in his manner towards me that we parted company at the first opportunity I could find. I joined a party of white traders returning to the West Coast. I stayed here among the Portuguese for many months. I then found that an English travelling party were going to explore a district adjoining that which I had formerly traversed with Sir Blount. They said they would be glad of my services, and I joined them. When we had crossed the territory to the south of Ulunda, and drew near to Marzambo,* I heard tidings of a man living there whom I suspected to be Sir Blount, although he was not known by that name. Being so near I was induced to seek him out, and found that he was indeed the same. He had dropped his old name altogether, and had married a native princess—'

'Married a native princess!' said Lady Constantine.

'That's what it says, my lady, –

'married a native princess according to the rites of the tribe, and was living very happily with her. He told me he should never return to England again. He also told me that having seen this princess just after I had left him, he had been attracted by her, and had thereupon decided to reside with her in that country, as being a land which afforded him greater happiness than he could hope to attain elsewhere. He asked me to stay with him, instead of going on with my party, and not reveal his real title to any of them. After some hesitation I did stay, and was not uncomfortable at first. But I soon found that Sir Blount drank much harder now than when I had known him, and that he was at times very greatly depressed in mind at his position. One morning in the middle of December last I heard a shot from his dwelling. His wife rushed frantically past me as I hastened to the spot, and when I entered I found that he had put an end to himself with his revolver. His princess was broken-hearted all that day. When we had buried him I discovered in his house a little box directed to his solicitors at Warborne, in England, and a note for myself, saying that I had better get the first chance of returning that offered, and requesting me to take the box with me. It is supposed to contain papers and articles for friends in England who have deemed him dead for some time.'

The clerk stopped his reading, and there was a silence. 'The middle of last December,' she at length said, in a whisper. 'Has the box arrived yet?'

'Not yet, my lady. We have no further proof of anything. As soon as the package comes to hand you shall know of it immediately.'

Such was the clerk's mission; and, leaving the paper with her, he withdrew. The intelligence amounted to thus much: that, Sir Blount having been alive till at least six weeks after her marriage with Swithin St Cleeve, Swithin St Cleeve was not her husband in the eyes of the law; that she would have to consider how her marriage with the latter might be instantly repeated, to establish herself legally as that young man's wife.

CHAPTER THIRTY-THREE

NEXT morning Viviette received a visit from Mr Cecil himself. He informed her that the box spoken of by the servant had arrived quite unexpectedly just after the departure of his clerk on the previous evening. There had not been sufficient time for him to thoroughly examine it as yet, but he had seen enough to enable him to state that it contained letters, dated memoranda in Sir Blount's handwriting, notes referring to events which had happened later than his supposed death, and other irrefragable proofs that the account in the newspapers was correct as to the main fact – the comparatively recent date of Sir Blount's decease.

She looked up, and spoke with the irresponsible helplessness of a child.

'On reviewing the circumstances, I cannot think how I could have allowed myself to believe the first tidings!' she said.

'Everybody else believed them, and why should you not have done so?' said the lawyer.

'How came the will to be permitted to be proved, as there could, after all, have been no complete evidence?' she asked. 'If I had been the executrix I would not have attempted it! As I was not, I know very little about how the business was pushed through. In a very unseemly way, I think.'

'Well, no,' said Mr Cecil, feeling himself morally called upon to defend legal procedure from such imputations. 'It was done in the usual way in all cases where the proof of death is only presumptive. The evidence, such as it was, was laid before the court by the applicants, your husband's cousins; and the servants who had been with him deposed to his death with a particularity that was deemed sufficient. Their error was, not that somebody died – for somebody did die at the time affirmed – but that they mistook one person for another; the person who died being not Sir Blount Constantine. The court was of opinion that the evidence led up to a reasonable inference that the deceased was actually Sir Blount, and probate was granted on the strength of it. As there was a doubt about the exact day of the month, the applicants were allowed to swear that he died on or after the date last given of his existence – which, in spite of their error then, has really come true, now, of course.'

'They little think what they have done to me by being so ready to swear!' she murmured.

Mr Cecil, supposing her to allude only to the pecuniary straits in which she had been prematurely placed by the will taking effect a year before its due time, said, 'True. It has been to your ladyship's loss, and to their gain. But they will make ample restitution, no doubt: and all will be wound up satisfactorily.'

Lady Constantine was far from explaining that this was not her meaning; and, after some further conversation of a purely technical nature, Mr Cecil left her presence.

When she was again unencumbered with the necessity of exhibiting a proper bearing, the sense that she had greatly suffered in pocket by the undue haste of the executors weighed upon her mind with a pressure quite inappreciable beside the greater gravity of her personal position. What was her position as legatee to her situation as a woman? Her face crimsoned with a flush which she was almost ashamed to show to the daylight, as she hastily penned the following note to Swithin at Greenwich – certainly one of the most informal documents she had ever written.

WELLAND, *Thursday*

O Swithin, my dear Swithin, what I have to tell you is so sad and so humiliating that I can hardly write it – and yet I must. Though we are dearer to each other than all the world besides, and as firmly united as if we were one, I am not legally your wife! Sir Blount did not die till some time after we in England supposed. The service must be repeated instantly. I have not been able to sleep all night. I feel so frightened and ashamed that I can scarcely arrange my thoughts. The newspapers sent with this will explain, if you have not seen particulars. Do come to me as soon as you can, that we may consult on what to do. Burn this at once.

Your VIVIETTE

When the note was despatched she remembered that there was another hardly less important question to be answered – the proposal of the Bishop for her hand. This communication had sunk into nothingness beside the momentous news that had so greatly distressed her. The two replies lay before her – the one she had first written, simply declining to become Dr Helmsdale's wife, without giving reasons; the second, which she had elaborated with so much care on the previous day, relating in confidential detail the history of her love for Swithin, their secret marriage, and their hopes for the future; asking his advice on what their procedure should be to escape the strictures of a censorious world. It was the letter she had barely finished writing when Mr Cecil's clerk announced news tantamount to a declaration that she was no wife at all.

This epistle she now destroyed – and with the less reluctance in knowing that Swithin had been somewhat averse to the confession as soon as he found that Bishop Helmsdale was also a victim to tender sentiment concerning her. The first, in which, at the time of writing, the *suppressio veri** was too strong for her conscience, had now become an honest letter, and sadly folding it she sent the missive on its way.

The sense of her undefinable position kept her from much repose on the second night also; but the following morning brought an unexpected letter from Swithin, written about the same hour as hers to him, and it comforted her much.

He had seen the account in the papers almost as soon as it had come to her knowledge, and sent this line to reassure her in the perturbation she must naturally feel. She was not to be alarmed at all. They two were husband and wife in moral intent and antecedent belief, and the legal flaw which accident had so curiously uncovered could be mended in half-an-hour. He would return on Saturday night at latest, but as the hour would probably be far advanced, he would ask her to meet him by slipping out of the house to the tower any time during service on Sunday morning, when there would be few persons about likely to observe them. Meanwhile he might provisionally state that their best course in the emergency would be, instead of confessing to anybody that there had already been a solemnization of marriage between them, to arrange their re-marriage in as open a manner as possible – as if it were the just-reached climax of a sudden affection, instead of a harking back to an old departure – prefacing it by a public announcement in the usual way.

This plan of approaching their second union with all the show and circumstance of a new thing, recommended itself to her strongly, but for one objection – that by such a course the wedding could not, without appearing like an act of unseemly haste, take place so quickly as she desired for her own moral satisfaction. It might take place somewhat early, say in the course of three or four months, without bringing down upon her the charge of levity; for Sir Blount, a notoriously unkind husband, had been out of her sight four years, and in his grave nearly one. But what she naturally desired was that there should be no more delay than was positively necessary for obtaining a new licence – two or three days at longest; and in view of this celerity it was next to impossible to make due preparation for a wedding of ordinary publicity, performed in her own church, from her own house, with a feast and amusements for the villagers, a tea for the school children, a bonfire, and other of those proclamatory accessories which, by meeting wonder half-way, deprive it of much of its intensity. It must be admitted, too, that she even now shrank from the shock of surprise that would inevitably be caused by her openly taking for husband such a mere youth of no position as Swithin still appeared, notwithstanding that in years he was by this time within a trifle of one-and-twenty.

The straightforward course had, nevertheless, so much to recommend it, so well avoided the disadvantage of future revelation which a private repetition of the ceremony would entail, that assuming she could depend upon Swithin, as she knew she could do, good sense counselled its serious consideration.

She became more composed at her queer situation: hour after hour passed, and the first spasmodic impulse of womanly decorum – not to let the sun go down upon her present improper state – was quite controllable. She could regard the strange contingency that had arisen with something like philosophy. The day slipped by: she thought of the awkwardness of the accident rather than of its humiliation; and, loving Swithin now in a far calmer spirit than at that past date when they had rushed into each other's arms and vowed to be one for the first time, she ever and anon caught herself reflecting, 'Were it not that for my honour's sake I must re-marry him, I should perhaps be a nobler woman in not allowing him to encumber his bright future by a union with me at all.'

This thought, at first artificially raised, as little more than a mental exercise, became by stages a genuine conviction; and while her heart enforced her reason regretted the necessity of abstaining from self-sacrifice – the being obliged, despite his curious escape from the first attempt, to lime Swithin's young wings* again solely for her credit's sake.

However, the deed had to be done; Swithin was to be made legally hers. Selfishness in a conjuncture of this sort was excusable, and even obligatory. Taking brighter views, she hoped that upon the whole this yoking of the young fellow with her, a portionless woman and his senior, would not greatly endanger his career. In such a mood night overtook her, and she went to bed conjecturing that Swithin had by this time arrived in the parish, was perhaps even at that moment passing homeward beneath her walls, and that in less than twelve hours she would have met him, have ventilated the secret which oppressed her, and have satisfactorily arranged with him the details of their reunion.

CHAPTER THIRTY-FOUR

SUNDAY morning came, and complicated her previous emotions by bringing a new and unexpected shock to mingle with them. The postman had delivered among other things an illustrated newspaper, sent by a hand she did not recognize; and on opening the cover the sheet that met her eyes filled her with a horror which she could not express. The print was one which drew largely on its imagination for its engravings, and it already contained an illustration of the death of Sir Blount Constantine. In this work of art he was represented as standing with his pistol to his mouth, his brains being in process of flying up to the roof of his chamber, and his native princess rushing terror-stricken away to a remote position in the thicket of palms which neighboured the dwelling.

The crude realism of the picture, possibly harmless enough in its effect upon others, overpowered and sickened her. By a curious fascination she would look at it again and again, till every line of the engraver's performance seemed really a transcript from what had happened before his eyes. With such details fresh in her thoughts she was going out of the door to make arrangements for confirming, by repetition, her marriage with another. No interval was available for serious reflection on the tragedy, or for allowing the softening effects of time to operate in her mind. It was as though her first husband had died that moment, and she was keeping an appointment with another in the presence of his corpse.*

So revived was the actuality of Sir Blount's recent life and death by this incident, that the distress of her personal relations with Swithin was the single force in the world which could have coerced her into abandoning to him the interval she would fain have set apart for getting over these new and painful impressions. Self-pity for ill-usage afforded her good reasons for ceasing to love Sir Blount; but he was yet too closely intertwined with her past life to be destructible on the instant as a memory.

But there was no choice of occasions for her now, and she steadily waited for the church bells to cease chiming. At last all was silent; the surrounding cottagers had gathered themselves within the walls of the adjacent building. Tabitha Lark's first voluntary then droned from the chancel, and Lady Constantine left the garden in which she had been loitering, and went towards Rings-Hill Speer.

The sense of her situation obscured the morning prospect. The country was unusually silent under the intensifying sun, the songless season of birds having just set in. Choosing her path amid the efts* that were basking upon the outer slopes of the plantation she wound her way up the tree-shrouded camp to the wooden cabin in the centre.

The door was ajar, but on entering she found the place empty. The tower door was also partly open; and listening at the foot of the stairs she heard Swithin above, shifting the telescope and wheeling round the rumbling dome, apparently in preparation for the next nocturnal reconnoitre. There was no doubt that he would descend in a minute or two to look for her, and not wishing to interrupt him till he was ready she re-entered the cabin, where she patiently seated herself among the books and papers that lay scattered about.

She did as she had often done before when waiting there for him; that is, she occupied her moments in turning over the papers and examining the progress of his labours. The notes were mostly astronomical, of course, and she had managed to keep sufficiently abreast of him to catch the meaning of a good many of these. The litter on the table, however, was somewhat more marked this morning than usual, as if it had been hurriedly overhauled. Among the rest of the sheets lay an open note, and, in the entire confidence that existed between them, she glanced over and read it as a matter of course.

It was a most business-like communication, and beyond the address and date contained only the following words: –

DEAR SIR, – We beg leave to draw your attention to a letter we addressed to you on the 26th ult., to which we have not yet been favoured with a reply. As the time for payment of the first moiety of the six hundred pounds per annum settled on you by your late uncle is now at hand, we should be obliged by your giving directions as to where and in what manner the money is to be handed over to you, and shall also be glad to receive any other definite instructions from you with regard to the future. – We are, dear Sir, yours faithfully,

HANNER & RAWLES

SWITHIN ST CLEEVE, Esq.

An income of six hundred a year for Swithin, whom she had hitherto understood to be possessed of an annuity of eighty pounds at the outside, with no prospect of increasing the sum but by hard work! What could this communication mean? He whose custom and delight it was to tell her all his heart, had breathed not a syllable of this matter to her, though it met the very difficulty towards which their discussions invariably tended – how to secure for him a competency that should enable him to establish his pursuits on a wider basis, and throw himself into more direct communion with the scientific world. Quite bewildered by the lack of any explanation she rose from her seat, and with the note in her hand ascended the winding tower-steps.

Reaching the upper aperture she perceived him under the dome, moving musingly about as if he had never been absent an hour, his light hair frilling out from under the edge of his velvet skull-cap as it was always wont to do. No question of marriage seemed to be disturbing the mind of this juvenile husband of hers. The *primum mobile** of his gravitation* was apparently the equatorial telescope which she had given him, and which he was carefully adjusting by means of screws and clamps. Hearing her movements he turned his head.

'O here you are, my dear Viviette! I was just beginning to expect you,' he exclaimed, coming forward. 'I ought to have been looking out for you, but I have found a little defect here in the instrument, and I wanted to set it right before evening comes on. As a rule it is not a good thing to tinker your glasses; but I have found that the diffraction-rings are not perfect circles.* I learnt at Greenwich how to correct them – so kind they have been to me there! – and so I have been loosening the screws and gently shifting the glass, till I think that I have at last made the illumination equal all round. I have so much to tell you about my visit; one thing is, that the astronomical world is getting quite excited about the coming Transit of Venus. There is to be a regular expedition fitted out. How I should like to join it!'

He spoke enthusiastically, and with eyes sparkling at the mental image of the said expedition; and as it was rather gloomy in the dome he rolled it round on its axis, till the shuttered slit for the telescope directly faced the morning sun, which thereupon flooded the concave interior, touching the bright metal-work of the equatorial, and lighting up her pale, troubled face.

'But Swithin!' she faltered; 'my letter to you – our marriage!'

'O yes, this marriage question,' he added. 'I had not forgotten it, dear Viviette – or at least only for a few minutes.'

'Can you forget it, Swithin, for a moment? O how can you!' she said reproachfully. 'It is such a distressing thing. It drives away all my rest!'

'Forgotten is not the word I should have used,' he apologized. 'Temporarily dismissed it from my mind, is all I meant. The simple fact is, that the vastness of the field of astronomy reduces every terrestrial thing to atomic dimensions. Do not trouble, dearest. The remedy is quite easy, as I stated in my letter. We can now be married in a prosy public way. Yes, early or late – next week, next month, six months hence – just as you choose. Say the word when, and I will obey.'

The absence of all anxiety or consternation from his face contrasted strangely with hers, which at last he saw, and, looking at the writing she held, inquired –

'But what paper have you in your hand?'

'A letter which to me is actually inexplicable,' said she, her curiosity returning to the letter, and overriding for the instant her immediate concerns. 'What does this income of six hundred a year mean? Why have you never told me about it, dear Swithin? or does it not refer to you?'

He looked at the note, flushed slightly, and was absolutely unable to begin his reply at once.

'I did not mean you to see that, Viviette,' he murmured.

'Why not?'

'I thought you had better not, as it does not concern me further now. The solicitors are labouring under a mistake in supposing that it does. I have to write at once and inform them that the annuity is not mine to receive.'

'What a strange mystery in your life!' she said, forcing a perplexed smile. 'Something to balance the tragedy in mine. I am absolutely in the dark as to your past history, it seems. And yet I had thought you told me everything.'

'I could not tell you that, Viviette, because it would have endangered our relations – though not in the way you may suppose. You would have reproved me. You, who are so generous and noble, would have forbidden me to do what I did; and I was determined not to be forbidden.'

'To do what?'

'To marry you.'

'Why should I have forbidden?'

'Must I tell – what I would not?' he said, placing his hands upon her arms, and looking somewhat sadly at her. 'Well, perhaps as it has come to this you ought to know all, since it can make no possible difference to my intentions now. We are one for ever – legal blunders notwithstanding; for happily they are quickly reparable – and this question of a devise* from my uncle Jocelyn only concerned me when I was a single man.'

Thereupon, with obviously no consideration of the possibilities that were reopened of the nullity of their marriage contract, he related in detail, and not without misgiving for having concealed them so long, the events that had occurred on the morning of their wedding-day; how he had met the postman on his way to Warborne after dressing in the cabin, and how he had received from him the letter his dead uncle had confided to his family lawyers, informing him of the annuity, and of the important provision attached – that he should be unmarried at his five-and-twentieth year; how in comparison with the possession of her dear self he had reckoned the income as nought, abandoned all idea of it there and then, and had come on to the wedding as if nothing had happened to interrupt for a moment the working out of their plan; how he had scarcely thought with any closeness of the circumstances of the case since, until reminded of them by this note she had seen, and a previous one of a like sort received from the same solicitors.

'O Swithin! Swithin!' she cried, bursting into tears as she realized it all, and sinking on the observing-chair; 'I have ruined you! yes, I have ruined you!'

The young man was dismayed by her unexpected grief, and endeavoured to soothe her; but she seemed touched by a poignant remorse which would not be comforted.

'And now,' she continued, as soon as she could speak, 'when you are once more free, and in a position – actually in a position to claim the annuity that would be the making of you, I am compelled to come to you, and beseech you to undo yourself again, merely to save me!'

'Not to save you, Viviette, but to bless me. You do not ask me to re-marry; it is not a question of alternatives at all; it is my straight course. I do not dream of doing otherwise. I should be wretched if you thought for one moment I could entertain the idea of doing otherwise.'

But the more he said the worse he made the matter. It was a state of affairs that would not bear discussion at all, and the unsophisticated view he took of his course seemed to increase her responsibility.

'Why did your uncle attach such a cruel condition to his bounty?' she cried bitterly. 'O, he little thinks how hard he hits me from the grave – me, who have never done him wrong; and you, too! Swithin, are you sure that he makes that condition indispensable? Perhaps he meant that you should not marry beneath you; perhaps he did not mean to object in such a case as your marrying (forgive me for saying it) a little above you.'

'There is no doubt that he did not contemplate a case which has led to such happiness as this has done,' the youth murmured with hesitation; for though he scarcely remembered a word of his uncle's letter of advice, he had a dim apprehension that it was couched in terms alluding specifically to Lady Constantine.

'Are you sure you cannot retain the money, and be my lawful husband too?' she asked piteously. 'O, what a wrong I am doing you! I did not dream that it could be as bad as this. I knew I was wasting your time by letting you have me, and hampering your projects; but I thought there were compensating advantages. This wrecking of your future at my hands I did not contemplate. You are sure there is no escape? Have you his letter with the conditions, or the will? Let me see the letter in which he expresses his wishes.'

'I assure you it is all as I say,' he pensively returned. 'Even if I were not legally bound by the conditions I should be morally.'

'But how does he put it? How does he justify himself in making such a harsh restriction? Do let me see the letter, Swithin. I shall think it a want of confidence if you do not. I may discover some way out of the difficulty if you let me look at the papers. Eccentric wills can be evaded in all sorts of ways.'

Still he hesitated. 'I would rather you did not see the papers,' he said.

But she persisted as only a fond woman can. Her conviction was that she who, as a woman many years his senior, should have shown her love for him by guiding him straight into the paths he aimed at, had blocked his attempted career for her own happiness. This made her more intent than ever to find out a device by which, while she still retained him, he might also retain the life-interest under his uncle's will.

Her entreaties were at length too potent for his resistance. Accompanying her downstairs to the cabin, he opened the desk from which the other papers had been taken, and against his better judgment handed her the ominous communication of Jocelyn St Cleeve which lay in the envelope just as it had been received three-quarters of a year earlier.

'Don't read it now,' he said. 'Don't spoil our meeting by entering into a subject which is virtually past and done with. Take it with you, and look it over at your leisure – merely as an old curiosity, remember, and not as a still operative document. I have almost forgotten what the contents are, beyond the general advice and stipulation that I was to remain a bachelor.'

'At any rate,' she rejoined, 'do not reply to the note I have seen from the solicitors till I have read this also.'

He promised. 'But now about our public wedding,' he said. 'Like certain royal personages, we shall have had the religious rite and the civil contract performed on independent occasions. Will you fix the day? When is it to be? and shall it take place at a registrar's office, since there is no necessity for having the sacred part over again?'

'I'll think,' replied she. 'I'll think it over.'

'And let me know as soon as you can how you decide to proceed.'

'I will write to-morrow, or come. I do not know what to say now. I cannot forget how I am wronging you. This is almost more than I can bear!'

To divert her mind he began talking about Greenwich Observatory, and the great instruments therein, and how he had been received by the astronomers, and the details of the expedition to observe the Transit of Venus, together with many other subjects of the sort, to which she had not power to lend her attention.

'I must reach home before the people are out of church,' she at length said wearily. 'I wish nobody to know I have been out this morning.' And forbidding Swithin to cross into the open in her company she left him on the edge of the isolated plantation, which had latterly known her tread so well.

CHAPTER THIRTY-FIVE

LADY CONSTANTINE crossed the field and the park beyond, and found on passing the church that the congregation was still within. There was no hurry for getting indoors, the open windows enabling her to hear that Mr Torkingham had only just given out his text. So instead of entering the house she went through the garden-door to the old bowling-green, and sat down in the arbour that Louis had occupied when he overheard the interview between Swithin and the Bishop. Not until then did she find courage to draw out the letter and papers relating to the bequest, which Swithin in a critical moment had handed to her.

Had he been ever so little older he would not have placed that unconsidered confidence in Viviette which had led him to give way to her curiosity. But the influence over him which nearly ten out-numbering years lent her was immensely increased by her higher position and wider experiences, and he had yielded the point, as he yielded all social points; while the same conditions exempted him from any deep consciousness that it was his duty to protect her even from herself.

The preamble of Dr St Cleeve's letter, in which he referred to his pleasure at hearing of the young man's promise as an astronomer, disturbed her not at all – indeed, somewhat prepossessed her in favour of the old gentleman who had written it. The first item of what he called 'unfavourable news', namely, the allusion to the inadequacy of Swithin's income to the wants of a scientific man, whose lines of work were not calculated to produce pecuniary emolument for many years, deepened the cast of her face to concern. She reached the second item of the so-called unfavourable news; and her face flushed as she read how the doctor had learnt 'that there was something in your path worse than narrow means, and that something was *a woman*'.

'To save you, if possible, from ruin on these heads,' she read on, 'I take the preventive measures entailed below.'

And then followed the announcement of the £600 a year settled on the youth for life, on the single condition that he was found to be unmarried at the age of twenty-five – just as Swithin had explained to her. She next learnt that the bequest was for a definite object – that he might have resources sufficient to enable him to travel in an inexpensive way, and begin a study of the southern constellations, which, according to the shrewd old man's judgment, were a mine not so thoroughly worked as the northern, and therefore to be recommended. This was followed by some sentences which hit her in the face like a switch: –

The only other preventive step in my power is that of exhortation.... Swithin St Cleeve, don't make a fool of yourself, as your father did. If your studies are to be worth anything, believe me they must be carried on without the help of a woman. Avoid her, and every one of the sex, if you mean to achieve any worthy thing. Eschew all of that sort for many a year yet. Moreover, I say, the lady of your acquaintance avoid in particular.... She has, in addition to her original disqualification as a companion for you (that is, that of sex), these two special drawbacks: she is much older than yourself—

Lady Constantine's indignant flush forsook her, and pale despair succeeded in its stead. Alas, it was true. Handsome, and in her prime, she might be; but she was too old for Swithin!

And she is so impoverished.... Beyond this, frankly, I don't think well of her. I don't think well of any woman who dotes upon a man so much younger than herself.... To care to be the first fancy of a young fellow like you shows no great common sense in her. If she were worth her salt she would have too much pride to be intimate with a youth in your unassured position, to say no worse. (Viviette's face by this time tingled hot again.) She is old enough to know that a *liaison* with her may, and almost certainly would, be your ruin; and, on the other hand, that a marriage would be preposterous – unless she is a complete goose; and in that case there is even more reason for avoiding her than if she were in her few senses.

A woman of honourable feeling, nephew, would be careful to do nothing to hinder you in your career, as this putting of herself in your way most certainly will. Yet I hear that she professes a great anxiety on this same future of yours as a physicist. The best way in which she can show the reality of her anxiety is by leaving you to yourself.

Leaving him to himself! She paled again, as if chilled by a conviction that in this the old man was right.

She'll blab your most secret plans and theories to every one of her acquaintance, and make them appear ridiculous by announcing them before they are matured. If you attempt to study with a woman, you'll be ruled by her to entertain fancies instead of theories, air-castles instead of intentions, qualms instead of opinions, sickly prepossessions instead of reasoned conclusions....

An experienced woman waking a young man's passions just at a moment when he is endeavouring to shine intellectually, is doing little less than committing a crime.

Thus much the letter; and it was enough for her, indeed. The flushes of indignation which had passed over her, as she gathered this man's opinion of herself, combined with flushes of grief and shame when she considered that Swithin – her dear Swithin – was perfectly acquainted with this cynical view of her nature; that, reject it as he might, and as he unquestionably did, such thoughts of her had been implanted in him, and lay in him. Stifled as they were, they lay in him like seeds too deep for germination, which accident might some day bring near the surface and aërate into life.

The humiliation of such a possibility was almost too much to endure; the mortification – she had known nothing like it till now. But this was not all. There succeeded a feeling in comparison with which resentment and mortification were happy moods – a miserable conviction that this old man who spoke from the grave was not altogether wrong in his speaking; that he was only half wrong; that he was, perhaps, virtually right. Only those persons who are by nature affected with that ready esteem for others' positions which induces an undervaluing of their own, fully experience the deep smart of such convictions against self – the wish for annihilation that is engendered in the moment of despair, at feeling that at length we, our best and firmest friend, cease to believe in our cause.

Viviette could hear the people coming out of church on the other side of the garden wall. Their footsteps and their cheerful voices died away; the bell rang for lunch; and she went in. But her life during that morning and afternoon was wholly introspective. Knowing the full circumstances of his situation as she knew them now – as she had never before known them – ought she to make herself the legal wife of Swithin St Cleeve, and so secure her own honour at any price to him? such was the formidable question which Lady

Constantine propounded to her startled understanding. As a subjectively honest woman alone, beginning her charity at home, there was no doubt that she ought. Save Thyself* was sound Old Testament doctrine, and not altogether discountenanced in the New. But was there a line of conduct which transcended mere self-preservation? and would it not be an excellent thing to put it in practice now?

That she had wronged St Cleeve by marrying him – that she would wrong him infinitely more by completing the marriage – there was, in her opinion, no doubt. She in her experience had sought out him in his inexperience, and had led him like a child. She remembered – as if it had been her fault, though it was in fact only her misfortune – that she had been the one to go for the licence and take up residence in the parish in which they were wedded. He was now just one-and-twenty. Without her, he had all the world before him, six hundred a year, and leave to cut as straight a road to fame as he should choose: with her, this story was negatived.

No money from his uncle; no power of advancement; but a bondage with a woman whose disparity of years, though immaterial just now, would operate in the future as a wet blanket upon his social ambitions; and that content with life as it was which she had noticed more than once in him latterly, a content imperilling his scientific spirit by abstracting his zeal for progress.

It was impossible, in short, to blind herself to the inference that marriage with her had not benefited him. Matters might improve in the future; but to take upon herself the whole liability of Swithin's life, as she would do by depriving him of the help his uncle had offered, was a fearful responsibility. How could she, an unendowed woman, replace such assistance? His recent visit to Greenwich, which had momentarily revived that zest for his pursuit that was now less constant than heretofore, should by rights be supplemented by other such expeditions. It would be true benevolence not to deprive him of means to continue them, so as to keep his ardour alive, regardless of the cost to herself.

It could be done. By the extraordinary favour of a unique accident she had now an opportunity of redeeming Swithin's seriously compromised future, and restoring him to a state no worse than his first. His annuity could be enjoyed by him, his travels undertaken, his studies pursued, his high vocation initiated, by one little sacrifice – that of herself. She only had to refuse to legalize their marriage, to part from him for ever, and all would be well with him thenceforward. The pain to him would after all be but slight, whatever it might be to his wretched Viviette.

The ineptness of retaining him at her side lay not only in the fact itself of injury to him, but in the likelihood of his living to see it as such, and reproaching her for selfishness in not letting him go in this unprecedented opportunity for correcting a move proved to be false. He wished to examine the southern heavens – perhaps his uncle's letter was the father of the wish – and there was no telling what good might not result to mankind at large from his exploits there. Why should she, to save her narrow honour, waste the wide promise of his ability?

That in immolating herself by refusing him, and leaving him free to work wonders for the good of his fellow-creatures, she would in all probability add to the sum of human felicity, consoled her by its breadth as an idea even while it tortured her by making herself the scapegoat or single unit on whom the evil would fall. Ought a possibly large number, Swithin included, to remain unbenefited because the one individual to whom his release would be an injury chanced to be herself? Love between man and woman, which in Homer, Moses,* and other early exhibitors of life, is mere desire, had for centuries past so far broadened as to include sympathy and friendship; surely it should in this advanced stage of the world include benevolence also. If so, it was her duty to set her young man free.

Thus she laboured, with a generosity more worthy even than its object, to sink her love for her own decorum in devotion to the world in general, and to Swithin in particular. To counsel her activities by her understanding, rather than by her emotions as usual, was hard work for a tender woman; but she strove hard, and made advance. The self-centred attitude natural to one in her situation was becoming displaced by the sympathetic attitude, which, though it had to be artificially fostered at first, gave her, by degrees, a certain sweet sense that she was rising above self-love. That maternal element which had from time to time evinced itself in her affection for the youth, and was imparted by her superior ripeness in experience and years, appeared now again, as she drew nearer the resolve not to secure propriety in her own social condition at the expense of this youth's earthly utility.

Unexpectedly grand fruits are sometimes forced forth by harsh pruning. The illiberal letter of Swithin's uncle was suggesting to Lady Constantine an altruism whose thoroughness would probably have amazed that queer old gentleman into a withdrawal of the conditions that had induced it. To love St Cleeve so far better than herself as this was to surpass the love of women* as conventionally understood, and as mostly existing.

Before, however, clinching her decision by any definite step she worried her little brain by devising every kind of ingenious scheme, in the hope of lighting on one that might show her how that decision could be avoided with the same good result. But to secure for him the advantages offered, and to retain him likewise; reflection only showed it to be impossible.

Yet to let him go *for ever* was more than she could endure, and at length she jumped at an idea which promised some sort of improvement on that design. She would propose that reunion should not be entirely abandoned, but simply postponed – namely, till after his twenty-fifth birthday – when he might be her husband without, at any rate, the loss to him of the income. By this time he would approximate to a man's full judgment, and that painful aspect of her as one who had deluded his raw immaturity would have passed for ever.

The plan somewhat appeased her disquieted honour. To let a marriage sink into abeyance for four or five years was not to nullify it; and though she would leave it to him to move its substantiation at the end of that time, without present stipulations, she had not much doubt upon the issue.

The clock struck five. This silent mental debate had occupied her whole afternoon. Perhaps it would not have ended now but for an unexpected incident – the entry of her brother Louis. He came into the room where she was sitting, or rather writhing, and after a few words to explain how he had got there and about the mistake in the date of Sir Blount's death, he walked up close to her. His next remarks were apologetic in form, but in essence they were bitterness itself.

'Viviette,' he said, 'I am sorry for my hasty words to you when I last left this house. I readily withdraw them. My suspicions took a wrong direction. I think now that I know the truth. You have been even madder than I supposed!'

'In what way?' she asked distantly.

'I lately thought that unhappy young man was only your too-favoured lover.'

'You thought wrong: he is not.'

'He is not – I believe you – for he is more. I now am persuaded that he is your lawful husband. Can you deny it!'

'I can.'

'On your sacred word!'

'On my sacred word he is not that either.'

'Thank heaven for that assurance!' said Louis, exhaling a breath of relief. 'I was not so positive as I pretended to be – but I wanted to know the truth of this mystery. Since you are not fettered to him in that way I care nothing.'

Louis turned away; and that afforded her an opportunity for leaving the room. Those few words were the last grains that had turned the balance, and settled her doom.

She would let Swithin go. All the voices in her world seemed to clamour for that consummation. The morning's mortification, the afternoon's benevolence, and the evening's instincts of evasion had joined to carry the point.

Accordingly she sat down, and wrote to Swithin a summary of the thoughts above detailed.

'We shall separate,' she concluded. 'You to obey your uncle's orders and explore the southern skies; I to wait as one who can implicitly trust you. Do not see me again till the years have expired. You will find me still the same. I am your wife through all time; the letter of the law is not needed to reassert it at present; while the absence of the letter secures your fortune.'

Nothing can express what it cost Lady Constantine to marshal her arguments; but she did it, and vanquished self-comfort by a sense of the general expediency. It may unhesitatingly be affirmed that the only ignoble reason which might have dictated such a step was non-existent; that is to say, a serious decline in her affection. Tenderly she had loved the youth at first, and tenderly she loved him now, as time and her after-conduct proved.

Women the most delicate get used to strange moral situations. Eve probably regained her normal sweet composure about a week after the Fall.* On first learning of her anomalous position Lady Constantine had blushed hot, and her pure instincts had prompted her to legalize her marriage without a moment's delay. Heaven and earth were to be moved at once to effect it. Day after day had passed; her union had remained unsecured, and the idea of its nullity had gradually ceased to be strange to her; till it became of little account beside her bold resolve for the young man's sake.

CHAPTER THIRTY-SIX

THE immediate effect upon St Cleeve of the receipt of her well-reasoned argument for retrocession was, naturally, a bitter attack upon himself for having been guilty of such cruel carelessness as to leave in her way the lawyer's letter that had first made her aware of his uncle's provision for him. Immature as he was, he could realize Viviette's position sufficiently well to perceive what the poor lady must suffer at having suddenly thrust upon her the responsibility of repairing her own situation as a wife by ruining his as a legatee. True, it was by the purest inadvertence that his pending sacrifice of means had been discovered; but he should have taken special pains to render such a mishap impossible. If on the first occasion, when a revelation might have been made with impunity, he would not put it in the power of her good nature to relieve his position by refusing him, he should have shown double care not to do so now when she could not exercise that benevolence without the loss of honour.

With a young man's inattention to issues he had not considered how sharp her feelings as a woman must be in this contingency. It had seemed the easiest thing in the world to remedy the defect in their marriage, and therefore nothing to be anxious about. And in his innocence of any thought of appropriating the bequest by taking advantage of the loophole in his matrimonial bond, he undervalued the importance of concealing the existence of that bequest.

The looming fear of unhappiness between them revived in Swithin the warm emotions of their earlier acquaintance. Almost before the sun had set he hastened to Welland House in search of her. The air was disturbed by stiff summer blasts, productive of windfalls and premature descents of leafage. It was an hour when unripe apples shower down in orchards, and unbrowned chestnuts descend in their husks upon the park glades. There was no help for it this afternoon but to call upon her in a direct manner, regardless of suspicions. He was thunderstruck when, while waiting in the full expectation of being admitted to her presence, the answer brought back to him was that she was unable to see him.

This had never happened before in the whole course of their acquaintance. But he knew what it meant, and turned away with a vague disquietude. He did not know that Lady Constantine was just above his head, listening to his movements with the liveliest emotions, and, while praying for him to go, longing for him to insist on seeing her and spoil all. But the faintest symptom being always sufficient to convince him of having blundered, he unwittingly took her at her word, and went rapidly away.

However, he called again the next day, and she, having gained strength by one victory over herself, was enabled to repeat her refusal with greater ease. Knowing this to be the only course by which her point could be maintained, she clung to it with strenuous and religious pertinacity.

Thus immured and self-controlling she passed a week. Her brother, though he did not live in the house (preferring the nearest watering-place at this time of the year), was continually coming there; and one day he happened to be present when she denied herself to Swithin for the third time. Louis, who did not observe the tears in her eyes, was astonished and delighted: she was coming to her senses at last. Believing now that there had been nothing more between them than a too plainly shown partiality on her part, he expressed his commendation of her conduct to her face. At this, instead of owning to its advantage also, her tears burst forth outright.

Not knowing what to make of this, Louis said –

'Well, I am simply upholding you in your course.'

'Yes, yes; I know it!' she cried. 'And it is my deliberately chosen course. I wish he – Swithin St Cleeve – would go on his travels at once, and leave the place! Six hundred a year has been left him for travel and study of the southern constellations; and I wish he would use it. You might represent the advantage to him of the course if you cared to.'

Louis thought he could do no better than let Swithin know this as soon as possible. Accordingly when St Cleeve was writing in the hut the next day he heard the crackle of footsteps over the fir-needles outside, and jumped up, supposing them to be hers; but, to his disappointment, it was her brother who appeared at the door.

'Excuse my invading the hermitage, St Cleeve,' he said in his careless way, 'but I have heard from my sister of your good fortune.'

'My good fortune?'

'Yes, in having an opportunity for roving; and with a traveller's conceit I couldn't help coming to give you the benefit of my experience. When do you start?'

'I have not formed any plan as yet. Indeed, I had not quite been thinking of going.'

Louis stared.

'Not going? Then I may have been misinformed. What I have heard is that a good uncle has kindly bequeathed you a sufficient income to make a second Isaac Newton* of you, if you only use it as he directs.'

Swithin breathed quickly, but said nothing.

'If you have not decided so to make use of it, let me implore you, as your friend, and one nearly old enough to be your father, to decide at once. Such a chance does not happen to a scientific youth once in a century.'

'Thank you for your good advice – for it is good in itself, I know,' said Swithin, in a low voice. 'But has Lady Constantine spoken of it at all?'

'She thinks as I do.'

'She has spoken to you on the subject?'

'Certainly. More than that; it is at her request – though I did not intend to say so – that I come to speak to you about it now.'

'Frankly and plainly,' said Swithin, his voice trembling with a compound of scientific and amatory emotion that defies definition, 'does she say seriously that she wishes me to go?'

'She does.'

'Then go I will,' replied Swithin firmly. 'I have been fortunate enough to interest some leading astronomers, including the Astronomer Royal; and in a letter received this morning I learn that the use of the Cape Observatory has been offered me for any southern observations I may wish to make. This offer I will accept. Will you kindly let Lady Constantine know this, since she is interested in my welfare?'

Louis promised, and when he was gone Swithin looked blankly at his own situation, as if he could scarcely believe in its reality. Her letter to him, then, had been deliberately written; she meant him to go.

But he was determined that none of those misunderstandings which ruin the happiness of lovers should be allowed to operate in the present case. He would see her, if he slept under her walls all night to do it, and would hear the order to depart from her own lips. This unexpected stand she was making for his interests was winning his admiration to such a degree as to be in danger of defeating the very cause it was meant to subserve. A woman like this was not to be forsaken in a hurry. He wrote two lines, and left the note at the house with his own hand.

THE CABIN, RINGS-HILL,
July 7th

DEAREST VIVIETTE – If you insist, I will go. But letter-writing will not do. I must have the command from your own two lips, otherwise I shall not stir. I am here every evening at seven. Can you come? – S.

This note, as fate would have it, reached her hands in the single hour of that week when she was in a mood to comply with his request, just when moved by a reactionary emotion after dismissing Swithin. She went upstairs to the window that had so long served purposes of this kind, and signalled 'Yes.'

St Cleeve soon saw the answer she had given, and watched her approach from the tower as the sunset drew on. The vivid circumstances of his life at this date led him ever to remember the external scenes in which they were set. It was an evening of exceptional irradiations, and the west heaven gleamed like a foundry of all metals common and rare. The clouds were broken into a thousand fragments, and the margin of every fragment shone. Foreseeing the disadvantage and pain to her of maintaining a resolve under the pressure of a meeting, he vowed not to urge her by word or sign; to put the question plainly and calmly, and to discuss it on a reasonable basis only, like the philosophers they assumed themselves to be.

But this intention was scarcely adhered to in all its integrity. She duly appeared on the edge of the field, flooded with the metallic radiance that marked the close of this day; whereupon he quickly descended the steps, and met her at the cabin door. They entered it together.

As the evening grew darker and darker he listened to her reasoning, which was precisely a repetition of that already sent him by letter, and by degrees accepted her decision, since she would not revoke it. Time came for them to say good-bye, and then –

> He turn'd and saw the terror in her eyes,
> That yearn'd upon him shining in such wise
> As a star midway in the midnight fix'd.*

It was the misery of her own condition that showed forth, hitherto obscured by her ardour for ameliorating his. They closed together, and kissed each other as though the emotion of their whole year-and-half's acquaintance had settled down upon that moment.

'I won't go away from you!' said Swithin huskily. 'Why did you propose it for an instant?'

Thus the nearly ended interview was again prolonged, and Viviette yielded to all the passion of her first union with him. Time, however, was merciless, and the hour approached midnight, and she was compelled to depart. Swithin walked with her towards the house, as he had walked many times before, believing that all was now smooth again between them, and caring, it must be owned, very little for his fame as an expositor of the southern constellations just then.

When they reached the silent house he said what he had not ventured to say before, 'Fix the day – you have decided that it is to be soon, and that I am not to go?'

But youthful Swithin was far, very far, from being up to the fond subtlety of Viviette this evening. 'I cannot decide here,' she said gently, releasing herself from his arm; 'I will speak to you from the window. Wait for me.'

She vanished; and he waited. It was a long time before the window opened, and he was not aware that, with her customary complication of feeling, she had knelt for some time inside the room before looking out.

'Well?' said he.

'It cannot be,' she answered. 'I cannot ruin you. But the day after you are five-and-twenty our marriage shall be confirmed, if you choose.'

'O, my Viviette, how is this!' he cried.

'Swithin, I have not altered. But I feared for my powers, and could not tell you whilst I stood by your side. I ought not to have given way as I did to-night. Take the bequest, and go. You are too young – to be fettered – I should have thought of it! Do not communicate with me for at least a year: it is imperative. Do not tell me your plans. If we part, we do part. I have vowed a vow not to further obstruct the course you had decided on before you knew me and my puling ways; and by Heaven's help I'll keep that vow.... Now go. These are the parting words of your own Viviette!'

Swithin, who was stable as a giant in all that appertained to nature and life outside humanity, was a mere pupil in domestic matters. He was quite awed by her firmncss, and looked vacantly at her for a time, till she closed the window. Then he mechanically turned, and went, as she had commanded.

CHAPTER THIRTY-SEVEN

A WEEK had passed away. It had been a time of cloudy mental weather to Swithin and Viviette, but the only noteworthy fact about it was that what had been planned to happen therein had actually taken place. Swithin had gone from Welland, and would shortly go from England.

She became aware of it by a note that he posted to her on his way through Warborne. There was much evidence of haste in the note, and something of reserve. The latter she could not understand, but it might have been obvious enough if she had considered.

On the morning of his departure he had sat on the edge of his bed, the sunlight streaming through the early mist, the house-martins scratching the back of the ceiling over his head as they scrambled out from the roof for their day's gnat-chasing, the thrushes cracking snails* on the garden stones outside with the noisiness of little smiths at work on little anvils. The sun, in sending its rods of yellow fire into his room, sent, as he suddenly thought, mental illumination with it. For the first time, as he sat there, it had crossed his mind that Viviette might have reasons for this separation which he knew not of. There might be family reasons – mysterious blood-necessities which are said to rule members of old musty-mansioned families, and are unknown to other classes of society – and they may have been just now brought before her by her brother Louis on the condition that they were religiously concealed.

The idea that some family skeleton, like those he had read of in memoirs, had been unearthed by Louis, and held before her terrified understanding as a matter which rendered Swithin's departure, and the neutralization of the marriage, no less indispensable to them than it was an advantage to himself, seemed a very plausible one to Swithin just now. Viviette might have taken Louis into her confidence at last, for the sake of his brotherly advice. Swithin knew that of her own heart she would never wish to get rid of him; but coerced by Louis, might she not have grown to entertain views of its expediency? Events made such a supposition on St Cleeve's part as natural as it was inaccurate, and, conjoined with his own excitement at the thought of seeing a new heaven overhead, influenced him to write but the briefest and most hurried final note to her, in which he fully obeyed her sensitive request that he would omit all reference to his plans. These at the last moment had been modified to fall in with the winter expedition formerly mentioned, to observe the Transit of Venus at a remote southern station.

The business being done, and himself fairly plunged into the preliminaries of an important scientific pilgrimage, Swithin acquired that lightness of heart which most young men feel in forsaking old love for new adventure, no matter how charming may be the girl they leave behind them.* Moreover, in the present case, the man was endowed with that schoolboy temperament which does not see, or at least consider with much curiosity, the effect of a given scheme upon others than himself. The bearing upon Lady Constantine of what was an undoubted predicament for any woman, was forgotten in his feeling that she had done a very handsome and noble thing for him, and that he was therefore bound in honour to make the most of it.

His going had resulted in anything but lightness of heart for her. Her sad fancy could, indeed, indulge in dreams of her yellow-haired laddie without that formerly besetting fear that those dreams would prompt her to actions likely to distract and weight him. She was wretched on her own account, relieved on his. She no longer stood in the way of his advancement, and that was enough. For herself she could live in retirement, visit the wood, the old camp, the column, and, like Œnone,* think of the life they had led there –

> Mournful Œnone, wandering forlorn
> Of Paris, once her playmate on the hills,

leaving it entirely to his goodness whether he would come and claim her in the future, or desert her for ever.

She was diverted for a time from these sad performances by a letter which reached her from Bishop Helmsdale. To see his handwriting again on an envelope, after thinking so anxiously of making a father-confessor of him, startled her out of her equanimity. She speedily regained it, however, when she read his note.

THE PALACE, MELCHESTER,
July 30, 18–

MY DEAR LADY CONSTANTINE – I am shocked and grieved that, in the strange dispensation of things here below, my offer of marriage should have reached you almost simultaneously with the intelligence that your widowhood had been of many months less duration than you and I, and the world, had supposed. I can quite understand that, viewed from any side, the news must have shaken and disturbed you; and your unequivocal refusal to entertain any thought of a new alliance at such a moment was, of course, intelligible, natural, and praiseworthy. At present I will say no more beyond expressing a hope that you will accept my assurances that I was quite ignorant of the news at the hour of writing, and a sincere desire that in due time, and as soon as you have recovered your equanimity, I may be allowed to renew my proposal. – I am, my dear Lady Constantine, yours ever sincerely,

C. MELCHESTER

She laid the letter aside, and thought no more about it, beyond a momentary meditation on the errors into which people fall in reasoning from actions back to motives. Louis, who was now again with her, became in due course acquainted with the contents of the letter, and was satisfied with the promising position in which matters seemingly stood all round.

Lady Constantine went her mournful ways as she had planned to do, her chief resort being the familiar column, where she experienced the unutterable melancholy of seeing two carpenters dismantle the dome of its felt covering, detach its ribs, and clear away the enclosure at the top till everything stood as it had stood before Swithin had been known to the place. The equatorial had already been packed in a box, to be in readiness if he should send for it from abroad. The cabin, too, was in course of demolition, such having been his directions, acquiesced in by her, before he started. Yet she could not bear the idea that these structures, so germane to the events of their romance, should be removed as if removed for ever. Going to the men she bade them store up the materials intact, that they might be re-erected if desired. She had the junctions of the timbers marked with figures, the boards numbered, and the different sets of screws tied up in independent papers for identification. She did not hear the remarks of the workmen when she had gone, to the effect that the young man would as soon think of buying a halter for himself as come back and spy at the moon from Rings-Hill Speer, after seeing the glories of other nations and the gold and jewels that were found there, or she might have been more unhappy than she was.

On returning from one of these walks to the column a curious circumstance occurred. It was evening, and she was coming as usual down through the sighing plantation, choosing her way between the ramparts of the camp towards the outlet giving upon the field, when suddenly in a dusky vista among the fir-trunks she saw, or thought she saw, a golden-haired, toddling child. The child moved a step or two, and vanished behind a tree. Lady Constantine, fearing it had lost its way, went quickly to the spot, searched, and called aloud. But no child could she perceive or hear anywhere around. She returned to where she had stood when first beholding it, and looked in the same direction, but nothing reappeared. The only object at all resembling a little boy or girl was the upper tuft of a bunch of fern, which had prematurely yellowed to about the colour of a fair child's hair, and waved occasionally in the breeze. This, however, did not sufficiently explain the phenomenon, and she returned to make inquiries of the man whom she had left at work, removing the last traces of Swithin's cabin. But he had gone with her departure and the approach of night. Feeling an indescribable dread she retraced her steps, and hastened homeward doubting, yet half believing, what she had seemed to see, and wondering if her imagination had played her some trick.

The tranquil mournfulness of her night of solitude terminated in a most unexpected manner.

The morning after the above-mentioned incident Lady Constantine, after meditating a while, arose with a strange personal conviction that bore curiously on the aforesaid hallucination. She realized a state of things that she had never anticipated, and for a moment the discovery of her condition so overwhelmed her that she thought she must die outright. In her terror she said she had sown the wind to reap the whirlwind.* Then the instinct of self-preservation flamed up in her like a fire. Her altruism in subjecting her self-love to benevolence, and letting Swithin go away from her, was demolished by the new necessity, as if it had been a gossamer web.

There was no resisting or evading the spontaneous plan of action which matured in her mind in five minutes. Where was Swithin? how could he be got at instantly? – that was her ruling thought. She searched about the room for his last short note, hoping, yet doubting, that its contents were more explicit on his intended movements than the few meagre syllables which alone she could call to mind. She could not find the letter in her room, and came downstairs to Louis as pale as a ghost.

He looked up at her, and with some concern said, 'What's the matter?'

'I am searching everywhere for a letter – a note from Mr St Cleeve – just a few words telling me when the *Occidental* sails, that I think he goes in.'

'Why do you want that unimportant document?'

'It is of the utmost importance that I should know whether he has actually sailed or not!' said she in agonized tones. 'Where *can* that letter be?'

Louis knew where that letter was, for having seen it on her desk he had, without reading it, torn it up and thrown it into the waste-paper basket, thinking the less that remained to remind her of the young philosopher the better.

'I destroyed it,' he said.

'O Louis! why did you?' she cried. 'I am going to follow him; I think it best to do so; and I want to know if he is gone – and now the date is lost!'

'Going to run after St Cleeve? Absurd!'

'Yes, I am!' she said with vehement firmness. 'I *must* see him; I want to speak to him as soon as possible.'

'Good Lord, Viviette! Are you mad?'

'O what was the date of that ship! But it cannot be helped. I start at once for Southampton. I have made up my mind to do it. He was going to his uncle's solicitors in the North first; then he was coming back to Southampton. He cannot have sailed yet.'

'I believe he has sailed,' muttered Louis sullenly.

She did not wait to argue with him, but returned upstairs, where she rang to tell Green to be ready with the pony to drive her to Warborne station in a quarter of an hour.

CHAPTER THIRTY-EIGHT

VIVIETTE'S determination to hamper Swithin no longer had led her, as has been shown, to balk any weak impulse to entreat his return, by forbidding him to furnish her with his foreign address. His ready disposition, his fear that there might be other reasons behind, made him obey her only too literally. Thus, to her terror and dismay, she had placed a gratuitous difficulty in the way of her present endeavour.

She was ready before Green, and urged on that factotum so wildly as to leave him no time to change his corduroys and 'skitty-boots'* in which he had been gardening; he therefore turned himself into a coachman as far down as his waist merely – clapping on his proper coat, hat, and waistcoat, and wrapping a rug over his horticultural half below. In this compromise he appeared at the door, mounted, and reins in hand.

Seeing how sad and determined Viviette was, Louis pitied her so far as to put nothing in the way of her starting, though he forbore to help her. He thought her conduct sentimental foolery, the outcome of mistaken pity and 'such a kind of gain-giving as would trouble a woman';* and he decided that it would be better to let this mood burn itself out than to keep it smouldering by obstruction.

'Do you remember the date of his sailing?' she said finally, as the pony-carriage turned to drive off.

'He sails on the 25th, that is, to-day. But it may not be till late in the evening.'

With this she started, and reached Warborne in time for the up-train. How much longer than it really is a long journey can seem to be, was fully learnt by the unhappy Viviette that day. The changeful procession of country seats past which she was dragged, the names and memories of their owners, had no points of interest for her now. She reached Southampton about midday, and drove straight to the docks.

On approaching the gates she was met by a crowd of people and vehicles coming out – men, women, children, porters, police, cabs, and carts. The *Occidental* had just sailed.

The adverse intelligence came upon her with such odds after her morning's tension that she could scarcely crawl back to the cab which had brought her. But this was not a time to succumb. As she had no luggage she dismissed the man, and, without any real consciousness of what she was doing, crept away and sat down on a pile of merchandise.

After long thinking her case assumed a more hopeful complexion. Much might probably be done towards communicating with him in the time at her command. The obvious step to this end, which she should have thought of sooner, would be to go to his grandmother in Welland Bottom, and there obtain his itinerary in detail – no doubt well known to Mrs Martin. There was no leisure for her to consider longer if she would be home again that night; and returning to the railway she waited on a seat without eating or drinking till a train was ready to take her back.

By the time she again stood in Warborne the sun rested his chin upon the meadows, and enveloped the distant outline of the Rings-Hill column in his humid rays. Hiring an empty fly that chanced to be at the station she was driven through the little town onward to Welland, which she approached about eight o'clock. At her request the man set her down at the entrance to the park, and when he was out of sight, instead of pursuing her way to the House, she went along the high road in the direction of Mrs Martin's.

Dusk was drawing on, and the bats were wheeling over the green basin called Welland Bottom by the time she arrived; and had any other errand instigated her call she would have postponed it till the morrow. Nobody responded to her knock, but she could hear footsteps going hither and thither upstairs, and dull noises as of articles moved from their places. She knocked again and again, and ultimately the door was opened by Hannah as usual.

'I could make nobody hear,' said Lady Constantine, who was so weary she could scarcely stand.

'I am very sorry, my lady,' said Hannah, slightly awed on beholding her visitor. 'But we was a putting poor Mr Swithin's room to rights, now that he is, as a woman may say, dead and buried to us; so we didn't hear your ladyship. I'll call Mrs Martin at once. She is up in the room that used to be his work-room.'

Here Hannah's voice implied moist eyes, and Lady Constantine's instantly overflowed.

'No, I'll go up to her,' said Viviette; and almost in advance of Hannah she passed up the shrunken ash stairs.

The ebbing light was not enough to reveal to Mrs Martin's aged gaze the personality of her visitor, till Hannah explained.

'I'll get a light, my lady,' said she.

'No, I would rather not. What are you doing, Mrs Martin?'

'Well, the poor misguided boy is gone – and he's gone for good to me! I am a woman of over four-score years, my Lady Constantine: my junketing days are over, and whether 'tis feasting or whether 'tis sorrowing in the land will soon be nothing to me. But his life may be long and active, and for the sake of him I care for what I shall never see, and wish to make pleasant what I shall never enjoy. I am setting his room in order, as the place will be his own lifehold when I am gone, so that when he comes back he may find all his poor jim-cracks* and trangleys* as he left 'em, and not feel that I have betrayed his trust.'

Mrs Martin's voice revealed that she had burst into such few tears as were left her, and then Hannah began crying likewise; whereupon Lady Constantine, whose heart had been bursting all day (and who, indeed, considering her coming trouble, had reason enough for tears), broke into bitterer sobs than either – sobs of absolute pain, that could no longer be concealed.

Hannah was the first to discover that Lady Constantine was weeping with them; and her feelings being probably the least intense among the three she instantly controlled herself.

'Refrain yourself, my dear woman, refrain!' she said hastily to Mrs Martin; 'don't ye see how it do raft* my lady?' And turning to Viviette she whispered, 'Her years be so great, your ladyship, that perhaps ye'll excuse her for busting out afore 'ee?* We know when the mind is dim, my lady, there's not the manners there should be; but decayed people can't help it, poor old soul!'

'Hannah, that will do now. Perhaps Lady Constantine would like to speak to me alone,' said Mrs Martin. And when Hannah had retreated Mrs Martin continued: 'Such a charge as she is, my lady, on account of her great age! You'll pardon her biding here as if she were one of the family. I put up with such things because of her long service, and we know that years lead to childishness.'

'What are you doing? Can I help you?' Viviette asked, as Mrs Martin, after speaking, turned to lift some large article.

'Oh, 'tis only the skeleton of a telescope that's got no works in his inside,' said Swithin's grandmother, seizing the huge pasteboard tube that Swithin had made, and abandoned because he could get no lenses to suit it. 'I am going to hang it up to these hooks, and there it will bide till he comes again.'

Lady Constantine took one end, and the tube was hung up against the whitewashed wall by strings that the old woman had tied round it.

'Here's all his equinoctial lines,* and his topics* of Capricorn, and I don't know what besides,' Mrs Martin continued, pointing to some charcoal scratches on the wall. 'I shall never rub 'em out; no, though 'tis such untidiness as I was never brought up to, I shall never rub 'em out.'

'Where has Swithin gone to first?' asked Viviette anxiously. 'Where does he say you are to write to him?'

'Nowhere yet, my lady. He's gone traipsing all over Europe and America, and then to the South Pacific Ocean about this Transit of Venus that's going to be done there. He is to write to us first – God knows when! – for he said that if we didn't hear from him for six months we were not to be gallied* at all.'

At this intelligence, so much worse than she had expected, Lady Constantine stood mute, sank down, and would have fallen to the floor if there had not been a chair behind her. Controlling herself by a strenuous effort, she disguised her despair and asked vacantly: 'From America to the South Pacific – Transit of Venus?' (Swithin's arrangement to accompany the expedition had been made at the last moment, and therefore she had not as yet been informed.)

'Yes, to a lone island, I believe.'

'Yes, a lone islant, my lady!' echoed Hannah, who had crept in and made herself one of the family again, in spite of Mrs Martin.

'He is going to meet the English and American astronomers there at the end of the year. After that he will most likely go on to the Cape.'

'But before the end of the year – what places did he tell you of visiting?'

'Let me collect myself; he is going to the observatory of Cambridge, United States,* to meet some gentlemen there, and spy through the great refractor.* Then there's the observatory of Chicago; and I think he has a letter to make him beknown to a gentleman in the observatory at Marseilles – and he wants to go to Vienna – and Poulkowa,* too, he means to take in his way – there being great instruments and a lot of astronomers at each place.'

'Does he take Europe or America first?' she asked faintly, for the account seemed hopeless.

Mrs Martin could not tell till she had heard from Swithin. It depended upon what he had decided to do on the day of his leaving England.

Lady Constantine bade the old people good-bye, and dragged her weary limbs homeward. The fatuousness of forethought had seldom been evinced more ironically. Had she done nothing to hinder him, he would have kept up an unreserved communication with her, and all might have been well.

For that night she could undertake nothing further, and she waited for the next day. Then at once she wrote two letters to Swithin, directing one to Marseilles observatory, one to the observatory of Cambridge, U.S., as being the only two spots on the face of the globe at which they were likely to intercept him. Each letter stated to him the urgent reasons which existed for his return, and contained a passionately regretful intimation that the annuity on which his hopes depended must of necessity be sacrificed by the completion of their original contract without delay.

But letter conveyance was too slow a process to satisfy her. To send an epitome of her epistles by telegraph was, after all, indispensable. Such an imploring sentence as she desired to address to him it would be hazardous to despatch from Warborne, and she took a dreary journey to a strange town on purpose to send it from an office at which she was unknown.

There she handed in her message, addressing it to the port of arrival of the *Occidental*, and again returned home.

She waited; and there being no return telegram, the inference was that he had somehow missed hers. For an answer to either of her letters she would have to wait long enough to allow him time to reach one of the observatories – a tedious while.

Then she considered the weakness, the stultifying nature of her attempt at recall.

Events mocked her on all sides. By the favour of an accident, and by her own immense exertions against her instincts, Swithin had been restored to the rightful heritage that he had nearly forfeited on her account. He had just started off to utilize it; when she, without a moment's warning, was asking him again to cast it away. She had set a certain machinery in motion – to stop it before it had revolved once.

A horrid apprehension possessed her. It had been easy for Swithin to give up what he had never known the advantages of keeping; but having once begun to enjoy his possession would he give it up now? Could he be depended on for such self-sacrifice? Before leaving, he would have done anything at her request; but the *mollia tempora fandi** had now passed. Suppose there arrived no reply from him for the next three months; and that when his answer came he were to inform her that, having now fully acquiesced in her original decision, he found the life he was leading so profitable as to be unable to abandon it, even to please her; that he was very sorry, but having embarked on this course by her advice he meant to adhere to it by his own.

There was, indeed, every probability that, moving about as he was doing, and cautioned as he had been by her very self against listening to her too readily, she would receive no reply of any sort from him for three or perhaps four months. This would be on the eve of the Transit; and what likelihood was there that a young man, full of ardour for that spectacle, would forego it at the last moment to return to a humdrum domesticity with a woman who was no longer a novelty?

If she could only leave him to his career, and save her own situation also! But at that moment the proposition seemed as impossible as to construct a triangle of two straight lines. O that last fatal evening with him!

In her walk home, pervaded by these hopeless views, she passed near the dark and deserted tower. Night in that solitary place, which would have caused her some uneasiness in her years of blitheness, had no terrors for her now. She went up the winding path, and, the door being unlocked, felt her way to the top. The open sky greeted her as in times previous to the dome-and-equatorial period; but there was not a star to suggest to her in which direction Swithin had gone. The absence of the dome suggested a way out of her difficulties. A leap in the dark, and all would be over. But she had not reached that stage of action as yet, and the thought was dismissed as quickly as it had come.

The new consideration which at present occupied her mind was whether she could have the courage to leave Swithin to himself, as in the original plan, and singly meet her impending trial, despising the shame,* till he should return at five-and-twenty and claim her? Yet was this assumption of his return so very safe? How altered things would be at that time! At twenty-five he would still be young and handsome; she would be five-and-thirty, fading to middle-age and homeliness,* from a junior's point of view. A fear sharp as a frost* settled down upon her, that in any such scheme as this she would be building upon the sand.*

She hardly knew how she reached home that night. Entering by the lawn door she saw a red coal* in the direction of the arbour. Louis was smoking there, and he came forward.

He had not seen her since the morning and was naturally anxious about her. She blessed the chance which enveloped her in night and lessened the weight of the encounter one half by depriving him of vision.

'Did you accomplish your object?' he asked.

'No,' said she.

'How was that?'

'He had sailed.'

'A very good thing for both, I say. I believe you would have married him, if you could have overtaken him.'

'That would I!' she said.

'Good God!'

'I would marry a tinker for that matter; I have physical reasons for being any man's wife,' she said recklessly, 'only I should prefer to drown myself!'

Louis held his breath, and stood rigid at the meaning her words conveyed.

'But Louis, you don't know all!' cried Viviette. 'I am not so bad as you think; mine has been folly – not vice. I thought I had married him – and then I found I had not; the marriage was invalid – Sir

Blount was alive! And now Swithin has gone away, and will not come back for my calling! How can he? His fortune is left him on condition that he forms no legal tie. O will he – will he, come again?'

'Never, if that's the position of affairs,' said Louis firmly, after a pause.

'What then shall I do?' said Viviette.

Louis escaped the formidable difficulty of replying by pretending to continue his Havannah;* and she, bowed down to dust* by what she had revealed, crept from him into the house. Louis's cigar went out in his hand as he stood looking intently at the ground.

CHAPTER THIRTY-NINE

LOUIS got up the next morning with an idea in his head. He had dressed for a journey, and breakfasted hastily.

Before he had started Viviette came downstairs. Louis, who was now greatly disturbed about her, went up to his sister and took her hand.

'*Aux grands maux les grands remèdes*,'* he said gravely. 'I have a plan.'

'I have a dozen!' said she.

'You have?'

'Yes. But what are they worth? And yet there must – there *must* be a way!'

'Viviette,' said Louis, 'promise that you will wait till I come home to-night, before you do anything.'

Her distracted eyes showed slight comprehension of his request as she said 'Yes.'

An hour after that time Louis entered the train at Warborne, and was speedily crossing a country of ragged woodland, which, though intruded on by the plough at places, remained largely intact from prehistoric times, and still abounded with yews of gigantic growth and oaks tufted with mistletoe. It was the route to Melchester.

On setting foot in that city he took the cathedral spire as his guide, the place being strange to him; and went on till he reached the archway dividing Melchester sacred from Melchester secular. Thence he threaded his course into the precincts of the damp and venerable Close,* level as a bowling-green, and beloved of rooks, who from their elm perches on high threatened any unwary gazer with the mishap of Tobit.* At the corner of this reposeful spot stood the episcopal palace.

Louis entered the gates, rang the bell, and looked around. Here the trees and rooks seemed older, if possible, than those in the Close behind him. Everything was dignified, and he felt himself like Punchinello in the king's chambers.* Verily in the present case

Glanville was not a man to stick at trifles any more than his illustrious prototype; and on the servant bringing a message that his lordship would see him at once, Louis marched boldly in.

Through an old dark corridor, roofed with old dark beams, the servant led the way to the heavily-moulded door of the Bishop's room. Dr Helmsdale was there, and welcomed Louis with considerable stateliness. But his condescension was tempered with a curious anxiety, and even with nervousness.

He asked in pointed tones after the health of Lady Constantine; if Louis had brought an answer to the letter he had addressed to her a day or two earlier; and if the contents of the letter, or of the previous one, were known to him.

'I have brought no answer from her,' said Louis. 'But the contents of your letter have been made known to me.'

Since entering the building Louis had more than once felt some hesitation, and it might now, with a favouring manner from his entertainer, have operated to deter him from going further with his intention. But the Bishop had personal weaknesses that were fatal to sympathy for more than a moment.

'Then I may speak in confidence to you as her nearest relative,' said the prelate, 'and explain that I am now in a position with regard to Lady Constantine which, in view of the important office I hold, I should not have cared to place myself in unless I had felt quite sure of not being refused by her. And hence it is a great grief, and some mortification to me, that I was refused – owing, of course, to the fact that I unwittingly risked making my proposal at the very moment when she was under the influence of those strange tidings, and therefore not herself, and scarcely able to judge what was best for her.'

The Bishop's words disclosed a mind whose sensitive fear of danger to its own dignity hindered it from criticism elsewhere. Things might have been worse for Louis's Puck-like idea of mismating his Hermia with this Demetrius.*

Throwing a strong colour of earnestness into his mien he replied: 'Bishop, Viviette is my only sister; I am her only brother and friend. I am alarmed for her health and state of mind. Hence I have come to consult you on this very matter that you have broached. I come absolutely without her knowledge, and I hope unconventionality may be excused in me on the score of my anxiety for her.'

'Certainly. I trust that the prospect opened up by my proposal, combined with this other news, has not proved too much for her?'

'My sister is distracted and distressed, Bishop Helmsdale. She wants comfort.'

'Not distressed by my letter?' said the Bishop, turning red. 'Has it lowered me in her estimation?'

'On the contrary; while your disinterested offer was uppermost in her mind she was a different woman. It is this other matter that oppresses her. The result upon her of the recent discovery with regard to the late Sir Blount Constantine is peculiar. To say that he ill-used her in his lifetime is to understate a truth. He has been dead now a considerable period; but this revival of his memory operates as a sort of terror upon her. Images of the manner of Sir Blount's death are with her night and day, intensified by a hideous picture of the supposed scene, which was cruelly sent her. She dreads being alone. Nothing will restore my poor Viviette to her former cheerfulness but a distraction – a hope – a new prospect.'

'That is precisely what acceptance of my offer would afford.'

'Precisely,' said Louis, with great respect. 'But how to get her to avail herself of it, after once refusing you, is the difficulty, and my earnest problem.'

'Then we are quite at one.'

'We are. And it is to promote our wishes that I am come; since she will do nothing of herself.'

'Then you can give me no hope of a reply to my second communication?'

'None whatever – by letter,' said Louis. 'Her impression plainly is that she cannot encourage your lordship. Yet, in the face of all this reticence, the secret is that she loves you warmly.'

'Can you indeed assure me of that? Indeed, indeed!' said the good Bishop musingly. 'Then I must try to see her, I begin to feel – to feel strongly – that a course which would seem premature and unbecoming in other cases would be true and proper conduct in this. Her unhappy dilemmas – her unwonted position – yes, yes – I see it all! I can afford to have some little misconstruction put upon my motives. I will go and see her immediately. Her past has been a cruel one; she wants sympathy; and with Heaven's help I'll give it.'

'I think the remedy lies that way,' said Louis gently. 'Some words came from her one night which seemed to show it. I was standing on the terrace: I heard somebody sigh in the dark, and found that it was she. I asked her what was the matter, and gently pressed her on this subject of boldly and promptly contracting a new marriage as a means of dispersing the horrors of the old. Her answer implied that she would have no objection to do it, and to do it at once, provided she could remain externally passive in the matter, that she would tacitly yield, in fact, to pressure, but would not meet solicitation half-way. Now, Bishop Helmsdale, you see what has prompted me. On the one hand is a dignitary of high position and integrity, to say no more, who is anxious to save her from the gloom of her situation; on the other is this sister, who will not make known to you her willingness to be saved – partly from apathy, partly from a fear that she may be thought forward in responding favourably at so early a moment, partly also, perhaps, from a modest sense that there would be some sacrifice on your part in allying yourself with a woman of her secluded and sad experience.'

'O, there is no sacrifice! Quite otherwise. I care greatly for this alliance, Mr Glanville. Your sister is very dear to me. Moreover, the advantages her mind would derive from the enlarged field of activity that the position of a bishop's wife would afford, are palpable. I am induced to think that an early settlement of the question – an immediate coming to the point – which might be called too early in the majority of cases, would be a right and considerate tenderness here. My only dread is that she should think an immediate following up of the subject premature. And the risk of a rebuff a second time is one which, as you must perceive, it would be highly unbecoming in me to run.'

'I think the risk would be small, if your lordship would approach her frankly. Write she will not, I am assured; and knowing that, and having her interest at heart, I was induced to come to you and make this candid statement in reply to your communication. If she could be married in a month or so it would save her from chronic melancholia – possibly from death itself. And her late husband having been virtually dead these four or five years, believed dead two years, and actually dead nearly one, no reproach could attach to her if she were to contract another union to-morrow.'

'I agree with you, Mr Glanville,' said the Bishop warmly. 'I will think this over. Her motive in not replying I can quite understand: your motive in coming I can also understand and appreciate in a brother. If I feel convinced that it would be a seemly and expedient thing I will come to Welland to-morrow.'

The point to which Louis had brought the Bishop being so satisfactory, he feared to endanger it by another word. He went away almost hurriedly, and at once left the precincts of the cathedral, lest another encounter with Dr Helmsdale should lead the latter to take a new and slower view of his duties as Viviette's suitor.

He reached Welland by dinner-time, and came upon Viviette in the same pensive mood in which he had left her. It seemed she had hardly moved since.

'Have you discovered Swithin St Cleeve's address?' she said, without looking up at him.

'No,' said Louis.

Then she broke out with indescribable anguish: 'But you asked me to wait till this evening; and I have waited through the long day, in the belief that your words meant something, and that you would bring good tidings! And now I find your words meant nothing, and you have *not* brought good tidings!'

Louis could not decide for a moment what to say to this. Should he venture to give her thoughts a new course by a revelation of his design? No: it would be better to prolong her despair yet another night, and spring relief upon her suddenly, that she might jump at it and commit herself without an interval for reflection on certain aspects of the proceeding.

Nothing, accordingly, did he say; and conjecturing that she would be hardly likely to take any desperate step that night, he left her to herself.

His anxiety at this crisis continued to be great. Everything depended on the result of the Bishop's self-communion. Would he or would he not come the next day? Perhaps instead of his important presence there would appear a letter postponing the visit indefinitely. If so, all would be lost.

Louis's suspense kept him awake, and he was not alone in his sleeplessness. Through the night he heard his sister walking up and down, in a state which betokened that for every pang of grief she had disclosed, twice as many had remained unspoken. He almost feared that she might seek to end her existence by violence, so unreasonably sudden were her moods; and he lay and longed for the day.

It was morning. She came down the same as usual, and asked if there had arrived any telegram or letter; but there was neither. Louis avoided her, knowing that nothing he could say just then would do her any good.

No communication had reached him from the Bishop, and that looked well. By one ruse and another, as the day went on, he led her away from contemplating the remote possibility of hearing from Swithin, and induced her to look at the worst contingency as her probable fate. It seemed as if she really made up her mind to this, for by the afternoon she was apathetic, like a woman who neither hoped nor feared.

And then a fly drove up to the door.

Louis, who had been standing in the hall the greater part of that day, glanced out through a private window, and went to Viviette. 'The Bishop has called,' he said. 'Be ready to see him.'

'The Bishop of Melchester?' said Viviette, bewildered.

'Yes. I asked him to come. He comes for an answer to his letters.'

'An answer – to – his – letters?' she murmured.

'An immediate reply of yes or no.'

Her face showed the workings of her mind. How entirely an answer of assent, at once acted on for better or for worse,* would clear the spectre from her path, there needed no tongue to tell. It would, moreover, accomplish that end without involving the impoverishment of Swithin – the inevitable result if she had adopted the legitimate road out of her trouble. Hitherto there had seemed to her dismayed mind, unenlightened as to any course save one of honesty, no possible achievement of *both* her desires – the saving of Swithin and the saving of herself. But behold, here was a way! A tempter had shown it to her. It involved a great wrong, which to her had quite obscured its feasibility. But she perceived now that it was indeed a way. Convention was forcing her hand at this game; and to what will not convention compel her weaker victims, in extremes?

Louis left her to think it out. When he reached the drawing-room Dr Helmsdale was standing there with the air of a man too good for his destiny – which, to be just to him, was not far from the truth this time.

'Have you broken my message to her?' asked the Bishop.

'Not your message; your visit,' said Louis. 'I leave the rest in your Lordship's hands. I have done all I can for her.'

She was in her own small room to-day; and, feeling that it must be a bold stroke or none, he led the Bishop across the hall till he reached her apartment and opened the door; but instead of following he shut it behind his visitor.

Then Glanville passed an anxious time. He walked from the foot of the staircase to the star of old swords and pikes on the wall; from these to the stags' horns; thence down the corridor as far as the door, where he could hear murmuring inside, but not its import. The longer they remained closeted the more excited did he become. That she had not peremptorily negatived the proposal at the outset was a strong sign of its success. It showed that she had admitted argument; and the worthy Bishop had a pleader on his side whom he knew little of. The very weather seemed to favour Dr Helmsdale in his suit. A blusterous wind had blown up from the west, howling in the smokeless chimneys, and suggesting to the feminine mind storms at sea, a tossing ocean, and the hopeless inaccessibility of all astronomers and men on the other side of the same.

The Bishop had entered Viviette's room at ten minutes past three. The long hand of the hall clock lay level at forty-five minutes past when the knob of the door moved, and he came out. Louis met him where the passage joined the hall.

Dr Helmsdale was decidedly in an emotional state, his face being slightly flushed. Louis looked his anxious inquiry without speaking it.

'She accepts me,' said the Bishop in a low voice. 'And the wedding is to be soon – the first week in September. Her long solitude and sufferings justify haste. What you said was true. Sheer weariness and distraction have driven her to me. She was quite passive at last, and agreed to anything I proposed – such is the persuasive force of trained logical reasoning! A good and wise woman, she perceived what a true shelter from sadness was offered in this, and was not the one to despise Heaven's gift.'

CHAPTER FORTY

THE silence of Swithin was to be accounted for by the fact that neither to the Mediterranean nor to America had he in the first place directed his steps. Feeling himself absolutely free he had, on arriving at Southampton, decided to make straight for the Cape, and hence had not gone aboard the *Occidental* at all. His object was to leave his heavier luggage there, examine the capabilities of the spot for his purpose, find out the necessity or otherwise of shipping over his own equatorial, and then cross to America as soon as there was a good opportunity. Here he might inquire the movements of the Transit expedition to the South Pacific, and join it at such a point as might be convenient.

Thus, though wrong in her premisses, Viviette had intuitively decided with sad precision. There was, as a matter of fact, a great possibility of her not being able to communicate with him for several months, notwithstanding that he might possibly communicate with her.

This excursive time was an awakening for Swithin. To altered circumstances inevitably followed altered views. That such changes should have a marked effect upon a young man who had made neither grand tour nor petty one – who had, in short, scarcely been away from home in his life – was nothing more than natural. New ideas struggled to disclose themselves; and with the addition of strange twinklers to his southern horizon came an absorbed attention that way, and a corresponding forgetfulness of what lay to the north behind his back, whether human or celestial. Whoever may deplore it few will wonder that Viviette, who till then had stood high in his heaven, if she had not dominated it, sank, like the North Star, lower and lower with his retreat southward. Master of a large advance of his first year's income in circular notes,* he perhaps too readily forgot that the mere act of honour, but for her self-suppression, would have rendered him penniless.

Meanwhile, to come back and claim her at the specified time, four years thence, if she should not object to be claimed, was as much a part of his programme as were the exploits abroad and elsewhere that were to prelude it. The very thoroughness of his intention for that advanced date inclined him all the more readily to shelve the subject now. Her unhappy caution to him not to write too soon was a comfortable licence in his present state of tension about sublime scientific things, which knew not woman, nor her sacrifices, nor her fears. In truth he was not only too young in years, but too literal, direct, and uncompromising in nature to understand such a woman as Lady Constantine; and she suffered for that limitation in him as it had been antecedently probable that she would do.

He stayed but a little time at Cape Town on this his first reconnoitring journey; and on that account wrote to no one from the place. On leaving he found there remained some weeks on his hands before he wished to cross to America; and feeling an irrepressible desire for further studies in navigation on shipboard, and under clear skies, he took the steamer for Melbourne; returning thence in due time, and pursuing his journey to America, where he landed at Boston.

Having at last had enough of great circles* and other nautical reckonings, and taking no interest in men or cities, this indefatigable scrutineer of the universe went immediately on to Cambridge, U.S.,* and there, by the help of an introduction he had brought from England, he revelled for a time in the glories of the gigantic refractor (which he was permitted to use on occasion), and in the pleasures of intercourse with the scientific group around. This brought him on to the time of starting with the Transit expedition, when he and his kind became lost to the eye of civilization behind the horizon of the Pacific Ocean.

To speak of their doings on this pilgrimage, of ingress and egress,* of tangent and parallax,* of external and internal contact,* would avail nothing. Is it not all written in the chronicles of the Astronomical Society? More to the point will it be to mention that Viviette's letter to Cambridge had been returned long before he reached that place, while her missive to Marseilles was, of course, misdirected altogether. On arriving in America, uncertain of an address in that country at which he would stay long, Swithin wrote his first letter to his grandmother; and in this he ordered that all communications should be sent to await him at Cape Town, as the only safe spot for finding him, sooner or later. The equatorial he also directed to be forwarded to the same place. At this time, too, he ventured to break Viviette's commands, and address a letter to her, not knowing of the strange results that had followed his absence from home.

It was February. The Transit was over,* the scientific company had broken up, and Swithin had steamed towards the Cape to take up his permanent abode there, with a view to his great task of surveying, charting and theorizing on those exceptional features in the southern skies which had been but partially treated by the younger Herschel.* Having entered Table Bay and landed on the quay, he called at once at the post-office.

Two letters were handed him, and he found from the date that they had been waiting there for some time. One of these epistles, which had a weather-worn look as regarded the ink, and was in old-fashioned penmanship, he knew to be from his grandmother. He opened it before he had as much as glanced at the superscription of the second.

Besides immaterial portions, it contained the following: –

J reckon* you know by now of our main news this fall,* but lest you should not have heard of it J send the exact thing snipped out of the newspaper. Nobody expected her to do it quite so soon; but it is said hereabout that my lord bishop and my lady had been drawing nigh to an understanding before the glum tidings of Sir Blount's taking of his own life reached her; and the account of this wicked deed was so sore afflicting to her mind, and made her poor heart so timid and low, that in charity to my lady her few friends agreed on urging her to let the bishop go on paying his court as before, notwithstanding she had not been a widow-woman near so long as was thought. This, as it turned out, she was willing to do; and when my lord asked her she told him she would marry him at once or never. That's as J was told, and J had it from those that know.

The cutting from the newspaper was an ordinary announcement of marriage between the Bishop of Melchester and Lady Constantine.

Swithin was so astounded at the intelligence of what for the nonce* seemed Viviette's wanton fickleness that he quite omitted to look at the second letter; and remembered nothing about it till an hour afterwards, when sitting in his own room at the hotel.

It was in her handwriting, but so altered that its superscription had not arrested his eye. It had no beginning, or date; but its contents soon acquainted him with her motive for the precipitate act. The few concluding sentences are all that it will be necessary to quote here: –

There was no way out of it, even if I could have found you, without infringing one of the conditions I had previously laid down. The long desire of my heart has been not to impoverish you or mar your career. The new desire was to save myself and, still more, another yet unborn. . . . I have done a desperate thing. Yet for myself I could do no better, and for you no less. I would have sacrificed my single self to honesty, but I was not alone concerned. What woman has a right to blight a coming life to preserve her personal integrity? . . . The one bright spot is that it saves you and your endowment from further catastrophes, and preserves you to the pleasant paths of scientific fame. I no longer lie like a log across your path, which is now as open as on the day before you saw me, and ere I encouraged you to win me. Alas, Swithin, I ought to have known better. The folly was great, and the suffering be upon my head! I ought not to have consented to that last interview: all was well till then! . . . Well, I have borne much, and am not unprepared. As for you, Swithin, by simply pressing straight on your triumph is assured. Do not communicate with me in any way – not even in answer to this. Do not think of me. Do not see me ever any more. – Your unhappy

VIVIETTE

Swithin's heart swelled within him in sudden pity for her, first; then he blanched with a horrified sense of what she had done, and at his own relation to the deed. He felt like an awakened somnambulist who should find that he had been accessory to a tragedy during his unconsciousness. She had loosened the knot of her difficulties by cutting* it unscrupulously through and through.

The big tidings rather dazed than crushed him, his predominant feeling being soon again one of keenest sorrow and sympathy. Yet one thing was obvious; he could do nothing – absolutely nothing. The event which he now heard of for the first time had taken place five long months ago. He reflected, and regretted – and mechanically went on with his preparations for settling down to work under the shadow of Table Mountain. He was as one who suddenly finds the world a stranger place than he thought; but is excluded by age, temperament, and situation from being much more than an astonished spectator of its strangeness.

The Royal Observatory was about a mile out of the town, and hither he repaired as soon as he had established himself in lodgings. He had decided, on his first visit to the Cape, that it would be highly advantageous to him if he could supplement the occasional use of the large instruments here by the use at his own house of his own equatorial, and had accordingly given directions that it might be sent over from England. The precious possession now arrived; and although the sight of it – of the brasses on which her hand had often rested, of the eyepiece through which her dark eyes had beamed – engendered some decidedly bitter regrets in him for a time, he could not long afford to give to the past the days that were meant for the future.

Unable to get a room convenient for a private observatory he resolved at last to fix the instrument on a solid pillar in the garden; and several days were spent in accommodating it to its new position. In this latitude there was no necessity for economizing clear nights as he had been obliged to do on the old tower at Welland. There it had happened more than once that, after waiting idle through days and nights of cloudy weather, Viviette would fix her time for meeting him at an hour when at last he had an opportunity of seeing the sky; so that in giving to her the golden moments of cloudlessness he was losing his chance with the orbs above.

Those features which usually attract the eye of the visitor to a new latitude are the novel forms of human and vegetable life, and other such sublunary things. But the young man glanced slightingly at these; the changes overhead* had all his attention. The old subject was imprinted there, but in a new type. Here was a heaven, fixed and ancient as the northern; yet much of it had never appeared above the Welland hills since they were heaved up from beneath. Here was an unalterable circumpolar* region; but the polar patterns stereotyped in history and legend – without which it had almost seemed that a polar sky could not exist – had never been seen therein.

St Cleeve, as was natural, began by cursory surveys, which were not likely to be of much utility to the world or to himself. He wasted several weeks – indeed above two months – in a comparatively idle survey of southern novelties; in the mere luxury of looking at stellar objects whose wonders were known, recounted, and classified, long before his own personality had been heard of. With a child's simple delight he allowed his instrument to rove, evening after evening, from the gorgeous glitter of Canopus* to the hazy clouds of Magellan.* Before he had well finished this optical prelude there floated over to him from the other side of the Equator the postscript to the epistle of his lost Viviette. It came in the vehicle of a common newspaper, under the head of 'Births': –

April 10th, 18–, at the Palace, Melchester, the wife of the Bishop of Melchester, of a son.

CHAPTER FORTY-ONE

THREE years passed away, and Swithin still remained at the Cape, quietly pursuing the work that had brought him there. His memoranda of observations had accumulated to a wheelbarrow load, and he was beginning to shape them into a treatise which should possess some scientific utility.

He had gauged the southern skies with greater results than even he himself had anticipated. Those unfamiliar constellations which, to the casual beholder, are at most a new arrangement of ordinary points of light were, to this professed astronomer as to his brethren, a far greater matter.

It was below the surface that his material lay. There, in regions revealed only to the instrumental observer, were suns of hybrid kind – fire-fogs, floating nuclei, globes that flew in groups like swarms of bees,* and other extraordinary sights – which, when decomposed by Swithin's equatorial, turned out to be the beginning of a new series of phenomena instead of the end of an old one.

There were gloomy deserts in those southern skies such as the north shows scarcely an example of; sites set apart for the position of suns which for some unfathomable reason were left uncreated, their places remaining ever since conspicuous by their emptiness.

The inspection of these chasms brought him a second pulsation of that old horror which he had used to describe to Viviette as produced in him by bottomlessness in the north heaven. The ghostly finger of limitless vacancy touched him now on the other side. Infinite deeps in the north stellar region had a homely familiarity about them, when compared with infinite deeps in the region of the south pole. This was an even more unknown tract of the unknown. Space here, being less the historic haunt of human thought than overhead at home, seemed to be pervaded with a more lonely loneliness.

Were there given on paper to these astronomical exercitations of St Cleeve a space proportionable to that occupied by his year with

Viviette at Welland, this narrative would treble its length; but not a single additional glimpse would be afforded of Swithin in his relations with old emotions. In these experiments with tubes and glasses, important as they were to human intellect, there was little food for the sympathetic instincts which create the changes in a life. That which is the foreground and measuring base of one perspective draught may be the vanishing-point of another perspective draught, while yet they are both draughts of the same thing. Swithin's doings and discoveries in the southern sidereal system were, no doubt, incidents of the highest importance to him; and yet from an inter-social point of view they served but the humble purpose of killing time, while other doings, more nearly allied to his heart than to his understanding, developed themselves at home.

In the intervals between his professional occupations he took walks over the sand-flats near, or among the farms which were gradually overspreading the country in the vicinity of Cape Town. He grew familiar with the outline of Table Mountain, and the fleecy 'Devil's Table-Cloth'* which used to settle on its top when the wind was south-east. On these promenades he would more particularly think of Viviette, and of that curious pathetic chapter in his life with her which seemed to have wound itself up and ended for ever. Those scenes were rapidly receding into distance, and the intensity of his sentiment regarding them had proportionately abated. He felt that there had been something wrong therein, and yet he could not exactly define the boundary of the wrong. Viviette's sad and amazing sequel to that chapter had still a fearful, catastrophic aspect in his eyes; but instead of musing over it and its bearings he shunned the subject, as we shun by night the shady scene of a disaster, and keep to the open road.

He sometimes contemplated her apart from the past – leading her life in the Cathedral Close at Melchester; and wondered how often she looked south and thought of where he was.

On one of these afternoon walks in the neighbourhood of the Royal Observatory he turned and gazed towards the signal-post on the Lion's Rump.* This was a high promontory to the north-west of Table Mountain, and overlooked Table Bay. Before his eyes had left the scene the signal was suddenly hoisted on the staff. It announced that a mail steamer had appeared in view over the sea. In the course of an hour he retraced his steps, as he had often done on such occasions, and strolled leisurely across the intervening mile and a half till he arrived at the post-office door.

There was no letter from England for him; but there was a newspaper, addressed in the seventeenth-century handwriting of his grandmother, who, in spite of her great age, still retained a steady hold on life. He turned away disappointed, and resumed his walk into the country, opening the paper as he went along.

A cross in black ink attracted his attention; and it was opposite a name among the 'Deaths'. His blood ran icily as he discerned the words 'The Palace, Melchester'. But it was not she. Her husband, the Bishop of Melchester, had, after a short illness, departed this life at the comparatively early age of fifty-four years.

All the enactments of the bygone days at Welland now started up like an awakened army from the ground. But a few months were wanting to the time when he would be of an age to marry without sacrificing the annuity which formed his means of subsistence. It was a point in his life that had had no meaning or interest for him since his separation from Viviette, for women were now no more to him than the inhabitants of Jupiter. But the whirligig of time* having again set Viviette free, the aspect of home altered, and conjecture as to her future found room to work anew.

But beyond the simple fact that she was a widow he for some time gained not an atom of intelligence concerning her. There was no one of whom he could inquire but his grandmother, and she could tell him nothing about a lady who dwelt far away at Melchester.

Several months slipped by thus; and no feeling within him rose to sufficient strength to force him out of a passive attitude. Then by the merest chance his granny stated in one of her rambling epistles that Lady Constantine was coming to live again at Welland in the old house, with her child, now a little boy between three and four years of age.

Swithin, however, lived on as before.

But by the following autumn a change became necessary for the young man himself. His work at the Cape was done. His uncle's wishes that he should study there had been more than observed. The materials for his great treatise were collected, and it now only remained for him to arrange, digest, and publish them, for which purpose a return to England was indispensable.

So the equatorial was unscrewed, and the stand taken down; the astronomer's barrow-load of precious memoranda, and rolls upon rolls of diagrams, representing three years of continuous labour, were safely packed; and Swithin departed for good and all from the shores of Cape Town.

He had long before informed his grandmother of the date at which she might expect him; and in a reply from her, which reached him just previous to sailing, she casually mentioned that she frequently saw Lady Constantine; that on the last occasion her ladyship had shown great interest in the information that Swithin was coming home, and had inquired the time of his return.

On a late summer day Swithin stepped from the train at Warborne, and, directing his baggage to be sent on after him, set out on foot for old Welland once again.

It seemed but the day after his departure, so little had the scene changed. True, there was that change which is always the first to arrest attention in places that are conventionally called unchanging – a higher and broader vegetation at every familiar corner than at the former time.

He had not gone a mile when he saw walking before him a clergyman whose form, after consideration, he recognized, in spite of a novel whiteness in that part of his hair that showed below the brim of his hat. Swithin walked much faster than this gentleman, and soon was at his side.

'Mr Torkingham! I knew it was,' said Swithin.

Mr Torkingham was slower in recognizing the astronomer, but in a moment had greeted him with a warm shake of the hand.

'I have been to the station on purpose to meet you!' cried Mr Torkingham, 'and was returning with the idea that you had not come. I am your grandmother's emissary. She could not come herself, and as she was anxious, and nobody else could be spared, I came for her.'

Then they walked on together. The parson told Swithin all about his grandmother, the parish, and his endeavours to enlighten it; and in due course said, 'You are no doubt aware that Lady Constantine is living again at Welland?'

Swithin said he had heard as much, and added, what was far within the truth, that the news of the Bishop's death had been a great surprise to him.

'Yes,' said Mr Torkingham, with nine thoughts to one word. 'One might have prophesied, to look at him, that Melchester would not lack a bishop for the next forty years. Yes; pale death knocks at the cottages of the poor and the palaces of kings with an impartial foot!'*

'Was he a particularly good man?' asked Swithin.

'He was not a Ken* or a Heber.* To speak candidly, he had his faults, of which arrogance was not the least. But who is perfect?'

Swithin, somehow, felt relieved to hear that the Bishop was not a perfect man.

'His poor wife, I fear, had not a great deal more happiness with him than with her first husband. But one might almost have foreseen it; the marriage was hasty – the result of a red-hot caprice, hardly becoming in a man of his position; and it betokened a want of temperate discretion which soon showed itself in other ways. That's all there was to be said against him; and now it's all over, and things have settled again into their old course. But the Bishop's widow is not the Lady Constantine of former days. No; put it as you will, she is not the same. There seems to be a nameless something on her mind – a trouble – a rooted melancholy, which no man's ministry* can reach. Formerly she was a woman whose confidence it was easy to gain; but neither religion nor philosophy avails with her now. Beyond that, her life is strangely like what it was when you were with us.'

Conversing thus they pursued the turnpike road till their conversation was interrupted by a crying voice on their left. They looked, and perceived that a child, in getting over an adjoining stile, had fallen on his face.

Mr Torkingham and Swithin both hastened up to help the sufferer, who was a lovely little fellow with flaxen hair, which spread out in a frill of curls from beneath a quaint, close-fitting velvet cap that he wore. Swithin picked him up, while Mr Torkingham wiped the sand from his lips and nose, and administered a few words of consolation, together with a few sweetmeats, which, somewhat to Swithin's surprise, the parson produced as if by magic from his pocket. One half the comfort rendered would have sufficed to soothe such a disposition as the child's. He ceased crying and ran away in delight to his unconscious* nurse, who was reaching up for blackberries at a hedge some way off.

'You know who he is, of course?' said Mr Torkingham, as they resumed their journey.

'No,' said Swithin.

'O, I thought you did. Yet how should you? It is Lady Constantine's boy – her only child. Remarkably fine boy, and yet he was a seven-months' baby. His fond mother little thinks he is so far away from home.'

'Dear me! – Lady Constantine's – ah, how interesting!' Swithin paused abstractedly for a moment, then stepped back again to the stile, while he stood watching the little boy out of sight.

'I can never venture out of doors now without sweets in my pocket,' continued the good-natured vicar: 'and the result is that I meet that young man more frequently on my rounds than any other of my parishioners.'

St Cleeve was silent, and they turned into Welland Lane, where their paths presently diverged, and Swithin was left to pursue his way alone. He might have accompanied the vicar yet further, and gone straight to Welland House; but it would have been difficult to do so then without provoking inquiry. It was easy to go there now: by a cross path he could be at the mansion almost as soon as by the direct road. And yet Swithin did not turn; he felt an indescribable reluctance to see Viviette. He could not exactly say why. True, before he knew how the land lay it might be awkward to attempt to call: and this was a sufficient excuse for postponement.

In this mood he went on, following the direct way to his grandmother's homestead. He reached the garden-gate, and, looking into the bosky* basin where the old house stood, saw a graceful female form moving before the porch, bidding adieu to some one within the door.

He wondered what creature of that mould his grandmother could know, and went forward with some hesitation. At his approach the apparition turned, and he beheld, developed into blushing womanhood, one who had once been known to him as the village maiden Tabitha Lark. Seeing Swithin, and apparently from an instinct that her presence would not be desirable just then, she moved quickly round into the garden.

The returned traveller entered the house, where he found awaiting him poor old Mrs Martin, to whose earthly course death stood rather as the asymptote* than as the end. She was perceptibly smaller in form than when he had left her, and she could see less distinctly.

A rather affecting greeting followed, in which his grandmother murmured the words of Israel:* '"Now let me die, since I have seen thy face, because thou art yet alive."'

The form of Hannah had disappeared from the kitchen, that ancient servant having been gathered to her fathers about six months before, her place being filled by a young girl who knew not Joseph.* They presently chatted with much cheerfulness, and his grandmother said, 'Have you heard what a wonderful young woman Miss Lark has become? – a mere fleet-footed, slittering* maid when you were last home.'

St Cleeve had not heard, but he had partly seen, and he was informed that Tabitha had left Welland shortly after his own departure, and had studied music with great success in London, where she had resided ever since till quite recently; that she played at concerts, oratorios – had, in short, joined the phalanx of Wonderful Women* who had resolved to eclipse masculine genius altogether, and humiliate the brutal sex to the dust.

'She is only in the garden,' added his grandmother. 'Why don't ye go out and speak to her?'

Swithin was nothing loth, and strolled out under the apple-trees, where he arrived just in time to prevent Miss Lark from going off by the back gate. There was not much difficulty in breaking the ice between them, and they began to chat with vivacity.

Now all these proceedings occupied time, for somehow it was very charming to talk to Miss Lark; and by degrees St Cleeve informed Tabitha of his great undertaking, and of the voluminous notes he had amassed, which would require so much rearrangement and recopying by an amanuensis as to absolutely appal him. He greatly feared he should not get one careful enough for such scientific matter; whereupon Tabitha said she would be delighted to do it for him. Then blushing, and declaring suddenly that it had grown quite late, she left him and the garden for her relation's house hard by.

Swithin, no less than Tabitha, had been surprised by the disappearance of the sun behind the hill; and the question now arose whether it would be advisable to call upon Viviette that night. There was little doubt that she knew of his coming; but more than that he could not predicate; and being entirely ignorant of whom she had around her, entirely in the dark as to her present feelings towards him, he thought it would be better to defer his visit until the next day.

Walking round to the front of the house he beheld the well-known agriculturists Hezzy Biles, Haymoss Fry, and some others of the same old school, passing the gate homeward from their work with bundles of wood at their backs. Swithin saluted them over the top rail.

'Well! do my eyes and ears—' began Hezzy; and then, balancing his faggot on end against the hedge, he came forward, the others following.

'Says I to myself as soon as I heerd his voice,' Hezzy continued (addressing Swithin as if he were a disinterested spectator and not himself), 'please God I'll pitch my nitch,* and go across and speak to en.'

'I knowed in a winking 'twas some great navigator that I see a standing there,' said Haymoss. 'But whe'r 'twere a sort of nabob,* or a diment-digger,* or a lion-hunter, I couldn't so much as guess till I heerd en speak.'

'And what changes have come over Welland since I was last at home?' asked Swithin.

'Well, Mr San Cleeve,' Hezzy replied, 'when you've said that a few stripling boys and maidens have busted into blooth,* and a few married women have plimmed and chimped* (my lady among 'em), why, you've said anighst* all, Mr San Cleeve.'

The conversation thus begun was continued on divers matters till they were all enveloped in total darkness, when his old acquaintances shouldered their faggots again and proceeded on their way.

Now that he was actually within her coasts again Swithin felt a little more strongly the influence of the past and Viviette than he had been accustomed to do for the last two or three years. During the night he felt half sorry that he had not marched off to the Great House to see her, regardless of the time of day. If she really nourished for him any particle of her old affection it had been the cruellest thing not to call. A few questions that he put concerning her to his grandmother elicited that Lady Constantine had no friends about her – not even her brother – and that her health had not been so good since her return from Melchester as formerly. Still, this proved nothing as to the state of her heart, and as she had kept a dead silence since the Bishop's death it was quite possible that she would meet him with that cold repressive tone and manner which experienced women know so well how to put on when they wish to intimate to the long-lost lover that past episodes are to be taken as forgotten.

The next morning he prepared to call, if only on the ground of old acquaintance, for Swithin was too straightforward to ascertain anything indirectly. It was rather too early for this purpose when he went out from his grandmother's garden-gate, after breakfast, and he waited in the garden. While he lingered his eye fell on Rings-Hill Speer.

It appeared dark, for a moment, against the blue sky behind it; then the fleeting cloud which shadowed it passed on, and the face of the column brightened into such luminousness that the sky behind sank to the complexion of a dark foil.

'Surely somebody is on the column,' he said to himself, after gazing at it awhile.

Instead of going straight to the Great House he deviated through the insulating field, now sown with turnips, which surrounded the plantation on Rings-Hill. By the time that he plunged under the trees he was still more certain that somebody was on the tower. He crept up to the base with proprietary curiosity, for the spot seemed again like his own.

The path still remained much as formerly, but the nook in which the cabin had stood was covered with undergrowth. Swithin entered the door of the tower, ascended the staircase about half-way on tip-toe, and listened, for he did not wish to intrude on the top if any stranger were there. The hollow spiral, as he knew from old experience, would bring down to his ears the slightest sound from above; and it now revealed to him the words of a duologue in progress at the summit of the tower.

'Mother, what shall I do?' a child's voice said. 'Shall I sing?'

The mother seemed to assent, for the child began –

> 'The robin has fled from the wood,
> To the snug habitation of man.'

This performance apparently attracted but little attention from the child's companion, for the young voice suggested, as a new form of entertainment, 'Shall I say my prayers?'

'Yes,' replied one whom Swithin had begun to recognize.

'Who shall I pray for?'

No answer.

'Who shall I pray for?'

'Pray for father.'

'But he is gone to heaven?'

A sigh from Viviette was distinctly audible.

'You made a mistake, didn't you, mother?' continued the little one.

'I must have. The strangest mistake a woman ever made!'

Nothing more was said, and Swithin ascended, words from above indicating to him that his footsteps were heard. In another half-minute he rose through the hatchway. A lady in black was sitting in the sun, and the boy with the flaxen hair whom he had seen yesterday was at her feet.

'Viviette!' he said.

'Swithin! – at last!' she cried.

The words died upon her lips, and from very faintness she bent her head. For instead of rushing forward to her he had stood still; and there appeared upon his face a look which there was no mistaking.

Yes; he was shocked at her worn and faded aspect. The image he had mentally carried out with him to the Cape he had brought home again as that of the woman he was now to rejoin. But another woman sat before him, and not the original Viviette. Her cheeks had lost for ever that firm contour which had been drawn by the vigorous hand of youth, and the masses of hair that were once darkness visible* had become touched here and there by a faint grey haze, like the Via Lactea* in a midnight sky.

Yet to those who had eyes to understand as well as to see, the chastened pensiveness of her once handsome features revealed more promising material beneath than ever her youth had done. But Swithin was hopelessly her junior. Unhappily for her he had now just arrived at an age whose canon of faith it is that the silly period of woman's life is her only period of beauty. Viviette saw it all, and knew that Time had at last brought about his revenges.* She had tremblingly watched and waited without sleep, ever since Swithin had re-entered Welland, and it was for this.

Swithin came forward, and took her by the hand, which she passively allowed him to do.

'Swithin, you don't love me,' she said simply.

'O Viviette!'

'You don't love me,' she repeated.

'Don't say it!'

'Yes, but I will! you have a right not to love me. You did once. But now I am an old woman, and you are still a young man; so how can you love me? I do not expect it. It is kind and charitable of you to come and see me here.'

'I have come all the way from the Cape,' he faltered, for her insistence took all power out of him to deny in mere politeness what she said.

'Yes; you have come from the Cape; but not for me,' she answered. 'It would be absurd if you had come for me. You have come because your work there is finished. . . . I like to sit here with my little boy – it is a pleasant spot. It was once something to us, was it not? but that was long ago. You scarcely knew me for the same woman, did you?'

'Knew you – yes, of course I knew you!'

'You looked as if you did not. But you must not be surprised at me. I belong to an earlier generation than you, remember.'

Thus, in sheer bitterness of spirit did she inflict wounds on herself by exaggerating the difference in their years. But she had nevertheless spoken truly. Sympathize with her as he might, and as he unquestionably did, he loved her no longer. But why had she expected otherwise? 'O woman,' might a prophet have said to her, 'great is thy faith if thou believest a junior lover's love will last five years!'*

'I shall be glad to know through your grandmother how you are getting on,' she said meekly. 'But now I would much rather that we part. Yes; do not question me. I would rather that we part. Good-bye.'

Hardly knowing what he did he touched her hand, and obeyed. He was a scientist, and took words literally. There is something in the inexorably simple logic of such men which partakes of the cruelty of the natural laws* that are their study. He entered the tower-steps, and mechanically descended; and it was not till he got half-way down that he thought she could not mean what she had said.

Before leaving Cape Town he had made up his mind on this one point; that if she were willing to marry him, marry her he would without let or hindrance. That much he morally owed her, and was not the man to demur. And though the Swithin who had returned was not quite the Swithin who had gone away, though he could not now love her with the sort of love he had once bestowed; he believed that all her conduct had been dictated by the purest benevolence to him, by that charity which 'seeketh not her own'.* Hence he did not flinch from a wish to deal with loving-kindness* towards her – a sentiment perhaps in the long-run more to be prized than lover's love.*

Her manner had caught him unawares; but now recovering himself he turned back determinedly. Bursting out upon the roof he clasped her in his arms, and kissed her several times.

'Viviette, Viviette,' he said, 'I came to marry you, and I will!'

She uttered a shriek – a shriek of amazed joy – such as never was heard on that tower before or since – and fell in his arms, clasping his neck.

There she lay heavily. Not to disturb her he sat down in her seat, still holding her fast. Their little son, who had stood with round conjectural eyes throughout the meeting, now came close; and presently looking up to Swithin said –

'Mother has gone to sleep.'

Swithin looked down, and started. Her tight clasp had loosened. A wave of whiteness, like that of marble which had never seen the sun, crept up from her neck, and travelled upwards and onwards over her cheek, lips, eyelids, forehead, temples, its margin banishing back the live pink till the latter had entirely disappeared.

Seeing that something was wrong, yet not understanding what, the little boy began to cry; but in his concentration Swithin hardly heard it. 'Viviette – Viviette!' he said.

The child cried with still deeper grief, and, after a momentary hesitation, pushed his hand into Swithin's for protection.

'Hush, hush! my child,' said Swithin distractedly. 'I'll take care of you! O Viviette!' he exclaimed again, pressing her face to his.

But she did not reply.

'What can this be?' he asked himself. He would not then answer according to his fear.

He looked up for help. Nobody appeared in sight but Tabitha Lark, who was skirting the field with a bounding tread – the single bright spot of colour and animation* within the wide horizon. When he looked down again his fear deepened to certainty. It was no longer a mere surmise that help was vain. Sudden joy after despair had touched an over-strained heart too smartly. Viviette was dead. The Bishop was avenged.

Notes

29 *several eminent pens.* Compare Hardy to Edmund Gosse, 10 December 1882: 'Eminent critics write and tell me in private that [*Two on a Tower*] is the most original thing I have done. . . . While other eminent critics (I wonder if they are the same) *print* the most cutting rebukes you can conceive – show me (to my amazement) that I am quite an immoral person: till I conclude that we are never again to be allowed to laugh and say with Launce – "it is a wise father that knows his own child" ' (R. L. Purdy, *Thomas Hardy: a bibliographical study* (1954) pp. 44–5). Hardy's answer to one of these critics is quoted in the Introduction, p. 15. See p. 311.

31 *landau.* A four-wheeled carriage, the upper part of which may be closed, open, or half-open.

31 *by inching and pinching.* By slow degrees, with difficulty.

32 *segmental.* Part of a circle (a term which came readily to an architect).

32 *the American war.* The War of Independence (1775–83): see also p. 37. The originals of the tower (see p. 317) were dated 1761 and 1790.

33 *castle.* Defensive position, series of earthworks.

33 *Witenagemote.* The supreme council of England in Anglo-Saxon times.

33 *vallum.* The Roman name for a ridge or bank thrown up from the fosse or ditch.

33 *overlapping ends.* Constructed in this way to make the prehistoric camp less accessible to the enemy.

33 *Tuscan.* Robust but unadorned, the simplest and rudest of the five classical orders, supposedly from the pillar style in Etruscan temples.

33 *rabbit-runs.* Tracks made by rabbits.

33 *exuviæ.* Cast-off skins.

35 *the times of the Classical Dictionary.* The period to which the Greek and Roman myths and legends belong.

35 *Lothario or Juan.* Handsome deceivers of women.

35 *Raffaelle.* Raphael, an Italian painter (1483–1520).

35 *son of Zacharias.* John the Baptist. He appears as an infant with a sun-tanned complexion in Raphael's 'Garvagh Madonna', which was acquired in 1865 by the National Gallery, where Hardy made a study of the paintings in his spare time while employed as an architect in London from 1862 to 1867.

35 *Romance.* She had the temperament more typical of southern Europe, where the Romance languages (derived from Latin or the Roman tongue) were spoken.

36 *terrene.* On earth.

36 *'Will it make any difference to us here?'* For the significance of the irony, see Hardy's Preface, p. 29.

36 *influence.* Hardy alludes to the old astrological belief that the stars' rays

influenced (literally flowed into) people; cf. the lines from John Milton's 'L'Allegro',

> . . . store of ladies, whose bright eyes
> Rain influence,

which Hardy included on the title-page of *A Group of Noble Dames* (1891).

37 *Rings-Hill Speer*. Named after the spire or obelisk within the earthworks encircling the top of the hill; see p. 317.

37 *Astronomer Royal*. The astronomer in charge of the Royal Greenwich Observatory.

38 *equatorial*. A mechanism which causes a telescope to move round in accordance with the apparent motion of the heavenly bodies, so that direct observation of a star or planet is possible at any time when it is visible.

38 *time is short, and science is infinite*. A variant of the first aphorism of Hippocrates, the famous Greek physician of the fourth century B.C.: 'Life is short, but the art is long.'

39 *'tempted*. i.e., no attempt had been made to beget her.

39 *Grammer*. (Dial.) Grandmother.

39 *gam'sters*. Fortune-seekers.

39 *draw . . . pan*. Force it to grow quickly.

39 *hit*. Force, drive.

39 *en . . . 'a*. (Dial.) him . . . he.

39 *talk like the day of Pentecost*. See Acts, II 1–4.

39 *plainest ciphering*. Capable only of the simplest arithmetic.

39 *bruckle hit*. (Dial.) mistake.

39 *the high*. The country gentry or 'toppermost folk'.

39 *limberish*. (Dial.) rather frail.

39 *mind*. (Dial.) remember.

39 *windling*. Wasting away (cf. 'dwindling').

39 *playward*. (Dial.) playful, lively.

40 *socked and sighed*. (Dial.) sighed loudly.

40 *snoff*. (Dial.) snuff of a candle.

40 *dazed*. (Dial.) damned.

40 *trumpery*. Rubbish, nonsense.

40 *as I say for*. As I said before.

40 *Eden of unconsciousness*. State of innocence, sexual unawareness.

40 *Caliban*. Ugly, monstrous; see Shakespeare's *The Tempest*.

41 *sweeping*. Surveying section by section.

41 *dormers*. Vertical windows projecting from a sloping roof.

41 *mob cap*. Indoor cap once worn by women and fastened under the chin.

42 *my old county*. This reminiscence is almost certainly based on Hardy's recollections of his paternal grandmother, who left the village of Fawley in Berkshire at the age of thirteen. In her old age she lived with the Hardys in Higher Bockhampton near Dorchester.

42 *dog how art*. (Dial.) an untraced expression meaning 'How are you?'

42 *'other station . . . blood'*. A reference to Amos Fry's remarks, p. 40.

43 *so many notches above her*. So much above her station.

43 *chaw high.* Have superior tastes.

44 *stoning of Stephen.* See Acts, VII 54–60.

44 *flick-flack.* Trippingly, without pause.

44 *the disobedient woman in Deuteronomy.* See Deuteronomy, XXVIII 67. 'A Ballad of Burdens', one of A. C. Swinburne's *Poems and Ballads,* which Hardy read with avid delight in 1866, helped to fix this passage in his memory.

44 *Tedious traipsing.* Slow, wearisome business.

45 *primest.* Best.

45 *St Martin's days.* St Martin's Day, or Martinmas, is 11 November.

45 *barley-mow.* Stack of barley.

45 *club-walking.* A 'club' was a parish 'friendly society', a benefit club which held a yearly 'walking' or procession at Whitsuntide. (Cf. William Barnes's poem 'Whitsuntide an' Club Walken' and also *Tess of the d'Urbervilles,* ch. 2.)

45 *jints.* (Dial.) joints.

45 *assembling myself.* Appearing.

45 *Welland Steeple.* The high tower of the church at Welland.

45 *clitch.* Crook.

45 *clots.* Turves.

46 *harnet's.* (Dial.) hornet's.

46 *send.* Grant.

46 *breast-ploughing.* Paring turf with an implement like a plough which was pushed from the chest.

46 *ground-dressing.* Spreading manure over the soil for ploughing in.

46 *mixens.* Manure heaps, which need turning to ensure even decomposition.

46 *wyndpipe.* Windpipe, or trachea.

46 *glutchpipe.* (Dial.) the passage from the throat down which food makes its way.

46 *'The Lord look'd ... view.'* From the Brady and Tate metrical version of the Psalms which was sung in churches. The psalm was chosen by Hardy to suit the theme of the novel.

46 *grater.* A rough-surfaced utensil for grating nutmeg, ginger, etc.

46 *hit up.* (Dial.) strike up.

46 *hawked.* Cleared (my) throat of phlegm.

47 *sol-fa.* Sing note by note, using the syllables *do, re, mi, fa, so, la, ti* for the notes of the major scale (C, D, E, F, G, A, B).

47 *nater.* (Dial.) nature.

47 *"His wife ... shall bring."* Psalm CXXVIII, 3 (metrical version).

47 *martel.* (Dial.) mortal. Used for emphasis only.

48 *have a slap at.* Attempt.

48 *brilliant.* Sparkling in tone.

49 *Hodge and Giles.* Both names are used generically to signify rustic labourers.

49 *at-home cards.* Invitations to receptions within stated times.

51 *rout.* Large evening party or reception.

52 *"An oath ... strife."* See Hebrews, VI 16. Hardy's quotations show a very close knowledge of the Bible. But for the loss of his faith in Christian theology, which resulted from the new scientific outlook of his age, he would almost certainly have entered the Church.

52 *"Pay . . . pay."* See Ecclesiastes, v 4–5.
53 *ecliptic.* The path of the sun as seen from the earth; the planets keep very close to it (within the Zodiac; see note to p. 62).
53 *early-Christian.* i.e., typical of early Christian art.
54 *Mont St Michel.* Steep-rising rocky island off the coast of Normandy, which Hardy visited in 1880.
55 *satellites or meteors.* The subject is the Rings of Saturn, which consist of multitudes of tiny satellites revolving round the planet.
55 *fly-wheel.* A fly-wheel is given momentum by its heavy rim, and for this reason is used to regulate the motion of machinery. The analogy is a simple one; 'close together as to seem solid matter' refers only to the satellites in the Rings of Saturn.
55 *achromatic.* Telescope with lenses which minimise colour distortion.
55 *bring its size up to zero.* Make it more than a point. Though its meaning is clear in the context, the expression 'up to zero' is odd.
55 *in the scrowl . . . constellations.* From *Hudibras,* pt II, canto III, ll. 429–32, the satirical poem by Samuel Butler (1612–80).
56 *Copernicus.* The Polish astronomer (1473–1543) whose revolutionary work overthrew the Ptolemaic theory, causing him to conclude that the sun, not the earth, was the centre of the universe. The thought here was suggested by R. A. Proctor (*Essays in Astronomy* (1872); see p. 13): 'The Copernicus of the sidereal system is not to be expected for many generations.'
56 *the Swan.* Cygnus, one of the northern constellations.
57 *the Coal Sack.* A region, apparently near the constellation of the Southern Cross, where the light of the stars is hidden by cosmic dust.
57 *leave alone.* Not to mention, much less.
58 *leading-strings.* Strings for holding and guiding children when they learn to walk.
58 *the Greater Bear.* Often known as Charles's Wain (see p. 155) or the Plough. It ends in two stars which form a pointer to the Pole Star.
59 *macrocosmic.* Pertaining to the universe at large.
59 *châtelaine.* (French) the lady of the castle or country mansion (with medieval associations.
61 *periodicity.* Regular occurrence.
62 *two stars in the Twins.* Castor and Pollux (Gemini, or the Twins), in the sign of the Zodiac named after them. The Zodiac is the celestial belt around which the sun appears to move; it extends eight or nine degrees on each side of the ecliptic (see note to p. 53) and is divided into twelve signs of equal length, through one of which the sun passes in a month.
64 *object-glass.* The lens in the telescope nearest the object viewed.
64 *wicket.* Small gate.
65 *Palissy.* A French potter of the sixteenth century who was often reduced to extreme poverty before he succeeded in discovering a method of making enamels.
66 *abacus.* The upper part of a column.
67 *Antinous.* There is a link with astronomy in the comparison. Antinous was an eastern youth of whom the Roman emperor Hadrian was so fond that he erected a temple to his memory and encouraged the belief that he had been changed into a constellation.

67 *amoroso.* (Italian) lover.

68 *Circe or Calypso.* After the Trojan War, Ulysses' return home was delayed by shipwrecks and by sojourns with seductive paramours. He stayed with Circe a year; she changed his companions into swine, but he was saved from her enchantment by the herb moly. With Calypso he stayed seven years; she had promised him immortality if he would remain with her. The reference to Ulysses is kept up in 'sailings'.

68 *Limbo.* Originally a region on the borders of Hell where all the just who lived before Christ's coming, and infants who died unbaptised, were once deemed to dwell. Here it has its usual modern meaning of oblivion, the place of all forgotten things.

69 *Cagliostros.* Famous charlatans. Count Cagliostro was the name assumed by an Italian during his European travels in the second half of the eighteenth century. He exploited his scientific knowledge to win wealth and fame as a physician, alchemist and necromancer, purveying among other things the elixir of youth.

70 *feverish fret.* From John Keats's 'the fever and the fret' in his 'Ode to a Nightingale'.

71 *Dorcas meeting.* Meeting of ladies for making and distributing clothes. See Acts, IX 36.

71 *watering-places.* Seaside resorts.

72 *right ascensions and declinations.* These co-ordinates, corresponding to lines of longitude and latitude, give the position of the heavenly bodies.

73 *Lord Angelo of Vienna.* Angelo in Shakespeare's *Measure for Measure*, Act II, sc. IV, ll. 1–4:

> When I would pray and think, I think and pray
> To several subjects. Heaven hath my empty words;
> Whilst my invention, hearing not my tongue,
> Anchors on Isabel.

73 *invention.* Thought, imagination.

73 *cribbed and confined.* From Shakespeare's *Macbeth*, Act III, sc. IV, ll. 24–5:

> But now I am cabin'd, cribb'd, confin'd, bound in
> To saucy doubts and fears.

73 *Astronomer Extraordinary.* A distinguished astronomer appointed as a supernumerary of lower status than an Astronomer Royal, generally for special investigations.

75 *weir-hatch ... inundated.* To prevent or minimise flooding at lower levels, weirs are constructed across rivers, often with a number of flood-gates or hatches to control the flow. Hardy was familiar with them in the Frome valley near Dorchester, e.g., the Ten Hatches Weir of *The Mayor of Casterbridge* and Shadwater Weir of *The Return of the Native.*

76 *'Shall be his Queen.'* Probably an echo of Alfred Tennyson's 'The Beggar Maid':

> So sweet a face, such angel grace,
>   In all the land had never been:
> Cophetua sware a royal oath:
>   'This beggar maid shall be my queen!'

76 *Cicero.* The Roman orator. The reference is to his *Ad Atticum*, bk IV, letter 8.

76 *Adonis.* A beautiful youth with whom Venus fell in love; he was killed while hunting.

77 *he modestly ventured on an apple.* The sequel may suggest an allusion to Eve and the fall of Adam, but the irony of the position is more obviously related to Swithin's boyish misdemeanours.

77 *the Ptolemaic System.* See note to p. 56.

77 *Eudoxus.* An astronomer of the fourth century B.C., the first among the Greeks to regulate the year.

77 *François Arago.* A French scientist and statesman who became director of the Paris Observatory in 1830.

77 *Humboldt.* In his *Cosmos* (1845–62) Friedrich Heinrich von Humboldt attempted to present a picture of the universe. 'In the tropics, where the air is more uniform in texture, so to speak, the stars do not scintillate unless they are quite close to the horizon, "a circumstance", says Humboldt, "which gives a peculiarly calm and serene character to the celestial depths in those countries"' (Proctor, *Essays on Astronomy*).

77 *Sirius ... Arcturus, and Capella.* These are all brilliant stars, the first in the northern hemisphere, the other two in the southern. Sirius may be seen in the northern sky on spring evenings or in autumn after midnight.

78 *lead-flat.* Flat roof covered with lead.

79 *plannards.* (Dial.) planets.

79 *a married example.* One who, as a married woman, ought to set an example.

79 *a Jericho shout.* This alludes to the capture of Jericho by the Israelites: 'the people shouted with a great shout, that the [city] wall fell down flat' (Joshua, VI).

82 *Lion ... Virgin.* Two of the signs of the Zodiac.

83 *like a nether Milky Way.* See p. 23.

83 *French casement.* A window which opens in two vertical halves.

83 *impish claws ... figuring in St Anthony's temptation.* St Anthony of Egypt (third century A.D.) was an ascetic who decided to become an anchorite. His abstinence, temptations and self-inflicted punishments were recorded by St Athanasius, and formed the subject of many religious paintings, where the tempters or devils appeared in the form of various beasts.

84 *bathing-machine.* A hut on wheels, used by bathers for changing, and drawn by horse to and from the edge of the sea.

84 *of lath-work.* Constructed of light strips of wood.

84 *the North Star.* Pole Star or Polaris, so called because it is over the North Pole. Around it, therefore, the heavenly bodies appear to move in the northern sky.

84 *Polaris.* See previous note.

84 *Castor and Pollux.* See note to p. 62.

86 *immortal shepherds ... Bethlehem.* See Matthew, II 1–12.

86 *Music drew an angel down.* From the final chorus of John Dryden's 'Alexander's Feast'.

86 *sidereal.* Of the stars.

87 *unvarnished.* Unpretentious.

87 *diurnal.* It would move a complete circle per day.

88 *Ash-Wednesday.* The first day of Lent, so called from the custom instituted by Pope Gregory the Great of observing that day by sprinkling ashes on the heads of the penitent.

88 *clerk.* One of the offices of the parish clerk was to take a leading part in services on behalf of the congregation, a necessary role when most of the parishioners could not read. In *Far from the Madding Crowd*, Laban Tall, the parish clerk, suffered 'mortal terror' on Sundays 'when he heard his lone voice among certain hard words of the Psalms, whither no man ventured to follow him'.

88 *Commination.* This 'denouncing of God's anger and judgements against Sinners' was read in the churches on Ash Wednesday and at other times.

88 *Adams and Leverrier.* The English astronomer John Adams (1819–92) and the French astronomer Urbain Jean Leverrier (1811–77) independently inferred the existence of a planet from disturbances or irregular movements in the planet Uranus. Proceeding from their calculations, the German astronomer Galle discovered Neptune in 1846.

90 *archivault.* Main vault or dome, the sky as a whole.

91 *Greenwich.* The Royal Observatory at Greenwich, London.

91 *the Royal Society.* Founded in 1660, it was the first scientific society in Great Britain.

91 *a chief office, five miles off.* At Warborne; see p. 151.

92 *American astronomer ... variable stars.* This probably alludes to the work of Prof. E. C. Pickering, whose paper on the subject was first presented in America in May 1880 and published in 1881. See p. 25.

92 *Philosophy.* Originally the study of wisdom and knowledge (including science).

92 *impishness of circumstance.* Compare Hardy's titles, *Satires of Circumstance*, *Life's Little Ironies.*

93 *Crusoe's large boat.* Robinson Crusoe, having built himself a boat, found it was too big to drag to the water.

95 *'Who lay ... ruining.'* From Shakespeare's Sonnet 125.

96 *Gambart's.* It was first seen in 1772 and 1805, but its orbit was calculated independently by Gambart, a French astronomer, and Wilhelm von Biela in 1826. It is usually known as Biela's Comet.

96 *Charles the Fifth's.* The comet of 1556 described by Fabricius, mathematician to Charles V, Holy Roman Emperor, and erroneously believed to have caused his abdication, which occurred in 1555.

96 *Halley's.* Edmund Halley calculated that the comet named after him would appear in 1758. It appeared in 1759 and again in 1835. As the interval between its appearances is about seventy-six years, Swithin must have been delirious.

96 *Faye's.* Faye discovered the comet named after him in 1843. He was made director of the Paris Observatory in 1878.

96 *seed en.* (Dial.) seen it.

96 *comet of 1811.* The first great comet of the nineteenth century, discovered by the French astronomer Flaugergues and observed in most European countries.

96 *Ujiji or Unyamwesi.* In Tanganyika (now Tanzania), east Africa.

97 *blue ocean.* Compare the 'nocturnal sailings', p. 68.

99 *many-chevroned.* With numerous zigzag mouldings.

100 *semi-Norman.* Transitional in style between the rounded Norman and the pointed Early English of the thirteenth century.

100 *blower.* Person working the bellows of the organ.

100 *one of those commandments on the second table.* The Ten Commandments were divided into two tables, the first four comprising duties towards God, and the remainder duties towards one's neighbour. The one which engaged Lady Constantine's attention was the seventh, 'Thou shalt not commit adultery.'

100 *its thunder.* God's voice is associated with thunder in the Bible.

101 *'Dear my love ... for me!'* Heinrich Heine (1797–1856), the German lyrical poet, had a special interest for Hardy, who owned at least two volumes of his verse in translation.

101 *poppy-head.* Carved finial at the end of a church pew.

102 *Zouga.* The Botletle river in Bechuanaland, north of the Kalahari Desert.

104 *personalty.* Personal belongings.

104 *an odd man.* One man only.

104 *donkey-chair.* Small, light, two-wheeled vehicle for one person.

104 *neat.* Strong, undiluted drink.

104 *visitant ... luminous streamer.* Tebbutt's Comet, which the Hardys observed on the night of 25 June 1881, their first in Wimborne. The season suggests this; see p. 51.

107 *ordinated.* Placed in order of precedence or importance.

109 *rathe.* Soon.

109 *Greenhill Fair.* See *Far from the Madding Crowd*, ch. 50.

109 *bain't.* Are not.

109 *backy.* (Dial.) tobacco.

109 *great tumult ... famine.* Cf. Shakespeare's *Julius Caesar*, Act II, sc. II, ll. 30–1, for similar Elizabethan superstitions.

109 *ten or a dozen shillings a week.* Throughout the greater part of the nineteenth century, the wages of agricultural labourers were low; Dorset was one of the depressed counties, and here, in the earlier part of the century, they were often no more than seven or eight shillings a week.

109 *gristing.* Flour from corn that is gleaned.

109 *faggots.* Bundles of sticks for fuel.

110 *randys.* (Dial.) celebrations, parties, enjoyment.

110 *'ooman.* (Dial.) woman.

110 *plannards ... rule them.* At one time it was believed that people's destinies were controlled by the planets.

110 *mid ha'.* (Dial.) may have.

111 *loop-hole.* Opening to admit light and (probably) air.

111 *the heaven above ... Earth beneath.* Hardy alludes to the fable of Aesop in which the astrologer (astronomer), seeing what is in the heavens but not what is on earth, falls into a well.

112 *I'd as lief that.* (Dial.) I should be just as pleased if.

113 *save her from unborn shame.* This, though in a lighter key, anticipates a crisis in the main story.

113 *jineral man.* Servant with general responsibilities, factotum.

115 *fellow-watcher of the skies.* Slightly adapted from Keats's sonnet 'On First

Looking into Chapman's Homer'.

115 *inamorato.* (Italian) young man in love.

115 *'I love you true!'* Suggested by Keats's 'La Belle Dame sans Merci'.

115 *'creep . . . kings'.* Shakespeare's Sonnet 115.

116 *Greek astronomer's.* In Aristophanes' satirical play, *The Clouds*, Socrates is presented as an astronomer enjoying a position so high in the sky to gaze upon the sun that he can look down on the Gods. The 'slight penalty of being consumed the next instant' seems to suggest another context, however.

119 *noble citizen of old Greece.* See Valerius Maximus, *Facta et Dicta Memorabilia*, bk III, ch. 3.

119 *by the card.* In exactly the manner. From Shakespeare's *Hamlet*, Act V, sc. I.

119 *the Eve in us.* The weaker side of woman's nature.

120 *Absalom's death.* During his unsuccessful insurrection against his father, David, King of Israel, Absalom rode on his mule through a wood. His head was caught in the boughs of an oak, 'and he was taken up between the heaven and the earth; and the mule that was under him went away'. While trapped in this position he was slain (II Samuel, XVIII).

122 *thousands of years.* This supports the view that Hardy had Tebbutt's Comet in mind. It is not expected to reappear until about the year 4300.

122 *like an armed man.* Cf. Proverbs, VI 11.

125 *Winstanley.* The architect who lost his life in the Eddystone lighthouse when it was swept away by a gale in 1703.

128 *sufficient time . . . requirements.* Fifteen days normally.

128 *two-and-thirty winds of heaven.* Winds blowing from all directions. The number comes from the points of the compass.

128 *"There is nothing . . . thinking makes it so."* From Shakespeare's *Hamlet*, Act II, sc. II, l. 255.

129 *pinion-end.* Gable end.

129 *'a 's.* (Dial.) she is.

129 *wambling on her pins.* (Dial.) unsteady on her feet.

130 *Sodom and Gomorrah.* Cities which were destroyed by fire from heaven because they were evil (Genesis, XIX 24).

130 *flitch.* Side of bacon.

130 *chine.* The back, including the spine.

130 *palæolithic dead men.* The site had been a prehistoric camp.

130 *apocalyptic.* Suggesting the end of the world. The Apocalypse is the book of Revelation at the end of the New Testament.

133 *drawing . . . covers.* A fox-hunting term which gives a hint of Louis Glanville's English background.

133 *realty.* Real property or estate.

134 *Apollo in person.* Hardy alludes to the intervention of classical gods and goddesses in mortal affairs (e.g., Venus in Virgil's *Aeneid*). Apollo is regarded here as the god of the sun.

135 *old plum-coloured brick street.* Most of Bath, from the late eighteenth century onwards, is in stone. Lady Constantine needed to economise and keep out of the public eye. See p. 311, however.

135 *postilions.* Riders of coach-horses.
136 *winders.* Windows.
136 *courage was screwed.* Cf. Shakespeare's *Macbeth,* Act I, sc. VII, ll. 60–1:

> But screw your courage to the sticking-place,
> And we'll not fail.

136 *surrogate's.* A surrogate was a person appointed by the Church to grant marriage licences which dispensed with banns.
140 *Little signified....* Hardy's vision of man was scientific in some aspects: the individual was insignificant in time and space. See note to p. 130 and the first paragraph of Hardy's preface, p. 29.
144 *air-castles.* Day-dreams.
145 *his bosom's lord ... throne.* Adapted from Shakespeare's *Romeo and Juliet,* Act V, sc. I, l. 3.
146 *fly.* One-horse carriage.
147 *deppity.* (Dial.) deputy.
147 *benefit.* Benefice (a malapropism).
147 *shaddery.* Shadowy, uncertain.
149 *phaeton.* Light, four-wheeled, open carriage.
152 *peculiar dialect of sylvan language.* As an example of Hardy's ability to interpret this language, see the opening lines of *Under the Greenwood Tree.*
152 *Delia's ... times.* Delia and Amanda were common names of heroines in eighteenth-century literature. A powder closet was a small room where powder was applied to the hair. The Georgian period extends from 1714–1830.
154 *buttery.* Pantry.
155 *Aurora Borealis.* The Northern Lights (caused by electrically charged particles from the sun which spiral down open magnetic field lines to form the circle of lights around the magnetic pole).
155 *Glenfinlas.* See Sir Walter Scott's 'Glenfinlas', one of his 'Imitations of the Ancient Ballad':

> Tall wax'd the Spirit's altering form,
> Till to the roof her stature grew;
> Then, mingling with the rising storm,
> With one wild yell away she flew.

155 *waggon ... constellation.* This refers to the configuration of the Greater Bear, and explains why it is often known as Charles's Wain.
158 *the lonely philosopher.* See note to p. 92.
159 *in good sooth.* (Archaic) to be sure, in truth.
160 *chamber organ.* Organ built for installation in a room of a mansion, particularly in the eighteenth century.
161 *dévote.* Devoutly religious woman.
161 *Communion Sunday.* The Communion service was held less frequently than is

the practice today, but it was expected at Christmas, Easter, and on Whit Sunday at least.

161 *habilimental.* Pertaining to clothes.

161 *hulls.* Shells.

167 *Jack-rag and Tom-straw.* Usually 'Jack-straw' for any common man and 'Tom-rig' for any common woman.

167 *telling.* Counting.

167 *thimble-rigger.* One who cheats at 'pea and thimble', a game played for money and rather similar to the three-card trick.

169 *Nothing is ominous ... causes.* This rational point of view rarely prevails in human affairs. Probably the most tragic illustration of this in Hardy is the dénouement of *Jude the Obscure.*

169 *brumal.* Wintry.

171 *bull's-eye lantern.* Lantern with sides made of inferior glass, containing protuberances ('bull's eyes') which created a strong beam.

173 *joyous poets.* It is no wonder that the Elizabethan poets, less protected from the rigours of winter than we are, celebrated the return of spring. May is the 'merry month' in the poems of Spenser, Dekker, and Breton, for example.

173 *compounded for.* Agreed to accept, after making concessions.

173 *laburnum ... Solomon's seal.* Hardy's memory played him false on seasonal flowering. In *The Mayor of Casterbridge* he presents a garden scene with wall-flowers ('bloody warriors') in bloom with such flowers as snapdragons, fuchsias, geraniums and dahlias.

173 *'skip ... counsel'.* From Shakespeare's *The Merchant of Venice*, Act I, sc. II, l. 21.

174 *reversed the ordained sequence of the Church services.* Cf. p. 160.

174 *lawn.* Fine linen used for a bishop's sleeves.

174 *Eastern and Western hemispheres.* Two halves of a globe.

175 *look the intelligence.* Express the idea by looks.

177 *aspect.* The relative position of the planet for observation, depending on how much of the side illuminated by the sun is visible.

179 *the new school.* The Pre-Raphaelites (?). Hardy had met such comparisons in Swinburne's *Poems and Ballads* (1866); but the Bishop would not have read Swinburne with approval, if at all.

179 *All Angels.* A college name suggested by All Souls, Oxford.

179 *taking up.* Adopting or accepting as one of their society.

180 *disgust.* Distaste, loss of interest.

180 *sustained fruition ... bias.* Lady Constantine is suiting her style to her company. Notice how the examples which follow show the leading interests of the speakers.

180 *Tycho Brahe.* Danish astronomer (1546–1601).

180 *Kepler.* Johann Kepler (1571–1630), a German astronomer.

180 *James Ferguson.* Scottish astronomer (1710–76).

180 *Fénelon.* François Fénelon (1651–1715), a French writer on education and religion, was ordained in 1675 and became Archbishop of Cambrai in 1695.

181 *face . . . book.* Cf. Shakespeare's *Macbeth,* Act I, sc. v, ll. 66–7.

> Your face, my thane, is as a book where men
> May read strange matters.

183 *Diocesan Synod.* Assembly of the clergy of a diocese or area over which a bishop presides.

184 *tithe question.* Originally tithes were a tenth of the land produce, which was paid for the use of church land; the Act of 1836 allowed the commutation of tithes by kind into rent charges, but the question remained unsettled in some parts of the country.

185 *Pharisee.* Self-righteous person; see Luke, XVIII 9–14.

187 *Arabian bedstead.* Divan.

191 *shovel-hat.* A stiff, broad-brimmed hat turned up at the sides.

191 *jack.* The smaller bowl, which serves as a mark for the players to aim at.

191 *Richard the Second.* See Shakespeare's *Richard II,* Act III, sc. IV.

191 *rubs.* Obstacles; in bowls, unevennesses in the lawn.

191 *bias.* A leaden weight in one side of the bowl which makes its course curve, especially as it slows down.

191 *mal à propos.* (French) inappropriately.

195 *meek as Moses.* See Numbers, XII 3.

197 *'Tra deri . . . nouvelle!'* 'It's an old story!' (The refrain of a contemporary French song?)

199 *turnpike road.* Road with toll-gates at intervals, where fees were collected to pay for road-making and maintenance.

200 *stepping-stone to higher things.* From Tennyson's *In Memoriam,* sect. I.

200 *grizzled.* Grey-haired.

202 *fencing.* Trying to put (me) off.

203 *excommunicating.* Making him feel unqualified to attend Communion.

206 *Timothy.* The Timothy to whom Paul sent epistles seems to have had pastoral oversight of the Church at Ephesus; in this sense he was a 'bishop', though he had no such title.

208 *the next Transit of Venus.* See p. 25. The 'transit' is the passage of the planet across the face of the sun.

211 *in folio.* In volumes with pages of the largest size, from sheets folded once only.

211 *en famille.* As if he were a member of the family.

211 *getting a few wrinkles.* Gaining some useful information, learning a few 'tips'.

212 *bibliophilist.* Book-lover.

212 *Bertius's Ptolemy.* This edition of Ptolemy's work in Greek and Latin, published in Leyden in 1618, was the standard work for a long time. Ptolemy lived in Alexandria in the second century A.D. He was regarded as the authority on astronomy until his 'system' was overthrown by Copernicus. See note to p. 56.

212 *Rees's Cyclopædia.* A standard encyclopaedia in five volumes, published 1778–88.

213 *jamb.* Doorpost.

213 *smoking-cap.* A light ornamental cap which it was fashionable to wear when smoking.

214 *Samson ... web.* See Judges, XVI 14.

215 *St Swithin.* Bishop of Winchester in the ninth century. His reburial in the new cathedral was due to take place on 15 July 971, but heavy rains delayed it. Hence the tradition that if it rains on St Swithin's Day (15 July) it will rain for forty days.

219 *flat.* Simpleton, 'soft' person.

224 *plain, unvarnished tale.* Cf. Shakespeare's *Othello*, Act I, sc. III, l. 90: 'I will a round unvarnish'd tale deliver.'

224 *plate of old gold.* Circular and of a dull golden yellow.

225 *Ulunda ... Marzambo.* The Portuguese were established on the west coast of Angola; Ulunda (or Lunda) is to the east of modern Angola. Marzambo has not been identified. The names probably show Hardy's interest in Livingstone's travels.

229 *suppressio veri.* (Latin) suppression of the truth.

231 *lime ... wings.* The expression comes from the old practice of smearing branches with sticky lime to catch birds. Cf. Shakespeare's *Twelfth Night*, Act III, sc. IV, where Malvolio, convinced that Olivia is in love with him, says, 'I have limed her.'

232 *appointment ... corpse.* Three years later (1885) Hardy turned this idea into the short story 'A Mere Interlude'.

233 *efts.* Small lizards. (Strictly, the word applies only to newts.)

234 *primum mobile.* The pre-Copernican universe was imagined as a series of concentric spheres with the earth at the centre. The moon, the sun and the planets were each fixed to an inner transparent sphere. Enclosing all these was a ninth which bore the stars. An outer sphere beyond this was called the *primum mobile* because it imparted motion to the inner spheres; cf. Hardy's own use of the term in *Tess of the d'Urbervilles*, ch. 47.

234 *gravitation.* The thought is conveyed in astronomical terms. Swithin's main interest, the prime cause of his concentration ('gravitation' is a 'moving or tending towards a centre of attraction') was the equatorial telescope.

234 *glasses ... circles.* When the telescope lenses are perfectly set, the diffraction rings caused by light waves are symmetrical about the centre of the image.

236 *devise.* Legacy, something bestowed in a will.

243 *Save Thyself.* This emphasis may be seen in the Ten Commandments. The key to the New Testament (for Hardy especially) is charity.

244 *Homer, Moses.* Though examples in the *Iliad* and the *Odyssey* substantiate this view, higher aspects of love are to be found in Homer. The 'Mosaic laws' in the books of the Old Testament illustrate steps which were necessary to make a primitive race more civilised in various ways of life, including marriage.

245 *surpass the love of women.* This recalls David's lament for the death of his great friend Jonathan (II Samuel, I 26): 'thy love to me was wonderful, passing the love of women'.

247 *Eve ... Fall.* See Genesis, III.

250 *Isaac Newton.* Scientist and mathematician (1642–1727), best known for his work on light and gravitation.

252 *He turn'd ... fix'd.* From Swinburne's *Tristram of Lyonesse*, pt I, which appeared in 1882, the year Hardy wrote *Two on a Tower*.

254 *gnat-chasing . . . cracking snails.* These Darwinian glimpses reinforce the harsher reality which Swithin accepts.

255 *the girl they leave behind them.* This recalls the popular military-band tune, 'The Girl I Left behind Me'.

255 *Œnone.* A nymph of Mount Ida who married Paris before it was discovered that he was the son of Priam, King of Troy, and the disastrous consequences of his voyages to Greece were foretold. See Tennyson's 'Œnone', from which the quotation derives.

257 *sown . . . whirlwind.* Based on Hosea, VIII 7.

259 *'skitty-boots'.* Heavy hobnailed boots.

259 *'such . . . woman'.* Shakespeare's *Hamlet*, Act V, sc. II, ll. 226–7.

261 *jim-cracks.* (Dial.) mechanical contrivances.

261 *trangleys.* (Dial.) toys and playthings.

261 *raft.* (Dial.) upset.

261 *busting out afore 'ee.* (Dial.) bursting into tears in front of you.

262 *equinoctial lines.* Lines showing the celestial equator.

262 *topics.* Mrs Martin had heard Swithin speak of the Tropic of Capricorn.

262 *gallied.* (Dial.) worried, alarmed.

263 *observatory of Cambridge, United States.* Harvard Observatory, founded in 1843 and known as 'the American Pulkowa'.

263 *refractor.* One of the two main types of telescope.

263 *Poulkowa.* Pulkowa near Leningrad. It had a large astronomical transit instrument in use in 1838.

264 *mollia tempora fandi.* The favourable time for speaking, the time when he was most likely to yield (from Virgil's *Aeneid*, bk IV, ll. 293–4: 'mollissima fandi tempora').

265 *despising the shame.* See Hebrews, XII 2.

265 *homeliness.* Plain looks.

265 *sharp as a frost.* Hardy frequently associates frost with adversity.

265 *building upon the sand.* See Matthew, VII 26–7.

265 *red coal.* See p. 19.

266 *Havannah.* A brand of cigar manufactured in Havanna(h), Cuba.

266 *bowed down to dust.* From Psalm XLIV, 25.

267 *'Aux grands maux . . . , remèdes.'* 'Great evils (setbacks) demand great remedies.' From the works of Michel de Montaigne, the French essayist (1533–92). Cf. Shakespeare's *Hamlet*, Act IV, sc. III, l. 9: 'Diseases desperate grown/By desperate appliance are reliev'd.'

267 *venerable Close.* The Close around Salisbury Cathedral.

267 *mishap of Tobit.* He was blinded by the droppings (faeces) of sparrows. See the Book of Tobit (ch. II) in the Apocrypha.

267 *Punchinello in the king's chambers.* So popular was the puppet drama of Punchinello (Punch) after its introduction from the Continent during the Restoration period that room for the part was found in stage performances, even in Biblical plays. When Solomon was presented, for example, Punch seated himself on the Queen of Sheba's lap. Whether Hardy had a particular occasion in mind is uncertain: the old traditional Punch was often associated for fun with kings and

people of high degree. The comic role of Louis at the Bishop's is hinted at in the reference to Puck which follows.

268 *Puck-like ... Demetrius.* The 'mismating' which Puck causes in error (in *A Midsummer Night's Dream*) occurs when he puts the love-juice, not on Demetrius's eyes, but on Lysander's, making him fall in love with Helena and spurn his true love Hermia.

272 *for better or for worse.* These words are from the Marriage Service.

274 *circular notes.* Letters of credit from an English bank which would enable Swithin to obtain money from banks in other countries.

275 *great circles.* In navigating long distances, great circles are followed as far as possible, simply because they are the shortest distances around the earth.

275 *U.S.* Since Cambridge is near Boston, this repetition (see p. 263) seems superfluous. It was made lest readers should think of Cambridge in England.

275 *ingress and egress.* The beginning and end of the transit, when Venus appears first to be invading the area of the sun's circle and when it begins to leave it.

275 *tangent and parallax.* The main reason for studying the transit of Venus was to determine the scale of the solar system, which was equivalent to finding the distance of the sun from the earth. Observations of transits for this purpose must be made from widely spaced points on the earth; hence the Pacific expedition. The results were usually expressed not in terms of the actual distance between the earth and the sun but in terms of the solar parallax, which is the very small angle subtended by the radius of the earth at the sun. In the calculations, trigonometric functions such as tangents could be used at several places.

275 *external and internal contact.* The first refers to the moment when Venus appears to be just in contact with the sun's circumference, either at the point when ingress begins or egress ends. The second applies to contact when the planet is seen wholly against the sun at the completion of ingress or precisely at the moment before egress begins. These four measurements are crucial.

276 *February. The Transit was over.* It took place in December; see p. 25.

276 *younger Herschel.* Sir John F. W. Herschel (1792–1871) travelled to the Cape to extend his father's sky-sweeps, and pioneered celestial photography.

276 *J reckon.* Only in the seventeenth century were *I* and *J* recognised as separate letters in the English alphabet. Swithin's grandmother had learned to write at home, as her ancestors had done, and so the old style was retained.

276 *fall.* Autumn.

276 *for the nonce.* At the time ('for then once').

277 *knot ... cutting.* An allusion to the Classical story of the Gordian Knot. An oracle declared that whoever loosened it would rule Asia; Alexander the Great cut through it with his sword.

278 *the changes overhead.* The new constellations of the southern sky; cf. Hardy's poem 'Drummer Hodge'.

278 *circumpolar.* The northern and southern skies each have their pole around which the stars seem to revolve as the earth turns on its axis.

279 *Canopus.* In the constellation Argo and second only to Sirius in its brilliance.

279 *clouds of Magellan.* The Large and Small Magellanic Clouds, galaxies named after the explorer, who described them in detail. They are prominent features of

the southern sky, the former remaining visible even in full moonlight.

280 *like swarms of bees.* Probably from stanzas originally intended by Tennyson for his poem 'The Palace of Art', and noticed by Hardy in Proctor's *Essays on Astronomy.* See Michael Millgate, *Thomas Hardy* (1971) pp. 187–9.

281 *'Devil's Table-Cloth'.* A white cloud which settles on Table Mountain when the winds blow from the south-east. They often attain gale force, and produce adverse conditions on land and at sea; hence probably the early attributions of the 'cloth' to the 'Devil'.

281 *Lion's Rump.* Signal Hill. Its popular name derives from its shape in conjunction with another feature known as the 'Lion's Head'.

282 *whirligig of time.* The revolutionary changes brought about by time; see note to p. 290.

284 *pale death . . . foot.* From Horace, *Odes*, bk I, ode IV.

284 *Ken.* Bishop Ken (1637–1711), the 'gentle-voiced prelate' of *Jude the Obscure*, pt II, ch. 1.

284 *Heber.* Reginald Heber (1783–1826), divine and hymn-writer, appointed to the See of Bombay.

284 *rooted melancholy . . . ministry.* Adapted from Shakespeare's *Macbeth*, Act V, sc. III, ll. 40–1:

> Canst thou not minister to a mind diseas'd,
> Pluck from the memory a rooted sorrow?

285 *unconscious.* Unaware of what had happened.

285 *bosky.* Full of thickets, bushy.

286 *asymptote.* A line which approaches a curve but never quite reaches it.

286 *Israel.* Jacob, when he saw his lost son Joseph again, in Egypt (Genesis, XLVI 30).

286 *knew not Joseph.* The quotation (Exodus, I 8) is linked with the context of the last.

286 *slittering.* (Dial.) skipping, never at rest.

286 *Wonderful Women.* An arch reference to the movement for women's rights, and especially to the contemporary development of opportunities in higher education for women. The first Mrs Hardy became an energetic supporter of their cause.

287 *pitch my nitch.* (Dial.) put my load on the ground.

287 *nabob.* One who had returned from India with great wealth (literally, an Indian governor).

287 *diment-digger.* Diamond-digger.

287 *blooth.* (Dial.) bloom.

287 *plimmed and chimped.* (Dial.) swollen and brought forth children.

287 *anighst.* (Dial.) almost.

289 *darkness visible.* From Milton's *Paradise Lost*, bk I, l. 63.

289 *Via Lactea.* The Milky Way.

290 *Time . . . revenges.* From Shakespeare's *Twelfth Night*, Act V, sc. I, l. 386: 'and thus the whirligig of time brings in his revenges'.

290 *'O woman . . . five years!'* An echo of Matthew, XV 28.

291 *cruelty of the natural laws.* The scientific view that the universe is subject to blind laws, not Providence, permeates Hardy's vision of life. It is their indifference to human fate which makes them seem cruel.

291 *charity which 'seeketh not her own'.* I Corinthians, XIII 5; see also note to p. 243.

291 *loving-kindness.* Charity, loving one's own kind or fellow-men. Without this great Christian virtue, Hardy saw little hope for mankind.

291 *lover's love.* From John Donne's 'Valediction: forbidding mourning'. With the anti-romantic thought here compare Hardy's remarks on the marriage of Bathsheba Everdene and Gabriel Oak in *Far from the Madding Crowd*, ch. 56.

292 *single bright spot of colour and animation.* Several pointers in the conclusion suggest that Swithin's future is with Tabitha Lark.

Note on the Text

ALTHOUGH *The Atlantic Monthly*, in which *Two on a Tower* appeared from May to December 1882, was printed and published in America, copies appeared simultaneously in London. Hardy's manuscript was sent month by month to Boston, and the editor was invited to correct any error he found. To 'guard against accidental loss' a duplicate copy followed. Some punctuation (which would have needed no attention had Hardy had more time to prepare his copy) was added, and other slight improvements were made, in the editorial office. Aldrich, a scrupulous editor, was in Europe when three intermediate numbers (chs 22–37) were prepared for the press. He seems to have overlooked a few loose constructions of the participial type or approximations to it (e.g. on pp. 34, 76); his deputy failed to spot a split infinitive (p. 187) The manuscript of the novel (at the Houghton Library, Harvard University) indicates that the printers' copies of the fifth, sixth and seventh instalments were lost during the editor's absence; and this portion consists of duplicate sheets containing revisions by Hardy which never entered the printed text.

For the first edition of the book (25 October 1882) the publishers in London received from Hardy a third manuscript copy of the seventh and eighth instalments, which did not make their serial appearance until the following November and December. Chapters 33–41 of the novel edition, therefore, were not subjected to editorial scrutiny, and this may account for an increase in split infinitives (pp. 227, 253, 286). The text of the earlier instalments was copied from *The Atlantic Monthly*, and, although other American spellings disappeared, 'license' remained throughout.

Manuscript changes which appear in the novel are of minor importance, e.g., 'Rings-Hill Speer' for 'Camphill Speer' and stylistic improvements such as (p. 31) 'weird multitude' for 'wilderness' (?), 'gleaming' for 'polished', 'placed itself in strong chromatic contrast' for 'contrasted', and 'tower in the form of a classical column' for 'pillar'. Greater or more accurate definition may also be seen in (p. 259): 'changeful procession of country seats past . . . the names and memories of their owners' for 'lovely scenes through', and the addition of 'and enveloped the distant outline of the Rings-Hill column in his humid rays'.[1]

In the second impression of the novel the two most important changes

[1] For manuscript evidence, see the article by Carl J. Weber in *Papers of the Bibliographical Society of America*, vol. 40 (1946).

were the increase of Swithin's annuity from £400 to £600, and the correction of 'Lady Helmsdale' to 'Lady Constantine'. The addition of the date (p. 251) was intended to show that the child of Swithin and Lady Constantine was conceived when they were knowingly no longer legally married (cf. p. 279). Two short passages were added to emphasise this in the 1895 edition: 'and Viviette yielded to all the passion of her first union with him' (p. 252) and 'I ought not to have consented to that last interview: all was well till then!' (p. 277).[1]

The quotation from Richard Crashaw's 'Love's Horoscope', which was suggested by Edmund Gosse, first appeared on the title-page of the single-volume edition of April 1883.

Suleiman M. Ahmad (to whom I am indebted for the following note) questions some of Weber's deductions relating to the duplicate manuscript. The whole manuscript shows numerous alterations and additions, some literary references being included in the latter. Swithin at first thought of finding some place for observation, not in the southern hemisphere, but near London; and the first appearance of the Bishop seems to have been an afterthought. Among the numerous revisions for the first edition are the deletion of 'the Byrons of firmamental celebrities' after 'dazzling and perplexing rangers' (p. 96), the addition of the paragraph 'He drew her yielding form ... days' (p. 127), of 'The best men ... odd jobs' (p. 147), of 'Before leaving ... now passed' (p. 264), and, very notably, of 'He looked up ... vain' (p. 292). Swithin's age was changed from eighteen to twenty, and the city chosen for the secret marriage from Melchester to Pumpminster (Bath), with 'Abbey' for 'Cathedral', 'aisles' for 'rooks' nests', and 'quarter' for 'Close' (pp. 135–6). In 1895 Hardy introduced more dialect, and substituted Bath for Pumpminster and Lornton for Horton. Most of the last sentence in the second paragraph of the 1895 preface was omitted in 1902; it ran, 'I was made to suffer in consequence from several eminent pens, such warm epithets as "hazardous", "repulsive", "little short of revolting", "a studied and gratuitous insult", being flung at the precarious volumes.' In the last revision, for the 1912 edition, the Bishop's age was increased from 'five-and-forty' to 'one-and-fifty' (p. 218) and from 'fifty' to 'fifty-four' (p. 282); 'fifteen' was changed to 'twenty' in consequence (p. 201). The ironical sentence 'Remarkably fine boy ... seven-months' baby' (p. 285) was added.

The text of the present edition is based on that of the Wessex Edition of 1912. One improvement in this was the substitution of 'The Lord look'd down from Heav'n's high tower' (p. 46) for the hymn 'Onward, Christian Soldiers'.

General Preface to the Wessex Edition of 1912

IN accepting a proposal for a definite edition of these productions in prose and verse I have found an opportunity of classifying the novels under heads that show approximately the author's aim, if not his achievement, in each book of the series at the date of its composition. Sometimes the aim was lower than at other times; sometimes, where the intention was primarily high, force of circumstances (among which the chief were the necessities of magazine publication) compelled a modification, great or slight, of the original plan. Of a few, however, of the longer novels, and of many of the shorter tales, it may be assumed that they stand to-day much as they would have stood if no accidents had obstructed the channel between the writer and the public. That many of them, if any, stand as they would stand if written *now* is not to be supposed.

In the classification of these fictitious chronicles – for which the name of 'The Wessex Novels' was adopted, and is still retained – the first group is called 'Novels of Character and Environment', and contains those which approach most nearly to uninfluenced works; also one or two which, whatever their quality in some few of their episodes, may claim a verisimilitude in general treatment and detail.

The second group is distinguished as 'Romances and Fantasies', a sufficiently descriptive definition. The third class – 'Novels of Ingenuity' – show a not infrequent disregard of the probable in the chain of events, and depend for their interest mainly on the incidents themselves. They might also be characterised as 'Experiments', and were written for the nonce simply; though despite the artificiality of their fable some of their scenes are not without fidelity to life.[1]

It will not be supposed that these differences are distinctly perceptible in

[1] Novels of Character and Environment: *Tess of the d'Urbervilles, Far from the Madding Crowd, Jude the Obscure, The Return of the Native, The Mayor of Casterbridge, The Woodlanders, Under the Greenwood Tree, Life's Little Ironies and A Few Crusted Characters, Wessex Tales.*

Romances and Fantasies: *A Pair of Blue Eyes, The Trumpet-Major, Two on a Tower, The Well-Beloved, A Group of Nobles Dames.*

Novels of Ingenuity: *Desperate Remedies, The Hand of Ethelberta, A Laodicean.* [General Editor's note]

every page of every volume. It was inevitable that blendings and alternations should occur in all. Moreover, as it was not thought desirable in every instance to change the arrangement of the shorter stories to which readers have grown accustomed, certain of these may be found under headings to which an acute judgment might deny appropriateness.

It has sometimes been conceived of novels that evolve their action on a circumscribed scene – as do many (though not all) of these – that they cannot be so inclusive in their exhibition of human nature as novels wherein the scenes cover large extents of country, in which events figure amid towns and cities, even wander over the four quarters of the globe. I am not concerned to argue this point further than to suggest that the conception is an untrue one in respect of the elementary passions. But I would state that the geographical limits of the stage here trodden were not absolutely forced upon the writer by circumstances; he forced them upon himself from judgment. I considered that our magnificent heritage from the Greeks in dramatic literature found sufficient room for a large proportion of its action in an extent of their country not much larger than the half-dozen counties here reunited under the old name of Wessex, that the domestic emotions have throbbed in Wessex nooks with as much intensity as in the palaces of Europe, and that, anyhow, there was quite enough human nature in Wessex for one man's literary purpose. So far was I possessed by this idea that I kept within the frontiers when it would have been easier to overleap them and give more cosmopolitan features to the narrative.

Thus, though the people in most of the novels (and in much of the shorter verse) are dwellers in a province bounded on the north by the Thames, on the south by the English Channel, on the east by a line running from Hayling Island to Windsor Forest, and on the west by the Cornish coast, they were meant to be typically and essentially those of any and every place where

> Thought's the slave of life, and life time's fool

– beings in whose hearts and minds that which is apparently local should be really universal.

But whatever the success of this intention, and the value of these novels as delineations of humanity, they have at least a humble supplementary quality of which I may be justified in reminding the reader, though it is one that was quite unintentional and unforeseen. At the dates represented in the various narrations things were like that in Wessex: the inhabitants lived in certain ways, engaged in certain occupations, kept alive certain customs, just as they are shown doing in these pages. And in particularizing such I have often been reminded of Boswell's remarks on the trouble to which he was put and the pilgrimages he was obliged to make to authenticate some detail, though the labour was one which would bring him no praise. Unlike his achievement, however, on which an error would as he says have brought discredit, if these country customs and vocations, obsolete and obsolescent, had been detailed wrongly, nobody would have discovered such errors to the end of Time. Yet I have instituted inquiries to correct tricks of memory, and striven against temptations to exaggerate, in order to preserve for my own satisfaction a fairly true record of a vanishing life.

It is advisable also to state here, in response to inquiries from readers interested in landscape, prehistoric antiquities, and especially old English architecture, that the description of these backgrounds has been done from the real – that is to say, has something real for its basis, however illusively treated. Many features of the first two kinds have been given under their existing names; for instance, the Vale of Blackmoor or Blakemore, Hambledon Hill, Bulbarrow, Nettlecombe Tout, Dogbury Hill, High-Stoy, Bubb-Down Hill, The Devil's Kitchen, Cross-in-Hand, Long-Ash Lane, Benvill Lane, Giant's Hill, Crimmercrock Lane, and Stonehenge. The rivers Froom, or Frome, and Stour, are, of course, well known as such. And the further idea was that large towns and points tending to mark the outline of Wessex – such as Bath, Plymouth, The Start, Portland Bill, Southampton, etc. – should be named clearly. The scheme was not greatly elaborated, but, whatever its value, the names remain still.

In respect of places described under fictitious or ancient names in the novels – for reasons that seemed good at the time of writing them – and kept up in the poems – discerning people have affirmed in print that they clearly recognise the originals: such as Shaftesbury in 'Shaston', Sturminster Newton in 'Stourcastle', Dorchester in 'Casterbridge', Salisbury Plain in 'The Great Plain', Cranborne Chase in 'The Chase', Beaminster in 'Emminster', Bere Regis in 'Kingsbere', Woodbury Hill in 'Greenhill', Wool Bridge in 'Wellbridge', Harfoot or Harput Lane in 'Stagfoot Lane', Hazlebury in 'Nuttlebury', Bridport in 'Port Bredy', Maiden Newton in 'Chalk Newton', a farm near Nettlecombe Tout in 'Flintcomb-Ash', Sherborne in 'Sherton Abbas', Milton Abbey in 'Middleton Abbey', Cerne Abbas in 'Abbot's Cernel', Evershot in 'Evershed', Taunton in 'Toneborough', Bournemouth in 'Sandbourne', Winchester in 'Wintoncester', Oxford in 'Christminster', Reading in 'Aldbrickham', Newbury in 'Kennetbridge', Wantage in 'Alfredston', Basingstoke in 'Stoke Barehills', and so on. Subject to the qualifications above given, that no detail is guaranteed – that the portraiture of fictitiously named towns and villages was only suggested by certain real places, and wantonly wanders from inventorial descriptions of them – I do not contradict these keen hunters for the real; I am satisfied with their statements as at least an indication of their interest in the scenes.

Thus much for the novels. Turning now to the verse – to myself the more individual part of my literary fruitage – I would say that, unlike some of the fiction, nothing interfered with the writer's freedom in respect of its form or content. Several of the poems – indeed many – were produced before novel-writing had been thought of as a pursuit; but few saw the light till all the novels had been published. The limited stage to which the majority of the latter confine their exhibitions has not been adhered to here in the same proportion, the dramatic part especially having a very broad theatre of action. It may thus relieve the circumscribed areas treated in the prose, if such relief be needed. To be sure, one might argue that by surveying Europe from a celestial point of vision – as in *The Dynasts* – that continent becomes virtually a province – a Wessex, an Attica, even a mere garden – and hence is made to conform to the principle of the novels, however far it outmeasures their region. But that may be as it will.

The few volumes filled by the verse cover a producing period of some eighteen years first and last, while the seventeen or more volumes of novels represent correspondingly about four-and-twenty years. One is reminded by this disproportion in time and result how much more concise and quintessential expression becomes when given in rhythmic form than when shaped in the language of prose.

One word on what has been called the present writer's philosophy of life, as exhibited more particularly in this metrical section of his compositions. Positive views on the Whence and the Wherefore of things have never been advanced by this pen as a consistent philosophy. Nor is it likely, indeed, that imaginative writings extending over more than forty years would exhibit a coherent scientific theory of the universe even if it had been attempted – of that universe concerning which Spencer owns to the 'paralyzing thought' that possibly there exists no comprehension of it anywhere. But such objectless consistency never has been attempted, and the sentiments in the following pages have been stated truly to be mere impressions of the moment, and not convictions or arguments.

That these impressions have been condemned as 'pessimistic' – as if that were a very wicked adjective – shows a curious muddle-mindedness. It must be obvious that there is a higher characteristic of philosophy than pessimism, or than meliorism, or even than the optimism of these critics – which is truth. Existence is either ordered in a certain way, or it is not so ordered, and conjectures which harmonize best with experience are removed above all comparison with other conjectures which do not so harmonize. So that to say one view is worse than other views without proving it erroneous implies the possibility of a false view being better or more expedient than a true view; and no pragmatic proppings can make that *idolum specus* stand on its feet, for it postulates a prescience denied to humanity.

And there is another consideration. Differing natures find their tongue in the presence of differing spectacles. Some natures become vocal at tragedy, some are made vocal by comedy, and it seems to me that to whichever of these aspects of life a writer's instinct for expression the more readily responds, to that he should allow it to respond. That before a contrasting side of things he remains undemonstrative need not be assumed to mean that he remains unperceiving.

It was my hope to add to these volumes of verse as many more as would make a fairly comprehensive cycle of the whole. I had wished that those in dramatic, ballad, and narrative form should include most of the cardinal situations which occur in social and public life, and those in lyric form a round of emotional experiences of some completeness. But

The petty done, the undone vast!

The more written the more seems to remain to be written; and the night cometh. I realize that these hopes and plans, except possibly to the extent of a volume or two, must remain unfulfilled.

October 1911 T.H.

Glossary of Place-names

BUDMOUTH. Weymouth.

GREENHILL. Woodbury Hill, immediately to the east of Bere Regis.

LORNTON COPSE. Near Horton, north of Wimborne Minster. Probably mentioned to baffle the reader since there is an observatory tower on a hill near Horton.

MELCHESTER. Salisbury.

OLD MELCHESTER ROAD. Hardy's poem 'My Cicely' indicates that his 'old Melchester Road' followed stretches of the Roman road, which passed only half a mile or so south of Weatherbury Castle or 'Rings-Hill Speer'. Less likely is the old road past Charborough Park (before the latter was extended to the north), which could have joined the route of the Roman road to Salisbury near Badbury Rings.

PUDDLE-SUB-MIXEN. An invented name. Hardy alludes humorously to Dorset villages, e.g. Puddletown, Piddlehinton, which are named after the Puddle or Piddle valley in which they are situated.

RINGS-HILL SPEER. The 'speer' was suggested by the obelisk memorial in the wood on the top of Weatherbury Castle east-north-east of Puddletown, the 'Weatherbury' of Wessex. 'Castle' derives from the ancient earthworks which ring the top of the hill.

The hill and its environs were imagined in the region of the tower in Charborough Park, west of Wimborne (cf. F. E. Hardy, *Life of Thomas Hardy 1840–1928* (1962) pp. 267, 441). In his copy of John Hutchins' *History and Antiquities of Dorset*, 3rd ed., 4 vols (1861–73) Hardy read that the Isle of Wight, much of Hampshire, Wiltshire, and western Dorset, and Alfred's Tower in Somerset could be seen from this tower (cf. p. 32).

WARBORNE. Wimborne Minster.

WELLAND BOTTOM. Largely imaginary, though the setting probably originated from the valley and stream below Weatherbury Castle.

WELLAND HOUSE. Suggested by Charborough House, though Hardy had not visited it. His policy of concealment may be seen in the inconsistency of its position with reference to Rings-Hill Speer on p. 80 and its being on the right of the road from Warborne (p. 152); the first is on the south side of the road, and the second on the north. Hardy learned from Hutchins that the village had been demolished (cf. p. 99) and that the park had been extended on the northern side of the old road when the new turnpike road was constructed. The church suggests not so much St Mary's near Charborough House as that attended by the Hardys at Stinsford, the tower of which overlooked Stinsford House.

The railway junction should perhaps be taken as imaginary. There were two routes from Bath to Wimborne, one via Salisbury, the other (from 1874, and more direct) via Templecombe Junction. Louis Glanville could have driven to either station, since he had been staying with a friend in the neighbourhood. Neither seems wholly convincing, especially when railway timetables are consulted. If Hardy intended Salisbury (with its adjacent stations), there seems to be no reason why he should have avoided the mention of 'Melchester'; it would have been risky also for the two lovers to make their way anywhere near 'Warborne' to the next station. Whether Hardy left any ambiguity in the sentence referring to this (p. 156) is uncertain. If he had Templecombe in mind, the next station would be at Blandford Forum, which is nine miles 'above' Wimborne; the train from Bath to Wimborne would have been a through train, however.

Originally the junction was 'Filton', and the line from Melchester to Warborne (see p. 311). This indicates that Hardy intended an imaginary junction from the outset. No change was necessary from Salisbury to Wimborne, and the only junction on this line was West Moors, the station nine miles from the fictional site of the tower.